PENGUIN BOOKS

BASIC BECH

John Updike was born in 1932 in Shillington, Pennsylvania. He attended Shillington High School, Harvard College and the Ruskin School of Drawing and Fine Art at Oxford, where he spent a year on a Knox Fellowship. From 1955 to 1957 he was a member of the staff of the *New Yorker*, to which he has contributed numerous poems, short stories, essays and book reviews. Since 1957 he has lived in Massachusetts as a freelance writer.

John Updike's first novel, *The Poorhouse Fair*, was published in 1959. It was followed by *Rabbit, Run*, the first volume of what have become known as the *Rabbit* books, which John Banville described as 'one of the finest literary achievements to have come out of the US since the war'. *Rabbit is Rich* (1981) and *Rabbit at Rest* (1990) were awarded the Pulitzer Prize for Fiction. Other novels by John Updike include *Marry Me*, *The Witches of Eastwick*, which was made into a major feature film, *Memories of the Ford Administration*, *Brazil*, *In the Beauty of the Lilies* and *Toward the End of Time*. He has written a number of volumes of short stories, and a selection entitled *Forty Stories*, taken from *The Same Door*, *Pigeon Feathers*, *The Music School* and *Museums and Women*, is published in Penguin, as is the highly acclaimed *The Afterlife and Other Stories*. His criticism and his essays, which first appeared in magazines such as the *New Yorker* and the *New York Review of Books*, have been collected in five volumes. *Golf Dreams*, a collection of his writings on golf, has also been published. His *Collected Poems 1953–1993* brings together almost all the poems from five previous volumes, including *Hoping for a Hoopoe*, *Telephone Poles* and *Tossing and Turning*, as well as seventy poems previously unpublished in book form. Many of his books are published in Penguin, including the recent *Bech at Bay: A Quasi-Novel*.

D1494395

BASIC BECH

BECH: A BOOK
BECH IS BACK

JOHN UPDIKE

PENGUIN BOOKS

PENGUIN BOOKS

Published by the Penguin Group
Penguin Books Ltd, 27 Wrights Lane, London W8 5TZ, England
Penguin Putnam Inc., 375 Hudson Street, New York, New York 10014, USA
Penguin Books Australia Ltd, Ringwood, Victoria, Australia
Penguin Books Canada Ltd, 10 Alcorn Avenue, Toronto, Ontario, Canada M4V 3B2
Penguin Books (NZ) Ltd, Private Bag 102902, NSMC, Auckland, New Zealand

Penguin Books Ltd, Registered Offices: Harmondsworth, Middlesex, England

Bech: A Book first published in the USA by Alfred A. Knopf Inc. 1970
First published in Great Britain by André Deutsch 1970
Published in Penguin Books 1972

Bech is Back first published in the USA by Alfred A. Knopf Inc. 1982
First published in Great Britain by André Deutsch 1983
Published in Penguin Books 1983

Originally published together as *The Complete Henry Bech* with the story 'Bech in Czech'
in Penguin Books 1992
Published as *Basic Bech* in Penguin Books 1999
10 9 8 7 6 5 4 3 2

'Bech in Czech' is included in *Bech at Bay* published in Penguin Books 1999

Six of these stories first appeared in the *New Yorker*: 'The Bulgarian Poetess', 'Bech in
Rumania', 'Bech Takes Pot Luck', 'Rich in Russia' (without appendix), 'Bech Swings' and
'Three Illuminations in the Life of an American Author'. 'Australia and Canada', 'Bech
Third-Worlds It' and 'The Holy Land' originally appeared in *Playboy* magazine.

Copyright © John Updike, 1965, 1966, 1968, 1970, 1975, 1979, 1982
All rights reserved

Printed in England by Clays Ltd, St Ives plc

Bech: A Book

(1970)

Contents

Foreword

Dear John,

Well, if you must commit the artistic indecency of writing about a writer, better I suppose about me than about you. Except, reading along in these, I wonder if it *is* me, enough me, purely me. At first blush, for example, in Bulgaria (eclectic sexuality, bravura narcissism, thinning curly hair), I sound like some gentlemanly Norman Mailer; then that London glimpse of *silver* hair glints more of gallant, glamorous Bellow, the King of the Leprechauns, than of stolid old homely yours truly. My childhood seems out of Alex Portnoy and my ancestral past out of I. B. Singer. I get a whiff of Malamud in your city breezes, and am I paranoid to feel my 'block' an ignoble version of the more or less noble renunciations of H. Roth, D. Fuchs, and J. Salinger? Withal, something Waspish, theological, scared, and insulatingly ironical that derives, my wild surmise is, from you.

Yet you are right. This monotonous hero who disembarks from an aeroplane, mouths words he doesn't quite mean, has vaguely to do with some woman, and gets back on the aeroplane, is certainly one Henry Bech. Until your short yet still not un-longish collection, no revolutionary has concerned himself with our oppression, with the silken mechanism whereby America reduces her writers to imbecility and cozenage. Envied like Negroes, disbelieved in like angels, we veer between the harlotry of the lecture platform and the torture of the writing desk, only to collapse, our five-and-dime Hallowe'en priests' robes a-rustle with economy-class jet-set tickets and honorary certificates from the Cunt-of-the-Month Club, amid a standing crowd of rueful, Lilliputian obituaries. Our language degenerating in the mouths of broadcasters and pop yellers, our formal designs crumbling

9

like sand castles under the feet of beach bullies, we nevertheless and incredibly support with our desperate efforts (just now, I had to look up 'desperate' in the dictionary for the ninety-ninth time, forgetting again if it is spelled with two 'a's or three 'e's) a flourishing culture of publishers, agents, editors, tutors, *Time*niks, media personnel in all shades of suavity, *chic*, and sexual gusto. When I think of the matings, the moaning, jubilant fornications between ectomorphic oversexed junior editors and svelte hot-from-Wellesley majored-in-English-minored-in-philosophy female coffee-fetchers and receptionists that have been engineered with the lever of some of my poor scratched-up and pasted-over pages (they arrive in the editorial offices as stiff with Elmer's glue as a masturbator's bedsheet; the office boys use them for tea-trays), I could mutilate myself like sainted Origen, I could keen like Jeremiah. Thank Jahweh these bordellos in the sky can soon dispense with the excuse of us entirely; already the contents of a book count as little as the contents of a breakfast cereal box. It is all a matter of the premium, and the shelf site, and the amount of air between the corn flakes. Never you mind. I'm sure that when with that blithe goyische brass I will never cease to grovel at you approached me for a 'word or two by way of preface', you were bargaining for a benediction, not a curse.

Here it is, then. My blessing. I like some of the things in these accounts very much. The Communists are all good – good *people*. There is a moment by the sea, I've lost the page, that rang true. Here and there passages seem overedited, constipated: you prune yourself too hard. With prose, there is no way to get it out, I have found, but to let it run. I liked some of the women you gave me, and a few of the jokes. By the way, I never – unlike retired light-verse writers – make puns. But if you [*here followed a list of suggested deletions, falsifications, suppressions, and rewordings, all of which have been scrupulously incorporated –* ED.], I don't suppose your publishing this little *jeu* of a book will do either of us drastic harm.

Henry Bech

Manhattan,
4–12 Dec. 1969

Rich in Russia

Students (not unlike yourselves) compelled to buy paperback copies of his novels – notably the first, *Travel Light*, though there has lately been some academic interest in his more surreal and 'existential' and perhaps even 'anarchist' second novel, *Brother Pig* – or encountering some essay from *When the Saints* in a shiny heavy anthology of mid-century literature costing $12.50, imagine that Henry Bech, like thousands less famous than he, is rich. He is not. The paperback rights to *Travel Light* were sold by his publisher outright for two thousand dollars, of which the publisher kept one thousand and Bech's agent one hundred (10 per cent of 50 per cent). To be fair, the publisher had had to remainder a third of the modest hard-cover printing and, when *Travel Light* was enjoying its vogue as the post-Golding pre-Tolkien fad of college undergraduates, would amusingly tell on himself the story of Bech's given-away rights, at sales meetings upstairs in '21'. As to anthologies – the average permissions fee, when it arrives at Bech's mailbox, has been eroded to $64.73, or some such suspiciously odd sum, which barely covers the cost of a restaurant meal with his mistress and a medium wine. Though Bech, and his too numerous interviewers, have made a quixotic virtue of his continuing to live for twenty years in a grim if roomy Riverside Drive apartment building (the mailbox, students should know, where his pitifully nibbled cheques arrive has been well scarred by floating urban wrath, and his last name has been so often ballpointed by playful lobby-loiterers into a somewhat assonant verb that Bech has left the name plate space blank and depends upon the clairvoyance of mailmen), he in truth lives there because he cannot afford to leave. He was rich just once in his life, and that was in Russia, in 1964, a thaw or so ago.

Russia, in those days, like everywhere else, was a slightly more innocent place. Khruschev, freshly deposed, had left an atmosphere, almost comical, of warmth, of a certain fitful openness, of inscrutable experiment and oblique possibility. There seemed no overweening reason why Russia and America, those lovable paranoid giants, could not happily share a globe so big and blue; there certainly seemed no reason why Henry Bech, the recherché but amiable novelist, artistically blocked but socially fluent, should not be flown into Moscow at the expense of our State Department for a month of that mostly imaginary activity termed 'cultural exchange'. Entering the Aeroflot plane at Le Bourget, Bech thought it smelled like his uncles' backrooms in Williamsburg, of swaddled body heat and proximate potatoes boiling.* The impression lingered all month; Russia seemed Jewish to him, and of course he seemed Jewish to Russia. He never knew how much of the tenderness and hospitality he met related to his race. His contact man at the American Embassy – a prissy, doleful ex-basketball-player from Wisconsin, with the all-star name of 'Skip' Reynolds – assured him that two out of every three Soviet intellectuals had suppressed a Jew in their ancestry; and once Bech did find himself in a Moscow apartment whose bookcases were lined with photographs (of Kafka, Einstein, Freud, Wittgenstein) pointedly evoking the glory of pre-Hitlerian *Judenkultur*. His hosts, both man and wife, were professional translators, and the apartment was bewilderingly full of kin, including a doe-eyed young hydraulics engineer and a grandmother who had been a dentist with the Red Army, and whose dental chair dominated the parlour. For a whole long toasty evening, Jewishness, perhaps also pointedly, was not mentioned. The subject was one Bech was happy to ignore. His own writing had sought to reach out from the ghetto of his heart towards the wider expanses across the Hudson; the artistic triumph of American Jewry lay, he thought, not in the novels of the fifties but in the movies of the thirties, those gargantuan, crass

* See Appendix A, section I.

contraptions whereby Jewish brains projected Gentile stars upon a Gentile nation and out of their own immigrant joy gave a formless land dreams and even a kind of conscience. The reservoir of faith, in 1964, was just going dry; through depression and world convulsion the country had been sustained by the *arriviste* patriotism of Louis B. Mayer and the brothers Warner. To Bech, it was one of history's great love stories, the mutually profitable romance between Jewish Hollywood and bohunk America, conducted almost entirely in the dark, a tapping of fervent messages through the wall of the San Gabriel Range; and his favourite Jewish writer was the one who turned his back on his three beautiful Brooklyn novels and went into the desert to write scripts for Doris Day. This may be, except for graduate students, neither here nor there. There, in Russia five years ago, when Cuba had been taken out of the oven to cool and Vietnam was still coming to a simmer, Bech did find a quality of life – impoverished yet ceremonial, shabby yet ornate, sentimental, embattled, and avuncular – reminiscent of his neglected Jewish past. Virtue, in Russia as in his childhood, seemed something that arose from men, like a comforting body odour, rather than something from above, that impaled the struggling soul like a moth on a pin. He stepped from the Aeroflot plane, with its notably hefty stewardesses, into an atmosphere of generosity. They met him with arms heaped with cold roses. On the first afternoon, the Writers' Union gave him as expense money a stack of rouble notes, pink-and-lilac Lenin and powder-blue Spasskaya Tower. In the following month, in the guise of 'royalties' (in honour of his coming they had translated *Travel Light*, and several of his *Commentary* essays ['M-G-M and the U.S.A.'; 'The Moth on the Pin'; 'Daniel Fuchs: An Appreciation'] had appeared in *I Nostrannaya Literatura*, but since no copyright agreements pertained the royalties were arbitrarily calculated, like showers of manna), more roubles were given to him, so that by the week of his departure Bech had accumulated over fourteen hundred roubles – by the official exchange rate, fifteen hundred and forty dollars. There was nothing to spend it on. All his hotels, his plane fares, his meals were paid for. He was a guest of the Soviet state. From morning to night he was never alone. That first afternoon, he had also been given, along with the roubles, a companion, a translator-escort: Ekaterina Alexandrovna Ryleyeva. She was a notably skinny red-headed woman with a flat chest and paper-coloured skin and a translucent wart above her left nostril. He grew to call her Kate.

'Kate,' he said, displaying his roubles in two fistfuls, letting some drift to the floor, 'I have robbed the proletariat. What can I do with my filthy loot?' He had developed, in this long time in which she was always with him, a clowning super-American manner that disguised all complaints as 'acts'. In response, she had strengthened her original pose – of schoolteacherish patience, with ageless peasant roots. Her normal occupation was translating English-language science fiction into Ukrainian, and he imagined this month with him was relatively a holiday. She had a mother, and late at night, after accompanying him to a morning-brandy session with the editors of *Yunost*, to lunch at the Writers' Union with its shark-mouthed chairman,* to Dostoevski's childhood home (next to a madhouse, and enshrining some agonized crosshatched manuscripts and a pair of oval tin spectacles, tiny, as if fashioned for a dormouse), a museum of folk art, an endless restaurant meal, and a night of ballet, Ekaterina would bring Bech to his hotel lobby, put a babushka over her bushy orange hair, and head into a blizzard towards this ailing mother. Bech wondered about Kate's sex life. Skip Reynolds solemnly told him that personal life in Russia was inscrutable. He also told Bech that Kate was undoubtedly a Party spy. Bech was touched, and wondered what in him would be worth spying out. From infancy on we all are spies; the shame is not this but that the secrets to be discovered are so paltry and few. Ekaterina was perhaps as old as forty, which could just give her a lover killed in the war. Was this the secret of her vigil, the endless paper-coloured hours she spent by his side? She was always translating for him, and this added to her neutrality and transparence. He, too, had never been married, and imagined that this was what marriage was like.

* See Appendix A, section II.

She answered, 'Henry' – she usually touched his arm, saying his name, and it never ceased to thrill him a little, the way the 'H' became a breathy guttural sound between 'G' and 'K' – 'you must not joke. This is your money. You earned it by the sweat of your brain. All over Soviet Union committees of people sit in discussion over *Travel Light*, its wonderful qualities. The printing of one hundred thousand copies has gone *poof!* in the bookstores.' The comic-strip colours of science fiction tinted her idiom unexpectedly.

'Poof!' Bech said, and scattered the money above his head; before the last bill stopped fluttering, they both stooped to retrieve the roubles from the rich red carpet. They were in his room at the Sovietskaya, the hotel for Party bigwigs and important visitors; all the suites were furnished in high tsarist style: chandeliers, wax fruit, and brass bears.

'We have banks here,' Kate said shyly, reaching under the satin sofa, 'as in the capitalist countries. They pay interest, you could deposit your money in such a bank. It would be here, enlarged, when you returned. You would have a numbered bankbook.'

'What?' said Bech, 'And help support the Socialist state? When you are already years ahead of us in the space race? I would be adding thrust to your rockets.'

They stood up, both a little breathless from exertion, betraying their age. The tip of her nose was pink. She passed the remainder of his fortune into his hands; her silence seemed embarrassed.

'Besides,' Bech said, 'when would I ever return?'

She offered, 'Perhaps in a space-warp?'

Her shyness, her pink nose and carroty hair, her embarrassment were becoming oppressive. He brusquely waved his arms. 'No, Kate, we must spend it! Spend, spend. It's the Keynesian way. We will make Mother Russia a consumer society.'

From the very still, slightly tipped way she was standing, Bech, bothered by 'space-warp', received a haunted impression – that she was locked into a colourless other dimension from which only the pink tip of her nose emerged. 'Is not so simple,' she ominously pronounced.

*

For one thing, time was running out. Bobochka and Myshkin, the two Writers' Union officials in charge of Bech's itinerary, had crowded the end of his schedule with compulsory cultural events. Fortified by relatively leisured weeks in Kazakhstan and the Caucasus,* Bech was deemed fit to endure a marathon of war movies (the hero of one of them had lost his Communist Party member's card, which was worse than losing your driver's licence; and in another a young soldier hitched rides in a maze of trains only to turn around at the end ['See, Henry,' Kate whispered to him, 'now he is home, that is his mother, what a good face, so much suffering, now they kiss, now he must leave, oh – ' and Kate was crying too much to translate further]) and museums and shrines and brandy with various writers who uniformly adored Gemingway. November was turning bitter, the Christmassy lights celebrating the Revolution had been taken down, Kate as they hurried from appointment to appointment had developed a sniffle. She constantly patted her nose with a handkerchief. Bech felt a guilty pang, sending her off into the cold towards her mother before he ascended to his luxurious hotel room, with its parqueted foyer stacked with gift books and its alabaster bathroom and its great brocaded double bed. He would drink from a gift bottle of Georgian brandy and stand by the window, looking down on the golden windows of an apartment building where young Russians were Twisting to Voice of America tapes. Chubby Checker's chicken-plucker's voice carried distinctly across the crevasse of sub-arctic night. In an adjoining window, a couple courteously granted isolation by the others was making love; he could see knees and hands and then a rhythmically kicking ankle. To relieve the pressure, Bech would sit down with his brandy and write to distant women boozy reminiscent letters that in the morning would be handed solemnly to the ex-basketball-player, to be sent out of Russia via diplomatic pouch.† Reynolds, himself something of a spy, was with them whenever Bech spoke to a group, as of translators (when asked who was America's best living writer, Bech said

* See Appendix A, section III.
† See Appendix A, section IV.

Nabokov, and there was quite a silence before the next question) or of students (whom he assured that Yevtushenko's *Precocious Autobiography* was a salubrious and patriotic work that instead of being banned should be distributed free to Soviet school-children). 'Did I put my foot in it?' Bech would ask anxiously afterwards – another 'act'.

The American's careful mouth twitched. 'It's good for them. Shock therapy.'

'You were charming,' Ekaterina Alexandrovna always said loy-ally, jealously interposing herself, and squeezing Bech's arm. She could not imagine that Bech did not, like herself, loathe all officials. She would not have believed that Bech approached this one with an intellectual's reverence for the athlete, and that they exchanged in private not anti-Kremlin poison but literary gossip and pro football scores, love letters and old copies of *Time*. Now, in her campaign to keep them apart, Kate had been given another weapon. She squeezed his arm smugly and said, 'We have an hour. We must rush off and *shop*.'

For the other thing, there was not much to buy. To begin, he would need an extra suitcase. He and Ekaterina, in their chauffeured Zil, drove to what seemed to Bech a far suburb, past flickerings of birch forest, to sections of new housing, perforated warehouses the colour of wet cement. Here they found a vast store, vast though each salesgirl ruled as a petty tyrant over her domain of shelves. There was a puzzling duplication of suitcase sections; each displayed the same squarish mountain of dark cardboard boxes, and each pouting princess responded with negative insouciance to Ekaterina's quest for a leather suitcase. 'I know there have been some,' she told Bech.

'It doesn't matter,' he said. 'I want a cardboard one. I love the metal studs and the little chocolate handle.'

'You have fun with me,' she said. 'I know what you have in the West. I have been to Science-Fiction Writers' Congress in Vienna. This great store, and not one leather suitcase. It is a disgrace upon the people. But come, I know another store.' They went back into the Zil, which smelled like a cloakroom, and in whose swaying stuffy depths Bech felt squeamish and chastened, having often been sent to the cloakroom as a child at P.S. 87, on West Seventy-seventh Street and Amsterdam Avenue. A dozen stuffy miles and three more stores failed to produce a leather suitcase; at last Kate permitted him to buy a paper one – the biggest, with gay plaid sides, and as long as an oboe. To console her, he also bought an astrakhan hat. It was not flattering (when he put it on, the haughty salesgirl laughed aloud) and did not cover his ears, which were cold, but it had the advantage of costing fifty-four roubles. 'Only a *boyar*,' said Kate, excited to flirtation by his purchase, 'would wear such a wow of a hat.'

'I look like an Armenian in it,' Bech said. Humiliations never come singly. On the street, with his suitcase and hat, Bech was stopped by a man who wanted to buy his overcoat. Kate translated and then scolded. During what Bech took to be a lengthy threat to call the police, the offender, a morose red-nosed man costumed like a New York chestnut vender, stared stubbornly at the sidewalk by their feet.

As they moved away, he said in soft English to Bech, 'Your shoes. I give forty roubles.'

Bech pulled out his wallet and said, '*Nyet, nyet*. For your shoes I give fifty.'

Kate with a squawk flew between them and swept Bech away. She told him in tears, 'Had the authorities witnessed that scene we would all be put in jail, biff, bang.'

Bech had never seen her cry in daylight – only in the dark of projection rooms. He climbed into the Zil feeling especially sick and guilty. They were late for their luncheon, with a cherubic museum director and his hatchet-faced staff. In the course of their tour through the museum, Bech tried to cheer her up with praise of Socialist realism. 'Look at that turbine. Nobody in America can paint a turbine like that. Not since the thirties. Every part so distinct you could rebuild one from it, yet the whole thing romantic as a sunset. Mimesis – you can't beat it.' He was honestly fond of these huge posterish oils; they reminded him of magazine illustrations from his adolescence.

Kate would not be cheered. 'It is stupid stuff,' she said. 'We have had no painters since Rublyov. You treat my country as a picnic.' Sometimes her English had a weird precision. 'It is not as if there is no talent. We are great, there are millions. The young are burning up with talent, it is annihilating them.' She pronounced it *anneeheel* – a word she had met only in print, connected with ray guns.

'Kate, I *mean* it,' Bech insisted, hopelessly in the wrong, as with a third-grade teacher, yet also subject to another pressure, that of a woman taking sensual pleasure in refusing to be consoled. 'I'm telling you, there is artistic passion here. This bicycle. Beautiful impressionism. No spokes. The French paint apples, the Russians paint bicycles.'

The parallel came out awry, unkind. Grimly patting her pink nostrils, Ekaterina passed into the next room. 'Once,' she informed him, 'this room held entirely pictures of *him*. At least that is no more.'

Bech did not need to ask who *he* was. The undefined pronoun had a constant value. In Georgia Bech had been shown a tombstone for a person described simply as Mother.

The next day, between lunch with Voznesensky and dinner with Yevtushenko (who both flatteringly seemed to concede to him a hemispheric celebrity equivalent to their own, and who feigned enchantment when he tried to explain his peculiar status, as not a lion, with a lion's confining burden of symbolic portent, but as a greying, furtively stylish rat indifferently permitted to gnaw and roam behind the wainscoting of a firetrap about to be demolished anyway), he and Kate and the impassive chauffeur managed to buy three amber necklaces and four wooden toys and two very thin wristwatches. The amber seemed homely to Bech – melted butter refrozen – but Kate was proud of it. The wristwatches he suspected would soon stop; they were perilously thin. The toys – segmented Kremlins, carved bears chopping wood – were good, but the only children he knew were his sister's in Cincinnati, and the youngest was nine. The Ukrainian needlework that Ekaterina hopefully pushed at him his imagination could not impose on any woman he knew, not even his mother; since his 'success', she had her hair done once a week and wore her hems just above the knee. Back in his hotel room, in the ten minutes before an all-Shostakovich concert, while Kate sniffed and sloshed in the bathroom (how could such a skinny woman be displacing all that water?), Bech counted his roubles. He had spent only a hundred and thirty-seven. That left one thousand two hundred and eighty-three, plus the odd kopecks. His heart sank; it was hopeless. Ekaterina emerged from the bathroom with a strange, bruised stare. Little burnt traces, traces of ashen tears, lingered about her eyes, which were by nature a washed-out blue. She had been trying to put on eye makeup, and had kept washing it off. Trying to be a rich man's wife. She looked blank and wounded. Bech took her arm; they hurried downstairs like criminals on the run.

The next day was his last full day in Russia. All month he had wanted to visit Tolstoy's estate, and the trip had been postponed until now. Since Yasnaya Polyana was four hours from Moscow, he and Kate left early in the morning and returned in the dark. After miles of sleepy silence, she asked, 'Henry, what did you like?'

'I liked the way he wrote *War and Peace* in the cellar, *Anna Karenina* on the first floor, and *Resurrection* upstairs. Do you think he's writing a fourth novel in Heaven?'

This reply, taken from a little *Commentary* article he was writing in his head (and would never write on paper), somehow renewed her silence. When she at last spoke, her voice was shy. 'As a Jew, you believe?'

His laugh had an ambushed quality he tried to translate, with a shy guffaw at the end, into self-deprecation. 'Jews don't go in much for Paradise,' he said. 'That's something you Christians cooked up.'

'We are not Christians.'

'Kate, you are saints. You are a land of monks and your government is a constant penance.' From the same unwritten article – tentatively titled 'God's Ghost in Moscow'. He went on, with Hollywood, Martin Buber, and his uncles all vaguely smiling in his mind, 'I think the Jewish feeling is that wherever they happen to be, it's rather paradisiacal, because they're there.'

'You have found it so here?'

'Very much. This must be the only country in the world you can be homesick for while you're still in it. Russia is one big case of homesickness.'

Perhaps Kate found this ground dangerous, for she returned to earlier terrain. 'It is strange,' she said, 'of the books I translate, how much there is to do with supernature. Immaterial creatures like angels, ideal societies composed of spirits, speeds that exceed that of light, reversals of time – all impossible, and perhaps not. In a way it is terrible to look up at the sky, on one of our clear nights of burning cold, at the sky of stars, and think of creatures alive in it.'

'Like termites in the ceiling.' Falling so short of the grandeur Kate might have had a right to expect from him, his simile went unanswered. The car swayed, dark gingerbread villages swooped by, the back of the driver's head was motionless. Bech idly hummed a bit of 'Midnight in Moscow', whose literal title, he had discovered, was 'Twilit Evenings in the Moscow Suburbs'. He said, 'I also liked the way Upton Sinclair was in his bookcase, and how his house felt like a farmhouse instead of a mansion, and his grave.'

'So super a grave.'

'Very graceful, for a man who fought death so hard.' It had been an unmarked oval of earth, rimmed green with frozen turf, at the end of a road in a birchwood where night was sifting in. It had been here that Tolstoy's brother had told him to search for the little green stick that would end war and human suffering. Because her importunate silence had begun to nag unbearably, Bech told Kate, 'That's what I should do with my roubles. Buy Tolstoy a tombstone. With a neon arrow.'

'Oh those roubles!' she exclaimed. 'You persecute me with those roubles. We have shopped more in one week than I shop in one year. Material things do not interest me, Henry. In the war we all learned the value of material things. There is no value but what you hold within yourself.'

'O.K., I'll swallow them.'

'Always the joke. I have one more desperate idea. In New York, you have women for friends?'

Her voice had gone shy, as when broaching Jewishness; she was asking him if he were a homosexual. How little, after a month, these two knew each other! 'Yes, I have *only* women for friends.'

'Then perhaps we could buy them some furs. Not a coat, the style would be wrong. But fur we have, not leather suitcases, no, you are right to mock us, but furs, the world's best, and dear enough for even a man so rich as you. I have often argued with Bobochka, he says authors should be poor for the suffering, it is how capitalist countries do it; and now I see he is right.'

Astounded by this tirade, delivered with a switching head so that her mole now and then darted into translucence – for they had reached Moscow's outskirts, and street lamps – Bech could only say, 'Kate, you've never read my books. They're *all* about women.'

'Yes,' she said, 'but coldly observed. As if extraterrestrial life.'

To be brief (I saw you, in the back row, glancing at your wristwatch, and don't think that glance will sweeten your term grade), fur it was. The next morning, in a scrambled hour before the ride to the airport, Bech and Ekaterina went to a shop on Gorky Street where a diffident Mongolian beauty laid pelt after pelt into his hands. The less unsuccessful of his uncles had been for a time a furrier, and after this gap of decades Bech again greeted the frosty luxuriance of silver fox, the more tender and playful and amorous amplitude of red fox, mink with its ugly mahogany assurance, svelte otter, imperial ermine tail-tipped in black like a writing plume. Each pelt, its soft tingling mass condensing acres of Siberia, cost several hundred roubles. Bech bought for his mother two mink still wearing their dried snarls, and two silver fox for his present mistress, Norma Latchett, to trim a coat collar in (her firm white Saxon chin *drowned* in fur, is how he pictured it), and some ermine as a joke for his house-slave sister in Cincinnati, and a sumptuous red fox for a woman he had yet to meet. The Mongolian salesgirl, magnificently unimpressed, added it up to over twelve hundred roubles and wrapped the furs in brown paper like fish. He paid her with a salad of pastel notes and was clean. Bech had not been so exhilarated, so aerated by prosperity, since he sold his first short story – in 1943, about boot camp, to *Liberty,* for a hundred and fifty dollars. It had been humorous, a New York Jew floundering among Southerners, and is omitted from most bibliographies.*

He and Ekaterina rushed back to the Sovietskaya and completed his packing. He tried to forget the gift books stacked in the foyer, but she insisted he take them. They crammed them into his new suitcase, with the furs, the amber, the wristwatches, the infuriatingly knobby and bulky wooden toys. When they were done, the suitcase bulged, leaked fur, and weighed more than his two others combined. Bech looked his last at the chandelier and the empty brandy bottle, the lovesick window and the bugged walls, and staggered out the door. Kate followed with a book and a sock she had found beneath the bed.

Everyone was at the airport to see him off – Bobochka with his silver teeth, Myshkin with his glass eye, the rangy American with his air of lugubrious caution. Bech shook Skip Reynolds's hand good-bye and abrasively kissed the two Russian men on the cheek. He went to kiss Ekaterina on the cheek, but she turned her face so that her mouth met his and he realized, horrified, that he should have slept with her. He had been expected to. From the complacent tiptoe smiles of Bobochka and Myshkin, they assumed he had. She had been provided to him for that purpose. He was a guest of the state. 'Oh Kate, forgive me; of course,' he said, but so stumblingly she seemed not to have understood him. Her kiss had been colourless but moist and good, like a boiled potato.

Then, somehow, suddenly, he was late, there was panic. His suitcases were not yet in the aeroplane. A brute in blue seized the two manageable ones and left him to carry the paper one himself. As he staggered across the runway, it burst. One catch simply

* See Appendix B.

tore loose at the staples, and the other sympathetically let go. The books and toys spilled; the fur began to blow down the concrete, pelts looping and shimmering as if again alive. Kate broke past the gate guard and helped him catch them; together they scooped all the loot back in the suitcase, but for a dozen fluttering books. They were heavy and slick, in the Cyrillic alphabet, like high-school yearbooks upside down. One of the watches had cracked its face. Kate was sobbing and shivering in excitement; a bitter wind was blowing streaks of grit and snow out of the coming long winter. 'Genry, the books!' she said, needing to shout. 'You must have them! They are souvenirs!'

'Mail them!' Bech thundered, and ran with the terrible suitcase under his arm, fearful of being burdened with more responsibilities. Also, though in some ways a man of our time, he has a morbid fear of missing aeroplanes, and of being dropped from the tail-end lavatory.

Though this was five years ago, the books have not yet arrived in the mail. Perhaps Ekaterina Alexandrovna kept them, as souvenirs. Perhaps they were caught in the cultural freeze-up that followed Bech's visit, and were buried in a blizzard. Perhaps they arrived in the lobby of his apartment building, and were pilfered by an émigré vandal. Or perhaps (you may close your notebooks) the mailman is not clairvoyant after all.

Bech in Rumania

or, The Rumanian Chauffeur

Deplaning in Bucharest wearing an astrakhan hat purchased in Moscow, Bech was not recognized by the United States Embassy personnel sent to greet him, and, rather than identify himself, sat sullenly on a bench, glowering like a Soviet machinery importer while these young men ran back and forth conversing with each other in dismayed English and shouting at the customs officials in what Bech took to be pidgin Rumanian. At last, one of these young men, the smallest and cleverest, Princeton '51 or so, noticing the rounded toes of Bech's American shoes, ventured suspiciously 'I beg your pardon, *pazhalusta*, but are you – ?'

'Could be,' Bech said. After five weeks of consorting with Communists, he felt himself increasingly tempted to evade, confuse, and mock his fellow Americans. Further, after attuning himself to the platitudinous jog of translatorese, he found rapid English idiom exhausting. So it was with some relief that he passed, in the next hours, from the conspiratorial company of his compatriots into the care of a monarchial Rumanian hotel and a smiling Party underling called Athanase Petrescu.

Petrescu, whose oval face was adorned by constant sunglasses and several round sticking plasters placed upon a fresh blue shave, had translated into Rumanian *Typee, Pierre, Life on the Mississippi, Sister Carrie, Winesburg, Ohio, Across the River and Into the Trees*, and *On the Road*. He knew Bech's work well and said, 'Although it was *Travel Light* that made your name illustrious, yet in my heart I detect a very soft spot for *Brother Pig*, which your critics did not so much applaud.'

Bech recognized in Petrescu, behind the blue jaw and sinister glasses, a man humbly in love with books, a fool for literature. As, that afternoon, they strolled through a dreamlike Bucharest park containing bronze busts of Goethe and Pushkin and Victor Hugo, beside a lake wherein the greenish sunset was coated with silver, the translator talked excitedly of a dozen things, sharing thoughts he had not been able to share while descending, alone at his desk, into the luminous abysses and profound crudities of American literature. 'With Hemingway, the difficulty of translating – and I speak to an extent of Anderson also – is to prevent the simplicity from seeming simple-minded. For we do not have here such a tradition of belle-lettrist fancifulness against which the style of Hemingway was a rebel. Do you follow the difficulty?'

'Yes. How did you get around it?'

Petrescu did not seem to understand. 'Get around, how? Circumvent?'

'How did you translate the simple language without seeming simple-minded?'

'Oh. By being extremely subtle.'

'Oh. I should tell you, some people in my country think Hemingway *was* simple-minded. It is actively debated.'

Petrescu absorbed this with a nod, and said, 'I know for a fact, his Italian is not always correct.'

When Bech got back to his hotel – situated on a square rimmed with buildings made, it seemed, of dusty pink candy – a message had been left for him to call Phillips at the U.S. Embassy. Phillips was Princeton '51. He asked, 'What have they got mapped out for you?'

Bech's schedule had hardly been discussed. 'Petrescu mentioned a production of *Desire Under the Elms* I might see. And he wants to take me to Braşov. Where is Braşov?'

'In Transylvania, way the hell off. It's where Dracula hung out. Listen, can we talk frankly?'

'We can try.'

'I know damn well this line is bugged, but here goes. This country is hot. Anti-Socialism is bursting out all over. My inkling is they want to get you out of Bucharest, away from all the liberal writers who are dying to meet you.'

'Are you sure they're not dying to meet Arthur Miller?'

'Kidding aside, Bech, there's a lot of ferment in this country, and we want to plug you in. Now, when are you meeting Taru?'

'Knock knock. Taru. Taru Who?'

'Jesus, he's the head of the Writer's Union – hasn't Petrescu even set up an appointment? Boy, they're putting you right around the old mulberry bush. I gave Petrescu a list of writers for you to latch on to. Suppose I call him and wave the big stick and ring you back. Got it?'

'Got it, tiger.' Bech hung up sadly; one of the reasons he had accepted the State Department's invitation was that he thought it would be an escape from agents.

Within ten minutes his phone rasped, in that dead rattly way it has behind the Iron Curtain, and it was Phillips, breathless, victorious. 'Congratulate me,' he said. 'I've been making like a thug and got *their* thugs to give you an appointment with Taru tonight.'

'This very night?'

Phillips sounded hurt. 'You're only here four nights, you know. Petrescu will pick you up. His excuse was he thought you might want some rest.'

'He's extremely subtle.'

'What was that?'

'Never mind, *pazhalusta*.'

Petrescu came for Bech in a black car driven by a hunched silhouette. The Writers' Union was housed on the other side of town, in a kind of castle, a turreted mansion with a flaring stone staircase and an oak-vaulted library whose shelves were twenty feet high and solid with leather spines. The stairs and chambers seemed deserted. Petrescu tapped on a tall panelled door of blackish oak, strap-hinged in the sombre Spanish style. The door soundlessly opened, revealing a narrow high room hung with tapestries, pale brown and blue, whose subject involved masses of attenuated soldiery unfathomably engaged. Behind a huge polished desk quite bare of furnishings sat an immaculate miniature man with a pink face and hair as white as a dandelion poll. His rosy hands, perfectly finished down to each fingernail, were folded on the shiny desk, reflected like water flowers; and his face wore a smiling expression that was also, in each neat crease, beyond improvement. This was Taru.

He spoke with magical suddenness, like a music box. Petrescu translated his words to Bech as, 'You are a literary man. Do you know the works of our Mihail Sadoveanu, of our noble Mihai Beniuc, or perhaps that most wonderful spokesman for the people, Tudor Arghezi?'

Bech said, 'No, I'm afraid the only Rumanian writer I know at all is Ionesco.'

The exquisite white-haired man nodded eagerly and emitted a length of tinkling sounds that was translated to Bech as simply 'And who is he?'

Petrescu, who certainly knew all about Ionesco, stared at Bech with blank expectance. Even in this innermost sanctum he had kept his sunglasses on. Bech said, irritated, 'A playwright. Lives in Paris. Theatre of the Absurd. Wrote *Rhinoceros*,' and he crooked a forefinger beside his heavy Jewish nose, to represent a horn.

Taru emitted a dainty sneeze of laughter. Petrescu translated, listened, and told Bech, 'He is very sorry he has not heard of this man. Western books are a luxury here, so we are not able to follow each new nihilist movement. Comrade Taru asks what you plan to do while in the People's Republic of Rumania.'

'I am told,' Bech said, 'that there are some writers interested in exchanging ideas with an American colleague. I believe my embassy has suggested a list to you.'

The musical voice went on and on. Petrescu listened with a cocked ear and relayed, 'Comrade Taru sincerely wishes that this may be the case and regrets that, because of the lateness of the hour and the haste of this meeting urged by your embassy, no secretaries are present to locate this list. He furthermore regrets that at this time of the year so many of our fine writers are bathing at the Black Sea. However, he points out that there is an excellent production of *Desire Under the Elms* in Bucharest, and that our Carpathian city of Braşov is indeed worthy of a visit.

Comrade Taru himself retains many pleasant youthful memories concerning Braşov.'

Taru rose to his feet – an intensely dramatic event within the reduced scale he had established around himself. He spoke, thumped his small square chest resoundingly, spoke again, and smiled. Petrescu said, 'He wishes you to know that in his youth he published many books of poetry, both epic and lyric in manner. He adds, "A fire ignited here"' – and here Petrescu struck his own chest in flaccid mimicry – ' "can never be quenched." '

Bech stood and responded, 'In my country we also ignite fires *here*.' He touched his head. His remark was not translated and, after an efflorescent display of courtesy from the brilliant-haired little man, Bech and Petrescu made their way through the empty mansion down to the waiting car, which drove them, rather jerkily, back to the hotel.

'And how did you like Mr Taru?' Petrescu asked on the way.

'He's a doll,' Bech said.

'You mean – a puppet?'

Bech turned curiously but saw nothing in Petrescu's face that betrayed more than a puzzlement over meaning. Bech said, 'I'm sure you have a better eye for the strings than I do.'

Since neither had eaten, they dined together at the hotel; they discussed Faulkner and Hawthorne while waiters brought them soup and veal a continent removed from the cabbagy cuisine of Russia. A lithe young woman on awkwardly high heels stalked among the tables singing popular songs from Italy and France. The trailing microphone wire now and then became entangled in her feet, and Bech admired the sly savagery with which she would, while not altering an iota her enamelled smile, kick herself free. Bech had been a long time without a woman. He looked forward to three more nights sitting at this table, surrounded by travelling salesmen from East Germany and Hungary, feasting on the sight of this lithe chanteuse. Though her motions were angular and her smile was inflexible, her high round bosom looked soft as a soufflé.

But tomorrow, Petrescu explained, smiling sweetly beneath his sad-eyed sunglasses, they would go to Braşov.

Bech knew little about Rumania. From his official briefing he knew it was 'a Latin island in a Slavic sea', that during World War II its anti-Semitism had been the most ferocious in Europe, that now it was seeking economic independence of the Soviet bloc. The ferocity especially interested him, since of the many human conditions it was his business to imagine, murderousness was among the more difficult. He was a Jew. Though he could be irritable and even vengeful, obstinate savagery was excluded from his budget of emotions.

Petrescu met him in the hotel lobby at nine and, taking his suitcase from his hand, led him to the hired car. By daylight, the chauffeur was a short man the colour of ashes – white ash for the face, grey cigarette ash for his close-trimmed smudge of a moustache, and the darker residue of a tougher substance for his eyes and hair. His manner was nervous and remote and fussy; Bech's impression was of a stupidity so severe that the mind is tensed to sustain the simplest tasks. As they drove from the city, the driver constantly tapped his horn to warn pedestrians and cyclists of his approach. They passed the prewar stucco suburbs, suggestive of southern California; the postwar Moscow-style apartment buildings, rectilinear and airless; the heretical all-glass exposition halls the Rumanians had built to celebrate twenty years of industrial progress under Socialism. It was shaped like a huge sailor's cap, and before it stood a tall Brancusi column cast in aluminium.

'Brancusi,' Bech said. 'I didn't know you acknowledged him.'

'Oh, much,' Petrescu said. 'His village is a shrine. I can show you many early works in our national museum.'

'And Ionesco? Is he really a non-person?'

Petrescu smiled. 'The eminent head of our Writers' Union,' he said, 'makes little jokes. He is known here but not much produced as yet. Students in their rooms perhaps read aloud a play like *The Singer Devoid of Hair*.'

Bech was distracted from the conversation by the driver's incessant mutter of tooting. They were in the country now, driving along a straight, slightly rising road lined with trees whose trunks were painted white. On the shoulder of the road walked bundle-shaped old women carrying knotted bundles, little boys tapping donkeys forward, men in French-blue work clothes sauntering empty-handed. At all of them the driver sounded his horn. His stubby, grey-nailed hand fluttered on the contact rim, producing an agitated stammer beginning perhaps a hundred yards in advance and continuing until the person, who usually moved only to turn and scowl, had been passed. Since the road was well travelled, the noise was practically uninterrupted, and after the first half hour nagged Bech like a toothache. He asked Petrescu, 'Must he do that?'

'Oh, yes. He is a conscientious man.'

'What good does it do?'

Petrescu, who had been developing an exciting thought on Mark Twain's infatuation with the apparatus of capitalism, which had undermined his bucolic genius, indulgently explained, 'The bureau from which we hire cars provides the driver. They have been precisely trained for this profession.'

Bech realized that Petrescu himself did not drive. He reposed in the oblivious trust of an aeroplane passenger, legs crossed, sunglasses in place, issuing smoother and smoother phrases, while Bech leaned forward anxiously, braking on the empty floor, twitching a wheel that was not there, trying to wrench the car's control away from this atrociously unrhythmic and brutal driver. When they went through a village, the driver would speed up and intensify the mutter of his honking; clusters of peasants and geese exploded in disbelief, and Bech felt as if gears, the gears that space and engage the mind, were clashing. As they ascended into the mountains, the driver demonstrated his technique with curves: he approached each like an enemy, accelerating, and at the last moment stepped on the brake as if crushing a snake underfoot. In the jerking and swaying, Petrescu grew pale. His blue jaw acquired a moist sheen and issued phrases less smoothly. Bech said to him, 'This driver should be locked up. He is sick and dangerous.'

'No, no, he is a good man. These roads, they are difficult.'

'At least please ask him to stop twiddling the horn. It's torture.'

Petrescu's eyebrows arched, but he leaned forward and spoke in Rumanian.

The driver answered; the language clattered in his mouth, though his voice was soft.

Petrescu told Bech, 'He says it is a safety precaution.'

'Oh, for Christ's sake!'

Petrescu was truly puzzled. He asked, 'In the States, you drive your own car?'

'Of course, everybody does,' Bech said, and then worried that he had hurt the feelings of this Socialist, who must submit to the aristocratic discomfort of being driven. For the remainder of the trip, he held silent about the driver. The muddy lowland fields with Mediterranean farmhouses had yielded to fir-dark hills bearing Germanic chalets. At the highest point, the old boundary of Austria-Hungary, fresh snow had fallen, and the car, pressed ruthlessly through the ruts, brushed within inches of some children dragging sleds. It was a short downhill distance from there to Braşov. They stopped before a newly built pistachio hotel. The jarring ride had left Bech with a headache. Petrescu stepped carefully from the car, licking his lips; the tip of his tongue showed purple in his drained face. The chauffeur, as composed as raked ashes no touch of wind has stirred, changed out of his grey driving coat, checked the oil and water, and removed his lunch from the trunk. Bech examined him for some sign of satisfaction, some betraying trace of malice, but there was nothing. His eyes were living smudges, and his mouth was the mouth of the boy in the class who, being neither strong nor intelligent, has developed insignificance into a positive character trait that does him some credit. He glanced at Bech without expression; yet Bech wondered if the man did not understand English a little.

In Braşov the American writer and his escort passed the time in harmless sightseeing. The local museum contained peasant costumes. The local castle contained armour. The Lutheran cathedral was surprising; Gothic lines and scale had been wedded to clear glass and an austerity of decoration, noble and mournful, that left one, Bech felt, much too alone with God. He felt the Reformation here as a desolating wind, four hundred years ago. From the hotel roof, the view looked sepia, and there was an empty swimming pool, and wet snow on the lacy metal chairs. Petrescu shivered and went down to his room. Bech changed neckties and went down to the bar. Champagne music bubbled from the walls. The bartender understood what a Martini was, though he used equal parts of gin and vermouth. The clientele was young, and many spoke Hungarian, for Transylvania had been taken from Hungary after the war. One plausible youth, working with Bech's reluctant French, elicited from him that he was *un écrivain*, and asked for his autograph. But this turned out to be the prelude to a proposed exchange of pens, in which Bech lost a sentimentally cherished Esterbrook and gained a nameless ball-point that wrote red. Bech wrote three and a half postcards (to his mistress, his mother, his publisher, and a half to his editor at *Commentary*) before the red pen went dry. Petrescu, who neither drank nor smoked, finally appeared. Bech said, 'My hero, where have you been? I've had four Martinis and been swindled in your absence.'

Petrescu was embarrassed. 'I've been shaving.'

'Shaving!'

'Yes, it is humiliating. I must spend each day one hour shaving, and even yet it does not look as if I have shaved, my beard is so obdurate.'

'Are you putting blades in the razor?'

'Oh, yes, I buy the best and use two upon each occasion.'

'This is the saddest story I've ever heard. Let me send you some decent blades when I get home.'

'Please, do not. There are no blades better than the blades I use. It is merely that my beard is phenomenal.'

'When you die,' Bech said, 'you can leave it to Rumanian science.'

'You are ironical.'

In the restaurant, there was dancing – the Tveest, the Hully

Gullee, and chain formations that involved a lot of droll hopping. American dances had become here innocently birdlike. Now and then a young man, slender and with hair combed into a parrot's peak, would leap into the air and seem to hover, emitting a shrill palatal cry. The men in Rumania appeared lighter and more fanciful than the women, who moved, in their bell-skirted cocktail dresses, with a wooden stateliness perhaps inherited from their peasant grandmothers. Each girl who passed near their table was described by Petrescu, not humorously at first, as a 'typical Rumanian beauty'.

'And this one, with the orange lips and eyelashes?'

'A typical Rumanian beauty. The cheekbones are very classical.'

'And the blonde behind her? The small plump one?'

'Also typical.'

'But they are so different. Which is more typical?'

'They are equally. We are a perfect democracy.' Between spates of dancing, a young chanteuse, more talented than the one in the Bucharest hotel, took the floor. She had learned, probably from free-world films, that terrible mannerism of strenuousness whereby every note, no matter how accessibly placed and how flatly attacked, is given a facial aura of immense accomplishment. Her smile, at the close of each number, triumphantly combined a conspiratorial twinkle, a sublime humility, and the dazed self-congratulation of post-coital euphoria. Yet, beneath the artifice, the girl had life. Bech was charmed by a number, in Italian, that involved much animated pouting and finger-scolding and placing of the fists on the hips. Petrescu explained that the song was the plaint of a young wife whose husband was always attending soccer matches and never stayed home with her. Bech asked, 'Is she also a typical Rumanian beauty?'

'I think,' Petrescu said, with a purr Bech had not heard before, 'she is a typical little Jewess.'

The drive, late the next afternoon, back to Bucharest was worse than the one out, for it took place partly in the dark. The chauffeur met the challenge with increased speed and redoubled honking. In a rare intermittence of danger, a straight road near

Ploesti where only the oil rigs relieved the flatness, Bech asked, 'Seriously, do you not feel the insanity in this man?' Five minutes before, the driver had turned to the back seat and, showing even grey teeth in a tight tic of a smile, had remarked about a dog lying dead beside the road. Bech suspected that most of the remark had not been translated.

Petrescu said, crossing his legs in the effete and weary way that had begun to exasperate Bech, 'No, he is a good man, an extremely kind man, who takes his work too seriously. In that he is like the beautiful Jewess whom you so much admired.'

'In my country,' Bech said, ' "Jewess" is a kind of fighting word.'

'Here,' Petrescu said, 'it is merely descriptive. Let us talk about Herman Melville. Is it possible to you that *Pierre* is a yet greater work than *The White Whale*?'

'No, I think it is yet not so great, possibly.'

'You are ironical about my English. Please excuse it. Being prone to motion sickness has discollected my thoughts.'

'Our driver would discollect anybody's thoughts. Is it possible that he is the late Adolf Hitler, kept alive by Count Dracula?'

'I think not. Our people's uprising in 1944 fortunately exterminated the Fascists.'

'That is fortunate. Have you ever read, speaking of Melville, *Omoo*?'

Melville, it happened, was Bech's favourite American author, in whom he felt united the strengths that were later to go the separate ways of Dreiser and James. Throughout dinner, back at the hotel, he lectured Petrescu about him. 'No one,' Bech said – he had ordered a full bottle of white Rumanian wine, and his tongue felt agile as a butterfly – 'more courageously faced our native terror. He went for it right between its wide-set little pig eyes, and it shattered his genius like a lance.' He poured himself more wine. The hotel chanteuse, who Bech now noticed had buck teeth as well as gawky legs, stalked to their table, untangled her feet from the microphone wire, and favoured them with a French version of 'Some Enchanted Evening'.

'You do not consider,' Petrescu said, 'that Hawthorne also

went between the eyes? And the laconic Ambrose Bierce?'

'*Quelque soir enchanté*,' the girl sang, her eyes and teeth and earrings glittering like the facets of a chandelier.

'Hawthorne blinked,' Bech pronounced, 'and Bierce squinted.'

'*Vous verrez l'étranger . . .*'

'I worry about you, Petrescu,' Bech continued. 'Don't you ever have to go home? Isn't there a Frau Petrescu, Madame, or whatever, a typical Rumanian, never mind.' Abruptly he felt steeply lonely.

In bed, when his room had stopped the gentle swaying motion with which it had greeted his entrance, he remembered the driver, and the man's neatly combed death-grey face seemed the face of everything foul, stale, stupid, and uncontrollable in the world. He had seen that tight tic of a smile before. Where? He remembered. West Eighty-sixth Street, coming back from Riverside Park, a childhood playmate, with whom he always argued, and was always right, and always lost. Their ugliest quarrel had concerned comic strips, whether or not the artist – Segar, say, who drew Popeye, or Harold Gray of Little Orphan Annie – whether or not the artist, in duplicating the faces from panel to panel, day after day, traced them. Bech had maintained, obviously, not. The other boy had insisted that some mechanical process was used. Bech tried to explain that it was not such a difficult feat, that just as one's handwriting is always the same – The other boy, his face clouding, said it wasn't possible. Bech explained, what he felt so clearly, that everything was possible for human beings, with a little training and talent, that the ease and variation of each panel proved – The other face had become totally closed, with a density quite inhuman, as it steadily shook 'No, no, no', and Bech, becoming frightened and furious, tried to behead the other boy with his fists, and the boy in turn pinned him and pressed his face into the bitter grits of pebble and glass that coated the cement passageway between two apartment buildings. These unswept jagged bits, a kind of city topsoil, had enlarged under his eyes, and this experience, the magnification amidst pain of those negligible mineral flecks, had formed, perhaps, a vision. At any rate, it seemed to Bech, as he skidded into sleep, that his artistic gifts had been squandered in the attempt to recapture that moment of stinging precision.

The next day was his last full day in Rumania. Petrescu took him to an art museum where, amid many ethnic posters posing as paintings, a few sketches and sculpted heads by the young Brancusi smelled like saints' bones. The two men went on to the twenty years' industrial exhibit and admired rows of brightly painted machinery – gaudy counters in some large international game. They visited shops, and everywhere Bech felt a desiccated pinkish elegance groping, out of eclipse, through the murky hardware of Sovietism, towards a rebirth of style. Yet there had been a tough and heroic naïveté in Russia that he missed here, where something shrugging and effete seemed to leave room for a vein of energetic evil. In the evening, they went to *Patima de Sub Ulmi*.

Their driver, bringing them to the very door of the theatre, pressed his car forward through bodies, up an arc of driveway crowded with pedestrians. The people caught in the headlights were astonished; Bech slammed his foot on a phantom brake and Petrescu grunted and strained backwards in his seat. The driver continually tapped his horn – a demented, persistent muttering – and slowly the crowd gave way around the car. Bech and Petrescu stepped, at the door, into the humid atmosphere of a riot. As the chauffeur, his childish small-nosed profile intent, pressed his car back through the crowd to the street, fists thumped on the fenders.

Safe in the theatre lobby, Petrescu took off his sunglasses to wipe his face. His eyes were a tender bulging blue, with jaundiced whites; a scholar's tremor pulsed in his left lower lid. 'You know,' he confided to Bech, 'that man our driver. Not all is well with him.'

'Could be,' Bech said.

O'Neill's starveling New England farmers were played as Russian muzhiks; they wore broad-belted coats and high black boots and kept walloping each other on the back. Abbie Cabot had become a typical Rumanian beauty, ten years past prime, with a beauty spot on one cheek and artful bare arms as supple as a swan's neck. Since their seats were in the centre of the second row, Bech had a good if infrequent view down the front of her dress, and thus, ignorant of when the plot would turn her his way, he contentedly manufactured suspense for himself. But Petrescu, his loyalty to American letters affronted beyond endurance, insisted that they leave after the first act. 'Wrong, wrong,' he complained. 'Even the pitchforks were wrong.'

'I'll have the State Department send them an authentic American pitchfork,' Bech promised.

'And the girl – the girl is not like that, not a coquette. She is a religious innocent, under economic stress.'

'Well, scratch an innocent, find a coquette.'

'It is your good nature to joke, but I am ashamed you saw such a travesty. Now our driver is not here. We are undone.'

The street outside the theatre, so recently jammed, was empty and dark. A solitary couple walked slowly towards them. With surrealist suddenness, Petrescu fell into the arms of the man, walloping his back, and then kissed the calmly proffered hand of the woman. The couple was introduced to Bech as 'a most brilliant young writer and his notably ravishing wife'. The man, stolid and forbidding, wore rimless glasses and a bulky checked topcoat. The woman was scrawny; her face, potentially handsome, had been worn to its bones by the nervous stress of intelligence. She had a cold and a command, quick but limited, of English. 'Are you having a liking for this?' she asked.

Bech understood her gesture to include all Rumania. 'Very much,' he answered. 'After Russia, it seems very civilized.'

'And who isn't?' she snapped. 'What are you liking most?'

Petrescu roguishly interposed, 'He has a passion for night-club singers.'

The wife translated this to her husband; he took his hands from his overcoat pockets and clapped them. He was wearing leather gloves, so the noise was loud on the deserted street. He spoke, and Petrescu translated, 'He says we should therefore, as hosts, escort you to the most celebrated night club in Bucharest, where you will see many singers, each more glorious than the preceding.'

'But,' Bech said, 'weren't they going somewhere? Shouldn't they go home?' It worried him that Communists never seemed to go home.

'For why?' the wife cried.

'You have a cold,' Bech told her. Her eyes didn't comprehend. He touched his own nose, so much larger than hers. '*Un rhume.*'

'Poh!' she said. 'Itself takes care of tomorrow.'

The writer owned a car, and he drove them, with the gentleness of a pedal boat, through a maze of alleys overhung by cornices suggestive of cake frosting, of waves breaking, of seashells, lion paws, unicorn horns, and cumulus clouds. They parked across the street from a blue sign, and went into a green doorway, and down a yellow set of stairs. Music approached them from one direction and a coat-check girl in net tights from the other. It was to Bech as if he were dreaming of an American night club, giving it the strange spaciousness of dreams. The main room had been conjured out of several basements – a cave hollowed from the underside of jeweller's shops and vegetable marts. Tables were set in shadowy tiers arranged around a central square floor. Here a man with a red wig and mascaraed eyes was talking into a microphone, mincingly. Then he sang, in the voice of a choirboy castrated too late. A waiter materialized. Bech ordered Scotch, the other writer ordered vodka. The wife asked for cognac and Petrescu for mineral water. Three girls dressed as rather naked bicyclists appeared with a dwarf on a unicycle and did some unsmiling gyrations to music while he pedalled among them, tugging bows and displacing straps. 'Typical Polish beauties,' Petrescu explained in Bech's ear. He and the writer's wife were seated on the tier behind Bech. Two women, one a girl in her teens and the other a heavy old blonde, perhaps her mother, both dressed identically in sequined silver, did a hypnotic, languorous act with tinted pigeons, throwing them up in the air, watching them wheel through the shadows of the night club, and holding out their wrists for their return. They juggled with the pigeons, passed them between their legs, and for a climax the elderly blonde fed an aquamarine pigeon with seeds held in her mouth and fetched, one by one, on to her lips. 'Czechs,' Petrescu explained. The master of ceremonies reappeared in a blue wig and a toreador's jacket, and did a comic act with the dwarf, who had been fitted with papier-mâché horns. An East German girl, flaxen-haired and apple-cheeked, with the smooth columnar legs of the very young, came to the microphone dressed in a minimal parody of a cowgirl outfit and sang, in English, 'Dip in the Hot of Texas' and 'Allo Cindy Lou, Gootbye Hot'. She pulled guns from her hips and received much pro-American applause, but Bech was on his third Scotch and needed his hands to hold cigarettes. The Rumanian writer sat at the table beside him, a carafe of vodka at his elbow, staring stolidly at the floor show. He looked like the young Theodore Roosevelt, or perhaps McGeorge Bundy. His wife leaned forward and said in Bech's ear, 'Is just like home, hey? Texas is ringing bells?' He decided she was being sarcastic. A fat man in a baggy maroon tuxedo set up a long table and kept eight tin plates twirling on the ends of flexible sticks. Bech thought it was miraculous, but the man was booed. A touching black-haired girl from Bulgaria hesitantly sang three atonal folk songs into a chastened silence. Three women behind Bech began to chatter hissingly. Bech turned to rebuke them and was stunned by the size of their wristwatches, which were man-sized, as in Russia. Also, in turning he had surprised Petrescu and the writer's wife holding hands. Though it was after midnight, the customers were still coming in, and the floor show refused to stop. The Polish girls returned dressed as ponies and jumped through hoops the dwarf held for them. The master of ceremonies reappeared in a striped bathing suit and black wig and did an act with the dwarf involving a stepladder and a bucket of water. A black dancer from Ghana twirled firebrands in the dark while slapping the floor with her bare feet. Four Latvian tumblers performed on a trampoline and a seesaw. The Czech mother and daughter came back in different costumes, spangled gold, but performed the identical act, the pigeons whirring, circling, returning, eating from the mother's lips. Then five Chinese girls from Outer Mongolia –

'My God,' Bech said, 'isn't this ever going to be over? Don't you Communists ever get tired of having fun?'

The writer's wife told him, 'For your money, you really gets.'

Petrescu and she conferred and decided it was time to go. One of the big wristwatches behind Bech said two o'clock. In leaving, they had to pass around the Chinese girls, who, each clad in a snug beige bikini, were concealing and revealing their bodies amid a weave of rippling coloured flags. One of the girls glanced sideways at Bech, and he blew her a pert kiss, as if from a train window. Their yellow bodies looked fragile to him; he felt that their bones, like the bones of birds, had evolved hollow, to save weight. At the mouth of the cave, the effeminate master of ceremonies, wearing a parrot headdress, was conferring with the hat-check girl. His intent was plainly heterosexual; Bech's head reeled at such duplicity. Though they added the weight of his coat to him, he rose like a balloon up the yellow stairs, bumped out through the green door, and stood beneath the street lamp inhaling volumes of the blue Rumanian night.

He felt duty-bound to confront the other writer. They stood, the two of them, on the cobbled pavement, as if on opposite sides of a transparent wall one side of which was lacquered with Scotch and the other with vodka. The other's rimless glasses were misted and the resemblance to Teddy Roosevelt had been dissipated. Bech asked him, 'What do you write about?'

The wife, patting her nose with a handkerchief and struggling not to cough, translated the question, and the answer, which was brief. 'Peasants,' she told Bech. 'He wants to know, what do *you* write about?'

Bech spoke to him directly. '*La bourgeoisie*,' he said; and that completed the cultural exchange. Gently bumping and rocking, the writer's car took Bech back to his hotel, where he fell into the deep, unapologetic sleep of the sated.

The plane to Sofia left Bucharest the next morning. Petrescu and the ashen-faced chauffeur came into the tall *fin-de-siècle* dining-room for Bech while he was still eating breakfast – *jus d'orange, des croissants avec du beurre* and *une omelette aux fines herbes*. Petrescu explained that the driver had gone back to the theatre, and waited until the ushers and the managers left, after midnight. But the driver did not seem resentful, and gave Bech, in the sallow morning light, a fractional smile, a *risus sardonicus*, in which his eyes did not participate. On the way to the airport, he scattered a flock of chickens an old woman was coaxing across the road, and forced a military transport truck on to the shoulder, while its load of soldiers gestured and jeered. Bech's stomach grovelled, bathing the fine herbs of his breakfast in acid. The ceaseless tapping of the horn seemed a gnawing on all of his nerve ends. Petrescu made a fastidious mouth and sighed through his nostrils. 'I regret,' he said, 'that we did not make more occasion to discuss your exciting contemporaries.'

'I never read them. They're too exciting,' Bech said, as a line of uniformed schoolchildren was narrowly missed, and a field-worker with a wheelbarrow shuffled to safety, spilling potatoes. The day was overcast above the loamy sunken fields and the roadside trees in their skirts of white paint. 'Why,' he asked, not having meant to be rude, 'are all these tree trunks painted?'

'So they are,' Petrescu said, 'I have not noticed this before, in all my years. Presumably it is a measure to defeat the insects.'

The driver spoke in Rumanian, and Petrescu told Bech, 'He says it is for the car headlights, at night. Always he is thinking about his job.'

At the airport, all the Americans were there who had tried to meet Bech four days ago. Petrescu immediately delivered to Phillips, like a bribe, the name of the writer they had met last night, and Phillips said to Bech, 'You spent the evening with *him*? That's fabulous. He's the top of the list, man. We've never laid a finger on him before; he's been inaccessible.'

'Stocky guy with glasses?' Bech asked, shielding his eyes. Phillips was so pleased it was like a bright light too early in the day.

'That's the boy. For our money he's the hottest Red writer this side of Solzhenitsyn. He's *waaay* out. Stream of consciousness, no punctuation, everything. There's even some sex.'

'You might say he's Red hot,' Bech said.

'Huh? Yeah, that's good. Seriously, what did he say to you?'

'He said he'll defect to the West as soon as his shirts come back from the laundry.'

'And we went,' Petrescu said, 'to La Caverne Bleue.'

'Say,' Phillips said, 'you really went underground.'

'I think of myself,' Bech said modestly, 'as a sort of low-flying U-2.'

'All kidding aside, Henry' – and here Phillips took Bech by the arms and squeezed – 'it sounds as if you've done a sensational job for us. Sensational. Thanks, friend.'

Bech hugged everyone in parting – Phillips, the chargé d'affaires, the junior chargé d'affaires, the ambassador's twelve-year-old nephew, who was taking archery lessons near the airport and had to be dropped off. Bech saved Petrescu for last, and walloped his back, for the man had led him to remember, what he was tempted to forget in America, that reading can be the best part of a man's life.

'I'll send you razor blades,' he promised, for in the embrace Petrescu's beard had scratched.

'No, no, I already buy the best. Send me books, any books!'

The plane was roaring to go, and only when safely, or fatally, sealed inside did Bech remember the chauffeur. In the flurry of formalities and baggage handling there had been no good-bye. Worse, there had been no tip. The leu notes Bech had set aside were still folded in his wallet, and his start of guilt gave way, as the runways and dark fields tilted and dwindled under him, to a vengeful satisfaction and glad sense of release. Clouds blotted out the country. He realized that for four days he had been afraid. The man next to him, a portly Slav whose bald brow was beaded with apprehensive sweat, turned and confided something unintelligible, and Bech said, '*Pardon, je ne comprends pas. Je suis Américain.*'

The Bulgarian Poetess

'Your poems. Are they difficult?'

She smiled and, unaccustomed to speaking English, answered carefully, drawing a line in the air with two delicately pinched fingers holding an imaginary pen. 'They are difficult – to write.'

He laughed, startled and charmed. 'But not to read?'

She seemed puzzled by his laugh, but did not withdraw her smile, though its corners deepened in a defensive, feminine way. 'I think,' she said, 'not so very.'

'Good.' Brainlessly he repeated 'Good', disarmed by her unexpected quality of truth. He was, himself, a writer, this fortyish young man, Henry Bech, with his thinning curly hair and melancholy Jewish nose, the author of one good book and three others, the good one having come first. By a kind of oversight, he had never married. His reputation had grown while his powers declined. As he felt himself sink, in his fiction, deeper and deeper into eclectic sexuality and bravura narcissism, as his search for plain truth carried him further and further into treacherous realms of fantasy and, lately, of silence, he was more and more thickly hounded by homage, by flat-footed exegetes, by arrogantly worshipful undergraduates who had hitchhiked a thousand miles to touch his hand, by querulous translators, by election to honorary societies, by invitations to lecture, to 'speak', to 'read', to participate in symposia trumped up by ambitious girlie magazines in shameless conjunction with venerable universities. His very government, in airily unstamped envelopes from Washington, invited him to travel, as an ambassador of the arts, to the other half of the world, the hostile, mysterious half. Rather automatically, but with some faint hope of shaking himself loose from the burden of himself, he consented, and found himself floating, with a passport so stapled with visas it fluttered when pulled from his pocket, down into the dim airports of Communist cities.

He arrived in Sofia the day after a mixture of Bulgarian and African students had smashed the windows of the American legation and ignited an overturned Chevrolet. The cultural officer, pale from a sleepless night of guard duty, tamping his pipe with trembling fingers, advised Bech to stay out of crowds and escorted him to his hotel. The lobby was swarming with Negroes in black wool fezzes and pointed European shoes. Insecurely disguised, he felt, by an astrakhan hat purchased in Moscow, Bech passed through to the elevator, whose operator addressed him in German, '*Ja, vier*,' Bech answered, '*danke*,' and telephoned, in his bad French, for dinner to be brought up to his room. He remained there all night, behind a locked door, reading Hawthorne. He had lifted a paperback collection of short stories from a legation window sill littered with broken glass. A few curved bright crumbs fell from between the pages on to his blanket. The image of Roger Malvin lying alone, dying, in the forest – 'Death would come like the slow approach of a corpse, stealing gradually towards him through the forest, and showing its ghastly and motionless features from behind a nearer and yet a nearer tree' – frightened him. Bech fell asleep early and suffered from swollen, homesick dreams. It had been the first day of Hanukkah.

In the morning, venturing downstairs for breakfast, he was surprised to find the restaurant open, the waiters affable, the eggs actual, the coffee hot, though syrupy. Outside, Sofia was sunny and (except for a few dark glances at his big American shoes) amenable to his passage along the streets. Lozenge-patterns of pansies, looking flat and brittle as pressed flowers, had been set in the public beds. Women with a touch of Western *chic* walked hatless in the park behind the mausoleum of Georgi Dimitrov. There was a mosque, and an assortment of trolleycars salvaged from the remotest corner of Bech's childhood, and a tree that talked – that is, it was so full of birds that it swayed under their weight and emitted volumes of chirping sound like a great leafy loudspeaker. It was the inverse of his hotel, whose silent walls presumably contained listening microphones. Electricity was somewhat enchanted in the Socialist world. Lights flickered off untouched and radios turned themselves on. Telephones rang in the dead of the night and breathed wordlessly in his ear. Six weeks ago, flying from New York City, Bech had expected Moscow to be a blazing counterpart and instead saw, through the plane window, a skein of hoarded lights no brighter, on that vast black plain, than a girl's body in a dark room.

Past the talking tree was the American legation. The sidewalk, heaped with broken glass, was roped off, so that pedestrians had to detour into the gutter. Bech detached himself from the stream, crossed the little barren of pavement, smiled at the Bulgarian militiamen who were sullenly guarding the jewel-bright heaps of shards, and pulled open the bronze door. The cultural officer was crisper after a normal night's sleep. He clenched his pipe in his teeth and handed Bech a small list. 'You're to meet with the Writers' Union at eleven. These are writers you might ask to see. As far as we can tell, they're among the more progressive.'

Words like 'progressive' and 'liberal' had a somewhat reversed sense in this world. At times, indeed, Bech felt he had passed through a mirror, a dingy flecked mirror that reflected feebly the capitalist world; in its dim depths everything was similar but left-handed. One of the names ended in '-ova'. Bech said, 'A woman.'

'A poetess,' the cultural officer said, sucking and tamping in a fury of bogus efficiency. 'Very popular, apparently. Her books are impossible to buy.'

'Have you read anything by these people?'

'I'll be frank with you. I can just about make my way through a newspaper.'

'But you always know what a newspaper will say anyway.'

'I'm sorry, I don't get your meaning.'

'There isn't any.' Bech didn't quite know why the Americans he met irritated him – whether because they garishly refused to blend into this shadow-world or because they were always so solemnly sending him on ridiculous errands.

At the Writers' Union, he handed the secretary the list as it had been handed to him, on US legation stationery. The secretary, a large stooped man with the hands of a stonemason, grimaced and shook his head but obligingly reached for the telephone. Bech's meeting was already waiting in another room. It was the usual one, the one that, with small differences, he had already attended in Moscow and Kiev, Yerevan and Alma-Ata, Bucharest and Prague: the polished oval table, the bowl of fruit, the morning light, the gleaming glasses of brandy and mineral water, the lurking portrait of Lenin, the six or eight patiently sitting men who would leap to their feet with quick blank smiles. These men would include a few literary officials, termed 'critics', high in the Party, loquacious and witty and destined to propose a toast to international understanding; a few selected novelists and poets, mustachioed, smoking, sulking at this invasion of their time; a university professor, the head of the Anglo-American Literature department, speaking in a beautiful withered English of Mark Twain and Sinclair Lewis; a young interpreter with a moist handshake; a shaggy old journalist obsequiously scribbling notes; and, on the rim of the group, in chairs placed to suggest that they had invited themselves, one or two gentlemen of ill-defined status, fidgety and tieless, maverick translators who would turn out to be the only ones present who had ever read a word by Henry Bech.

Here this type was represented by a stout man in a tweed coat leather-patched at the elbows in the British style. The whites of his eyes were distinctly red. He shook Bech's hand eagerly, made of it almost an embrace of reunion, bending his face so close that Bech could distinguish the smells of tobacco, garlic, cheese, and alcohol. Even as they were seating themselves around the table, and the Writers' Union chairman, a man elegantly bald, with very pale eyelashes, was touching his brandy glass as if to lift it, this anxious red-eyed interloper blurted at Bech, 'Your *Travel*

Light was so marvellous a book. The motels, the highways, the young girls with their lovers who were motorcyclists, so marvellous, so American, the youth, the adoration for space and speed, the barbarity of the advertisements in neon lighting, the very poetry. It takes us truly into another dimension.'

Travel Light was the first novel, the famous one. Bech disliked discussing it. 'At home,' he said, 'it was criticized as despairing.'

The man's hands, stained orange with tobacco, lifted in amazement and plopped noisily to his knees. 'No, no, a thousand times. Truth, wonder, terror even, vulgarity, yes. But despair, no, not at all, not one iota. Your critics are dead wrong.'

'Thank you.'

The chairman softly cleared his throat and lifted his glass an inch from the table, so that it formed with its reflection a kind of playing card.

Bech's admirer excitedly persisted. 'You are not a *wet* writer, no. You are a dry writer, yes? You have the expressions, am I wrong in English, dry, hard?'

'More or less.'

'I want to translate you!'

It was the agonized cry of a condemned man, for the chairman coldly lifted his glass to the height of his eyes, and like a firing squad the others followed suit. Blinking his white lashes, the chairman gazed mistily in the direction of the sudden silence, and spoke in Bulgarian.

The young interpreter murmured in Bech's ear. 'I wish to propose now, ah, a very brief toast. I know it will seem doubly brief to our honoured American guest, who has so recently enjoyed the, ah, hospitality of our Soviet comrades.' There must have been a joke here, for the rest of the table laughed. 'But in seriousness permit me to say that in our country we have seen in years past too few Americans, ah, of Mr Bech's progressive and sympathetic stripe. We hope in the next hour to learn from him much that is interesting and, ah, socially useful about the literature of his large country, and perhaps we may in turn inform him of our own proud literature, of which perhaps he knows regrettably little. Ah, so let me finally, then, since there is a saying that too long a courtship spoils the marriage, offer to drink, in our native plum brandy *slivovica*, ah, firstly to the success of his visit and, in the second place, to the mutual increase of international understanding.'

'Thank you,' Bech said and, as a courtesy, drained his glass. It was wrong; the others, having merely sipped, stared. The purple burning revolved in Bech's stomach and a severe distaste for himself, for his role, for this entire artificial and futile process, focused into a small brown spot on a pear in the bowl so shiningly posed before his eyes.

The red-eyed fool smelling of cheese was ornamenting the toast. 'It is a personal honour for me to meet the man who, in *Travel Light*, truly added a new dimension to American prose.'

'The book was written,' Bech said, 'ten years ago.'

'And since?' A slumping, moustached man sat up and sprang into English. 'Since, you have written what?'

Bech had been asked that question often in these weeks and his answer had grown curt. 'A second novel called *Brother Pig*, which is St Bernard's expression for the body.'

'Good. Yes, and?'

'A collection of essays and sketches called *When the Saints*.'

'I like the title less well.'

'It's the beginning of a famous Negro song.'

'We know the song,' another man said, a smaller man, with the tense, dented mouth of a hare. He lightly sang, 'Lordy, I just want to be in that number.'

'And the last book,' Bech said, 'was a long novel called *The Chosen* that took five years to write and that nobody liked.'

'I have read reviews,' the red-eyed man said. 'I have not read the book. Copies are difficult here.'

'I'll give you one,' Bech said.

The promise seemed, somehow, to make the recipient unfortunately conspicuous; wringing his stained hands, he appeared to swell in size, to intrude grotesquely upon the inner ring, so that the interpreter took it upon himself to whisper, with the haste of an apology, into Bech's ear, 'This gentleman is well known as the translator into our language of *Alice in Wonderland*.'

'A marvellous book,' the translator said, deflating in relief, pulling at his pockets for a cigarette. 'It truly takes us into another dimension. Something that must be done. We live in a new cosmos.'

The chairman spoke in Bulgarian, musically, at length. There was polite laughter. Nobody translated for Bech. The professorial type, his hair like a flaxen toupee, jerked forward. 'Tell me, is it true, as I have read' – his phrases whistled slightly, like rusty machinery – 'that the stock of Sinclair Lewis has plummeted under the Salinger wave?'

And so it went, here as in Kiev, Prague, and Alma-Ata, the same questions, more or less predictable, and his own answers, terribly familiar to him by now, mechanical, stale, irrelevant, untrue, claustrophobic. Then the door opened. In came, with the rosy air of a woman fresh from a bath, a little breathless, having hurried, hatless, a woman in a blond coat, her hair also blond. The secretary, entering behind her, seemed to make a cherishing space around her with his large curved hands. He introduced her to Bech as Vera Something-ova, the poetess he had asked to meet. None of the others on the list, he explained, had answered their telephones.

'Aren't you kind to come?' As Bech asked it, it was a genuine question, to which he expected some sort of an answer.

She spoke to the interpreter in Bulgarian. 'She says,' the interpreter told Bech, 'she is sorry she is so late.'

'But she was just called!' In the warmth of his confusion and pleasure Bech turned to speak directly to her, forgetting he would not be understood. 'I'm terribly sorry to have interrupted your morning.'

'I am pleased,' she said, 'to meet you. I heard of you spoken in France.'

'You speak English!'

'No. Very little amount.'

'But you *do*.'

A chair was brought for her from a corner of the room. She

yielded her coat, revealing herself in a suit also blond, as if her clothes were an aspect of a total consistency. She sat down opposite Bech, crossing her legs. Her legs were visibly good; her face was perceptibly broad. Lowering her lids, she tugged her skirt to the curve of her knee. It was his sense of her having hurried, hurried to *him*, and of being, still, graciously flustered, that most touched him.

He spoke to her very clearly, across the fruit, fearful of abusing and breaking the fragile bridge of her English. 'You are a poetess. When I was young, I also wrote poems.'

She was silent so long he thought she would never answer; but then she smiled and pronounced, 'You are not old now.'

'Your poems. Are they difficult?'

'They are difficult – to write.'

'But not to read?'

'I think – not so very.'

'Good. Good.'

Despite the decay of his career, Bech had retained an absolute faith in his instincts; he never doubted that somewhere an ideal course was open to him and that his intuitions were pre-dealt clues to his destiny. He had loved, briefly or long, with or without consummation, perhaps a dozen women; yet all of them, he now saw, shared the trait of approximation, of narrowly missing an undisclosed prototype. The surprise he felt did not have to do with the appearance, at last, of this central woman; he had always expected her to appear. What he had not expected was her appearance here, in this remote and abused nation, in this room of morning light, where he discovered a small knife in his fingers and on the table before him, golden and moist, a precisely divided pear.

Men travelling alone develop a romantic vertigo. Bech had already fallen in love with a freckled embassy wife in Prague, a buck-toothed chanteuse in Rumania, a stolid Mongolian sculptress in Kazakhstan. In the Tretyakov Gallery he had fallen in love with a recumbent statue, and at the Moscow Ballet School with an entire roomful of girls. Entering the room, he had been struck by the aroma, tenderly acrid, of young female sweat. Sixteen and seventeen, wearing patchy practice suits, the girls were twirling so strenuously their slippers were unravelling. Demure student faces crowned the unconscious insolence of their bodies. The room was doubled in depth by a floor-to-ceiling mirror. Bech was seated on a bench at its base. Staring above his head, each girl watched herself with frowning eyes frozen, for an instant in the turn, by the imperious delay and snap of her head. Bech tried to remember the lines of Rilke that expressed it, this snap and delay: *did not the drawing remain/that the dark stroke of your eyebrow/swiftly wrote on the wall of its own turning?* At one point the teacher, a shapeless old Ukrainian lady with gold canines, a *prima* of the thirties, had arisen and cried something translated to Bech as, 'No, no, the arms free, *free!*' And in demonstration she had executed a rapid series of pirouettes with such proud effortlessness that all the girls, standing this way and that like deer along the wall, had applauded. Bech had loved them for that. In all his loves, there was an urge to rescue – to rescue the girls from the slavery of their exertions, the statue from the cold grip of its marble, the embassy wife from her boring and unctuous husband, the chanteuse from her nightly humiliation (she could not sing), the Mongolian from her stolid race. But the Bulgarian poetess presented herself to him as needing nothing, as being complete, poised, satisfied, achieved. He was aroused and curious and, the next day, inquired about her of the man with the vaguely contemptuous mouth of a hare – a novelist turned playwright and scenarist, who accompanied him to the Rila Monastery. 'She lives to write,' the playwright said. 'I do not think it is healthy.'

Bech said, 'But she seems so healthy.' They stood beside a small church with whitewashed walls. From the outside it looked like a hovel, a shelter for pigs or chickens. For five centuries the Turks had ruled Bulgaria, and the Christian churches, however richly adorned within, had humble exteriors. A peasant woman with wildly snarled hair unlocked the door for them. Though the church could hardly ever have held more than thirty worshippers, it was divided into three parts, and every inch of wall was covered with eighteenth-century frescoes. Those in the narthex depicted a Hell where the devils wielded scimitars. Passing through the tiny nave, Bech peeked through the iconostasis into the screened area that, in the symbolism of Orthodox architecture, represented the next, the hidden world – Paradise. He glimpsed a row of books, an easy chair, a pair of ancient oval spectacles. Outdoors again, he felt released from the unpleasantly tight atmosphere of a children's book. They were on the side of a hill. Above them was a stand of pines whose trunks were shelled with ice. Below them sprawled the monastery, a citadel of Bulgarian national feeling during the years of the Turkish Yoke. The last monks had been moved out in 1961. An aimless soft rain was falling in these mountains, and there were not many German tourists today. Across the valley, whose little silver river still turned a water wheel, a motionless white horse stood silhouetted against a green meadow, pinned there like a brooch.

'I am an old friend of hers,' the playwright said. 'I worry about her.'

'Are the poems good?'

'It is difficult for me to judge. They are very feminine. Perhaps shallow.'

'Shallowness can be a kind of honesty.'

'Yes. She is very honest in her work.'

'And in her life?'

'As well.'

'What does her husband do?'

The other man looked at him with parted lips and touched his arm, a strange Slavic gesture, communicating an underlying racial urgency, that Bech no longer shied from. 'But she has no husband. As I say, she is too much for poetry to have married.'

'But her name ends in "-ova".'

'I see. You are mistaken. It is not a matter of marriage; I am Petrov, my unmarried sister is Petrova. All females.'

'How stupid of me. But I think it's such a pity, she's so charming.'

'In America, only the uncharming fail to marry?'

'Yes, you must be very uncharming not to marry.'

53

'It is not so here. The government indeed is alarmed; our birth rate is one of the lowest in Europe. It is a problem for economists.'

Bech gestured at the monastery. 'Too many monks?'

'Not enough, perhaps. With too few of monks, something of the monk enters everybody.'

The peasant woman, who seemed old to Bech but who was probably younger than he, saw them to the edge of her domain. She huskily chattered in what Petrov said was very amusing rural slang. Behind her, now hiding in her skirts and now darting away, was her child, a boy not more than three. He was faithfully chased, back and forth, by a small white pig, who moved, as pigs do, on tiptoe, with remarkably abrupt changes of direction. Something in the scene, in the open glee of the woman's parting smile and the unselfconscious way her hair thrust out from her head, something in the mountain mist and spongy rutted turf into which frost had begun to break at night, evoked for Bech a nameless absence to which was attached, like a horse to a meadow, the image of the poetess, with her broad face, her good legs, her Parisian clothes, and her sleekly brushed hair. Petrov, in whom he was beginning to sense, through the wraps of foreignness, a clever and kindred mind, seemed to have overheard his thoughts, for he said, 'If you would like, we could have dinner. It would be easy for me to arrange.'

'With her?'

'Yes, she is my friend, she would be glad.'

'But I have nothing to say to her. I'm just curious about such an intense conjunction of good looks and brains. I mean, what does a soul do with it all?'

'You may ask her. Tomorrow night?'

'I'm sorry, I can't. I'm scheduled to go to the ballet, and the next night the legation is giving a cocktail party for me, and then I fly home.'

'Home? So soon?'

'It does not feel soon to me. I must try to work again.'

'A drink, then. Tomorrow evening before the ballet? It is possible? It is not possible.'

Petrov looked puzzled, and Bech realized that it was his fault, for he was nodding to say Yes, but in Bulgarian nodding meant No, and a shake of the head meant Yes. 'Yes,' he said. 'Gladly.'

The ballet was entitled *Silver Slippers*. As Bech watched it, the word 'ethnic' kept coming to his mind. He had grown accustomed, during his trip, to this sort of artistic evasion, the retreat from the difficult and disappointing present into folk dance, folk tale, folk song, with always the implication that, beneath the embroidered peasant costume, the folk was really one's heart's own darling, the proletariat.

'Do you like fairy tales?' It was the moist-palmed interpreter who accompanied him to the theatre.

'I *love* them,' Bech said, with a fervour and gaiety lingering from the previous hour. The interpreter looked at him anxiously, as when Bech had swallowed the brandy in one swig, and throughout the ballet kept murmuring explanations of self-evident events on the stage. Each night, a princess would put on silver slippers and dance through her mirror to tryst with a wizard, who possessed a magic stick that she coveted, for with it the world could be ruled. The wizard, as a dancer, was inept, and once almost dropped her, so that anger flashed from her eyes. She was, the princess, a little redhead with a high round bottom and a frozen pout and beautiful free arm motions, and Bech found it oddly ecstatic when, preparatory to her leap, she would dance towards the mirror, an empty oval, and another girl identically dressed in pink, would emerge from the wings and perform as her reflection. And when the princess, haughtily adjusting her cape of invisibility, leaped through the oval of gold wire, Bech's heart leaped backwards into the enchanted hour he had spent with the poetess.

Though the appointment had been established, she came into the restaurant as if, again, she had been suddenly summoned and had hurried. She sat down between Bech and Petrov slightly breathless and fussed, but exuding, again, that impalpable warmth of intelligence and virtue.

'Vera, Vera,' Petrov said.

'You hurry too much,' Bech told her.

'Not so very much,' she said.

Petrov ordered her a cognac and continued with Bech their discussion of the newer French novelists. 'It is tricks,' Petrov said. 'Good tricks, but tricks. It does not have enough to do with life, it is too much verbal nervousness. Is that sense?'

'It's an epigram,' Bech said.

'There are just two of their number with whom I do not feel this: Claude Simon and Samuel Beckett. You have no relation, Bech, Beckett?'

'None.'

Vera said, 'Nathalie Sarraute is a very modest woman. She felt motherly to me.'

'You have met her?'

'In Paris I heard her speak. Afterwards there was the coffee. I liked her theories, of the, oh, *what*? Of the *little* movements within the heart.' She delicately measured a pinch of space and smiled, through Bech, back at herself.

'Tricks,' Petrov said. 'I do not feel this with Beckett; there, in a low form, believe it or not, one has human content.'

Bech felt duty-bound to pursue this, to ask about the theatre of the absurd in Bulgaria, about abstract painting (these were the touchstones of 'progessiveness'; Russia had none, Rumania some, Czechoslovakia plenty), to subvert Petrov. Instead, he asked the poetess, 'Motherly?'

Vera explained, her hands delicately modelling the air, rounding into nuance, as it were, the square corners of her words. 'After her talk, we – talked.'

'In French?'

'And in Russian.'

'She knows Russian?'

'She was born Russian.'

'How is her Russian?'

'Very pure but – old-fashioned. Like a book. As she talked, I felt in a book, safe.'

'You do not always feel safe?'

'Not always.'

'Do you find it difficult to be a woman poet?'

'We have a tradition of woman poets. We have Elisaveta Bagriana, who is very great.'

Petrov leaned towards Bech as if to nibble him. 'Your own works? Are they influenced by the *nouvelle vague*? Do you consider yourself to write anti-*romans*?'

Bech kept himself turned towards the woman. 'Do you want to hear about how I write? You don't, do you?'

'Very much yes,' she said.

He told them, told them shamelessly, in a voice that surprised him with its steadiness, its limpid urgency, how once he had written, how in *Travel Light* he had sought to show people skimming the surface of things with their lives, taking tints from things the way that objects in a still life colour one another, and how later he had attempted to place beneath the melody of plot a counter-melody of imagery, interlocking images which had risen to the top and drowned his story, and how in *The Chosen* he had sought to make of this confusion the theme itself, an epic theme, by showing a population of characters whose actions were all determined, at the deepest level, by nostalgia, by a desire to get back, to dive, each, into the springs of their private imagery. The book probably failed; at least, it was badly received. Bech apologized for telling all this. His voice tasted flat in his mouth; he felt a secret intoxication and a secret guilt, for he had contrived to give a grand air, as of an impossibly noble and quixotically complex experiment, to his failure when at bottom, he suspected, a certain simple laziness was the cause.

Petrov said, 'Fiction so formally sentimental could not be composed in Bulgaria. We do not have a happy history.'

It was the first time Petrov had sounded like a Communist. If there was one thing that irked Bech about these people behind the mirror, it was their assumption that, however second-rate elsewhere, in suffering they were supreme. He said, 'Believe it or not, neither do we.'

Vera calmly intruded. 'Your personae are not moved by love?'

'Yes, very much. But as a form of nostalgia. We fall in love, I tried to say in the book, with women who remind us of our first landscape. A silly idea. I used to be interested in love. I once wrote an essay on the orgasm – you know the word? – '

She shook her head. He remembered that it meant Yes.

' – on the orgasm as perfect memory. The one mystery is, what are we remembering?'

She shook her head again, and he noticed that her eyes were grey, and that in their depths his image (which he could not see) was searching for the thing remembered. She composed her finger tips around the brandy glass and said, 'There is a French poet, a young one, who has written of this. He says that never else do we, do we so gather up, collect into ourselves, oh – ' Vexed, she spoke to Petrov in rapid Bulgarian.

He shrugged and said, 'Concentrate our attention.'

' – concentrate our attention,' she repeated to Bech, as if the words, to be believed, had to come from her. 'I say it foolish – foolishly – but in French it is very well put and – *correct*.'

Petrov smiled neatly and said, 'This is an enjoyable subject for discussion, love.'

'It remains,' Bech said, picking his words as if the language were not native even to him, 'one of the few things that still deserve meditation.'

'I think it is good,' she said.

'Love?' he asked, startled.

She shook her head and tapped the stem of her glass with a fingernail, so that Bech had an inaudible sense of ringing, and she bent as if to study the liquor, so that her entire body borrowed a rosiness from the brandy and burned itself into Bech's memory – the silver gloss of her nail, the sheen of her hair, the symmetry of her arms relaxed on the white tablecloth, everything except the expression on her face.

Petrov asked aloud Bech's opinion of Dürrenmatt.

Actuality is a running impoverishment of possibility. Though he had looked forward to seeing her again at the cocktail party and had made sure that she was invited, when it occurred, though she came, he could not get to her. He saw her enter, with Petrov, but he was fenced in by an attaché of the Yugoslav Embassy and his burnished Tunisian wife; and, later, when he was worming his way towards her diagonally, a steely hand closed on his arm and a rasping American female told him that her fifteen-year-old nephew had decided to be a writer and desperately needed advice. Not the standard crap, but real brass-knuckles advice. Bech found himself balked. He was surrounded by America: the voices, the narrow suits, the watery drinks, the clatter, the glitter. The mirror had gone opaque and gave him back only himself. He managed, in the end, as the officials were thinning out, to break through and confront her in a corner. Her coat, blond, with a rabbit collar, was already on; from its side pocket she pulled a pale volume of poems in the Cyrillic alphabet. 'Please,' she said. On the flyleaf she had written, 'to H. Beck, sincerely, with bad spellings but much' – the last word looked like 'leave' but must have been 'love'.

'Wait,' he begged, and went back to where his ravaged pile of presentation books had been and, unable to find the one he wanted, stole the legation library's jacketless copy of *The Chosen*. Placing it in her expectant hands, he told her, 'Don't look,' for inside he had written, with a drunk's stylistic confidence.

Dear Vera Glavanakova –
  It is a matter of earnest regret for me that you and I must live on opposite sides of the world.

Bech Takes Pot Luck

Though Henry Bech's few persistent admirers among the critics praised his 'highly individual and refractory romanticism', his 'stubborn refusal to mount, in this era of artistic coup d'état and herd movement, any bandwagon but that of his own quixotic, excessively tender, strangely anti-Semitic Semitic sensibility', the author nevertheless had a sneaking fondness for the fashionable. Each August, he deserted his shabby large apartment at Ninety-ninth and Riverside and rented a cottage on a Massachusetts island whose coves and sandy lanes were crammed with other writers, television producers, museum directors, under-secretaries of State, old *New Masses* editors possessively squatting on seaside acreage bought for a song in the Depression, movie stars whose forties films were now enjoying a Camp revival, and hordes of those handsome, entertaining, professionless prosperous who fill the chinks between celebrities. It innocently delighted Bech, a child of the lower middle class, to see these luxurious people padding in bare feet along the dirty sidewalks of the island's one town, or fighting for overpriced groceries in the tiny general store of an up-island hamlet. It gratified him to recognize some literary idol of his youth, shrunken and frail, being tumbled about by the surf; or to be himself recognized by some faunlike bikinied girl who had been assigned *Travel Light* at the Brearley School, or by a cosy Westchester matron, still plausible in her scoop-back one-piece, who amiably confused Bech's controversial chef-d'œuvre *The Chosen* with a contemporary best-seller of the same title. Though often thus accosted, Bech had never before been intercepted by a car. The little scarlet Porsche, the long blond hair of its driver flapping, cut in front of Bech's old Ford as he was driving to the beach, and forced him to brake within inches of two mailboxes painted with flowers and lettered, respectively, 'Sea Shanty' and 'Avec du Sel'. The boy – it was a boy's long blond hair – hopped out and raced back to Bech's window, extending a soft hand that, as Bech docilely shook it, trembled like a bird's breast. The boy's plump face seemed falsified by the uncut mane; it engulfed his ears and gave his mouth, perhaps because it was unmistakably male, an assertive quarrelsome look. His eyebrows were sun-bleached to invisibility; his pallid blue eyes were all wonder and love.

'Mr Bech, hey. I couldn't believe it was you.'

'Suppose it hadn't been me. How would you explain forcing me into this ditch?'

'I bet you don't remember who I am.'

'Let me guess. You're not Sabu, and you're not Freddie Bartholomew.'

'Wendell Morrison, Mr Bech. English 1020 at Columbia, 1963.' For one spring term Bech, who belonged to the last writing generation that thought teaching a corruption, had been persuaded to oversee – it amounted to little more than that – the remarkably uninhibited conversations of fifteen undergraduates and to read their distressingly untidy manuscripts. Languid and clever, these young people had lacked not only patriotism and faith but even the coarse morality competitiveness imposes. Living off fathers they despised, systematically attracted to the outrageous, they seemed ripe for Fascism. Their politics burlesqued the liberal beliefs dear to Bech; their literary tastes ran to chaotic second-raters like Miller and Tolkien and away from those saints of formalism – Eliot, Valéry, Joyce – whose humble suppliant Bech had been. Bech even found fault with them physically: though the girls were taller and better endowed than the girls of his youth, with neater teeth and clearer skins, there was something doughy about their beauty; the starved, conflicted girls of Bech's generation had had distinctly better legs. He slowly remembered Wendell. The boy always sat on Bech's left, a fair-haired young Wasp from Stamford, crewcut, a Connecticut Yankee, more grave and respectful than the others, indeed so courteous Bech wondered if some kind of irony were intended.

He appeared to adore Bech; and Bech's weakness for Wasps was well known. 'You wrote in lower case,' Bech said. 'An orgy with some girls in a house full of expensive furniture. Glints of pink flesh in a chandelier. Somebody defecated on a polar-bear rug.'

'That's right. What a great memory.'

'Only for fantasies.'

'You gave it an A, you said it really shook you up. That meant a hell of a lot to me. I couldn't tell you then, I was playing it cool, that was my hang-up, but I can tell you now, Mr Bech, it was real encouragement, it's really kept me going. You were great.'

As the loosening of the boy's vocabulary indicated a prolonged conversation, the woman beside Bech shifted restlessly. Wendell's clear blue eyes observed the movement, and obligated Bech to perform introductions. 'Norma, this is Wendell Morris. Miss Norma Latchett.'

'Morrison,' the boy said, and reached in past Bech's nose to shake Norma's hand. 'He's beautiful, isn't he, Ma'am?'

She answered dryly, 'He'll do.' Her thin brown hand rested in Wendell's white plump one as if stranded. It was a sticky day.

'Let's *go*,' a child exclaimed from the back seat, in that dreadful squeezed voice that precedes a tantrum. Helplessly Bech's hands tightened on the steering wheel, and the hairs on the back of his neck stiffened. After two weeks, he was still unacclimated to the pressures of surrogate paternity. The child grunted, stuffed with fury; Bech's stomach sympathetically clenched.

'Hush,' the child's mother said, slow-voiced, soothing. 'Uncle Harry's talking to an old student of his. They haven't seen each other for years.'

Wendell bent low to peer into the back seat, and Bech was obliged to continue introductions. 'This is Norma's sister, Mrs Beatrice Cook, and her children – Ann, Judy, Donald.'

Wendell nodded four times in greeting. His furry plump hand clung tenaciously to the sill of Bech's window. 'Quite a scene,' he said.

Bech told him, 'We're trying to get to the beach before it clouds over.' Every instant, the sky grew less transparent. Often the island was foggy while the mainland, according to the radio, blissfully baked.

'Where's everybody staying?' The boy's assumption that they were all living together irritated Bech, since it was correct.

'We've rented a shoe,' Bech said, 'from an old lady who's moved up to a cigar box.'

Wendell's eyes lingered on the three fair children crammed, along with sand pails and an inflated air mattress, into the back seat beside their mother. He asked them, 'Uncle Harry's quite a card, huh, kids?'

Bech imagined he had hurt Wendell's feelings. In rapid atonement he explained, 'We're in a cottage rented from Andy Spofford, who used to be in war movies – before your time, he played sidekicks that got killed – and lives mostly in Corsica now. Blue mailbox, third dirt road past the Up-Island Boutique, take every left turning except the last, when you go right, not *hard* right. Mrs Cook is up from Ossining visiting for the week.' Bech restrained himself from telling Wendell that she was going through a divorce and cried every evening and lived on pills. Bea was an unspectacular middle-sized woman two years younger than Norma; she wore dull clothes that seemed designed to set off her sister's edgy beauty.

Wendell understood Bech's apologetic burst as an invitation, and removed his hand from the door. 'Hey, I know this is an imposition, but I'd love to have you just glance at the stuff I'm doing now. I'm out of that lower-case bag. In fact I'm into something pretty classical. I've seen the movie of *Ulysses* twice.'

'And you've let your hair grow. You're out of the barbershop bag.'

Wendell spoke past Bech's ear to the children. 'You kids like to Sunfish?'

'Yes!' Ann and Judy chorused; they were twins.

'What's Sunfish?' Donald asked.

Going to the beach had been the children's only entertainment. Their mother was drugged and dazed, Norma detested physical activity before dark, and Bech was frightened of the water. Even the ferry ride over to the island felt precarious to him. He never sailed, and rarely swam in water higher than his hips. From his apartment on Riverside Drive, he looked across to New Jersey as if the Hudson were a wide flat black street.

'Let's do it tomorrow,' Wendell said. 'I'll come for them around one, if that's O.K., Ma'am.'

Bea, flustered to find herself addressed – for Bech and Norma had almost enforced invisibility upon her, staging their fights and reconciliations as if she were not in the cottage – answered in her melodious grief-slowed voice, 'That would be lovely of you, if you really want to bother. Is there any danger?'

'Not a bit, ma'am. I have life jackets. I used to be a camp councillor.'

'That must have been when you shot your polar bear,' Bech said, and pointedly restarted the motor.

They arrived at the beach just as the sun went behind one of those irregular expanding clouds whose edges hold blue sky at bay for hours. The children, jubilant at freedom and the prospect of Sunfishing, plunged into the surf. Norma, as if unwrapping a fragile gift in faintly poor taste, removed her beach robe, revealing a mauve bikini, and, inserting plastic eyecups in her sockets, arranged herself in the centre of a purple towel the size of a double bed. Bea, disconsolate in a loose brown suit that did not do her figure justice, sat down on the sand with a book – one of Bech's curiously. Though her sister had been his mistress for two and a half years, she had just got around to doing her homework. Embarrassed, fearful that the book, so near his actual presence, would somehow detonate, Bech moved off a few strides and stood, bare-chested, gazing at his splendid enemy the sea, an oblivious hemisphere whose glitter of whitecaps sullenly persisted without the sun. Shortly, a timid adolescent voice, the voice he had been waiting for, rustled at his shoulder, 'I beg your pardon, sir, but by any chance are you . . . ?'

Wendell found Bech's diffident directions no obstacle and came for the children promptly at one the next day. The expedition was so successful Beatrice prolonged her visit another week. Wendell took the children clamming and miniature-golfing, he took them to an Indian burial ground, to an abandoned windmill, to grand beaches fenced with No Trespassing signs. The boy had that Wasp knowingness, that facility with things: he knew how to insert a clam knife, how to snorkle (just to put on the mask made Bech gasp for breath), how to bluff and charm his way on to private beaches (Bech believed everything he read), how to excite children with a few broken shell bits that remotely might be remnants of ceremonially heaped conch shells. He was connected to the land in a way Bech could only envy. Though so young, he had been everywhere – Italy, Scandinavia, Mexico, Alaska – whereas Bech, except for Caribbean holidays and a State Department-sponsored excursion to some Communist countries, had hardly been anywhere. He lived twenty blocks north of where he had been born, and couldn't sleep for nervousness the night before he and Norma and his rickety Ford risked the journey up the seaboard to the ferry slip. The continent-spanning motorcyclists of *Travel Light* had been daydreams based upon his Cincinnati sister's complaints about her older son, a college dropout. Wendell, a mere twenty-three, shamed Bech with his Yankee ingenuity, his native woodcraft – the dozen and one tricks of a beach picnic, for instance; the oven of scooped sand, the corn salted in seawater, the fire of scavenged driftwood. It all seemed adventurous to Bech, as did the boy's removal, in the amber summer twilight, of his bathing suit to body-surf. Wendell was a pudgy yet complete Adonis stiff-armed in the waves, his buttocks pearly, his genitals distinctly visible when he stood in the wave troughs. The new generation was immersed in the world that Bech's, like a foolish old bridegroom full of whisky and dogma, had tried to mount and master. Bech was shy of things, and possessed few, not even a wife; Wendell's room, above a garage on the summer property of some friends of his parents, held everything from canned anchovies and a Bible to pornographic photographs and a grain of LSD.

Ever since Bech had met her, Norma had wanted to take LSD. It was one of her complaints against him that he had never got her any. He, who knew that all her complaints were in truth that he would not marry her, told her she was too old. She was thirty-six; he was forty-three, and, though flirting with the senility that comes early to American authors, still absurdly wary of anything that might damage his brain. When, on their cottage porch, Wendell let slip the fact that he possessed some LSD, Bech recognized Norma's sudden new mood. Her nose sharpened, her wide mouth rapidly fluctuated between a heart-melting grin and a severe down-drawn look almost of anger. It was the mood in which, two Christmases ago, she had come up to him at a party, ostensibly to argue about *The Chosen*, in fact to conjure him into taking her to dinner. She began to converse exclusively with Wendell.

'Where did you get it?' she asked. 'Why haven't you used it?'

'Oh,' he said, 'I knew a turned-on chemistry major. I've had it for a year now. You just don't take it, you know, before bedtime like Ovaltine. There has to be somebody to take the trip with. It can be very bad business' – he had his solemn whispering voice, behind his boyish naïve one – 'to go on a trip alone.'

'You've been,' Bech said politely.

'I've been.' His shadowy tone matched the moment of day. The westward sky was plunging towards rose; the sailboats were taking the final tack towards harbour. Inside the cottage, the children, happy and loud after an expedition with Wendell to the lobster hatchery, were eating supper. Beatrice went in to give them dessert, and to get herself a sweater.

Norma's fine lean legs twitched, recrossing, as she turned to Wendell with her rapacious grin. Before she could speak, Bech asked a question that would restore to himself the centre of attention. 'And is this what you write about now? In the classic manner of *Ulysses* movies?'

Under the embarrassment of having to instruct his instructor, Wendell's voice dropped another notch. 'It's not really writable. Writing makes distinctions, and this breaks them down. For example, I remember once looking out of my window at Columbia. Someone had left a green towel on the gravel roof. From sunbathing, I suppose. I thought, Mmm, pretty green towel, nice shade of green, *beau*tiful shade of green – and the colour at*tacked* me!'

Norma asked, 'How attacked you? It grew teeth? Grew bigger? What?' She was having difficulty, Bech felt, keeping herself out of Wendell's lap. The boy's innocent eyes, browless as a Teddy bear's, flicked a question towards Bech.

'Tell her,' Bech told him. 'She's curious.'

'I'm *horribly* curious,' Norma exclaimed. 'I'm *so* tired of being myself. Liquor doesn't do anything for me anymore, sex, *any-thing*.'

Wendell glanced again towards Bech, worried. 'It – attacked me. It tried to become me.'

'Was it wonderful? Or terrible?'

'It was borderline. You must understand, Norma, it's not a playful experience. It takes everything you have.' His tone of voice had become the unnaturally, perhaps ironically, respectful one he had used in English 1020.

'It'll even take,' Bech told her, 'your Saks charge-a-plate.'

Bea appeared in the doorway, dim behind the screen. 'As long as I'm on my feet, does anybody want another drink?'

'Oh, *Bea*,' Norma said, leaping up, 'stop being a martyr. It's my turn to cook, let me help you.' To Bech, before going in, she said, '*Please* arrange my trip with Wendell. He thinks I'm a nuisance, but he *adores* you. Tell him how good I'll be.'

Her departure left the men silent. Sheets of mackerel shards were sliding down the sky towards a magenta sunset; Bech felt himself being sucked into a situation where nothing, neither tact nor reason nor the morality he had learned from his father and Flaubert, afforded leverage. Wendell at last asked, 'How stable is she?'

'Very un–.'

'Any history of psychological disturbance?'

'Nothing but the usual psychiatry. Quit analysis after four months. Does her work apparently quite well – layout and design for an advertising agency. Likes to show her temper off but underneath has a good hard eye on the main chance.'

'I'd really need to spend some time alone with her. It's very important that people on a trip together be congenial. They last at least twelve hours. Without rapport, it's a nightmare.' The boy was so solemn, so blind to the outrageousness of what he was proposing, that Bech laughed. As if rebuking Bech with his greater seriousness, Wendell whispered in the dusk. 'The people you've taken a trip with become the most important people in your life.'

'Well,' Bech said, 'I want to wish you and Norma all the luck in the world. When should we send out announcements?'

Wendell intoned, 'I feel you disapprove. I feel your fright.'

Bech was speechless. Didn't he know what a mistress was? No sense of private property in this generation. The early Christians; Brook Farm.

Wendell went on carefully, considerately, 'Let me propose this. Has she ever smoked pot?'

'Not with me around. I'm an old-fashioned father figure. Two parts Abraham to one part Fagin.'

'Why don't she and I, Mr Bech, smoke some marijuana together as a dry run? That way she can satisfy her female curiosity and I can see if we could stand a trip together. As I size her up, she's much too practical-minded to be ahead; she just wants to make the sixties scene, and maybe to bug you.'

The boy was so hopeful, so reasonable, that Bech could not help treating him as a student, with all of a student's purchased prerogatives, a student's ruthless power to intrude and demand. Young American minds. The space race with Russia. Bech heard himself yield. 'O.K. But you're not taking her over into that sorcerer's-apprentice cubbyhole of yours.'

Wendell puzzled; he seemed in the half light a blameless furry creature delicately nosing his way through the inscrutable maze of the other man's prejudices. At last he said, 'I think I see your worry. You're wrong. There is absolutely no chance of sex. All these things of course are sexual depressants. It's a medical fact.'

Bech laughed again. 'Don't you dare sexually depress Norma. It's all she and I have any more.' But in making this combination of joke and confession, he had absolved the boy of the maze and admitted him more deeply into his life than he had intended – all because, Bech suspected, at bottom he was afraid of being out-of-date. They agreed that Wendell would bring back some marijuana and they would give him supper. 'You'll have to take pot luck,' Bech told him.

Norma was not pleased by his arrangements. 'How ridiculous of you,' she said, 'not to trust me alone with that child. You're so immature and proprietorial. You don't own me. I'm a free agent, by your preference.'

'I wanted to save you embarrassment,' he told her. 'I've read the kid's stories, you don't know what goes on in his mind.'

'No, after keeping you company for three years I've forgotten what goes on in any normal man's mind.'

'Then you admit he *is* a normal man. *Not* a child. O.K. You stay out of that bastard's atelier, or whatever he thinks it is. A pad.'

'My, aren't *you* the fierce young lover? I wonder how I survived thirty-odd years out from under your wing.'

'You're so self-destructive, I wonder too. And by the way it's not been three years we've been keeping company, it's two and a half.'

'You've been counting the minutes. Is my time about up?'

'Norma, *why* do you want to cop out with all these drugs? It's so insulting to the world, to me.'

'I want to have an *experi*ence. I've never had a *ba*by, the only wedding ring I've ever worn is the one you loan me when we go to St Croix in the winter, I've never been to Pakistan, I'm *never* going to get to Antarctica.'

'I'll buy you a freezer.'

'That *is* your solution, isn't it? – buy another box. You go from box to box, each one snugger than the last. Well I for one *don't* think your marvellous life-style, your heady mixture of art for art's sake and Depression funk, entirely covers the case. My life is closing in and I hate it and I thought this way I could open it up a little. Just a *little*. Just a teeny *crack*, a splinter of sunshine.'

'He's coming back, he's coming back. Your fix is on the way.'

'How can I *pos*sibly get high with you and Bea sitting there watching with long faces? It's too grotesque. It's too limiting. My kid sister. My kindly protector. I might as well call my mother – she can fly up from West Orange with the smelling salts.'

Bech was grateful to her, for letting her anger, her anguish, recede from the high point reached with the wail that she had never had a baby. He promised, 'We'll take it with you.'

'Who will? You and Bea?' Norma laughed scornfully. 'You two nannies. You're the two most careful people I've ever met.'

'We'd *love* to smoke pot. Wouldn't we, Bea? Come on, take a holiday. Break yourself of Nembutal.'

Beatrice, who had been cooking lamb chops and setting the table for four while Bech and her sister were obstructively gesturing in the passageway between the kitchen and the dining area, stopped and considered. 'Rodney would have a fit.'

'Rodney's divorcing you,' Bech told her. 'Think for yourself.'

'It makes it *too* ridiculous,' Norma protested. 'It takes *all* the adventure out of it.'

Bech asked sharply, 'Don't you love us?'

'Well,' Bea was saying. 'On one condition. The children must be asleep. I don't want them to see me do anything wild.'

It was Wendell's ingenious idea to have the children sleep on the porch, away from what noise and fumes there might be. He had brought from his magical cache of supplies two sleeping bags, one a double, for the twins. He settled the three small Cooks by pointing out the constellations and the area of the sky where they might, according to this week's newspapers, see shooting stars. 'And when you grow tired of that,' Wendell said, 'close your eyes and listen for an owl.'

'Are there owls?' one twin asked.

'Oh, sure.'

'On this island?' asked the other.

'One or two. Every island has to have an owl, otherwise the mice would multiply and multiply and there would be no grass, just mice.'

'Will it get us?' Donald was the youngest, five.

'You're no mouse,' Wendell whispered. 'You're a man.'

Bech, eavesdropping, felt a pang, and envied the new Americans their easy intermingling with children. How terrible it seemed for him, a Jew, not to have children, to lack a father's dignity. The four adults ate a sober and unconversational meal. Wendell asked Bech what he was writing now, and Bech said nothing, he was proofreading his old books, and finding lots of typos. No wonder the critics had misunderstood him. Norma had changed into a shimmering housecoat, a peacock-coloured silk kimono Bech had bought her last Christmas – their second anniversary. He wondered if she had kept on her underclothes, and finally glimpsed, as she bent frowning over her overcooked lamb chop, the reassuring pale edge of a bra. During coffee, he cleared his throat. 'Well, kids. Should the séance begin?'

Wendell arranged four chairs in a rectangle, and produced a pipe. It was an ordinary pipe, the kind that authors, in the corny days when Bech's image of the literary life had been formed, used to grip on dust-jacket photographs. Norma took the best chair, the wicker armchair, and impatiently smoked a cigarette while Beatrice cleared away the dishes and checked on the children. They were asleep beneath the stars. Donald had moved his sleeping bag against the girls' and lay with his thumb in his mouth and the other hand on Judy's hair. Beatrice and Bech sat down, and Wendell spoke to them as if they were children, showing them the magic substance, which looked like a residue of pencil shavings in a dirty tobacco pouch, instructing them how to suck in air and smoke simultaneously, how to 'swallow' the smoke and hold it down so the precious narcotic permeated the lungs and stomach and veins and brain. The thoroughness of these instructions aroused in Bech the conviction that something was going to go wrong. He found Wendell as an instructor pompous. In a fury of puffing and expressive inhaling the boy got the pipe going, and offered first drag to Norma. She had never smoked a pipe, and suffered a convulsion of coughing. Wendell leaned forward and greedily inhaled from midair the smoke she had wasted. He had become, seen sidewise, with his floppy blond hair, a baby lion above a bone; his hungry quick movements were padded with a sinister silence. 'Hurry,' he hoarsely urged

Norma, 'don't waste it. It's all I have left from my last trip to Mexico. We may not have enough for four.'

She tried again – Bech felt her as tense, rebellious, all too aware that, with the pipe between her teeth, she became a sharp-nosed crone – and coughed again, and complained, 'I'm not *getting* any.'

Wendell whirled, barefoot, and, stabbing with the pipestem, said, 'Mr Bech.'

The smoke was sweet and circular and soft, softer than Bech could have imagined, ballooning in his mouth and throat and chest like a benevolent thunderhead, like one of those valentines from his childhood that unfolded into a three-dimensional tissue-paper fan. 'More,' Wendell commanded, thrusting the pipe at him again, ravenously sniffing into himself the shreds of smoke that escaped Bech's sucking. This time there was a faint burning – a ghost of tobacco's unkind rasp. Bech felt himself as a domed chamber, with vaults and upward recesses, welcoming the cloud; he shut his eyes. The colour of the sensation was yellow mixed with blue yet in no way green. The base of his throat satisfyingly burned.

While his attention was turned inward, Beatrice was given the pipe. Smoke leaked from her compressed lips; it seemed intensely poignant to Bech that even in depravity she was wearing no lipstick. 'Give it to *me*,' Norma insisted, greedily reaching. Wendell snatched the pipe against his chest and, with the ardour of a trapped man breathing through a tube, inhaled marijuana. The air began to smell sweetish, flowery, and gentle. Norma jumped from her chair and, kimono shimmering, roughly seized the pipe, so that precious sparks flew. Wendell pushed her back into her chair and, like a mother feeding a baby, insinuated the pipestem between her lips. 'Gently gently,' he crooned, 'take it in, feel it press against the roof of your mouth, blossoming inside you, hold it fast, fast.' His s's were extremely sibilant.

'What's all this hypnosis?' Bech asked. He disliked the deft way Wendell handled Norma. The boy swooped to him and eased the wet pipe into his mouth. 'Deeper, deeper, that's it, good ... good ...'

'It burns,' Bech protested.

'It's supposed to,' Wendell said. 'That's beautiful. You're really getting it.'

'Suppose I get sick.'

'People never get sick on it, it's a medical fact.'

Bech turned to Beatrice and said, 'We've raised a generation of amateur pharmacologists.'

She had the pipe; handing it back to Wendell, she smiled and pronounced, 'Yummy.'

Norma kicked her legs and said savagely, 'Nothing's *happening*. It's not *do*ing anything to me.'

'It will, it will,' Wendell insisted. He sat down in the fourth chair and passed the pipe. Fine sweat beaded his plump round face.

'Did you ever notice,' Bech asked him, 'what nifty legs Norma has? She's old enough to be your biological mother, but condescend to take a gander at her gams. We were the Sinewy Generation.'

'What's this generation bag you're in?' Wendell asked him, still rather respectfully English 1020. 'Everybody's people.'

'*Our* biological mother,' Beatrice unexpectedly announced. 'thought actually *I* had the better figure. She used to call Norma nobby.'

'I *won't* sit here being discussed like a piece of meat,' Norma said. Grudgingly she passed the pipe to Bech.

As Bech smoked, Wendell crooned, 'Yes, deeper, let it fill you. He really has it. My master, my guru.'

'Guru you,' Bech said, passing the pipe to Beatrice. He spoke with a rolling slowness, sonorous as an idol's voice. 'All you flower types are incipient Fascists.' The a's and s's had taken on a private richness in his mouth. 'Fascists *manqués*,' he said.

Wendell rejected the pipe Beatrice offered him. 'Give it back to our teacher. We need his wisdom. We need the fruit of his suffering.'

'*Manqué* see, *manqué* do,' Bech went on, puffing and inhaling. What a woman must feel like in coitus. More, more.

73

'*Mon maître*,' Wendell sighed, leaning forward, breathless, awed, loving.

'Suffering,' Norma sneered. 'The day Henry Bech lets himself suffer is a day I'm dying to see. He's the safest man in America, since they retired Tom Dewey. Oh, this is horrible. You're all being so silly and here I sit perfectly sober. I hate it. I hate *all* of you, absolutely.'

'Do you hear music?' Bech asked, passing the pipe directly across to Wendell.

'Look at the windows, everybody people,' Beatrice said. 'They're coming into the room.'

'*Stop* pretending,' Norma told her. 'You *always* played up to Mother. I'd rather be nobby Norma than bland Bea.'

'She's beautiful,' Wendell said, to Norma, of Beatrice. 'But so are you. The Lord Krishna bestows blessings with a lavish hand.'

Norma turned to him and grinned. Her tropism to the phony like a flower's to the sun. Wide warm mouth wherein memories of pleasure have become poisonous words.

Carefully Bech asked the other man, 'Why does your face resemble the underside of a colander in which wet lettuce is heaped?' The image seemed both elegant and precise, cruel yet just. But the thought of lettuce troubled his digestion. Grass. All men. Things grow in circles. Stop the circles.

'I sweat easily,' Wendell confessed freely. The easy shamelessness purchased for an ingrate generation by decades of poverty and war.

'And write badly,' Bech said.

Wendell was unabashed. He said, 'You haven't seen my new stuff. It's really terrifically controlled. I'm letting the things dominate the emotions instead of vice versa. Don't you think, since the "Wake", emotions have about had it in prose?'

'Talk to *me*,' Norma said. '*He's* absolutely self-obsessed.'

Wendell told her simply, 'He's my god.'

Beatrice was asking, 'Whose turn is it? Isn't anybody else worried about the windows?' Wendell gave her the pipe. She smoked and said, 'It tastes like dregs.'

When she offered the pipe to Bech, he gingerly waved it away. He felt that the summit of his apotheosis had slipped by, replaced by a widespread sliding. His perceptions were clear, he felt them all trying to get through to him, Norma seeking love, Wendell praise, Beatrice a few more days of free vacation; but these arrows of demand were directed at an object in metamorphosis. Bech's chest was sloping upward, trying to lift his head into steadiness, as when, thirty years ago, carsick on the long subway ride to his Brooklyn uncles, he would fix his eyes in a death grip on his own reflection in the shuddering black glass. The funny wool Buster Brown cap his mother made him wear, his pale small face, old for his age. The ultimate deliverance of the final stomach-wrenching stop. In the lower edge of his vision Norma leaped up and grabbed the pipe from Beatrice. Something fell. Sparks. Both women scrambled on the floor. Norma arose in her shimmering kimono and majestically complained, 'It's out. It's all gone. Damn you, greedy Bea!'

'Back to Mexico,' Bech called. His own voice came from afar, through blankets of a gathering expectancy, the expanding motionlessness of nausea. But he did not know for a certainty that he was going to be sick until Norma's voice, a few feet away in the sliding obfuscation, as sharp and small as something seen in reversed binoculars, announced, 'Henry, you're absolutely yellow!'

In the bathroom mirror he saw that she was right. The blood had drained from his long face, leaving like a scum the tallow of his summer tan, and a mauve blotch of sunburn on his melancholy nose. Face he had glimpsed from a thousand pits, in barbershops and bar rooms, in subways and aeroplane windows above the Black Sea, before shaving and after lovemaking, it witlessly smiled, the eyes very tired. Bech kneeled and submitted to the dark ecstasy of being eclipsed, his brain shouldered into nothingness by the violence of the inversion whereby his stomach emptied itself, repeatedly, until a satisfying pain scraped tears from his eyes, and he was clean.

Beatrice sat alone in the living room, beside the dead fireplace. Bech asked her, 'Where is everybody?'

She said, unmoving, uncomplaining. 'They went outside and about two minutes ago I heard his car motor start.'

Bech, shaken but sane, said, 'Another medical fact exploded.'

Beatrice looked at him questioningly. Flirting her head, Bech thought, like Norma. A stick refracted in water. Our biological mother.

He explained, 'A, the little bastard tells me it won't make me sick, and B, he solemnly swears it's a sexual depressant.'

'You don't think – they went back to his room?'

'Sure. Don't you?'

Beatrice nodded. 'That's how she is. That's how she's always been.'

Bech looked around him, and saw that the familiar objects – the jar of dried bayberry; the loose shell collections, sandy and ill-smelling; the damp stack of books on the sofa – still wore one final gossamer thickness of the mystery in which marijuana had clothed them. He asked Bea, 'How are you feeling? Do the windows still worry you?'

'I've been sitting here watching them,' she said. 'I keep thinking they're going to tip and fall into the room, but I guess they won't really.'

'They might,' Bech told her. 'Don't sell your intuitions short.'

'Please, could you sit down beside me and watch them with me? I know it's silly, but it would be a help.'

He obeyed, moving Norma's wicker chair close to Bea, and observed that indeed the window frames, painted white in unpainted plank walls, did have the potentiality of animation, and a disturbing pressingness. Their centre of gravity seemed to shift from one corner to the other. He discovered he had taken Bea's hand – limp, cool, less bony than Norma's – into his. She gradually turned her head, and he turned his face away, embarrassed that the scent of vomit would be still on his breath. 'Let's go outside on the porch,' he suggested.

The stars overhead were close and ripe. What was that sentence from *Ulysses*? Bloom and Stephen emerging from the house to urinate, suddenly looking up – *The heaventree of stars hung with humid nightblue fruit*. Bech felt a sadness, a terror, that he had not written it. Not ever. A child whimpered and rustled in its sleep. Beatrice was wearing a loose pale dress luminous in the air of the dark porch. The night was moist, alive; lights along the horizon pulsed. The bell buoy clanged on a noiseless swell. She sat in a chair against the shingled wall and he took a chair facing her, his back to the sea. She asked, 'Do you feel betrayed?'

He tried to think, scanned the scattered stars of his decaying brain for the answer. 'Somewhat. But I've had it coming to me. I've been getting on her nerves deliberately.'

'Like me and Rodney.'

He didn't answer, not comprehending and marvelling instead how, when the woman crossed and recrossed her legs, it could have been Norma – a gentler, younger Norma.

She clarified, 'I forced the divorce.'

The child who had whimpered now cried aloud; it was little Donald, pronouncing hollowly, 'The owl!'

Beatrice, struggling for control against her body's slowness, rose and went to the child, kneeled and woke him. 'No owl,' she said. 'Just Mommy.' With that ancient strange strength of mothers she pulled him from the sleeping bag and carried him back in her arms to her chair. 'No owl,' she repeated, rocking gently, 'just Mommy and Uncle Harry and the bell buoy.'

'You smell funny,' the child told her.

'Like what funny?'

'Like sort of candy.'

'Donald,' Bech said, 'we'd never eat any candy without telling you. We'd never be so mean.'

There was no answer; he was asleep again.

'I admire you,' Beatrice said at last, the lulling rocking motion still in her voice, 'for being yourself.'

'I've tried being other people,' Bech said, fending, 'but nobody was convinced.'

'I love your book,' she went on. 'I didn't know how to tell you, but I always rather sneered at you, I thought of you as part of

Norma's phony crowd, but your writing, it's terribly tender. There's something in you that you keep safe from all of us.'

As always when his writing was discussed to his face, a precarious trembling entered Bech's chest. A case of crystal when heavy footsteps pass. He had the usual wild itch to run, to disclaim, to shut his eyes in ecstasy. More, more. He protested, 'Why didn't anybody at least knock on the door when I was dying in the bathroom? I haven't whoopsed like that since the army.'

'I wanted to, but I couldn't move. Norma said it was just your way of always being the centre of attention.'

'That bitch. Did she really run off with that woolly little prep-school snot?'

Beatrice said, with an emphatic intonation dimly, thrillingly familiar, 'You *are* jealous. You *do* love her.'

Bech said, 'I just don't like creative-writing students pushing me out of my bed. I make a good Phoenician Sailor but I'm a poor Fisher King.'

There was no answer; he sensed she was crying. Desperately changing the subject, he waved towards a distant light, whirling, swollen by the mist. 'That whole headland,' he said, 'is owned by an ex-member of the Communist Party, and he spends all his time putting up No Trespassing signs.'

'You're nice,' Beatrice sobbed, the child at rest in her arms.

A motor approached down the muffling sandy road. Headlights raked the porch rail, and doubled footsteps crashed through the cottage. Norma and Wendell emerged on to the porch, Wendell carrying a messy thickness of typewriter paper. 'Well,' Bech said, 'that didn't take long. We thought you'd be gone for the night. Or is it dawn?'

'Oh, Henry,' Norma said, 'you think *every*thing is sex. We went back to Wendell's place to flush his LSD down the toilet, he felt so guilty when you got sick.'

'Never again for me, Mr Bech. I'm out of that subconscious bag. Hey, I brought along a section of my thing, it's not exactly a novel, you don't have to read it now if you don't want to.'

'I couldn't,' Bech said. 'Not if it makes distinctions.'

Norma felt the changed atmosphere and accused her sister, 'Have you been boring Henry with what an awful person I am? How could the two of you *imagine* I'd misbe*have* with this *boy* under your noses? Surely I'm subtler than *that*.'

Bech said, 'We thought you might be high on pot.'

Norma triumphantly complained, 'I never got *anything*. And I'm *positive* the rest of you faked it.' But, when Wendell had been sent home and the children had been tucked into their bunks, she fell asleep with such a tranced soundness that Bech, insomniac, sneaked from her side and safely slept with Beatrice. He found her lying awake waiting for him. By fall the word went out on the literary circuit that Bech had shifted mistresses again.

Bech Panics

This moment in Bech's pilgrimage must be approached reverently, hesitantly, as befits a mystery. We have these few slides: Bech posing before a roomful of well-groomed girls spread seraglio-style on the floor, Bech lying awake in the frilly guest room of a dormitory, Bech conversing beside a granite chapel with a woman in a purple catsuit, Bech throwing himself like a seed upon the leafy sweet earth of Virginia, within a grove of oaks on the edge of the campus, and mutely begging Someone, Something, for mercy. Otherwise, there is semi-darkness, and the oppressive roar of the fan that cools the projector, and the fumbling, snapping noises as the projectionist irritably hunts for slides that are not there. What made Bech panic? That particular March, amid the ripening aromas of rural Virginia, in that lake of worshipful girls?

All winter he had felt uneasy, idle, irritable, displaced. He had broken with Norma and was seeing Bea. The train ride up to Ossining was dreary, and the children seemed, to this bachelor, surprisingly omnipresent; the twin girls sat up watching television until 'Uncle Harry' himself was nodding, and then in the heart of the night little Donald would sleepwalk, sobbing, into the bed where Bech lay with his pale, gentle, plump beloved. The first time the child, in blind search of his mother, had touched Bech's hairy body, he had screamed, and in turn Bech had screamed. Though Donald, who had few preconceptions, soon grew adept at sorting out the muddle of flesh he sometimes found in his mother's bed, Bech on his side never quite adjusted to the smooth transition between Bea's lovemaking and her mothering. Her tone of voice, the curve of her gestures, seemed the same. He Bech, forty-four and internationally famous, and this towheaded male toddler depended parallel from the same broad body, the same silken breasts and belly, the same drowsy croons and intuitive caresses. Of course, abstractly, he knew it to be so – Freud tells us, all love is one, indivisible, like electricity – but concretely this celibate man of letters, who had been an only son and who saw his sister's family in Cincinnati less than once a year, felt offended at his immersion in the ooze of familial.promiscuity. It robbed sex of grandeur if, with Bech's spunk still dribbling from her vagina and her startled yips of pleasure still ringing in his dreams, Bea could rouse and turn and almost identically minister to a tot's fit of night-fright. It made her faintly comical and unappetizing, like the giant milk dispenser in a luncheonette. Sometimes, when she had not bothered to put on her nightie, or had been unable to find where their amorous violence had tossed it, she nestled the boy to sleep against her naked breasts and Bech would find himself curled against her cool backside, puzzled by priorities and discomfited by the untoward development of jealousy's adamant erection.

His attempts to separate her from her family were not successful. Once he stayed at a motel near the railroad station, and took her out, in her own car, on a 'date' that was to proceed, after dinner, to his hired room, and was to end with Bea's return home no later than midnight, since the babysitter was the fifteen-year-old daughter of the local Methodist minister. But the overfilling meal at a boorish roadside restaurant, and their furtive decelerated glide through the crackling gravel courtyard of the motel (where a Kiwanis banquet was in progress, and had hogged all the parking spaces), and his fumbly rush to open the tricky aluminoid lock-knob of his door and to stuff his illicit guest out of sight, and the macabre interior of oak-imitating wallboard and framed big-eyed pastels that embowered them proved in sum withering to Bech's potency. Though his suburban mistress graciously, following less her own instincts than the exemplary drift of certain contemporary novels, tried to bring his weakling member to strength by wrapping it in the velvet bandages of her lips, Bech couldn't achieve more than a two-thirds hard-on, which diminished to an even less usable fraction whenever the starchy fare within their stomachs rumbled, or his gaze met that of a pastel waif, or the Kiwanis broke into another salvo of applause, or Bea's beginning yips frightened him up from the primordial level where he was, at last, beginning to thrive. Who, as a rabbi once said, by taking thought can add a cubit to his height? Not Bech, though he tried. The minister's freckle-faced daughter was asleep on the sofa when he and Bea finally returned, as stiff with dried sweat as a pair of squash players.

In Manhattan, on Bech's cosy turf, the problem was different: Bea underwent a disquieting change. At home in Bech's drab large rooms at Riverside and Ninety-ninth, she became slangy, bossy, twitchy, somewhat sluttish, too much at home – she became in short like her rejected sister Norma. The Latchett blood ran tart at the scent of marriage; old Judge Latchett, when alive, had been one of the hanginger magistrates in Jersey City. Bea, as her underwear and Bech's socks dried together on the bathroom radiator, tended to pontificate. 'You should get out of these dreary rooms, Henry. They're half the reason you're blocked.'

'Am I blocked? I'd just thought of myself as a slow typist.'

'What do you do, hit the space bar once a day?'

'Ouch.'

'I'm sorry, that did sound bitchy. But it makes me *sad*, to see someone of your beautiful gifts just stagnating.'

'Maybe I have a beautiful gift for stagnation.'

'Come live with me.'

'What about the neighbours? What about the children?'

'The neighbours don't care. The children love you. Come live with us and see in the spring. You're dying of carbon monoxide down here.'

'I'd drown in flesh up there. You pin me down and the others play pile-on.'

'Only Donald. And aren't you funny about that? Rodney and I absolutely agreed, a child shouldn't be excluded from *any*thing physical. We thought *noth*ing of being nude in front of them.'

'Spare me the picture, it's like a Grünewald. You and Rodney, as I understand it, agreed about everything.'

'Well at least neither of us were squeamish old maids.'

'Unlike a certain *écrivain juif, n'est-ce pas?*'

'You're very good at making me sound like a bitch. But I honestly *do* believe, Henry, you need to do something different with yourself.'

'Such as integrating Suburbia. Henry Bech, Ossining's one-man ghetto.'

'It's not like that. It's not like a Polish village. Nobody thinks in these categories any more.'

'Will I be asked to join the Kiwanis? Does a mama's lover qualify to join the P.-T.A.?'

'They don't call it the P.-T.A. any more.'

'Bea baby, here I stand, I can do no other. I've lived here twenty years.'

'That is precisely your problem.'

'Every shop on Broadway knows me. From the Chinese laundry to the Swedish bakery. From Fruit House to Japanese Foodland. There he goes, they say, Old Man Bech, a legend in his lifetime. Or, as the coloured on the block call me, Cheesecake Charley, the last of the Joe Louis liberals.'

'You're really terrified, aren't you,' Bea said, 'of having a serious conversation?'

The telephone rang. Without the telephone, Bech wondered, how would we ever avoid proposing marriage? The instrument sat by a window, on a table with a chessboard inlaid into veneer warped by years of disuse and steam heat. A dust-drenched shaft of four o'clock sun dwelt tepidly upon a split seam in the sofa cover, a scoop-shaped dent in the lampshade, a yellowing stack of unread presentation copies of once-new novels, arranged to lend stability to the chess table's rickety, dried-out legs. The phone directory was years old and its cover was scrawled with numbers that Bech no longer called including, in happy crimson greedily inked early one morning, Norma's. The receiver, filmed by air pollution, held a history of fingerprints. 'Hello?'

'Mistah Bech? Is that Hainry Bech the authuh?'

'Could be,' Bech said. The Southern voice, delightfully female, went on, with a lacy interweave of cajoling and hysterical intonations, to propose that he come and speak or read, which-eveh he prefuhhed, to a girl's college in Virginia. Bech said, 'I'm sorry, I don't generally do that sort of thing.'

'Oh Mistah Bech, Ah *knew* you'd say that, ouah English in-structah, a Miss Eisenbraun, ah don't suppose you know heh, *sayd* you were immensely hard to gait, but you have *so* many fayuns among the girls heah, we're all just hopin' against hope.'

'Well,' Bech said – a bad word choice, in the situation.

The voice must have sensed he found the accent seductive, for it deepened. 'Oueh countrehsaad round heah is eveh so pretteh, the man who wrote *Travel Laaht* owes it to himself to see it, and though to be shooah we all know moneh is no temptation foh a man of yoh statchuh, we have a *goood* speakeh's budget this ye-ah and kin offeh you – ' And she named a round figure that did give Bech pause.

He asked, 'When would this be?'

'Oh!' – her yip was almost coital – 'oh, Misteh Bech, you mean you *maaht?*' Before she let him hang up he had agreed to appear in Virginia next month. Bea was indignant. 'You've lost all your principles. You let yourself be sweet-talked into that.'

Bech shrugged. 'I'm trying to do something different with myself.'

Bea said, 'Well I didn't mean letting yourself be cooed at by an auditorium full of fluffy-headed racists.'

'I think of it more as being an apostle to the Gentiles.'

'You won't speak at Columbia when it's two subway stops away and full of people on your own wavelength, but you'll fly a thousand miles to some third-rate finishing school on the remote chance you can sack out with Scarlett O'Hara. You are sick, Henry. You are weak, and sick.'

'Actually,' Bech told Bea, 'I'll be there two nights. So I can sack out with Melanie too.'

Bea began to cry. The inner slump he felt, seeing her proud Saxon chin crumple and her blonde head bow, was perhaps a premonition of his panic. He tried to joke through it: 'Bea baby, I'm just following your orders, I'm going to see spring in in the suburbs. They offered me an even grand. I'll buy a triple bed for you, me, and Donald.'

Her blue eyes went milky; her lips and lids became the rubbed pink colour of her nipples. She had washed her hair and was wearing only his silk bathrobe, one Norma had given him in response to the gift of a kimono, and when Bea bowed her head and pressed the heels of her hands into her eyes, the lapels parted and her breasts hung lustrous in his sight. He tried to fetch up some words of comfort but knew that none would be comfort enough but the words, 'Marry me'. So he looked away, past the dented lampshade, at the framed rectangle of city that he knew better than he knew his own soul – the fragile forest of television aerials, the stunted courtyards of leafless ailanthus, the jammed clockwork of fire escapes. His slump hung nervously suspended within him, like a snagged counterweight.

Two petite, groomed, curried girls met him at the airport and drove him in a pink convertible, at great speed, through the rolling, burgeoning landscape. Spring had arrived here. New York had been windy and raw. The marzipan monuments of Washington, seen from the airport, had glittered above cherry blossoms. Piedmont Air Lines had lifted him and rocked him above hills dull evergreen on the ridges and fresh deciduous green in the valleys, where streams twinkled. The shadow of the plane crossed racetrack ovals and belts of ploughed land. Dot-sized horses slowly traced lines of gallop within fenced diagrams. Looking down, Bech was vertiginous; twice they bumped down into small airports cut into hillsides. On the third stop, he alighted. The sun stood midway down the sky, as it had the day the phone had rung and Bea had mocked his acceptance, but now the time stood an hour later in the day; it was after five. The two girls, giggling, gushing, met him and drove him, in a deafening rush of speed (if the convertible flipped, his head would be scraped from his shoulders; he foresaw the fireman hosing his remains from the highway) to a campus, once a great plantation. Here many girls in high heels and sheer stockings and, Bech felt, girdles strolled across acres of hilly lawn overswept by the strong smell of horse manure. In his urban nostrils, the stench rampaged, but nothing in the genteel appearance of the place acknowledged it – not the scrubbed and powdered faces of the girls, nor the brick-and-trim façades of the buildings, nor the magnolia trees thick and lumpy with mauve-and-cream, turnip-shaped buds. It was as if one of his senses had short-circuited to another channel, or as if a school of deaf-mutes were performing a minuet to the mistaken accompaniment of a Wagnerian storm. He felt suddenly, queasily hollow. The declining sun nubbled the lawn's texture with shadowed tufts, and as Bech was led along a flagstone path to his first obligation (an 'informal' hour with the Lanier Club, a branch of budding poetesses) profound duplicity seemed to underlie the landscape. Along with the sun's reddening rays and the fecal stench a devastating sadness swept in. He knew that he was going to die. That his best work was behind him. That he had no business here, and was frighteningly far from home.

Bech had never gone to college. War had come when he was eighteen, and a precocious acceptance from *Liberty* two years later. He stayed in Germany a year after V-E day, editing a newssheet for the U.S. occupation forces in Berlin, and returned home to find his father dying. When in time the man – not even old, merely in his fifties – had surrendered the last shred of his trachea to the surgeon's knife and had beat his way back from the underworld of anaesthesia for the final time, Bech felt he knew too much for college. He joined the army of vets who believed they had earned the right to invent their lives. He entered a tranced decade of abstract love, of the exhilarations of type and gossip and nights spent sitting up waiting for the literary renaissance that would surely surpass that of the twenties by just as much as this war had surpassed, in nobility and breadth and conclusiveness, its predecessor. But it was there, with the gaunt Titans of modernism, with Joyce and Eliot and Valéry and Rilke, that one must begin. *Make it new. The intolerable wrestle with words and meanings.* Bech weaned himself from the slicks and wormed his way into the quarterlies. *Commentary* let him use a desk. As he confessed to Vera Glavanakova, he wrote poems: thin poems scattered on the page like soot on snow. He reviewed books, any books, history, mysteries, almanacs, pornography – anything printed had magic. For some months he was the cinema critic for an ephemeral journal titled *Displeasure*. Bech was unprepossessing then, a scuttler, a petty seducer, a bright-eyed bug of a man in those days before whisky and fame fleshed him out, his head little more than a nose and a cloud of uncombable hair. He was busy and idle, melancholy and happy. Though he rarely crossed the water necessary to leave Manhattan, he was conscious of freedom – his freedom to sleep late, to eat ham, to read the *Arabian Nights* in the 42nd Street library, to sit an hour in the Rembrandt room at the Metropolitan, to chisel those strange early paragraphs, not quite stories, which look opaque when held in the lap but held up to the window reveal a symmetrical translucence of intended veins. In the years before *Travel Light*, he paced his grey city with a hope in his heart, the expectation that, if not this day the next, he would perfectly fuse these stone rectangles around him with the grey rectangles of printed prose. Self-educated, street-educated, then, he was especially vulnerable to the sadness of schools. They stank of country cruelty to him – this herding, this cooping up of people in their animal prime, stunning them with blunt classics, subjecting them to instructors deadened and demented by the torrents of young blood that pass through their years; just the lip-licking reverence with which professors pronounce the world 'students' made Bech recoil.

Our slide shows him posturing in a sumptuous common room whose walls are padded with leatherbound editions of Scott and Carlyle and whose floor is carpeted with decorously arranged specimens of nubility. He was, possibly, as charming and witty as usual – the florid letter of thanks he received in New York from the Lanier Club's secretary suggested so. But to himself his tongue seemed to be moving strangely, as slowly as one of those galloping horses he had seen from a mile in the air, while his real attention was turned inwards towards the swelling of his dread, his unprecedented recognition of horror. The presences at his feet – those seriously sparkling eyes, those earnestly flushed cheeks, those demurely displayed calves and knees – appalled him with the abyss of their innocence. He felt dizzy, stunned. The essence of matter, he saw, is dread. Death hung behind everything, a real skeleton about to leap through a door in these false walls of books. He saw himself, in this nest of delicate limbs, limbs still ripening towards the wicked seductiveness Nature intended, as a seed among too many eggs, as a gross thrilling intruder, a genuine male intellectual Jew, with hairy armpits and capped molars, a man from the savage North, the North that had once fucked the South so hard it was still trembling – Bech saw himself thus, but as if in a *trompe-l'œil* box whose painted walls counterfeit, from the single perspective of the peephole, three-dimensional furnishings and a succession of archways. He felt what was expected of him, and felt himself performing it, and felt the fakery of the performance, and knew these levels of perception as the shifting sands of absurdity, nullity, death. His death gnawed inside him like a foul parasite while he talked to these charming daughters of fertile Virginia.

One asked him, 'Suh, do you feel there is any place left in modern poetry for *rhaam*?'

'For what?' Bech asked, and educed a gale of giggles.

The girl blushed violently, showing blood suddenly as a wound. 'For rhy-em,' she said. She was a delicate creature, with a small head on a long neck. Her blue eyes behind glasses felt to be on stalks. The sickness in Bech bit deeper as he apologized, 'I'm sorry, I simply didn't hear what you said. You ask about rhyme. I write only prose – '

A sweet chorus of mutters protested that No, his prose was a poet's, was poetry.

He went on, stooping with the pain inside him, dazed to hear himself make a kind of sense, ' – but it seems to me rhyme is one of the ways we make things hard for ourselves, make a game out of nothing, so we can win or lose and lighten the, what?, the *indeterminacy* of life. Paul Valéry, somewhere, discusses this, the first line that comes as a gift from the gods and costs nothing, and then the second line that we make ourselves, word by word, straining all our resources, so that it harmonizes with the supernatural first, so that it *rhymes*. He thought, as I remember, that our lives and thoughts and language are all a 'familiar chaos' and that the arbitrary tyranny of a strict prosody goads us to feats of, as it were, rebellion that we couldn't otherwise perform. To this I would only add, and somewhat in contradiction, that rhyme is very ancient, that it marks rhythm, and that much in our natural lives is characterized by rhythm.'

'Could you give us an example?' the girl asked.

'For example, lovemaking,' Bech said, and to his horror beheld her blush surging up again, and beheld beyond her blush an entire seething universe of brainless breeding, of moist inter-penetration, of slippery clinging copulation, of courtship dances and come-on signals, of which her hapless blush, unknown to her, was one. He doubted that he could stand here another minute without fainting. Their massed fertility was overwhelm-ing; their bodies were being broadened and readied to generate from their own cells a new body to be pushed from the old, and in time to push bodies from itself, and so on into eternity, an ocean of doubling and redoubling cells within which his own conscious moment was soon to wink out. He had had no child. He had spilled his seed upon the ground. Yet we are all seed spilled upon the ground. These thoughts, as Valéry had predi-cated, did not come neatly, in chiming packets of language, but as slithering, overlapping sensations, micro-organisms of thought setting up in sum a panicked sweat on Bech's palms and a palpable nausea behind his belt. He attempted to grin, and the pond of young ladies shuddered, as if a pebble had been dropped among them. In rescue an unseen clock chimed the half-hour, and a matronly voice, in the accents of Manhattan, called, 'Girls, we must let our guest eat!'

Bech was led to a cathedral-sized dining-room and seated at a table with eight young ladies. A coloured girl sat on his right. She was one of two in the school. The student body, by its own petition, in the teeth of parental protest and financial cur-tailments from the state legislature, had integrated itself. The girl was rather light-skinned, with an Afro hair-do cut like an up-right loaf of bread; she spoke to Bech in a voice from which all traces of Dixie had been clipped. 'Mr Bech,' she said, 'we admire your gifts of language but wonder if you aren't, now and then, somewhat racist?'

'Oh? When?' The presence of food – shrimp salad nested in lettuce, in tulip glasses – had not relieved his panic; he wondered if he dared eat. The shrimps seemed to have retained their legs and eyes.

'In *Travel Light*, for example, you keep calling Roxanne a Negress.'

'But she was one.' He added, 'I loved Roxanne.'

'The fact is, the word had distinctly racist overtones.'

'Well, what should we call them?'

'I suppose you might say "Black women".' But her primness of tone implied that she, like a spinster lecturing on male anatomy, would rather not call certain things anything at all. Bech was momentarily roused from his funk by this threat, that there were holes in language, things that could not be named. He told her, 'Calling you a black woman is as inexact as calling me a pink man.'

She responded promptly. 'Calling me a Negress is as insulting as calling you a kike.'

He liked the way she said it. Flat, firm, clear. Fuck you. Black is beautiful. Forced by the argument to see her colour, he saw that her loaf of hair was cinnamon-tinted and a spatter of freckles saddled the bridge of her nose. Through this he saw, in a sliding succession of imagery that dumped him back into terror, an Irish overseer raping a slave, vomiting slaves packed beneath the deck of a bucking ship, Africans selling Africans, tribes of all colours torturing one another, Iroquois thrusting firebrands down the throats of Jesuits, Chinese skinning each other in careful strips, predation and cruelty reaching back past Man to the dawn of life, paramecia in a drop of water, aeons of evolution, each turn of beak or stretch of toe shaped by a geological patter of individual deaths. His words echoed weakly in the deep well of this vision. 'A black woman could be a woman who's painted herself black. "Negro" designates a scientific racial grouping, like Caucasian or Mongolian. I use it without prejudice.'

'How do you feel then about "Jewess"?'

Bech lied; the word made him wince. 'Just as I do about "duchess".'

'As to your love,' the girl went on, still with deliberate dignity, holding her head erect as if balancing something upon it and addressing the entire table in full consciousness of dominating, 'we've had enough of your love. You've been loving us down in Georgia and Mississippi for hundreds of years. We've been loved to death, we want now to be respected.'

'By which you mean,' Bech told her, 'you want to be feared.'

A white girl at the table broke in with hasty politeness. 'Pahdon me, Beth Ann, but Misteh Bech, do you *realleh* believe in races? The school I went to befoh, they made us read a Misteh Carleton Coon? He says, I don't believe a word of it but he says, black folks have longer *heel*s, thet's wahah the men run fastuh in *sprints?*'

'Black *people*, Cindy,' Beth Ann corrected. 'Not black "folks".' At her prim shudder the ring of pink faces broke into relieved, excessive laughter.

Cindy blushed but was not deflected; she continued, 'Also he says, Misteh Bech, that they have thinneh *skulls*, thet's whah so many dah in the prahz ring? We used to be told they had *thick*eh!'

Puzzled by the intensity of her blush, Bech saw that for this excited young convert to liberalism anthropology was as titillating as pornography. He saw that even in an age of science and unbelief our ideas are dreams, styles, superstitions, mere animal noises intended to repel or attract. He looked around the ring of munching females and saw their bodies as a Martian or a mollusc might see them, as pulpy stalks of bundled nerves oddly pinched to a bud of concentration in the head, a hairy bone knob holding some pounds of jelly in which a trillion circuits, mostly dead, kept records, coded motor operations, and generated an excess of electricity that pressed into the hairless side of the head and leaked through the orifices, in the form of pained, hopeful noises and a simian dance of wrinkles. Impossible mirage! A blot on nothingness. And to think that all the efforts of his life – his preening, his lovemaking, his typing – boiled down to the attempt to displace a few sparks, to bias a few circuits, within some random other scoops of jelly that would, in less time than it takes the Andreas Fault to shrug or the tail-tip star of Scorpio to crawl an inch across the map of Heaven, be utterly dissolved. The widest fame and most enduring excellence shrank to nothing in this perspective. As Bech ate, mechanically offering votive bits of dead lamb to the terror enthroned within him, he saw that the void should have been left unvexed, should have been spared this trouble of matter, of life, and, worst, of consciousness.

Slide Two. His bedroom was the corner first-floor room of a large new neo-Georgian dorm. Locked glass doors discreetly separated his quarters from the corridors where virginity slept in rows. But frilly touches whispered and giggled in the room – the beribboned lampshade, the petticoat curtains of dotted swiss beneath the velvet drapes, the abundance of lace runners and china figurines on dainty tables. His bed, with its two plumped pillows one on top of the other like a Pop Art sandwich, its brocaded coverlet turned down along one corner like an Open Here tab on a cereal box, seemed artificially crisp and clean: a hospital bed. And indeed, like an infirm man, he discovered he could lie only in one position, on his back. To turn on to either side was to tip himself towards the edge of a chasm; to roll over on to his belly was to risk drowning in the oblivion that bubbled up from the darkness heated by his own body. The college noises beyond his windows drifted into silence. The last farewell was called, the last high heels tapped down a flagstone path. Chapel bells tolled the quarter hours. The land beyond the campus made itself heard in the sounds of a freight train, an owl, a horse faintly whinnying in some midnight meadow where manure and grass played yin and yang. Bech tried concentrating on these noises, pressing from them, by sheer force of attention, the balm of their undeniability, the innocence that somehow characterized their simple existence, apart from their attributes. All things have the same existence, share the same atoms, reshuffled: grass into manure, flesh into worms. A blackness beneath this thought like glass from which frost is rubbed. He tried to relive pleasantly his evening triumph, his so warmly applauded reading: he had read a long section from *Brother Pig*, the part where the hero rapes his stepdaughter in the bowling alley, behind the pin-setting machine, and had been amazed, as he read, by the coherence of the words, by their fearless onward march. The blanket of applause, remembered, oppressed him. He tried word games. He went through the alphabet with world saviours: Attila, Buddha, Christ, Danton ... Woodrow Wilson, Xerxes the Great, Brigham Young, Zoroaster. There was some slight comfort in the realization that the world had survived all its saviours, but Bech had not put himself to sleep. His panic, like a pain which intensifies when we dwell upon it, when we inflame it with undivided attention, felt worse away from the wash of applause; yet, like a wound tentatively defined by the body's efforts of asepsis and rejection, it was revealing a certain shape. It felt pasty and stiff. Mixed with the fear, a kind of coagulant, was shame: shame at his having a 'religious crisis' that, by all standard psychology, should have been digested in early adolescence, along with post-masturbatory guilt; shame at the degradation of a one-time disciple of those great secreters Flaubert and Joyce into a slick crowd-pleaser at whistle-stop colleges; shame at having argued with a Negress, at having made Bea cry, at having proved himself, in his relations with all women from his mother on, a thin-skinned, fastidious, skittish, slyly clowning cold-blooded ingrate. Now that she was too anginal and arthritic to live alone, he had stuck his mother into a Riverdale nursing home, instead of inviting her into his own spacious rooms, site of his dreary, sterile privacy. His father, in his position, would have become his mother's nurse. His grandfather would have become her slave. Six thousand years of clan loyalty were overturned in Bech. He denied even his characters the final measure of love, that would enable them to break free of his favourite tropes, the ruts of his phrases, the chains that rattled whenever he sat down at the typewriter. He tried to analyse himself. He reasoned that since the id cannot entertain the concept of death, which by being not-being is nothing to be afraid of, his fear must be of something narrower, more pointed and printed. He was afraid that his critics were right. That his works were indeed flimsy, unfelt, flashy, and centrifugal. That the proper penance for his artistic sins was silence and reduction; that his id, in collaboration with the superego figures of Alfred Kazin and Dwight Macdonald, had successfully reduced him to artistic impotence and was now seeking, in its rambling, large-hearted way, his personal extinction: hence his pip-squeak ego's present flutter of protest. As soon sleep in a cement mixer as amid these revelations. Sleep, the foreshadow of death, the dab of poison we daily take to forestall convulsion, became impossible. The only position in which Bech could even half-relax was on his back, his head propped on both pillows to hold him above smothering, his limbs held steady in the fantasy that he was a china figurine, fragile, cool, and miniature, cupped in a massive hand. Thus Bech tricked himself, a moment after the chapel bells had struck three, into sleep – itself a devastating testimony to the body's power to drag us down with it. His dreams, strange to report, were light as feathers, and blew this way and that. In one of them, he talked fluid French with Paul Valéry, who looked like the late Mischa Auer.

He awoke stiff. He moved from bed to suitcase to bathroom with an old man's self-dramatizing crouch. By the light of this new day, through the murky lens of his panic, objects – objects, those atomic mirages with edges that hurt – appeared mock-heroic in their persistence, their quixotic loyalty to the shapes in which chance has cast them. They seemed to be watching him, to be animated by their witness of his plight. Thus, like primitive Man, he began to personify the universe. He shat plenteously, hot gaseous stuff acidified into diarrhoea, he supposed, by his fear. He reflected how, these last unproductive years, his output of excrement had grown so that instead of an efficient five minutes he seemed to spend most of his work morning trapped on the toilet, leafing sadly through *Commentary* and *Encounter*. Elimination had become Bech's forte: he answered letters with the promptness of a backboard, he mailed his loose-paper files to the Library of Congress twice a year. He had become a compulsive wastebasket-emptier. Toilets, mailboxes, cunts were all the receptacles of a fanatic and incessant attempt to lighten himself, as if to fly. Standing at the basin of lavender porcelain (which, newly installed, boasted one of those single faucet controls that blends hot and cold like a joy stick on the old biplanes) Bech, far from his figurine fantasy of last night, felt precariously tall: a sky-high prodigy about to topple, or crumple. His self-ministrations – brushing his teeth, wiping his anus, shaving his jaw – seemed laid upon his body from a cosmic distance, amid the held breath of inert artifacts, frozen presences he believed were wishing him well. He was especially encouraged, and touched, by the elfin bar of motel-size mauve soap his fingers unwrapped across an interstellar gap.

But stepping, dressed, into the sunshine, Bech was crushed by the heedless scale of outdoors. He was overwhelmed by the multiple transparent signs – the buds, the twittering, the springtide glisten – of growth and natural process, the inhuman mutual consumption that is Nature. A zephyr stained by manure recalled his first flash of terror. He ate breakfast stunned, with a tickling in his nose that might have been the wish to cry. Yet the eight girls seated with him – eight new ones, all Caucasian – pretended to find his responses adequate, even amusing. As he was being led to his first display case of the day, a seminar in the post-war American novel, a *zoftig* woman in a purple catsuit accosted him by the chapel. She was lithe, rather short, in her thirties, with brushed-back black hair of which some strands kept drifting on to her temple and cheeks and needed to be brushed back with her fingers, which she did lithely, cleverly, continuously. Her lips were long; the upper bore a faint moustache. Her nose too was long, with something hearteningly developed and intelligent about the modulations from tip to nostril wing. When she spoke, it was not with a Southern accent but with Bech's own, the graceless but rapid and obligingly enunciating accent of New York. She was Jewish.

She said, 'Mr Bech, I know you're being rushed to some important destination, but my girls, the girls you spoke to last night, the Lanier Club, were so, I guess the word is impressed, that they cooked up a rather impertinent, not to say importunate, request that none of them had the nerve to deliver. So they asked me to. I'm their adviser. I was impressed, too, by the way. The name is Ruth Eisenbraun.' She offered her hand.

Bech accepted the offer. Her hand was warmer than porcelain, yet exact, and firm. He asked, 'What are you doing amid all this alien corn, Ruth?'

The woman said, 'Don't knock it, it's a living. This is my fourth year, actually. I like it here. The girls are immensely sweet, and not all of them are dumb. It's a place where you can see things happening, you can actually *see* these kids loosening up. Your consenting to come down here is a tremendous boost to the cause.' She took her hand back from his to make the gestures needed to dramatize 'loosening up' and 'tremendous'. In the sunshine glare reflected from the granite chapel Bech could admire the nimble and even flow of her expressiveness; he enjoyed the sensation, as of a tailor's measurements, of her coolly sizing him up even as she maintained a screen of patter, every dry and rapid turn of phrase a calibrated, unembarrassed offer of herself. 'In fact,' she was saying, 'the society as a whole is loosening up. If I were a black, the South is where I'd prefer to be. Nobody in the North believes now in integration because they've never had it, but here, in an economic and social way, they've had integration all along, though of course entirely on the Man's terms. My girls, at least until they marry the local sheriff or Coke distributor, are really very naïvely' – again, arabesques with her hands – 'sin*cere*ly excited about the idea that black people are *people*. I find them sweet. After five years at CCNY, this has been a gigantic breath of fresh air. You can honestly tell yourself you're *teach*ing these girls.' And by repeating 'girls' so often, she was burning into Bech's fogged brain awareness that she, something of a girl herself, was also something more.

'What did they want to ask me?'

'Oh, yes. And that seminar is waiting. You know what their nickname for it is? – "Bellow's Belles". Now *that's* been turned into "Bellow's Balls". Isn't that a good sign, that they can be obscene? *My* girls delegated me to ask *you*' – and Bech inwardly questioned the source of that delegation – 'if you'd please, please,

*pret*ty please be willing to judge a poetry contest of theirs. I got
your schedule from Dean Coates and see you have a big empty
slot late this afternoon; if you could *poss*ibly make it over to
Ruffin Hall at five, they will recite for you in their best Sunday
School manner some awful doggerel you can take back to your
room, and give us the verdict before you go tomorrow. It is an
imposition, I know. I know, I know. But they'll be so thrilled
they'll *melt*.'

The zipper of her catsuit was open three inches below the base
of her throat. If he pulled the zipper down six inches more, Bech
estimated, he would discover that she was wearing no bra. Not to
mention no girdle. 'I'd be pleased to,' he said. 'Honoured, you
can tell them.'

'God that's swell of you,' Miss Eisenbraun responded briskly.
'I hope you weren't hoping to have a nap this afternoon.'

'In fact,' he told her, 'I didn't get much sleep. I feel very
strange.'

'In what way strange?' She looked up into his face like a dentist who had asked him to open his mouth. She was interested. If
he had said haemorrhoids, she would still be interested. Part
mother, part clinician. He should have more to do with Jewish
women.

'I can't describe it. *Angst.* I'm afraid of dying. Everything is so implacable. Maybe it's all these earth-smells so suddenly.'

She smiled and deeply inhaled. When she sniffed, her upper
lip broadened, furry. The forgotten downiness of Jewish women.
Their hairy thighs. 'It's worst in spring,' she said. 'You get ac-
climated. May I ask, have you ever been in analysis?'

His escort of virgins, which had discreetly withdrawn several
yards when Miss Eisenbraun had pulled her ambush, rustled
nervously. Bech bowed. 'I am awaited.' Trying to rise to jaunti-
ness from in under her implication that he was mad, he added,
'See you later, alligator.'

'In a while, crocodile': streetcorner yids yukking it up in the
land of milk and honey, giving the gentle indigenes something to
giggle about. But with her he had been able to ignore, for an

absent-minded moment, the gnawing of the worm inside.

How strange, really, his condition was! As absorbing as pain, yet painless. As world-transforming as drunkenness, yet with no horizon of sobriety. As debilitating, inwardly, as a severed spine yet permitting him, outwardly, a convincing version of his usual performance. Which demonstrated, if demonstration were needed, how much of a performance it was. Who was he? A Jew, a modern man, a writer, a bachelor, a loner, a loss. A con artist in the days of academic modernism undergoing a Victorian shudder. A white monkey hung far out on a spindly heaventree of stars. A fleck of dust condemned to know it is a fleck of dust. A mouse in a furnace. A smothered scream.

His fear, like a fever or deep humiliation, bared the beauty veiled by things. His dead eyes, cleansed of healthy egotism, discovered a startled tenderness, like a virgin's whisper, in every twig, cloud, brick, pebble, shoe, ankle, window mullion, and bottle-glass tint of distant hill. Bech had moved, in this compressed religious evolution of his, from the morning's raw animism to an afternoon of natural romanticism, of pantheistic pangs. Between lunch (creamed asparagus, French fries, and meatloaf) and the poetry contest he was free; he took a long solitary walk around the edges of the campus, inhaling the strenuous odours, being witness to myriad thrusts of new growth through the woodland's floor of mulching leaves. Life chasing its own tail. Bech lifted his eyes to the ridges receding from green to blue, and the grandeur of the theatre in which Nature stages its imbecile cycle struck him afresh and enlarged the sore accretion of fear he carried inside him as unlodgeably as an elastic young wife carries within her womb her first fruit. He felt increasingly hopeless; he could never be delivered of this. In a secluded, sloping patch of oaks, he threw himself with a grunt of decision on to the damp earth, and begged Someone, Something, for mercy. He had created God. And now the silence of the created universe acquired for Bech a miraculous quality of willed reserve, of divine tact that would let him abjectly pray on a patch of mud and make no answer but the familiar ones of rustle, of whisper, of invisible growth like a net sinking slowly deeper into the sea of the sky; of gradual realization that the earth is populated infinitely, that a slithering slug was slowly causing a dead oak leaf to lift and a research team of red ants were industriously testing a sudden morsel, Bech's thumb, descended incarnate.

Eventually the author arose and tried to brush the dirt from his knees and elbows. To his fear, and shame, was added anger, anger at the universe for having extracted prayer from him. Yet his head felt lighter; he walked to Ruffin Hall in the mood of a condemned spy who, entering the courtyard where the firing squad waits, at least leaves behind his dank cell. When the girls read their poetry, each word hit him like a bullet. The girl with the small head and the long neck read:

> *Air, that transparent fire*
> *our red earth burns*
> *as we daily expire,*
> *sing ! As water in urns*
> *whispers of rivers and wharves,*
> *sing, life, within the jar*
> *each warm soul carves*
> *from this cold star.*

There was more to this poem, about Nature, about fine-veined leaves and twigs sharp as bird feet, and more poems, concerning meadows and horses and Panlike apparitions that Bech took to be college boys with sticks of pot, and then more poets, a heavy mannish girl with an unfortunate way of rolling her lips after each long Roethkësque line, and a nun-pale child who indicted our bombing of thatched villages with Lowellian ruminations, and a budding Tallulah swayed equally by Allen Ginsberg and Edna St Vincent Millay; but Bech's ears closed, his scraped heart flinched. These youthful hearts, he saw, knew all that he knew, but as one knows the rules of a game there is no obligation to play; the sealed structure of naturalism was a school to them, a prison to him. In conclusion, a splendid, goggle-eyed beauty incanted some Lanier, from 'The Marshes of Glynn', the great hymn that begins

> *As the marsh-hen secretly builds on the watery sod,*
> *Behold I will build me a nest on the greatness of God:*

and goes on

> *And the sea lends large, as the marsh: lo, out of his plenty the sea*
> *Pours fast: full soon the time of the flood-tide must be:*

and ends

> *The tide is in his ecstasy.*
> *The tide is at his highest height:*
> *And it is night.*

Something filmed Bech's eyes, less full-formed tears than the blurry reaction pollen excites in the allergic.

After the poetry reading, there was supper at Madame President's – you know her: hydrangea hair and sweeping manners and a listening smile as keen and neat as an ivory comb. And then there was a symposium, with three students and two members of the English faculty and Bech himself, on 'The Destiny of the Novel in a Non-Linear Future'. And then a party at the home of the chairman of the department, a bluff old Chaucerian with a flesh-coloured hearing aid tucked behind his ear like a wad of chewing gum. The guests came up and performed obeisances, jocular or grave, to Bech, their distinguished interloper, and then resumed seething among each other in the fraught patterns of rivalry and erotic attraction that prevail in English departments everywhere. Amid them Bech felt slow-witted and paunchy; writers are not scholars but athletes, who grow beerbellies after thirty. Miss Eisenbraun detached herself and walked him back across the campus. A fat Southern moon rode above the magnolias and the cupolas.

'You were wonderful tonight,' she told him.

'Oh?' Bech said. 'I found myself very lumpish.'

'You're just marvellously kind to children and bores,' she pursued.

'Yes. Fascinating adults are where I fall down.'

A little pause, three footsteps' worth, as if to measure the depth of the transaction they were contemplating. One, two, three: a moderate reading. Yet to lift them back over the sill of silence into conversation, a self-conscious effort, something kept in a felt-lined drawer, was needed. She pulled out French.

'*Votre malaise – est-il passé?*' The language of diplomacy.

'*Il passe, mais très lentement,*' Bech said. 'It's becoming part of me.'

'Maybe your room has depressed you. Their guest accommodations are terribly little-girly and sterile.'

'Exactly. Sterile. I feel I'm an infection. I'm the only germ in a porcelain universe.'

She laughed, uncertain. They had reached the glass doors of the dormitory where he slept. An owl hooted. The moon frosted with silver a distant ridge. He wondered if in his room his fear would make him pray again. A muffled radio somewhere played country rock.

'Don't worry,' he reassured her. 'I'm not catching.'

Her laugh changed quality; it became an upwards offer of her throat, followed by her breasts, her body. She was not wearing the catsuit but a black cocktail dress with a square neckline, yet the effect was the same, of a loose slipperiness about her that invited a peeling. She was holding to her breasts a manilla envelope full of poems awaiting his verdict. 'I think your room is underfurnished,' she told him.

'My rooms in New York are too.'

'You need something to sleep beside.'

'An oxygen tent?'

'Me.'

Bech said, 'I don't think we should,' and cried. He seemed to mean, to himself, that he was too hideous, too sick; yet also in his mind was the superstition that they must not defile the sleeping dormitory, this halcyon Lesbos, with copulation. Ruth Eisenbraun stared amazed, her hands tightening on the envelope of poems, at the moonlight making ice of Bech's impotent tears. Her firm willing body, silhouetted against the dewy smell of sleeping grass, seemed to him another poem abysmal in its ignorance, deceitful in its desire to mitigate the universe. Poetry and love, twin attempts to make the best of a bad job. Impotent; yet in his stance, his refusal to embrace, we must admire a type of rigidity, an erect pride in his desolation, a determination to defend it as his territory. A craven pagan this morning, he had become by midnight a stern monk.

This is all speculation. Truly we are in the dark here. Knowing Bech on other, better lit occasions, we doubt that, given this importunate woman, the proximity of the glass doors, and the key in his pocket, he did not for all his infirmity take her inside to his sickbed and let her apply to his wound the humid poultice of her flesh. Also, on her side, Ruth was a professor of literature; she would not have misread the works so badly as to misjudge the man. Picture them then. Above Bech and Ruth hangs the black dome of their sepulchre; the nipples of her breasts also appear black, as they swing above him, teasing his mouth, his mouth blind as a baby's, though his eyes, when he shuts them, see through the succulent padding to the calcium xylophone of her rib cage. His phallus a counterfeit bone, a phantasmal creature, like Man, on the borderline of substance and illusion, of death and life. They establish a rhythm. Her socket becomes a positive force, begins to suck, to pound. Enough. Like Bech, we reach a point where words seem horrible, maggots on the carcass of reality, feeding, proliferating; we seek peace in silence and reduction.

Wait, wait. Here is another slide, a fifth, found hiding under a stack of gold domes from Russia. It shows Bech the next morning. Again, he has slept on his back, his head held high by two pillows, a china figurine through which dreams idly blow. The pillows having been piled one on top of the other prevent our knowing whether or not two heads lay down on the bed. He rises grudgingly, stiffly. Again, he is wonderfully productive of excrement. His wound feels scabbier, drier; he knows now he can get through a day with it, can live with it. He performs his toilet – washes, wipes, brushes, shaves. He sits down at the little pseudo-Sheraton desk and shuffles the sheaf of poems as if they are physically hot. He awards the first prize, a cheque for $25, to the girl with the small head and blue eyes on stalks, writing as his citation:

Miss Haynsworth's poems strike me as technically accomplished, making their way as good loyal citizens under the tyranny of rhyme, and as precociously rich in those qualities we associate with poetesses from Sappho on – they are laconic, clear-eyed, gracious towards the world, and in their acceptance of our perishing frailty, downright brave.

Bech arranged to have the envelope delivered to Miss Eisenbraun by someone else, and was driven to the airport by a homely, tall, long-toothed woman whose voice, he realized, was the voice that beguiled him over the telephone. 'Ah'm *so* sorreh, Misteh Bech, evrehbodeh saiys you were *dah*lin, but Ah had to attend mah sisteh's weddin in Roanoke, it was one of those sudden affaihs, and jes got back this mawnin! Believe me, suh, Ah am *moht*ifahd!'

'Neveh you mind,' Bech told her, and touched his inside breast pocket to make sure his cheque was in it. The landscape, unwinding in reverse, seemed greener than when he arrived, and their speed less dangerous. Bea, who with much inconvenience had hired a babysitter so she could meet him at La Guardia, sensed, just seeing him emerge from the giant silver belly and scuttle across the tarmac in the rain, that something had happened to him, that there wasn't enough of him left for her to have any.

Bech Swings?

Bech arrived in London with the daffodils; he knew that he must fall in love. It was not his body that demanded it, but his art. His first novel, *Travel Light*, had become a minor classic of the fifties, along with *Picnic*, *The Search for Bridey Murphy*, and the sayings of John Foster Dulles. His second novel, a lyrical gesture of disgust, novella-length, called *Brother Pig*, did his reputation no harm and cleared his brain, he thought, for a frontal assault on the wonder of life. The assault, surprisingly, consumed five years, in which his mind and work habits developed in circles, or loops, increasingly leisurely and whimsical; when he sat down at his desk, for instance, his younger self, the somehow fictitious author of his earlier fictions, seemed to be not quite displaced, so that he became an uneasy, blurred composite, like the image left on film by too slow an exposure. The final fruit of his distracted struggles, *The Chosen*, was universally judged a failure – one of those 'honourable' failures, however, that rather endear a writer to the race of critics, who would rather be reassured of art's noble difficulty than cope with a potent creative verve. Bech felt himself rise from the rubble of bad reviews bigger than ever, better known and in greater demand. Just as the id, according to Freud, fails to distinguish between a wish-image and a real external object, so does publicity, another voracious idiot, dismiss all qualitative distinctions and feast off good and bad alike. Now five – no, six – years had passed, and Bech had done little but pose as himself, and scribble reviews and 'impressionistic' journalism for *Commentary* and *Esquire*, and design a series of repellent rubber stamps.

HENRY BECH REGRETS THAT HE DOES NOT SPEAK IN PUBLIC.

SORRY, PETITIONS
AREN'T MY METIER.

HENRY BECH IS TOO OLD AND ILL
AND DOUBTFUL TO SUBMIT TO
QUESTIONNAIRES AND INTERVIEWS.

IT'S YOUR PH.D. THESIS;
PLEASE WRITE IT YOURSELF.

By appropriately stamping the letters he received and returning them to the sender, Bech simplified his correspondence. But six years had passed, and his third stamp pad had gone dry, and the age of fifty was in sight, and it was high time to write something to justify his sense of himself as a precious and useful recluse. A stimulus seemed needed.

Love? Travel? As to love, he had been recently processed by a pair of sisters, first the one, and then the other; the one was neurotic and angular and harsh and glamorous and childless and exhausting, and the other had been sane and soft and plain and maternal and exhausting. Both had wanted husbands. Both had mundane, utilitarian conceptions of themselves that Bech could not bring himself to corroborate. It was his charm and delusion to see women as deities – idols whose jewel was set not in the centre of their foreheads but between their legs, with another between their lips, and pairs more sprinkled up and down, from ankles to eyes, the length of their adorable, alien forms. His transactions with these supernatural creatures imbued him, more keenly each time, with his own mortality. His life seemed increasingly like that sinister fairy story in which each granted wish diminishes a magic pelt that is in fact the wisher's life. But perhaps, Bech thought, one more woman, one more leap would bring him safe into that high calm pool of immortality where Proust and Hawthorne and Catullus float, glassy-eyed and belly up. One more wasting love would release his genius from the bondage of his sagging flesh.

As to travel: his English publisher, J. J. Goldschmidt, Ltd, who had sidestepped Bech's collected essays (published in the United

States and Canada as *When the Saints*) and had remaindered
Brother Pig with the haste usually reserved for bishops' memoirs
and albums of Pharaonic art, now, possibly embarrassed by the
little novel's creeping success in its Penguin edition, and guilty
over the minuscule advances and scrimped printings with which
he had bound Bech's thriving name, decided to bring out a
thirty-shilling anthology called, all too inevitably, *The Best of
Bech*. To support this enterprise he asked the author to come to
London for the week before publication and permit himself to 'be
lionized'. The phrase snaked in less time than an eyeblink along
three thousand miles of underwater cable.

'I'd rather be lambified,' Bech answered.

'What, Henry? Sorry, I can hardly hear you.'

'Forget it, Goldy. It was a hard word.'

'You heard what?'

'Nothing. This is a very wet connection.'

'Dead?'

'Not yet, but let's kill it. I'll come.' He arrived with the
daffodils. The VC-10 banked over Hampton Court, and the
tinge of their yellow was visible from the air. In Hyde Park beside
the Serpentine, along Birdcage Walk in St James's, in Grosvenor
Square beneath the statue of Roosevelt and in Russell Square
beneath the statue of Gandhi, in all the fenced squares from
Fitzroy to Pembroke, the daffodils made a million golden curt-
seys to those tourists who, like our hero, wandered dazed by jet-
lag and lonely as a cloud. *A poet could not but be gay*, Bech
recalled, *In such a jocund company*. And the people in the
streets, it seemed to him, whether milling along Oxford Street or
sauntering from lion to lion in Trafalgar Square, formed another
golden host, beautiful in the antique cold-faced way of Blake's
pastel throngs, pale Dionysiacs, bare thighs and gaudy cloth,
lank hair and bell-bottoms, *Continuous as the stars that shine /
And twinkle on the milky way*. And, the next morning, watching
Merissa move nude to the window and to her closet, he felt her
perfections – the parallel tendons at the backs of her knees, the
kisslike leaps of shadow among the muscles of her shoulders –
flow outdoors and merge with the lacy gauze of the grey British

air. A VC-10 hung in silent descent above the treetops of Regent's Park. He rose and saw that this park too had its pools of gold, its wandering beds of daffodils, and that under the sunless noon sky lovers, their heads androgynous masses of hair, had come to lie entwined on the cold greening grass. *Cold greening grass,* Bech heard. The echo disturbed and distracted him. The papery daytime world, cluttered with books he had not written, cut into the substantial dreams of drunkenness and love.

Jørgen Josiah Goldschmidt, a bustling small anxious man with an ambitiously large head and the pendulous profile of a Florentine banker, had arranged a party for Bech the very evening of his arrival. 'But, Goldy, by your time I've been awake since two this morning.'

They had met several times in New York. Goldschmidt had evidently sized up Bech as a clowner to be chuckled and shushed into line. In turn Bech had sized up Goldschmidt as one of those self-made men who have paid the price (for not letting God make them) of minor defects like inner deafness and constant neuralgia. Goldschmidt's was a success story. A Danish Jew, he had arrived in England in the late thirties. In twenty years, he had gone from the Ministry of Information to the B.B.C. to an editorship in a venerable publishing house to the founding, in the mid-fifties, of one of his own, specializing in foreign avant-garde writers no one else wanted and dainty anthologies of poetic matter lapsed from copyright. A lucky recipe book (health food soups) and a compendium of Prayers for Humanists staved off bankruptcy. Now he was prosperous, thanks mostly to his powers of persuading his lawyers and printers to let him publish increasingly obscene American authors. Though devoid of any personal taste for obscenity, he had found a wave and was riding it. His accent and dress were impeccably British. In tune with the times he had sprouted bushy sideburns. His face was always edged with the grey of nagging pain. He said, his brown eyes (in repose, they revealed lovely amber depths, lit by the fire of his brain, but were rarely in repose) flicking past Bech's shoulder towards the next problem, 'Henry, you must come. Everyone is dying to meet you.

I've invited just the very dearest nicest people. Ted Heath might drop in later, and Princess Margaret was so sorry she must be in Ceylon. You can have a nice nap in your hotel. If you don't like the room, we can change it. I thought from your books you would enjoy a view of the traffic. Your interview isn't until five, a terribly nice intelligent boy, a compatriot of yours. If you don't like him, just give him a half hour of the usual and he'll be on his way.'

Bech protested, 'I have no usual,' but the other man said deafly, 'Bless you,' and left.

Too excited by the new city, and by having survived another aeroplane flight, Bech instead of sleeping walked miles looking at the daffodils, at the Georgian rows plastered with demolition notices and peace slogans, at the ruffled shirts and Unisex pants in the shop windows, at the bobbies resembling humourless male models, at the dingy band of hippies sharing Eros's black island in Piccadilly Circus with pigeons the colour of exhaust fumes. On Great Russell Street, down from the British Museum, past a Hindu luncheonette, a plaque marked the site of a Dickens novel as if the characters had occupied the same time-space in which Bech walked. Back in his hotel lobby, he was offended by the American voices, the pseudo-Edwardian decor, the illustrated chart of acceptable credit cards. A typical Goldschmidt snap decision, to stuff him into a tourist trap. A pale young man, plainly American from his round-headed haircut and his clever hangdog way of sidling forward, came up to Bech. 'My name is Tuttle, Mr Bech. I guess I'm going to interview you.'

'Your guess is as good as mine,' Bech said.

The boy tipped his head slightly, like a radar dish, as if to decipher the something acerb in Bech's tone, and said, 'I don't generally do this sort of thing, actually I have as low an opinion of interviews as you do – '

'How do you know I have a low opinion?' Jet-lag was getting to Bech; irritability was droning in his ears.

'You've said so' – the boy smiled shyly, cleverly – 'in your other interviews.' He went on hastily, pursuing his advantage. 'But this wouldn't be like your others. It would be all you, I have no axe to grind, no axe at all. A friend of mine on the staff of the Sunday *Observer* begged me to do it, actually I'm in London researching a thesis on eighteenth-century printers. It would be a sort of full spread to go with *The Best of Bech*. Let me frankly confess, it seemed a unique opportunity. I've written you letters in the past, in the States, but I suppose you've forgotten.'

'Did I answer them?'

'You hit them with a rubber stamp and sent them back.' Tuttle waited, perhaps for an apology, then went on. 'What I have in mind now is a chance for you to explain yourself, to say everything you want to say. *You* want to say. Your *name* is known over here, Mr Bech, but they don't really know *you*.'

'Well, that's their privilege.'

'I beg your pardon, sir, I think it's their loss.'

Bech felt himself slippingly, helplessly relenting. 'Let's sit over here,' he said. To take the boy up to his room would, he thought groggily, simulate pederasty and risk the fate of Wilde.

They sat in facing lobby chairs; Tuttle perched on the edge of his as if he had been called into the principal's office. 'I've read every word you've written five or six times. Frankly, I think you're *it*.' This sounded to Bech like the safest praise he had ever heard; one appetite that had not diminished with the years was for unambiguous, blood-raw superlatives.

He reached over and tagged the boy. 'Now you're it,' he said.

Tuttle blushed. 'I mean to say, what other people *say* they're doing, you really *do*.' An echo troubled Bech; he had heard this before, but not applied to himself. Still, the droning had ceased. The blush had testified to some inner conflict, and Bech could maintain his defences only in the face of a perfectly simple, resolute attack. Any sign of embarrassment or self-doubt he confused with surrender.

'Let's have a drink,' he said.

'Thank you, no.'

'You mean you're on duty?'

'No, I just don't ever drink.'

'Never?'

'No.'

Bech thought, They've sent me a Christer. That's what Tuttle's pallor, his sidling severity, his embarrassed insistence reminded Bech of: the Pentecostal fanatic who comes to the door. 'Well, let me frankly confess, I sometimes do. Drink.'

'Oh, I know. Your drinking is famous.'

'Like Hitler's vegetarianism.'

In his haste to put Bech at ease, Tuttle neglected to laugh. 'Please go ahead,' the boy insisted. 'If you become incoherent, I'll just stop taking notes, and we can resume another day.'

Poor Henry Bech, to whom innocence, in its galoshes of rudeness and wet raincoat of presumption, must always appear as possibly an angel to be sheltered and fed. He ordered a drink ('Do you know what a whisky sour is?' he asked the waiter, who said 'Absolutely, sir' and brought him a whisky-and-soda) and tried for one more degrading time to dig into the rubbish of his 'career' and come up with the lost wristwatch of truth. Encouraged by the fanatic way the boy covered page after page of his notebook with wildly oscillating lines, Bech talked of fiction as an equivalent of reality, and described how the point of it, the justification, seemed to lie in those moments when a set of successive images locked and then one more image arrived and, as it were, superlocked, creating a tightness perhaps equivalent to the terribly tight knit of reality, e.g., the lightning ladder of chemical changes in the body cell that translates fear into action or, say, the implosion of mathematics consuming the heart of a star. And the down-grinding thing is the realization that no one, not critics or readers, ever notices these moments but instead prattles, in praise or blame, of bits of themselves glimpsed in the work as in a shattered mirror. That it is necessary to begin by believing in an ideal reader and that slowly he is proved not to exist. He is not the daily reviewer skimming a plastic-bound set of raggedy advance proofs, nor the bulk-loving housewife who buys a shiny new novel between the grocer's and the hairdresser's, nor the diligent graduate student with his heap of index cards and Xerox applications, nor the plump-scripted young ballpointer who sends a mash note via *Who's Who*, nor, in the weary end, even oneself. In short, one loses heart in the discovery that one is not being read. That the ability to read, and therefore to write, is being lost, along with the abilities to listen, to see, to smell, and to breathe. That all the windows of the spirit are being nailed shut. Here Bech gasped for air, to dramatize his point. He said, then, that he was sustained, insofar as he was sustained, by the memory of laughter, the specifically Jewish, embattled, religious, sufficiently desperate, not quite belly laughter of his father and his father's brothers, his beloved Brooklyn uncles; that the American Jews had kept the secret of this laughter a generation longer than the Gentiles, hence their present domination of the literary world; that unless the Negroes learned to write there was nowhere else it could come from; and that in the world today only the Russians still had it, the Peruvians possibly, and Mao Tse-tung but not any of the rest of the Chinese. In his, Bech's, considered judgement.

Tuttle scribbled another page and looked up hopefully. 'Maoism does seem to be the coming mood,' he said.

'The mood of t'mao,' Bech said, rising. 'Believe it or not, my lad, I must take a shower and go to a party. Power corrupts.'

'When could we resume? I think we've made a fascinating beginning.'

'Be*gin*ning? You want *more*? For just a little puff in the *Observer*?'

When Tuttle stood, though he was skinny, with a round head like a newel knob, he was taller than Bech. He got tough. 'I want it to be much more than that, Mr Bech. Much more than a little puff. They've promised me as much space as we need. You have a chance here, if you *use* me hard enough, to make a d-definitive t-t-testament.'

If the boy hadn't stammered, Bech might have escaped. But the stammer, those little spurts of helpless silence, hooked him. Stalling, he asked, 'You never drink?'

'Not really.'

'Do you smoke?'

'No.'

'Matter of principle?'

'I just never acquired the taste.'

'Do you eat between meals?'

'I guess once in a while.'

'Call me tomorrow,' Bech conceded, and hated himself. Strange, how dirty the attempt to speak seriously made him feel. Comparable to his sensation when he saw someone press an open book flat and complacently, irreparably crack the spine.

Bech's tuxedo over the years had developed a waxen sheen and grown small; throughout Goldy's party, his waist was being cruelly pinched. The taxicab, so capacious that Bech felt like ballast, turned down a succession of smaller and smaller streets and stopped on a dead-end loop, where, with the mystic menace of a Christmas tree, a portico blazed. The doorknocker was a goldsmith's hammer inscribed with a florid double 'J'. A servant in blue livery admitted Bech. Goldy bustled forward in a red velvet jacket and flopping ruffles. Another servant poured Bech a warm Scotch. Goldy, his eyes shuttling like a hockey player's, steered Bech past a towering pier glass into a room where beautiful women in cream and saffron and magenta drifted and billowed in soft slow motion. Men in black stood like channel markers in this sea. 'Here's a lovely person you must meet,' Goldy told Bech. To her he said, 'Henry Bech. He's very shy. Don't frighten him away, darling.'

She was an apparition – wide powdery shoulders, long untroubled chin ever so faintly cleft, lips ghostly in their cushioned perfection, grey eyes whose light flooded their cages of false lash and painted shadow. Bech asked her, 'What do you do?'

She quivered; the corners of her lips trembled wryly, and he realized that the question had been consummately stupid, that merely to rise each morning and fill her skin to the brim with such loveliness was enough for any woman to do.

But she said, 'Well, I have a husband, and five children, and I've just published a book.'

'A novel?' Bech could see it now: robin's-egg-blue jacket, brisk adultery on country week-ends, comic relief provided by precocious children.

'No, not really. It's the history of labour movements in England before 1860.'

'Were there many?'

'Some. It was very difficult for them.'

'How lovely of you,' Bech said, 'to care; that is, when you look so' – he rejected 'posh' – 'unlaborious.'

Again, her face underwent, not a change of expression, which was unvaryingly sweet and attentive, but a seismic tremor, as if her composure restrained volcanic heat. She asked, 'What are your novels about?'

'Oh, ordinary people.'

'Then how lovely of *you*; when you're so extraordinary.'

A man bored with being a channel marker came and touched her elbow, and statelily she turned, leaving Bech her emanations, like an astronomer flooded by radio waves from a blank part of the sky. He tried to take a fix on her flattery by looking, as he went for another drink, into a mirror. His nose with age had grown larger and its flanges had turned distinctly red; his adaption of the hair style of the young had educed woolly bursts of grey above his ears and a tallowish mass of white curling outwards at the back of his collar: he looked like a mob-controlled congressman from Queens hoping to be taken for a Southern senator. His face was pasty with fatigue, though his eyes seemed frantically alive. He observed in the mirror, observing him, a slim young African woman in see-through pyjamas. He turned and asked her, 'What *can* we do about Biafra?'

'*Je le regrette, Monsieur,*' she said, '*mais maintenant je ne pense jamais. Je vis, simplement.*'

'*Parce que,*' Bech offered, '*le monde est trop effrayant?*'

She shrugged. '*Peut-être.*' When she shrugged, her silhouetted breasts shivered with their weight; it took Bech back to his avid youthful perusals of the *National Geographic*. He said, '*Je pense, comme vous, que le monde est difficile à comprendre, mais certainement, en tout cas, vous êtes très sage, très belle.*' But his French was not good enough to hold her, and she turned, and was wearing bikini underpants, with tiger stripes, beneath the saffron gauze of her pantaloons. Blue servants rang chimes for dinner. He gulped his drink, and avoided the sideways eye of the congressman from Queens.

On his right was seated a middle-aged Lady of evident importance, though her beauty could never have been much more than a concentrate of sharpness and sparkle. 'You American Jews,' she said, 'are so romantic. You think every little dolly bird is Delilah. I hate the "pity me" in all your books. Women don't want to be complained at. They want to be screwed.'

'I'll have to try it,' Bech said.

'Do. Do.' She pivoted towards a long-toothed gallant waiting grinning on her right; he exclaimed 'Darling!' and their heads fell together like bagged oranges. On Bech's left sat a magenta shape his first glance had told him to ignore. It glittered and was young. Bech didn't trust anyone under thirty; the young now moved with the sacred and dangerous assurance of the old when he had been young. She was toying with her soup like a child. Her head was small as a child's, with close-cut fingernails and endearing shadows around the knuckles. He felt he had seen the hand before. In a novel. *Lolita? Magic Mountain?* Simple etiquette directed that he ask her how she was.

'Rotten, thanks.'

'Think of me,' Bech said. 'By the time I woke up in, it's four o'clock in the morning.'

'I hate sleep. I don't sleep for days sometimes and feel wonderful. I think people sleep too much, that's why their arteries harden.' In fact, he was to discover that she slept as the young do, in long easy swings that gather the extra hours into their arc and override all noise – though she had every woman's tendency to stir at dawn. She went on, as if politely, 'Do you have hard arteries?'

'Not to my knowledge. Just impotence and gout.'

'That sounds come-ony.'

'Forgive me. I was just told women don't like being complained to.'

'I heard the old tart say that. Don't believe her. They love it. Why are you impotent?'

'Old age?' A voice inside him said, *Old age? he tentatively said*.

'Come off it.' He liked her voice, one of those British voices produced half-way down the throat, rather than obliquely off the sinuses, with alarming octave jumps. She was wearing gold granny glasses on her little heart-shaped face. He didn't know if her cheeks were flushed or rouged. He was pleased to observe that, though she was petite, her breasts pushed up plumply from her dress, which was ornamented with small mirrors. Her lips, chalky and cushioned, with intelligent tremulous corners, seemed taken from the first woman he had met, as if one had been a preliminary study for the other. He noticed she had a little moustache, faint as two erased pencil lines. She told him, 'You write.'

'I used to.'

'What happened?'

A gap in the dialogue. Fill in later. 'I don't seem to know.'

'I used to be a wife. My husband was an American. Still is, come to think of it.'

'Where did you live?' The girl and Bech simultaneously glanced down and began to hurry to finish the food on their plates.

'New York.'

'Like it?'

'Loved it.'

'Didn't it seem dirty to you?'

'Gloriously.' She chewed. He pictured sharp small even teeth lacerating and compressing bloody beef. He set down his fork. She swallowed and asked, 'Love London?'

'Don't know it.'

'You don't?'

'Been here only long enough to look at daffodils.'

'I'll show it to you.'

'How can you? How can I find you again?' Victorian novel? Rewrite.

'You're in London alone?'

A crusty piece of Yorkshire pudding looked too good to leave. Bech picked up his fork again, agreeing, 'Mm. I'm alone everywhere.'

'Would you like to come home with me?'

The lady on his right turned and said, 'I must say, you're a stinker to let this old fag monopolize me.'

'Don't complain. Men hate it.'

She responded, 'Your hair is smashing. You're almost Santa Claus.'

'Tell me, love, who's this, what do you say, bird on my left?'

'She's Little Miss Poison. Her father bought himself a peerage from Macmillan.'

The girl at Bech's back tickled the hairs of his neck with her breath and said, 'I withdraw my invitation.'

'Let's all,' Bech said loudly, 'have some more wine,' pouring. The man with long teeth put his hand over the top of his glass. Bech expected a magician's trick but was disappointed.

And at the door, as Bech tried to sneak past the voracious pier glass with the girl, Goldy seemed disappointed. 'But did you meet *everybody?* These are the nicest people in London.'

Bech hugged his publisher. Waxy old tux, meet velvet and ruffles. Learn how the other half lives. 'Goldy,' he said, 'the party was nice, nicey, niciest. It couldn't have been nicer. Like, wow, out of sight.' He saw drunken noise as the key to his exit. Otherwise this velvet gouger would milk him for another hour of lionization. Grr.

Coldly displayed the racial gracefulness in defeat. His limpid eyes, as busy as if he were playing blitz chess, flicked past Bech's shoulder to the girl. 'Merissa dear, *do* take decent care of our celebrity. My fortune rides on his charm.' Thus Bech learned her first name.

The taxi, with two in it, felt less like a hollow hull and more like a small drawing-room, where voices needn't be raised. They did not, perhaps oddly, touch. *Perhaps oddly?* He had lost all ability to phrase. He was on the dark side of the earth in a cab with a creature whose dress held dozens of small mirrors. Her legs were white like knives, crossed and recrossed. A triangular

bit of punctuation where the thighs ended. The cab moved
through empty streets, past wrought-iron gates inked on to the
sky and granite museums frowning beneath the weight of their
entablatures, across the bright loud gulch of Hyde Park Corner
and Park Lane, into darker quieter streets. They passed a shut-
tered building that Merissa identified as the Chinese Communist
Embassy. They entered a region where the shaggy heads of trees
seemed to be dreaming of fantastically long colonnades and of
high white wedding-cake façades receding to infinity. The cab
stopped. Merissa paid. She let him in by a door whose knob,
knocker, and mail slot were silken with polishings. Marble stairs.
Another door. Another key. The odours of floor wax, of stale
cigarette smoke, of narcissi in a pebbled bowl. Brandy with its
scorched, expensive smell was placed beneath his nose. Obediently he drank. He was led into a bedroom. Perfume and powder,
leather and an oil-clothy scent that took him back into English
children's books that his mother, bent on his 'improvement', used
to buy at the Fifth Avenue Scribner's. A window opened. Chill
April smells. *Winter kept us warm.* She brushed back curtains. A
slice of slate night yellowish above the trees. The lights of an
aeroplane winking in descent. A rustling all around him. The
candy taste of lipstick. Clean air, warm skin. *Feeding a little life
with dried tubers.* Her bare back a lunar surface beneath his
hands. The forgotten impression of intrusion, of subtle monstrous assault, that the particularities of a new woman's body
make upon us. *Summer surprised us.* Must find out her last
name. There are rings of release beyond rings, Bech discovered in
the bliss – the pang of relief around his waist – of taking off his
tuxedo. Must see a tailor.

'When you were writing *The Chosen*,' Tuttle asked, 'did you
deliberately set out to create a more flowery style?' This time he
had brought a tape recorder. They were in Bech's hotel rooms, an
extensive corner suite with a fake fireplace and a bed that hadn't
been slept in. The fireplace was not entirely fake; it held a kind of
crinkly plastic sculpture of a coal fire that glowed when plugged
in and even gave off an imitation of heat.

'I never think about style, about creating one,' Bech dictated into the baby microphone of the tape recorder. 'My style is always as simple as the subject matter permits. As you grow older, though, you find that few things are simple.'

'For example?'

'For example, changing a tyre. I'm sorry, your question seems inane to me. This interview seems inane.'

'Let me try another approach,' Tuttle said, as maddeningly patient as a child psychiatrist. 'In *Brother Pig*, were you conscious of inserting the political resonances?'

Bech blinked. 'I'm sorry, when you say "resonances" all I see is dried grapes. *Brother Pig* was about what its words said it was about. It was not a mask for something else. I do not write in code. I depend upon my reader for a knowledge of the English language and some acquired vocabulary of human experience. My books, I hope, would be unintelligible to baboons, or squid. My books are human transactions – flirtations, quarrels.'

'You're tired,' Tuttle told him.

He was right. Merissa had taken him to a restaurant along Fulham Road run by fairies and then to Revolution, where big posters of Ho and Mao and Engels and Lenin watched from the walls as young people dressed in sequins and bell-bottoms jogged up and down within a dense, throbbing, coruscating fudge of noise. Bech knew something was happening here, a spiritual upthrusting like Christianity among the slaves of Rome or cabalism among the peasant Jews of stagnant Slavic Europe, but his old-fashioned particularizing vision kept dissolving the mob into its components: working girls resigned to a groggy tomorrow at their typewriters; neutered young men in fashion or photography to whom coming here was work; the truly idle, the rich and the black, escaping from the empty-eye-socket state of spooked hours; the would-be young like himself, ancient lecherous woolly-haired Yanks whose willy-nilly charm and backwards success had prevented their learning ever to come in out of the rain; enigmatic tarty birds like Merissa, whose flat, he had discovered, held a room full of electric toys and teddy bears, with a bed where a child slept, her child, she confessed, a son, eight years old, born in America, when Merissa was nineteen, a child sent off to boarding school and even on vacations, Bech suspected, mostly taken to the park and the zoo by Isabella, Merissa's Spanish maid, an old round woman who peeked at Bech through doorways and then quickly, quietly shut the door ... it was confusing. Revolution was the cave of a new religion but everyone had come, Bech saw, for reasons disappointingly reasonable and opportunistic. To make out. To be seen. To secure advancement. To be improved. That girl in the chain-link tunic and nothing else was working off her Yorkshire accent. That man flicking his arm like a dervish under the blue battering of the strobe lights was swinging a real-estate deal in his head. Bech doubted that the men on the wall approved what they saw. They were simple failed librarians like himself, schooled in the pre-Freudian verities. Hunger and pain are bad. Work is good. Men were made for the daylight. Orgasms are private affairs. *Down in Loosiana/Where the alligators swim so mean* ... Opposite him Merissa, who had a way of suddenly looking tall, though her smallness was what enchanted him, twinkled through the holes of her dress and moved her limbs and turned to him a shuddering profile, eyes shut as if better to feel the beat between her legs, that fluttering elusive beat: *What we are witnessing*, Bech announced inside his own head, in his role of college circuit-rider, *is the triumph of the clitoral, after three thousand years of phallic hegemony.* She called over to him, through the flashing din, 'It gets to be rather same-y, doesn't it?' And he felt then his heart make the motion he had been waiting for, of love for her; like the jaws of a clam when the muscle is sliced, his heart opened. He tasted it, the sugary nip of impossibility. For he was best at loving what he could never have.

'Lord, you're lovely,' he said. 'Let's go home.'

She accused him: 'You don't love London, only me.'

His conversations with Merissa did have a way of breaking into two-liners. For example,

MERISSA: 'I'm terribly tired of being white.'

BECH: 'But you're so good at it.'

Or:

BECH: 'I've never understood what sex is like for a woman.'
MERISSA: (*thinking hard*): 'It's like – fog.'

The phone rang at nine the next morning. It was Tuttle. Goldschmidt had given him Merissa's number. Bech thought of ex-
postulating but since the boy never drank he would have no idea
how Bech's head felt. With some dim idea of appeasing those
forces of daylight and righteous wrath that he had seen mocked
on the walls of Revolution last night, he consented to meet Tuttle
at his hotel at ten. Perhaps this stab at self-abnegation did him
good, for, on his way to the West End in the lurching, swaying
upstairs of a 74 bus, nauseated by the motion, having breakfasted
on unbuttered toast and reheated tea (Merissa had observed his
departure by sighing and rolling over on her stomach, and her
refrigerator held nothing but yoghurt and champagne), gazing
down upon the top of the shoppers in Baker Street – shimmering
saris, polka-dot umbrellas – Bech was visited by inspiration. The
title of his new novel abruptly came to him: Think Big. It bal-
anced the title of his first, *Travel Light*. It held in the girders of
its consonants, braced by those two stark 'i's, America's promise,
pathos, crassness, grandeur. As *Travel Light* had been about a
young man, so *Think Big* must be about a young woman, about
openness and confusion, coruscation and the loss of the breeding
function. Merissa could be the heroine. But she was British.
Transposing her into an American would meet resistance at a
hundred points, as for instance when she undressed, and was as
white as an Artemis of marble, whereas any American girl that
age carries all winter the comical ghost of last summer's bikini,
emphasizing her erogenous zones like a diagram. And Merissa's
enchanting smallness, the manner in which her perfection
seemed carried out on an elfin scale, so that Bech could study by
lamplight the bones of an ankle and foot as he would study an
ivory miniature, a smallness excitingly violated when her mouth
swam into the dimensions of the normal – this too was un-Am-
erican. Your typical Bennington girl wore a 9½ sneaker and carried her sex as in a knapsack, to be unpacked at night. A rugged

Boy/Girl Scout was the evolutionary direction, not the perfumed, faintly treacherous femininity Merissa exuded from each dear pore. Still, Bech reasoned while the bus manoeuvred into Oxford Street and the shoppers danced in psychedelic foreshortening, she was not quite convincing as she was (what did she *do*? for instance, to warrant that expensive flat, and Isabella, and a dinner invitation from Goldy, and the closets full of swinging clothes, not to mention riding chaps and mud-crusted golf shoes) and Bech was sure he could fill in her gaps with bits of American women, could indeed re-create her from almost nothing, needing less than a rib, needing only the living germ of his infatuation, of his love. Already small things from here and there, kept alive by some kink in his forgetting mechanism, had begun to fly together, to fit. A dance hall he had once walked upstairs to, off of war-darkened Broadway. A rabid but deft Trotskyite barber his father had patronized. The way New York's side streets seek the sunset and the way on Fifth Avenue hard-shinned women in sunglasses hurry past languorous mannequins in gilded robes, black-velvet cases of jewels wired to burglar alarms, shop windows crying out ignored. But what would be the action of the book (it was a big book, he saw, with a blue jacket of coated stock and his unsmiling photo full on the back, bled top and bottom), its conflict, it issue, its outcome? The answer, like the title, came from so deep within him that it seemed a message from beyond: Suicide. His heroine must kill herself. Think big. His heart trembled in excitement, at the enormity of his crime.

'You're tired,' Tuttle said, and went on, 'I've seen the point raised about your work, that the kind of ethnic loyalty you display, loyalty to a narrow individualistic past, is divisive, and encourages war, and helps account for your reluctance to join the peace movement and the social revolution. How would you rebut this?'

'Where did you see this point raised, did you say?'

'Some review.'

'*What* review? Are you sure you just didn't make it up? I've seen some dumb things written about me, but never anything quite that vapid and doctrinaire.'

'My attempt, Mr Bech, is to elicit from you your opinions. If you find this an unfruitful area, let's move on. Maybe I should stop the machine while you collect your thoughts. We're wasting tape.'

'Not to mention my lifeblood.' But Bech groggily tried to satisfy the boy; he described his melancholy feelings in the go-go place last night, his intuition that self-aggrandizement and entrepreneurial energy were what made the world go and that slogans and movements to the contrary were evil dreams, evil in that they distracted people from particular, concrete realities, whence all goodness and effectiveness derive. He was an Aristotelian and not a Platonist. Write him down, if he must write him down as something, as a disbeliever; he disbelieved in the Pope, in the Kremlin, in the Vietcong, in the American eagle, in astrology, Arthur Schlesinger, Eldridge Cleaver, Senator Eastland, and Eastman Kodak. Nor did he believe overmuch in his disbelief. He thought intelligence a function of the individual and that groups of persons were intelligent in inverse proportion to their size. Nations had the brains of an amoeba whereas a committee approached the condition of a trainable moron. He believed, if this tape recorder must know, in the goodness of something $v.$ nothing, in the dignity of the inanimate, the intricacy of the animate, the beauty of the average woman, and the common sense of the average man. The tape spun out its reel and ran flapping.

Tuttle said, 'That's great stuff, Mr Bech. One more session, and we should have it.'

'Never, never, never, never,' Bech said. Something in his face drove Tuttle out the door. Bech fell asleep on his bed in his clothes. He awoke and found that *Think Big* had died. It had become a ghost of a book, an empty space beside the four faded spines that he had already brought to exist. *Think Big* had no content but wonder, which was a blankness. He thought back through his life, so many dreams and wakings, so many faces encountered and stoplights obeyed and streets crossed, and there was nothing solid; he had rushed through his life as through a badly chewed meal, leaving an ache of indigestion. In the beginning, the fresh flame of his spirit had burned everything clean – the entire grey city, stone and soot and stoops. Miles of cracked pavement had not been too much. He had gone to sleep on the sound of sirens and woken to the cries of fruit carts. There had been around him a sheltering ring of warm old tall bodies whose droning appeared to be wisdom, whose crooning and laughter seemed to be sifted down from the God who presided above the smouldering city's tip lights. There had been classrooms smelling of eraser crumbs, and strolling evenings when the lights of New Jersey seemed strung gems, and male pals from whom to learn loyalty and stoicism, and the first dizzying drag on a cigarette, and the first girl who let his hands linger, and the first joys of fabrication, of invention and completion.

Then unreality had swept in. It was his fault; he had wanted to be noticed, to be praised. He had wanted to be a man in the world, a 'writer'. For his punishment they had made from the sticks and mud of his words a coarse large doll to question and torment, which would not have mattered except that he was trapped inside the doll, shared a name and bank account with it. And the life that touched and brushed other people, that played across them like a saving breeze, could not break through the crust to him. He was, with all his brave talk to Tuttle of individual intelligence and the foolishness of groups, too alone.

He telephoned Goldschmidt, Ltd, and was told Goldy was out to lunch. He called Merissa but her number did not answer. He went downstairs and tried to talk to the hotel doorman about the weather. 'Well, sir, weather is weather, I find to be the case generally. Some days is fine, and others a bit dim. This sky today you'll find is about what we generally have this time of the year. It'll all average out when we're in the grave, isn't that the truth of it, sir?' Bech disliked being humoured, and the grave-digger scene had never been one of his favourites. He went walking beneath the dispirited, homogeneous sky, featureless but for some downward wisps of nimbus promising rain that never arrived. Where were the famous English clouds, the clouds of Constable and Shelley? He tried to transplant the daffodils to Riverside Park, for his novel, but couldn't see them there, among those littered thickets hollowed by teen-aged layabouts bloodless with heroin, these British bulbs laid out in their loamy bed by ancient bowed men, the great-grandchildren of feudalism, who swept the paths where Bech walked with brooms, yes, and this was cheering, with brooms fashioned of twigs honestly bound together with twine. It began to rain.

Bech became a docile tourist and interviewee. He bantered on the B.B.C. Third Programme with a ripe-voiced young Welshman. He read from his works to bearded youths at the London School of Economics, between strikes. He submitted to a cocktail party at the U.S. Embassy. He participated in a television discussion on the Collapse of the American Dream with an edgy homosexual historian whose toupee kept slipping; a mug-shaped small man who thirty years ago had invented a donnish verse-form resembling the limerick; a preposterously rude young radical with puffed-out lips and a dominating stammer; and, chairing their discussion, a tall B.B.C. girl whose elongated thighs kept arresting Bech in mid-sentence – she had pop eyes and a wild way of summing up, as if all the while she had been attending to angel-voices entirely her own. Bech let Merissa drive him, in her beige Fiat, to Stonehenge and Canterbury. At Canterbury she got into a fight with a verger about exactly where Becket had been stabbed. She took Bech to a concert in the Albert Hall, whose cavernous interior Bech drowsily confused with Victoria's womb, and where he fell asleep. Afterwards they went to a club with gaming rooms where Merissa, playing two blackjack hands simultaneously, lost sixty quid in twenty minutes. There was a professional fierceness about the way she sat at the green felt table that requickened his curiosity as to what she *did*. He was sure she did something. Her flat held a swept-off desk, and a bookcase shelf solid with reference works. Bech would have snooped, but he felt Isabella always watching him, and the daylight hours he spent here were few. Merissa told him her last name – Merrill, the name of her American husband – but fended off his other inquiries with the protest that he was being 'writery' and the disarming request that he consider her as simply his 'London episode'. But how did she live? She and her son and her maid. 'Oh,' Merissa told him, 'my father owns things. Don't ask me what things. He keeps buying different ones.'

He had not quite given up the idea of making her the heroine of his masterpiece. He must understand what it is like to be young now. 'The other men you sleep with – what do you feel towards them?'

'They seem nice at the time.'

'At the time; and then afterwards not so nice?'

The suggestion startled her; from the way her eyes widened, she felt he was trying to insert evil into her world. 'Oh yes, then too. They're so grateful. Men are. They're so grateful if you just make them a cup of tea in the morning.'

'But where is it all going? Do you think about marrying again?'

'Not much. That first go was pretty draggy. He kept saying things like, "Pick up your underwear," and, "In Asia they live on ninety dollars a year." ' Merissa laughed.

Her hair was a miracle, spread out on the pillow in the morning light, a lustrous mass measured in infinity, every filament the same lucid black, a black that held red light within it as matter holds heat – whereas even of the hairs on his toes some had turned white. Gold names on an honour roll. As a character, Merissa would become a redhead, with that vulnerable freckled pallor and overlarge, uneven, earnest front teeth. Merissa's teeth were so perfectly spaced they seemed machined. Like her eyelashes. *Stars with a talent for squad-drill.* As she laughed, divulging the slippery grotto beyond her palate, Bech felt abhorrence rising in his throat. He looked towards the window; an aeroplane was descending from a ceiling of grey. He asked, 'Do you take drugs?'

'Not really. A little grass to be companionable. I don't believe in it.'

Her American counterpart would, of course. Bech saw this counterpart in his mind: a pale Puritan, self-destructive, her blue eyes faded like cotton work clothes too often scrubbed. Merissa's green eyes sparkled, her hectic cheeks burned. 'What do you believe in?' he asked.

'Different things at different times,' she said. 'You don't seem all that pro-marriagey yourself.'

'I am, for other people.'

'I know why sleeping with you is so exciting. It's like sleeping with a parson.'

'Dear Merissa,' Bech said. He tried to crush her into himself. To suck the harlot's roses from her cheeks. He slobbered on her wrists, pressed his forehead against the small of her spine. He did all this in ten-point type, upon the warm white paper of her sliding skin. Poor child, under this old ogre, who had chewed his life so badly his stomach hurt, whose every experience was harassed by a fictional version of itself, whose waking life was a weary dream of echoes and erased pencil lines; he begged her forgiveness, while she moaned with anticipated pleasure. It was no use; he could not rise, he could not love her, could not perpetuate a romance or *roman* without seeing through it to the sour parting and the mixed reviews. He began, in lieu of performance, to explain this.

She interrupted: 'Well, Henry, you must learn to replace ardour with art.'

The cool practicality of this advice, its smug recourse to millennia of peasant saws and aristocratic maxims, to all that civilized wisdom America had sought to flee and find an alternative to, angered him. 'Art *is* ardour,' he told her.

'Bad artists hope that's true.'

'Read your Wordsworth.'

'In tran*quil*lity, darling.'

Her willingness to debate was beginning to excite him. He saw that wit and logic might survive into the lawless world coming to birth. 'Merissa, you're so clever.'

'The weak must be. That's what England is learning.'

'Do you think I'm necessarily impotent? As an artist?'

'Unnecessarily.'

'Merissa, tell me: what do you *do?*'

'You'll see,' she said, pressing her head back into the pillow and smiling in assured satisfaction, as his giant prick worked back and forth. The tail wagging the dog.

Tuttle caught him at his hotel the day before he left and asked him if he felt any affinity with Ronald Firbank. 'Only the affinity,' Bech said, 'I feel with all Roman Catholic homosexuals.'

'I was hoping you'd say something like that. How are you feeling, Mr Bech? The last time I saw you, you looked awful. Frankly.'

'I feel better now that you've stopped seeing me.'

'Great. It was a real privilege and delight for me, I tell you. I hope you like the way the piece shaped up; I do. I hope you don't mind my few reservations.'

'No, you can't go anywhere these days without reservations.'

'Ha ha.' It was the only time Bech ever heard Tuttle laugh.

Merissa didn't answer her telephone. Bech hoped she'd be at the farewell party Goldy threw for him – a modest affair, without blue servants, and Bech in his altered tuxedo the sole man present in formal dress – but she wasn't. When Bech asked where she was, Goldy said tersely, 'Working. She sends her love and regrets.' Bech called her at midnight, at one in the morning, at two, at five when the birds began singing, at seven when the earliest church bells rang, at nine and at ten, while packing to catch his plane. Not even Isabella answered. She must be off on a country week-end. Or visiting the boy at school. Or vanished like a good paragraph in a book too bulky to reread.

Goldschmidt drove him to the airport in his maroon Bentley, and with an urgent prideful air pressed a number of Sunday newspapers upon him. 'The *Observer* gave us more space,' he said, 'but *The Times* seemed to like it more. All in all, a very fine reception for a, let's be frank, a rather trumped-up mishmash of a book. Now you must do us a blockbuster.' He said this, but his eyes were darting over Bech's shoulder towards the stream of fresh arrivals.

'I have just the title,' Bech told him. He saw he must put

Goldy into it, as a Jewish uncle. A leatherworker, his right palm hard as a turtle shell from handling an awl. That heavy pampered Florentine head bent full of greedy dreams beneath a naked light bulb, as pocket-books, belts, and sandals tumbled from the slaughter of screaming calves. The baroque beauty of the scraps piled neglected at his feet. A fire escape out the window. Some of the panes were transparent wire-glass and others, unaccountably, were painted opaque.

Goldschmidt added a folded tabloid to Bech's supply of aeroplane reading.

PEER, BRIDE NABBED
IN DORSET DOPE RAID

the headline said. Goldschmidt said, 'Page seventeen might amuse you. As you know, this is the paper Merissa's father bought last year. Millions read it.'

'No, I didn't know. She told me nothing about her father.'

'He's a dear old rascal. Almost the last of the true Tories.'

'I could have sworn she was a Lib-Lab.'

'Merissa is a very clever lamb,' Goldschmidt stated, and pinched his lips shut. In our long Diaspora we have learned not to tattle on our hosts. Goldy's right hand, shaken farewell, was unreally soft.

Bech saved page seventeen for the last. *The Times* review was headlined 'More Ethnic Fiction from the New World' and lumped *The Best of Bech* with a novel about Canadian Indians by Leonard Cohen and a collection of protest essays and scatalogical poems by LeRoi Jones. The long *Observer* piece was titled 'Bech's Best Not Good Enough' and was signed L. Clark Tuttle. Bech skimmed, as a fakir walks on hot coals, pausing nowhere long enough to burn the moisture from the soles of his feet. Almost none of the quotes he had poured into the boy's notebook and tape recorder were used. Instead, an aggrieved survey of Bech's *œuvre* unfolded, smudged by feeble rebuttals.

... Queried concerning the flowery, not to say fruity, style of *The Chosen*, Bech shrugged off the entire problem of style, claiming (facetiously?) that he never thinks about it. ... Of the book's profound failure, the crippling irreconcilability of its grandiose intentions and the triviality of its characters' moral concerns, Bech appears blissfully unaware, taking refuge in the charming, if rather automatically gnomic, disclaimer that 'as you grow older, life becomes complicated'. . . . This interviewer was struck, indeed, by the defensive nature of Bech's breezy garrulousness; his charm operates as a screen against others – their menacing opinions, the raw *stuff* of their life – just as, perhaps, drink operates within him as a screen against his own deepest self-suspicions . . . counter-revolutionary nostalgia . . . possibly ironical faith in 'entrepreneurism' . . . nevertheless, undoubted verbal gifts . . . traumatized by the economic collapse of the 1930s . . . a minor master for the space of scattered pages . . . not to be classed, Bech's faithful *New York Review* claque to the contrary, with the early Bellow or the late Mailer . . . reminded, in the end, after the butterfly similes and overextended, substanceless themes of this self-anointed 'Best', of (and the comparison may serve English readers as an index of present relevance) Ronald Firbank!

Bech let the paper go limp. The aeroplane had taxied out and he braced himself for the perilous plunge into flight. Only when aloft, with Hampton Court securely beneath him, a delicate sepia diagram of itself, and London's great stone mass dissolved into a cloud behind him, did Bech turn to page seventeen. A column there was headed MERISSA'S WEEK. The line drawing of the girl reminded Bech erotically of the spaces in her face – the catlike span between her eyes, the painted circles of her cheeks, the sudden moist gap of her mouth, which in the caricature existed as a wry tilde, a ~

Merissa had a tamey week * * * The daffodils were just like olde tymes, eh, W. W. ? * * * Beware: the blackjack dealer at L'Ambassadeur draws to sixteen and always makes it * * * A verger down at Canterbury C. is such an ignoramus I took him for a Drugs Squad agent * * * The new acoustics in Albert Hall are still worse than those on Salisbury Plain * * * John & Oko will cut their next record standing on their heads, their bottoms painted to resemble each other * * * Swinging L. was a shade more swingy this week when the darling American author Henry (*Travel Light*, *Brother Pig* and don't look blank they're in Penguins) Bech dropped in at Revolution and other In spots. The heart of many a jaded bird beat brighter to see Bech's rabbinical curls bouncing in time to 'Poke Salad Annie' and other Now hits. Merissa says: Hurry Back, H. B., transatlantic men are the most existential ★ ★ ★ He was visiting Londinium to help push la crème of his crème, *Bech's Best*, a J. J. Goldschmidt release, with a dull, dull jacket – the author's pic is missing. Confidentially, his heart belongs to dirty old New York ★ ★ ★

Bech closed his eyes, feeling his love for her expand as the distance between them increased. Entrepreneurism rides again. *Rabbinical curls:* somehow he had sold her that. *Automatically gnomic:* he had sold that too. *As a screen against others.* Firbank dead at forty. Still gaining altitude, he realized he was not dead; his fate was not so substantial. He had become a character by Henry Bech.

Bech Enters Heaven

When Henry Bech was an impressionable pre-adolescent of thirteen, more bored than he would admit with the question of whether or not the 1936 Yankees could wrest the pennant back from Detroit, his mother one May afternoon took him out of school, after consultation with the principal; she was a hardened consulter with the principal. She had consulted when Henry entered the first grade, when he came back from the second with a bloody nose, when he skipped the third, when he was given a 65 in Penmanship in the fifth, and when he skipped the sixth. The school was P.S. 87, at Seventy-seventh and Amsterdam – a bleak brick building whose interior complexity of smells and excitement, especially during a snowstorm or around Hallowe'en, was transcendent. None but very young hearts could have withstood the daily strain of so much intrigue, humour, desire, personality, mental effort, emotional current, of so many achingly important nuances of prestige and impersonation. Bech, rather short for his age, yet with a big nose and big feet that promised future growth, was recognized from the first by his classmates as an only son, a mother's son more than a father's, pampered and bright though not a prodigy (his voice had no pitch, his mathematical aptitude was no Einstein's); naturally he was teased. Not all the teasing took the form of bloody noses; sometimes the girl in the adjacent desk-seat tickled the hair on his forearms with her pencil, or his name was flaunted through the wire fence that separated the sexes at recess. The brownstone neighbourhoods that supplied students to the school were in those years still middle-class, if by middle-class is understood not a level of poverty (unlike today's poor, they had no cars, no credit and delivery arrangements with the liquor store) but of self-esteem. Immersed in the Great Depression, they had kept their families together, kept their feet from touching bottom, and kept their faith in the future – their children's future more than their own. These children brought a giddy relief into the sanctum of the school building, relief that the world, or at least this brick cube carved from it, had survived another day. How fragile the world felt to them! – as fragile as it seems sturdy to today's children, who wish to destroy it. Predominately Jewish, Bech's grammar school classes had a bold bright dash of German Gentiles, whose fathers also kept a small shop or plied a manual craft, and some Eastern Europeans, whose fey manners and lisped English made them the centres of romantic frenzy and wild joking attacks. At this time Negroes, like Chinese, were exotic oddities, created, like zebras, in jest. All studied, by the light of yellowish overhead globes and of the 48-star flag nailed above the blackboard, penmanship, the spice routes, the imports and exports of the three Guianas, the three cases of percentage, and other matters of rote given significance by the existence of breadlines and penthouses, just as the various drudgeries of their fathers were given dignity, even holiness, by their direct connection with food and survival. Although he would have been slow to admit this also, little Bech loved the school; he cherished his citizenship in its ragged population, was enraptured by the freckled chin and cerulean eyes of Eva Hassel across the aisle, and detested his mother's frequent interference in his American education. Whenever she appeared outside the office of the principal (Mr Linnehan, a sore-lidded spoiled priest with an easily mimicked blink and stammer), he was teased in the cloakroom or down on the asphalt at recess; whenever she had him skipped a grade, he became all the more the baby of the class. By the age of thirteen, he was going to school with girls that were women. That day in May, he showed his anger with his mother by not talking to her as they walked from the scarred school steps, down Seventy-eighth, past a mock-Tudor apartment house like some evilly enlarged and begrimed fairy-tale chalet, to Broadway and Seventy-ninth and the IRT kiosk with its compounded aroma of hot brakes, warm bagels, and vomit.

Extraordinarily, they took a train *north*. The whole dift of their lives was *south* – south to Times Square and to the Public Library, south to Gimbels, south to Brooklyn where his father's two brothers lived. North, there was nothing but Grant's Tomb, and Harlem, and Yankee Stadium, and Riverdale where a rich cousin, a theatre manager, inhabited an apartment full of glass furniture and an array of leering and scribbled photographs. North of that yawned the foreign vastness, first named New York State but melting westward into other names, other states, where the *goyim* farmed their farms and drove their roadsters and swung on their porch swings and engaged in the countless struggles of moral heroism depicted continuously in the Hollywood movies at the Broadway RKO. Upon the huge body of the United States, swept by dust storms and storms of Christian conscience, young Henry knew that his island of Manhattan existed like a wart; relatively, his little family world was an immigrant enclave, the religion his family practised was a tolerated affront, and the language of this religion's celebration was a backwards-running archaism. He and his kin and their kindred were huddled in shawls within an overheated back room while outdoors a huge and beautiful wilderness rattled their sashes with wind and painted the panes with frost; and all the furniture they had brought with them from Europe, the foot-stools and phylacteries, the copies of Tolstoy and Heine, the ambitiousness and defensiveness and love, belonged to this stuffy back room.

Now his mother was pointing him north, into the cold. Their reflections shuddered in the black glass as the express train slammed through local stops, wan islands of light where fat coloured women waited with string shopping bags. Bech was always surprised that these frozen vistas did not shatter as they pierced them; perhaps it was the multi-levelled sliding, the hurtling metal precariously switched aside from collision, more than the odours and subterranean claustrophobia, that made the boy sick on subways. He figured that he was good for eight stops before nausea began. It had just begun when she touched his arm. High, high on the West Side they emerged, into a region where cliffs and windy hilltops seemed insecurely suppressed by the asphalt grid. A boisterous shout of spring rolled upwards from

the river, and unexpected bridges of green metal arched sera-
phically overhead. Together they walked, the boy and his
mother, he in a wool knicker suit that scratched and sang between his legs, she in a tremulous hat of shining black straw, up a
broad pavement bordered with cobblestones and trees whose bark
was scabbed brown and white like a giraffe's neck. This was the
last year when she was taller than he; his sideways glance reaped
a child's cowing impression of, beneath the unsteady flesh of her
jaw, the rose splotches at the side of her neck that signalled
excitement or anger. He had better talk. 'Where are we going?'

'So,' she said, 'the cat found his tongue.'

'You know I don't like your coming into the school.'

'Mister Touch-Me-Not,' she said, 'so ashamed of his mother
he wants all his blue-eyed *shikses* to think he came out from
under a rock, I suppose. Or better yet lives in a tree like Sieg-
fried.'

Somewhere in the past she had wormed out of him his admiration of the German girls at school. He blushed. 'Thanks to you,'
he told her, 'they're all two years older than me.'

'Not in their empty golden heads, they're not so old. Maybe in
their pants, but that'll come to you soon enough. Don't hurry the
years, soon enough they'll hurry you.'

Homily, flattery, and humiliation: these were what his mother
applied to him, day after day, like a sculptor's pats. It deepened
his blush to hear her mention Eva Hassel's pants. Were they what
would come to him soon enough? This was her style, to mock his
reality and stretch his expectations. 'Mother, don't be fantastic.'

'Ai, nothing fantastic. There's nothing one of those golden
girls would like better than fasten herself to some smart little
Jewish boy. Better that than some sausage-grinding Fritz who'll
go to beer and beating her before he's twenty-five. You keep your
nose in your books.'

'That's where it was. Where are you taking me?'

'To see something more important than where to put your
putz.'

'Mother, don't be vulgar.'

'Vulgar is what I call a boy who wants to put his mother under a rock. His mother and his people and his brain, all under a rock.'

'Now I understand. You're taking me to look at Plymouth Rock.'

'Something like it. If you have to grow up American, at least let's not look only at the underside. Arnie' – the Riverdale cousin – 'got me two tickets from Josh Glazer, to I don't know quite what it is. We shall see.'

The hill beneath their feet flattened; they arrived at a massive building of somehow unsullied granite, with a paradoxical look of having been here forever yet having been rarely used. Around its top ran a ribbon of carved names: PLATO · NEWTON · AESCHYLUS · LEONARDO · AQUINAS · SHAKESPEARE · VOLTAIRE · COPERNICUS · ARISTOTLE · HOBBES · VICO · PUSHKIN · LINNAEUS · RACINE and infinitely on, around cornices and down the receding length of the building's two tall wings. Courtyard followed courtyard, each at a slightly higher level than the last. Conical evergreens stood silent guard; an unseen fountain played. For entrance, there was a bewildering choice of bronze doors. Bech's mother pushed one and encountered a green-uniformed guard; she told him, 'My name is Hannah Bech and this is my son Henry. These are our tickets, it says right here this is the day, they were obtained for us by a close associate of Josh Glazer's, the playwright. Nobody forewarned me it would be such a climb from the subway, that's why I'm out of breath like this.' The guard, and then another guard, for they several times got lost, directed them (his mother receiving and repeating a full set of directions each time) up a ramifying series of marble stairways into the balcony of an auditorium whose ceiling, the child's impression was, was decorated with plaster toys – scrolls, masks, seashells, tops, and stars.

A ceremony was already in progress. Their discussions with the guards had consumed time. The bright stage far below them supported a magical tableau. On a curved dais composed of six or seven rows a hundred persons, mostly men, were seated. Though some of the men could be seen to move – one turned his

head, another scratched his knee – their appearance in sum had
an iron unity; they looked engraved. Each face, even at the distance of the balcony, displayed the stamp of extra precision that
devout attention and frequent photography etch upon a visage;
each had suffered the crystallization of fame. Young Henry saw
that there were other types of Heaven, less agitated and more
elevated than the school, more compact and less tragic than
Yankee Stadium, where the scattered players, fragile in white,
seemed about to be devoured by the dragon-shaped crowd. He
knew, even before his mother, with the aid of a diagram provided
on her programme, began to name names, that under his eyes was
assembled the flower of the arts in America, its rabbis and chieftains, souls who while still breathing enjoyed their immortality.

The surface of their collective glory undulated as one or
another would stand, shuffle outwards from his row, seize the
glowing lectern, and speak. Some rose to award prizes; others
rose to accept them. They applauded one another with a polite
rustle eagerly echoed and thunderously amplified by the anonymous, perishable crowd on the other side of the veil, a docile
cloudy multitude stretching backwards from front rows of cor-
saged loved ones into the dim regions of the balcony where mere
spectators sat, where little Bech stared dazzled while his mother
busily bent above the identifying diagram. She located, and
pointed out to him, with that ardour for navigational detail that
had delayed their arrival here, Emil Nordquist, the Bard of the
Prairie, the beetle-browed celebrant in irresistible *vers libre* of
shocked corn and Swedish dairymaids; John Kingsgrant Forbes,
New England's dapper novelist of manners; Hannah Ann
Collins, the wispy, mystical poet of impacted passion from Alabama, the most piquant voice in American verse since the passing
of the Amherst recluse; the massive Jason Honeygale, Ten-
nessee's fabled word-torrent; hawk-eyed Torquemada Langguth,
lover and singer of California's sheer cliffs and sere unpopulated
places; and Manhattan's own Josh Glazer, Broadway wit, comedy-
wright, lyricist, and Romeo. And there were squat bald sculp-
tors with great curved thumbs; red-bearded painters like

bespattered prophets; petite, gleaming philosophers who piped Greek catchwords into the microphone; stooped and drawling historians from the border states; avowed Communists with faces as dry as paper and black ribbons dangling from their *pinces-nez*; atonal composers delicately exchanging awards and reminiscences of Paris, the phrases in French nasally cutting across their speech like accented trombones; sibylline old women with bronze faces – all of them unified, in the eyes of the boy Bech, by not only the clothy dark mass of their clothes and the brilliance of the stage but by their transcendence of time: they had attained the haven of lasting accomplishment and exempted themselves from the nagging nuisance of growth and its twin (which he precociously felt in himself even then, especially in his teeth), decay. He childishly assumed that, though unveiled every May, they sat like this eternally, in the same iron arrangement, beneath this domed ceiling of scrolls and stars.

At last the final congratulation was offered, and the final modest acceptance enunciated. Bech and his mother turned to re-navigate the maze of staircases. They were both shy of speaking, but she sensed, in the abstracted way he clung to her side, neither welcoming nor cringing from her touch when she reached to reassure him in the crowd, that his attention had been successfully turned. His ears were red, showing that an inner flame had been lit. She had set him on a track, a track that must be – Mrs Bech ignored a sudden qualm, like a rude jostling from behind – the right one.

Bech never dared hope to join that pantheon. Those faces of the thirties, like the books he began to read, putting aside baseball statistics forever, formed a world impossibly high and apart, an immutable text graven on the stone brow – his confused impression was – of Manhattan. In middle age, it would startle him to realize that Louis Bromfield, say, was no longer considered a sage, that van Vechten, Cabell, and John Erskine had become as obscure as the famous gangsters of the same period, and that an entire generation had grown to wisdom without once chuckling over a verse by Arthur Guiterman or Franklin P. Adams. When

Bech received, in an envelope not so unlike those containing solicitations to join the Erotica Book Club or the Associated Friends of Apache Education, notice of his election to a society whose title suggested that of a merged church, with an invitation to its May ceremonial, he did not connect the honour with his truant afternoon of over three decades ago. He accepted, because in his fallow middle years he hesitated to decline any invitation, whether it was to travel to Communist Europe or to smoke marijuana. His working day was brief, his living day was long, and there always lurked the hope that around the corner of some impromptu acquiescence he would encounter, in a flurry of apologies and excitedly mis-aimed kisses, his long-lost mistress, Inspiration. He took a taxi north on the appointed day. By chance he was let off at a side entrance in no way reminiscent of the august frontal approach he had once ventured within the shadow of his mother. Inside the bronze door, Bech was greeted by a mini-skirted secretary who, licking her lips and perhaps unintentionally bringing her pelvis to within an inch of his, pinned his name in plastic to his lapel and, as a tantalizing after-thought, the tip of her tongue exposed in playful concentration, adjusted the knot of his necktie. Other such considerate houris were supervising arrivals, separating antique *belle-lettrists* from their overcoats with philatelic care, steering querulously nodding poetesses towards the elevator, administering the distribution of gaudy heaps of name tags, admission cards, and coded numerals.

His girl wore a button that said GOD FREAKS OUT.

Bech asked her, 'Am I supposed to do anything?'

She said, 'When your name is announced, stand.'

'Do I take the elevator?'

She patted his shoulders and tugged one of his earlobes. 'I think you're a young enough body,' she judged, 'to use the stairs.'

He obediently ascended a thronged marble stairway and found himself amid a cloud of murmuring presences; a few of the faces were familiar – Tory Ingersoll, a tireless old fag, his prim features rigid in their carapace of orangish foundation, who had in recent years plugged himself into hipsterism and become a

copious puffist and anthologist for the 'new' poetry, whether
concrete, non-associative, neo-gita, or plain protest; Irving
Stern, a swarthy, ruminative critic of Bech's age and background, who for all his strenuous protests of McLuhanite openness had never stopped squinting through the dour goggles of
Leninist aesthetics, and whose own prose style tasted like aspirin
tablets being chewed; Mildred Belloussovsky-Dommergues, her
name as polyglot as her marriages, her weight-lifter's shoulders
and generous slash of a wise whore's mouth perversely dwindled
in print to a trickle of elliptic dimeters; Char Ecktin, the revolutionary young dramatist whose foolish smile and high-pitched
chortle consorted oddly with the facile bitterness of his
dénouements – but many more were half-familiar, faces dimly
known, like those of bit actors in B movies, or like those faces
which emerge from obscurity to cap a surprisingly enthusiastic
obituary, or those names which figure small on title pages, as
translator, co-editor, or 'as told to', faces whose air of recogni-
zability might have been a matter of ghostly family resemblance,
or of a cocktail party ten years ago, or a P.E.N. meeting, or of a
moment in a bookstore, an inside flap hastily examined and then
resealed into the tight bright row of the unpurchased. In this
throng Bech heard his name softly called, and felt his sleeve
lightly plucked. But he did not lift his eyes for fear of shattering
the spell, of disturbing the penumbral decorum and rustle
around him. They came to the end of their labyrinthine climb,
and were ushered down a dubiously narrow corridor. Bech hesitated, as even the dullest steer hesitates in the slaughterer's chute,
but the pressure behind moved him on, outwards, into a spotlit
tangle of groping men and scraping chairs. He was on a stage.
Chairs were arranged in curved tiers. Mildred Belloussovsky-
Dommergues waved an alabaster, muscular arm: 'Yoo-hoo,
Henry, over here. Come be a B with me.' She even spoke now – so
thoroughly does art corrupt the artist – in dimeters. Willingly he
made his way upwards towards her. Always, in his life, no matter
how underfurnished in other respects, there had been a woman to
shelter beside. The chair beside her bore his name. On the seat
of the chair was a folded programme. On the back of the pro-

gramme was a diagram. The diagram fitted a memory, and looking outward, into the populated darkness that reached backwards into a balcony, beneath a ceiling dimly decorated with toylike protrusions of plaster, Bech suspected, at last, where he was. With the instincts of a literary man he turned to printed matter for confirmation; he bent over the diagram and, yes, found his name, his number, his chair. He was here. He had joined that luminous, immutable tableau. He had crossed to the other side.

Now that forgotten expedition with his mother returned to him, and their climb through those ramifications of marble, a climb that mirrored, but profanely, the one he had just taken within sacred precincts; and he deduced that this building was vast twice over, an arch-like interior meeting in this domed auditorium where the mortal and the immortal could behold one another, through a veil that blurred and darkened the one and gave to the other a supernatural visibility, the glow and precision of Platonic forms. He studied his left hand – his partner in numerous humble crimes, his delegate in many furtive investigations – and saw it partaking, behind the flame-blue radiance of his cuff, joint by joint, to the quicks of his fingernails, in the fine articulation found less in reality than in the Promethean anatomical studies of Leonardo and Raphael.

Bech looked around; the stage was filling. He seemed to see, down front, where the stage light was most intense, the oft-photographed (by Steichen, by Karsh, by Cartier-Bresson) profile and vivid cornsilk hair of – it couldn't be –Emil Nordquist. The Bard of the Prairie still lived! He must be a hundred. No, well, if in the mid-thirties he was in his mid-forties, he would be only eighty now. While Bech, that pre-adolescent, was approaching fifty: time had treated him far more cruelly.

And now, through the other wing of the stage, from the elevator side, moving with the agonized shuffle-step of a semi-paralytic but still sartorially formidable in double-breasted chalkstripes and a high starched collar, entered John Kingsgrant Forbes, whose last perceptive and urbane examination of Beacon Hill mores had appeared in World War II, during the paper shortage. Had Bech merely imagined his obituary?

'Arriveth our queen,' Mildred Belloussovsky-Dommergues sardonically murmured on his left, with that ambiguous trace of a foreign accent, the silted residue of her several husbands. And to Bech's astonishment in came, supported on the courtly arm of Jason Honeygale, whose epic bulk had shrivelled to folds of veined hide draped over stegosaurian bones, the tiny tottering figure of Hannah Ann Collins, wearing the startled facial expression of the blind. She was led down front, where the gaunt figure of Torquemada Langguth, his spine bent nearly double, his falconine crest now white as an egret's, rose to greet her and feebly to adjust her chair.

Bech murmured leftwards, 'I thought they were all dead.'

Mildred airily answered, 'We find it easier, not to die.'

A shadow plumped brusquely down in the chair on Bech's right; it was – O, monstrous! – Josh Glazer. His proximity seemed to be a patron's, for he told Bech windily, 'Jesus Christ, Bech, I've been plugging you for years up here, but the bastards always said, "Let's wait until he writes another book, that last one was such a flop." Finally I say to them, "Look. The son of a bitch, he's *never* going to write another book," so they say, "O.K., let's let him the hell in." Welcome aboard, Bech. Christ I've been a raving fan of yours since the Year One. When're you gonna try a comedy, Broadway's dead on its feet.' He was deaf, his hair was dyed black, and his teeth were false too, for his blasts of breath carried with them a fetid smell of trapped alcohol and of a terrible organic something that suggested to Bech – touching a peculiar fastidiousness that was all that remained of his ancestors' orthodoxy – the stench of decayed shellfish. Bech looked away and saw everywhere on this stage dissolution and riot. The furrowed skulls of philosophers lolled in a Bacchic stupor. Wicked smirks flickered back and forth among faces enshrined in textbooks. Eustace Chubb, America's poetic conscience throughout the Cold War, had holes in his socks and mechanically chaffed a purple sore on his shin. Anatole Husač, the Father of Neo-Figurism, was sweating out a drug high, his hands twitching like suffocating fish. As the ceremony proceeded, not a classroom of trade-school dropouts could have been more impudently inattentive. Mildred Belloussovsky-Dommergues persistently tickled the hairs on Bech's wrist with the edge of her programme; Josh Glazer offered him a sip from a silver flask signed by the Gershwin brothers. The leonine head – that of a great lexicographer – directly in front of Bech drifted sideways and emitted illegible snores. The Medal for Modern Fiction was being awarded to Kingsgrant Forbes; the cello-shaped critic (best known for his scrupulous editorship of the six volumes of Hamlin Garland's correspondence) began his speech, 'In these sorry days of so-called Black Humour, of the fictional apotheosis of the underdeveloped,' and a Negro in the middle of Bech's row stood, spoke a single black expletive, and, with much scraping of chairs, made his way from the stage. A series of grants was bestowed. One of the recipients, a tiptoeing fellow in a mauve jump suit, hurled paper streamers towards the audience and bared his chest to reveal painted there a psychedelic pig labelled Milhaus; at this, several old men, an Arizona naturalist and a New Deal muralist, stamped off, and for a long time could be heard buzzing for the elevator. The sardonic hubbub waxed louder. Impatience set in. 'Goddammit,' Josh Glazer breathed to Bech, 'I'm paying a limousine by the hour downstairs. Jesus and I've got a helluva cute little fox waiting for me at the Plaza.'

At last the time came to introduce the new members. The citations were read by a far-sighted landscape painter who had trouble bringing his papers, the lectern light, and his reading glasses into mutual adjustment at such short focus. 'Henry Bech,' he read, pronouncing it 'Betch', and Bech confusedly stood. The spotlights dazzled him; he had the sensation of being microscopically examined, and of being strangely small. When he stood, he had expected to rear into a man's height, and instead rose no taller than a child.

'A native New Yorker,' the citation began, 'who has chosen to sing of the continental distances – '

Bech wondered why writers in official positions were always supposed to 'sing'; he couldn't remember the last time he had even hummed.

' – a son of Israel loyal to Melville's romanticism – '

He went around telling interviewers Melville was his favourite author, but he hadn't got a third of the way through *Pierre*.

' – a poet in prose whose polish precludes pre – pro – pardon me, these are new bifocals – '

Laughter from the audience. Who was out there in that audience?

' – let me try again: whose polish precludes prolifigacy – '

His mother was out there in that audience!

' – a magician of metaphor – '

She was there, right down front, basking in the reflected stage-light, an orchid corsage pinned to her bosom.

' – and a friend of the human heart.'

But she had died four years ago, in a nursing home in Riverdale. As the applause washed in, Bech saw that the old lady with the corsage was applauding only politely, she was not his mother but somebody else's, maybe of the boy with the pig on his stomach, though for a moment, a- trick of the light, something determined and expectant in the tilt of her head, something hopeful. ... The light in his eyes turned to warm water. His applause ebbed away. He sat down. Mildred nudged him. Josh Glazer shook his hand, too violently. Bech tried to clear his vision by contemplating the backs of the heads. They were blank: blank shabby backs of a cardboard tableau lent substance only by the credulous, by old women and children. His knees trembled, as if after an arduous climb. He had made it, he was here, in Heaven. Now what?

Appendix A

We are grateful for permission to reprint corroborating excerpts from the unpublished Russian journal of Henry Bech. The journal, physically, is a faded red Expenses diary, measuring 7⅝" by 4¼", stained by Moscow brandy and warped by Caucasian dew. The entries, of which the latter are kept in red ballpoint pen, run from 20 October 1964 to 6 December 1964. The earliest are the fullest.

I

20 Oct. Flight from NY at midnight, no sleep, Pan Am kept feeding me. Beating against the sun, soon dawn. Paris strange passing through by bus, tattered tired sepia sets of second-rate opera being wheeled through, false cheer of café awnings, waiting for chorus of lamplighters. Orly to Le Bourget. Moscow plane a new world. Men in dark coats waiting bunched. Solemn as gangsters. Overhead first understood Russian word, *Americanski*, pronounced with wink towards me by snaggle-toothed gent putting bulky black coat in overhead rack. Rack netted cord, inside ribs of plane show, no capitalist plastic. Stewardesses not our smoothly extruded tarts but hefty flesh; served us real potatoes, beef sausage, borsch. Aeroflot a feast afloat. Crowded happy stable smell, animal heat in cold stable, five miles up. Uncles' back rooms in Wmsburg. Babble around me, foreign languages strangely soothing, at home in Babel. Fell asleep on bosom of void, grateful to be alive, home. Woke in dark again. Earth's revolution full in my face. Moscow dim on ocean of blackness, delicate torn veil, shy of electricity, not New York, that rude splash. Prémonition: no one will meet. Author Disappears Behind Iron Curtain. Bech Best Remembered for Early

Work. A delegation with roses waiting for me on other side of glass pen, wait for hours, on verge of Russia, decompressing, time different here, steppes of time, long dully lit terminal, empty of ads. Limousine driven by voiceless back of head, sleigh driver in Tolstoy, long haul to Moscow, a wealth of darkness, grey birches, slim, young, far from gnarled American woods. In hotel spelled out этáж waiting for elevator, French hidden beneath the Cyrillic. Everywhere, secrets.

II

23 Oct. Met Sobaka, head of Writers' U. Building Tolstoy's old manse, dining-room baronial oak. Litterateurs live like aristocrats. Sobaka has lipless mouth, wild bark, must have strangled men with bare hands. Tells me long story of love of his poetry expressed by coalminers in the Urals. Skip translating: '. . . then, here in . . . the deepest part of the mine . . . by only the light of, uh, carbon lights in the miners' caps . . . for three hours I recited . . . from the works of my youth, lyrics of the fields and forests of Byelorussia. Never have I known such enthusiasm. Never have I possessed such inspiration, such, ah, powers of memory. At the end . . . they wept to see me depart . . . these simple miners . . . their coal-blackened faces streaked, ah, veined with the silver of tears.'

'Fantastic,' I say.

'*Fantastichni,*' Skip translates.

Sobaka makes Skip ask me if I like the image, their faces of coal veined with silver.

'It's good,' say I.

'*Korosho,*' says Skip.

'The earth weeps precious metal,' I say. 'The world's working people weep at the tyranny of capital.'

Skip guffaws but translates, and Sobaka reaches under table and seizes my thigh in murderous pinch of conspiracy.

12 Nov. Back in Moscow, lunch at W.U. Sobaka in fine form, must have chopped off somebody's index finger this morning. Says trip to Irkutsk hazardous, airport might get snowed in. Hee

hee hee. Suggests Kazakhstan instead, I say why not? – *nichyvo*. Eyeball to eyeball. He toasts Jack London, I toast Pushkin. He does Hemingway, I do Turgenev. I do Nabokov, he counters with John Reed. His mouth engulfs the glass and crunches. I think of what my dentist would say, my beautiful gold caps . . .

19 Nov. . . . I ask Kate where Sobaka is, she pretends not to hear. Skip tells me later he was friend of Khrush., hung on for while, now non-person. I miss him. My strange weakness for cops and assassins: their sense of craftsmanship?

III

1 Nov. Off to Caucasus with Skip, Mrs R., Kate. Fog, no planes for twenty-four hours. Airport crammed with hordes of sleeping. Soldiers, peasants, an epic patience. Sleeping on clothy heaps of each other, no noise of complaint. Many types of soldier uniform, long coats. Kate after twelve hours bullies way on to plane, pointing to me as Guest of the State, fierce performance. Engines screaming, officials screaming, she screaming. Get on plane at 2 a.m., amid bundles, chickens, gypsies, sit opposite pair of plump fortune tellers who groan and (very discreetly) throw up all the way to Tbilisi. Ears ache in descent; no pressurization. Birds in airport, in and out, remind of San Juan. Happy, sleepless. Sun on hills, flowers like oleanders. Hotel as in Florida Keys in Bogart movies, sour early morning service, a bracing sense of the sinister. Great fist-shaking Lenin statue in traffic circle. Flies buzz in room.

2 Nov. Slept till noon. Reynolds wakes with phone call. He and Mrs caught later plane. Cowboys and Indians, even my escorts have escorts. We go in two cars to Pantheon on hill, Georgian escort lantern-jawed professor of aesthetics. Cemetery full of funny alphabet, big stone he says with almost tear in eye called simply 'Mother'. Reynolds clues me sotto voce it's Stalin's mother. Had been statue of S. here so big it killed two workmen when they pulled it down. Supper with many Georgian poets, toasts in white wine, my own keep calling them 'Russians' which Kate corrects in translation to 'Georgians'. Author of epic in-

fatuated with Mrs R., strawberry blonde from Wisconsin, puts hands on thighs, kisses throat, Skip grins sheepishly, what he's here for, to improve relations. Cable car down the mountain, Tbilisi a-spangle under us, all drunk, singing done in pit of throat, many vibrations, hillbilly mournfulness, back to bed. Same flies buzz.

3 Nov. Car ride to Muxtyeta, oldest church in Christendom, professor of aesthetics ridicules God, chastity, everybody winces. Scaldingly clear blue sky, church a ruddy octagonal ruin with something ancient and pagan in the centre. Went to lunch with snowy-haired painter of breasts. These painters of a sleazy ethnic softness, of flesh like pastel landscapes, landscapes like pastel flesh. Where are the real artists, the cartoonists who fill *Krokodil* with fanged bankers and cadaverous Adenauers, the anonymous Chardins of industrial detail? Hidden from me, like missile sites and working ports. Of the Russian cake they give me only frosting. By train to Armenia. We all share a four-bunk sleeper. Ladies undress below me, see Kate's hand dislodge beige buttoned canvasy thing, see circlet of lace flick past Ellen Reynolds's pale round knee. Closeted with female flesh and Skip's supercilious snore expect to stay awake, but fall asleep in top bunk like child among nurses. Yerevan station at dawn. The women, puffy-eyed and mussed, claim night of total insomnia. Difficulty of women sleeping on trains, boats, where men are soothed. Distrust of machinery? Sexual stimulation, Claire saying she used to come just from sitting on vibrating subway seat, never the IRT, only the IND. Took at least five stops.

4 Nov. Svartz-Notz. Armenian cathedral. Old bones in gold bands. Our escort has withered arm, war record, dear smile, writing long novel about 1905 uprising. New city pink and mauve stone, old one Asiatic heaped rubble. Ruins of Alexander's palace, passed through on way to India. Gorgeous gorge.

5 Nov. Lake Sevan, grim grey sulphuric beach, lowered lake six feet to irrigate land. Land dry and rosy. Back at hotel, man

stopped in lobby, recognized me, here from Fresno visiting relatives, said he couldn't finish *The Chosen*, asked for autograph. Dinner with Armenian science fiction writers, Kate in her element, they want to know if I know Ray Bradbury, Marshall McLuhan, Vance Packard, Mitchell Wilson. I don't. Oh. I say I know Norman Podhoretz and they ask if he wrote *Naked and Dead*.

6 Nov. Long drive to 'working' monastery. Two monks live in it. Chapel carved from solid rock, bushes full of little strips of cloth, people make a wish. Kate borrows my handkerchief, tears off strip, ties to bush, makes a wish. Blushes when I express surprise. Ground littered with sacrificial bones. In courtyard band of farmers having ceremonial cookout honouring birth of son. Insist we join them, Reynoldses tickled pink, hard for American diplomats to get to clambake like this, real people. Priest scruffy sly fellow with gold fangs in beard. Armenians all wearing sneakers, look like Saroyan characters. Flies in wine, gobbets of warm lamb, blessings, toasts heavily directed towards our giggling round-kneed strawberry-blonde Ellen R. As we left we glimpsed real monk, walking along tumbledown parapet. Unexpectedly young. Pale, expressionless, very remote. A spy? Dry lands make best saints. Reynoldses both sick from effects of peoples' feast, confined to hotel while Kate and I, hardened sinners, iron stomachs, go to dinner with white-haired artist, painter of winsome faces, sloe eyes, humanoid fruit, etc.

7 Nov. Woke to band music; today Revolution Day. Should be in Red Square, but Kate talked me out of it. Smaller similar parade here, in square outside hotel. Overlooking while eating breakfast of blini and caviar parade of soldiers, red flags, equipment enlarging phallically up to rockets, then athletes in different colours like gumdrops, swarm at end of children, people, citizens, red dresses conspicuous. Kate kept clucking tongue and saying she hates war. Reynoldses still rocky, hardly eat. Ellen admires my digestive toughness, I indifferent to her praise. Am I falling in love with Kate? Feel insecure away from her side, listen to her

clear throat and toss in hotel room next to me. We walk in sun, I jostle to get between her and withered arm, jealous when they talk in Rooski, remember her blush when she tied half my torn hanky to that supernatural bush. What was her wish? Time to leave romantic Armenia. Back to Moscow by ten, ears ache fearfully in descent. Bitter cold, dusting of snow. Napoleon trembles.

IV

This sample letter, never sent, was found enclosed in the journal. 'Claire' appears to have been the predecessor, in Bech's affections, of Miss Norma Latchett. Reprinted by permission, all rights © Henry Bech.

Dear Claire:

I am back in Moscow, after three days in Leningrad, an Italian opera set begrimed by years in an arctic warehouse and populated by a million out-of-work baritone villains. Today, the American Ambassador gave me a dinner to which no Russians came, because of something they think we did in the Congo, and I spent the whole time discussing shoes with Mrs Ambassador, who hails originally, as she put it, from Charleston. She even took her shoe off so I could hold it – it was strange, warm, small. How are you? Can you feel my obsolete ardour? Can you taste the brandy? I live luxuriously, in the hotel where visiting plenipotentiaries from the Emperor of China are lodged, and Arabs in white robes leave oil trains down the hall. There may be an entire floor of English homosexual defectors, made over on the model of Cambridge digs. Lord, it's lonely, and bits of you – the silken depression beside each anklebone, the downy rhomboidal small of your back – pester me at night as I lie in exiled majesty, my laborious breathing being taped by three-score OGPU rookies. You were so beautiful. What happened? Was it all me, my fearful professional gloom, my Flaubertian syphilitic impotence? Or was it your shopgirl go-go brass, that held like a pornographic novel in a bureau (your left nipple was the drawer pull) a Quaker A-student from Darien? We turned each other inside out, it seemed to me, and made all those steak restaurants in the East Fifties light up like seraglios under bombardment. I will never be so young again. I am transported around here like a brittle curio; plug me into the nearest socket and I spout red, white, and blue. The Soviets like me because I am redolent of the oppressive thirties. I like them for the same reason. You, on the other hand, were all sixties, a bath of sequins and glowing pubic tendrils. Forgive my unconscionable distance, our preposterous prideful parting, the way our miraculously synchronized climaxes came to nothing, like novae. Oh, I send you such airmail lost love, Claire, from this very imaginary place, the letter may beat the plane home, and jump into your refrigerator, and nestle against the illuminated parsley as if we had never said unforgivable things.

H.

Folded into the letter, as a kind of postscript, a picture postcard. On the obverse, in bad colour, a picture of an iron statue, male. On the reverse, this message:

Dear Claire: What I meant to
say in my unsent letter was that
you were so good to me, good for
me, there was a goodness in me you
brought to birth. Virtue is so rare,
I thank you forever. The man on the
other side is Mayakovsky, who shot
himself and thereby won Stalin's un-
dying love. Henry

Gay with Sputnik stamps, it passed through the mails un-censored and was waiting for him when he at last returned from his travels and turned the key of his stifling, airless, unchanged apartment. It lay on the floor, strenuously cancelled. Claire had slipped it under the door. The lack of any accompanying note was eloquent. They never communicated again, though for a time Bech would open the telephone directory to the page where her number was encircled and hold it on his lap. – ED.

Appendix B

1. Books by Henry Bech (b. 1923, d. 19—)

Travel Light, novel. New York: The Vellum Press, 1955. London: J. J. Goldschmidt, 1957.

Brother Pig, novella. New York: The Vellum Press, 1957. London: J. J. Goldschmidt, 1958.

When the Saints, miscellany. [*Contents:* 'Uncles and Dybbuks', 'Subway Gum', 'A Vote For Social Unconsciousness', 'Soft-Boiled Sergeants', 'The Vanishing Wisecrack', 'Graffiti', 'Sunsets Over Jersey', 'The *Arabian Nights* At Your Own Pace', 'Orthodoxy and Orthodontics', 'Rag Bag' [collection of book reviews], 'Displeased in the Dark' [collection of cinema reviews], forty-three untitled paragraphs under the head of 'Tumblers Clicking'.] New York: The Vellum Press, 1958.

The Chosen, novel. New York: The Velum Press, 1963. London: J. J. Goldschmidt, 1963.

The Best of Bech, anthology. London: J. J. Goldschmidt, 1968. [Contains *Brother Pig* and selected essays from *When the Saints*.]

Think Big, novel. New York: The Vellum Press, 1979. London: J. J. Goldschmidt, 1980.

2. Uncollected Articles and Short Stories

'Stee-raight'n Yo' Shoulduhs, Boy!', *Liberty*, XXXIV.33 (21 August 1943), 62–3.

'Home for Hannukah', *Saturday Evening Post*, CCXVII.2 (8 January 1944), 45–6, 129–33.

'Kosher Konsiderations', *Yank*, IV.4 (26 January 1944), 6.

'Rough Crossing', *Collier's*, XLIV (22 February 1944), 23–5.

'London Under Buzzbombs', *New Leader*, XXVII.11 (11 March 1944), 9.

'The Cockney Girl', *Story*, XIV.3 (May–June 1944), 68–75.

'V-Mail from Brooklyn', *Saturday Evening Post*, CCXVII.25 (31 June 1944), 28–9, 133–7.

'Letter from Normandy', *New Leader*, XXVII.29 (15 July 1944), 6.

'Hey, Yank!', *Liberty*, XXXV.40 (17 September 1944), 48–9.

'Letter from the Bulge', *New Leader*, XXVIII.1 (3 January 1945), 6.

'Letter from the Reichstag', *New Leader*, XXVIII.23 (9 June 1945), 4.

'Fräulein, kommen Sie her, bitte', *The Partisan Review*, XII (October 1945), 413–31.

'Rubble' [poem], *Tomorrow*, IV.7 (December 1945), 45.

'Soap' [poem], *The Nation*, CLXII (22 June 1946), 751.

'Ivan in Berlin', *Commentary*, I.5 (August 1946), 68–77.

'Jig-a-de-Jig', *Liberty*, XXVII.47 (15 October 1946), 38–9.

'Novels from the Wreckage', *New York Times Book Review*, LII (19 January 1947), 6.

☞ *The bulk of Bech's reviews, articles, essays, and prose-poems 1947–58 were reprinted in* When the Saints (*see above*). *Only exceptions are listed below.*

'My Favorite Reading in 1953', *New York Times Book Review*, LXVII (25 December 1953), 2.

'Smokestacks' [poem], *Poetry*, LXXXIV.5 (August 1954), 249–50.

'*Larmes d'huile*' [poem], *Accent*, XV.4 (Autumn 1955), 101.

'Why I Will Vote for Adlai Stevenson Again' [part of paid political advertisement printed in various newspapers], October 1956.

'My Favorite Salad', *McCall's*, XXXIV.4 (April 1957), 88.

'Nihilistic? Me?' [interview with Lewis Nichols], *New York Times Book Review*, LXI (12 October 1957), 17–18, 43.

'Rain King for a Day', *New Republic*, CXL.3 (19 January 1959), 22–3.

'The Eisenhower Years: Instant Nostalgia', *Esquire*, LIV.8 (August 1960), 51–4.

'Lay Off, Norman', *The New Republic*, CXLI.22 (14 May 1960), 19–20.

'Bogie: The Tic That Told All', *Esquire*, LV.10 (October 1960), 44–5, 108–111.

'The Landscape of Orgasm', *House and Garden*, XXI.3 (December 1960), 136–41.

'Superscrew', *Big Table*, II.3 (Summer, 1961), 64–79.

'The Moth on the Pin', *Commentary*, XXXI (March 1961), 223–4.

'Iris and Muriel and Atropos', *New Republic*, CXLIV.20 (15 May 1961), 16–17.

'M-G-M and the USA', *Commentary*, XXXII (October 1961), 305–316.

'My Favoriteh Cristmas Carol', *Playboy*, VIII.12 (December 1961), 289.

'The Importance of Beginning with a B: Barth, Borges, and Others', *Commentary*, XXXIII (February 1962), 136–42.

'Down in Dallas' [poem], *New Republic*, CXLVI.49 (2 December 1963), 28.

'My Favorite Three Books of 1963', *New York Times Book Review*, LXVII (19 December 1963), 2.

'Daniel Fuchs: An Appreciation', *Commentary*, XLI.2 (February 1964), 39–45.

'Silence', *The Hudson Review*, XVII (Summer 1964), 258–75.

'Rough Notes from Tsardom', *Commentary*, XLI.2 (February 1965), 39–47.

'Frightened Under Kindly Skies' [poem], *Prairie Schooner*, XXXIX.2 (Summer 1965), 134.

'The Eternal Feminine As It Hits *Me*' [contribution to a symposium], *Rogue*, III.2 (February 1966), 69.

'What Ever Happened to Jason Honeygale ?' *Esquire*, LXI.9 (September 1966), 70–73, 194–8.

'Romanticism Under Truman: A Reminiscence', *New American Review*, III (April 1968), 59–81.

'My Three Least Favorite Books of 1968', *Book World*, VI (20 December 1968), 13.

3. Critical Articles Concerning (Selected List)

Prescott, Orville, 'More Dirt', *New York Times*, 12 October 1955.

Weeks, Edward, '*Travel Light* Heavy Reading', *Atlantic* Monthly, CCI.10 (October 1955), 131–2.

Kirkus Service, Virginia, 'Search for Meaning in Speed', XXIV (11 October 1955).

Time, 'V-v-vrooom!', LXXII.17 (12 October 1955), 98.

Macmanaway, Fr. Patrick X., 'Spiritual Emptiness Found Behind Handlebars', *Commonweal*, LXXII.19 (12 October 1955), 387–8.

Engels, Jonas, 'Consumer Society Burlesqued', *Progressive*, XXI.35 (20 October 1955), 22.

Kazin, Alfred, 'Triumphant Internal Combustion', *Commentary*, XXIX (December 1955), 90–96.

Time, 'Puzzling Porky', LXXIV.3 (19 January 1957), 75.

Hicks, Granville, 'Bech Impressive Again', *Saturday Review*, XLIII.5 (30 January 1957), 27–8.

Callaghan, Joseph, S.J., 'Theology of Despair Dictates Dark Allegory', *Critic*, XVII.7 (8 February 1957), 61–2.

West, Anthony, 'Oinck, Oinck', *New Yorker*, XXXIII.4 (14 March 1957), 171–3.

Steiner, George, 'Candide as Schlemiel', *Commentary*, XXV (March 1957), 265–70.

Maddocks, Melvin, 'An Unmitigated Masterpiece', *New York Herald Tribune Book Review*, 6 February 1957.

Hyman, Stanley Edgar, 'Bech Zeroes In', *New Leader*, XLII.9 (1 March 1957), 38.

Poore, Charles, 'Harmless Hodgepodge', *New York Times*, 19 August 1958.

Marty, Martin, 'Revelations Within the Secular', *Christian Century*, LXXVII (20 August 1958), 920.

Aldridge, John, 'Harvest of Thoughtful Years', Kansas City *Star*, 17 August 1958.

Time, 'Who Did the Choosing?' LXXXIII.26 (24 May 1963), 121.

Klein, Marcus, 'Bech's Mighty Botch', *Reporter*, XXX.13 (23 May 1963), 54.

Thompson, John, 'So Bad It's Good', *New York Review of Books*, II.14 (15 May 1963), 6.

Dilts, Susan, 'Sluggish Poesy, Murky Psychology', Baltimore *Sunday Sun*, 20 May 1963.

Miller, Jonathan, 'Oopsie!', *Show*, III.6 (June 1963), 49–52.

Macdonald, Dwight, 'More in Sorrow', *Partisan Review*, XXVIII (Summer 1963), 271–9.

Kazin, Alfred, 'Bech's Strange Case Reopened', *Evergreen Review*, VII.7 (July 1963), 19–24.

Podhoretz, Norman, 'Bech's Noble Novel: A Case Study in the Pathology of Criticism', *Commentary*, XXXIV (October 1963), 277–86.

Gilman, Richard, 'Bech, Gass, and Nabokov: The Territory Beyond Proust', *Tamarack Review*, XXXIII.1 (Winter 1963), 87–99.

Minnie, Moody, 'Myth and Ritual in Bech's Evocations of Lust and Nostalgia', *Wisconsin Studies in Contemporary Literature*, V.2 (Winter–Spring 1964), 1267–79.

Terral, Rufus, 'Bech's Indictment of God', *Spiritual Rebels in Post-Holocaustal Western Literature*, ed. Webster Schott (Las Vegas: University of Nevada Press, 1964).

L'Heureux, Sister Marguerite, 'The Sexual Innocence of Henry Bech', *America*, CX (11 May 1965), 670–74.

Brodin, Pierre, 'Henri Bech, le juif réservé', *Écrivains Americains d'aujourd'hui* (Paris: N.E.D., 1965).

Elbek, Leif, 'Damer og dæmoni', *Vindrosen*, Copenhagen (January–February 1965), 67–72.

Wagenback, Dolf, 'Bechkritic und Bechwissenschaft', *Neue Rundschau*, Frankfurt am Main, September–January 1965–6), 477–81.

Fiedler, Leslie, '*Travel Light*: Synopsis and Analysis', *E-Z Outlines*, No. 403 (Akron, O.: Hand-E Student Aids, 1966).

Tuttle, L. Clark, 'Bech's Best Not Good Enough', *Observer* (London), 22 April 1968.

Steinem, Gloria, 'What Ever Happened to Henry Bech?', *New York* II.46 (14 November 1969), 17–21.

Bech is Back
(1982)

BECQUE (Henry) . . . Après des débuts poétiques assez
obscurs . . . à travers des inexpériences et des brutalités
voulues, un talent original et vigoureux. Toutefois,
l'auteur ne reparut que beaucoup plus tard avec [œuvres
nombreuses], où la critique signala les mêmes défauts et
la même puissance. . . . M. Becque a été décoré de la
Légion d'Honneur en 1887.

LA GRANDE ENCYCLOPÉDIE

Contents

Three Illuminations in the Life of an American Author

Though Henry Bech, the author, in his middle years had all but ceased to write, his books continued, as if ironically, to live, to cast shuddering shadows towards the centre of his life, where that thing called his reputation cowered. To have once imagined and composed fiction, it seemed, laid him under an indelible curse of unreality. The phone rang in the middle of the night and it was a kid on a beer trip wanting to argue about the ambivalent attitude towards Jewishness expressed (his professor felt) in *Brother Pig*. 'Embrace your ethnicity, man,' Bech was advised. He hung up, tried to estimate the hour from the yellowness of the Manhattan night sky, and as the yellow turned to dawn's pearl grey succumbed to the petulant embrace of interrupted sleep. Next morning, he looked to himself, in the bathroom mirror, markedly reduced. His once leonine head, and the frizzing hair expressive of cerebral energy, and the jowls testimonial to companionable bourbon taken in midnight discourse with Philip Rahv were all being whittled by time, its relentless wizening. The phone rang and it was a distant dean, suddenly a buddy, inviting him to become a commencement speaker in Kansas. 'Let me be brutally frank,' the dean said in his square-shouldered voice. 'The seniors' committee voted you in unanimously, once Ken Kesey turned us down. Well, there was one girl who had to be talked around. But it turned out she had never read your stuff, just Kate Millett's condemnation of the rape bits in *Travel Light*. We gave her an old copy of *When the Saints*, and now she's your staunchest fan. Not to put any unfair pressure on, but you don't want to break that girl's heart. Or do you?'

'I do,' Bech solemnly affirmed. But since the dean denied him the passing grade of a laugh, the author had to babble on, digging himself deeper into the bottomless apology his unproductive life had become. He heard himself, unreally, consenting. The date was months away, and World War III might intervene. He hung up, reflecting upon the wonderful time warps of the literary life. You stay young and merely promising forever. Five years of silence, even ten, pass as a pause unnoticed by the sluggish, reptilian race of critics. An eighteen-year-old reads a book nearly as old as he is and in his innocent mind you are born afresh, your pen just lifted from the page. Bech could rattle around forever amid the persisting echoes, being 'himself', going to parties and openings in his Henry Bech mask. He had his friends, his fans, even his collectors. Indeed, his phone over the lengthening years acknowledged no more faithful agitator than that foremost collector of Bechiana, Marvin Federbusch, of Cedar Meadow, Pennsylvania.

The calls had begun to come through shortly after the publication of his first novel in 1955. Would Mr Bech be so kind as to consider signing a first edition if it were mailed with a stamped, self-addressed padded envelope? Of course, the young author agreed, flattered by the suggestion that there had been a second edition and somewhat amused by the other man's voice, which was peculiarly rich and slow, avuncular and patient, with a consonant-careful accent Bech associated with his own German–Jewish forebears. Germanic thoroughness characterized, too, the bibliographical rigour as, through the years, the invisible Federbusch kept up with Bech's once burgeoning production and even acquired such ephemera as Bech's high-school yearbook and those wartime copies of *Collier's* and *Liberty* in which his first short stories had appeared. As Bech's creativity – checked by the rude critical reception given his massive chef-d'oeuvre, *The Chosen*;* and then utterly stymied within the mazy ambitions

---

*Not to be confused with *The Chosen*, by Chaim Potok (New York, Simon & Schuster, 1967). Nor with *The Chosen*, by Edward J. Edwards (London, P. Davies, 1950); *The Chosen*, by Harold Uriel Ribalow (London, Abelard-Schuman, 1959); *Chosen Country*, by John Dos Passos (Boston, Houghton Mifflin, 1951); *A Chosen*

of his work in progress, tentatively titled *Think Big* – ceased to supply objects for collection, a little flurry of reprinting occurred, and unexpected foreign languages (Korean, Turkish) shyly nudged forward and engorged some one of those early works which Bech's celebrated impotence had slowly elevated to the status of minor classics. Federbusch kept a retinue of dealers busy tracking down these oddments, and the books all came in time to the author's draughty, underpopulated apartment at Ninety-ninth and Riverside for him to sign and send back. Bech learned a lot about himself this way. He learned that in Serbo-Croatian he was bound with Washington Irving as a Hudson Valley regionalist, and that in Paraguay *The Chosen* was the choice of a book club whose honorary chairman was General Alfredo Stroessner. He learned that the Japanese had managed to issue more books by him than he had written, and that the Hungarians had published on beige paper a bulky symposium upon Kerouac, Bech, and Isaac Asimov. On his Brazilian jackets Bech looked swarthy, on his Finnish pale and icy-eyed, and on his Australian a bit like a kangaroo. All these varied volumes arrived from Federbusch and returned to Federbusch; the collector's voice gradually deepened over the years to a granular, all-forgiving grandfatherliness. Though Bech as man and artist had turned skimpy and scattered, Federbusch was out there in the blue beyond the Hudson gathering up what pieces there were. What Federbusch didn't collect deserved oblivion – deserved to fall, the dross of Bech's days, into the West Side gutters and be whipped into somebody's eye by the spring winds.

Few, by Frank R. Stockton (New York, Charles Scribner's Sons, 1895); *The Chosen Four*, by John Theodore Tussaud (London, Jonathan Cape, 1928); *The Chosen Highway*, by Lady Blomfield (London, The Bahá'i Publishing Trust, 1940); *Chôsen-koseki-kenkyû-kwai* (Seoul, Keijo, 1934); *The Chosen One*, by Rhys Davies (London, Heinemann, 1967); *The Chosen One*, by Harry Simonhoff (New York, T. Yoseloff, 1964); *The Chosen People*, by Sidney Lauer Nyburg (Philadelphia; J. B. Lippincott, 1917); *The Chosen Place, the Timeless People*, by Paule Marshall (New York, Harcourt, Brace & World, 1969); *The Chosen Valley*, by Margaret Irene Snyder (New York, W. W. Norton, 1948); *Chosen Vessels*, by Parthene B. Chamberlain (New York, T. Y. Crowell & Co., 1882); *Chosen Words*, by Ivor Brown (London, Jonathan Cape, 1955); or *Choses d'autrefois*, by Ernest Gagnon (Quebec, Dussault & Proulx, 1905).

The author in these thin times supported himself by appearing at colleges. There, he was hauled from the creative-writing class to the faculty cocktail party to the John D. Benefactor Memorial Auditorium and thence, baffled applause still ringing in his ears, back to the Holiday Inn. Once, in central Pennsylvania, where the gloomy little hilltop schools are stocked with starch-fed students blinking like pupfish after their recent emergence from fundamentalism, Bech found himself with an idle afternoon, a rented car, and a map that said he was not far from Cedar Meadow. The fancy took him to visit Federbusch. He became, in his mind's eye, a god descending – whimsical as Zeus, radiant as Apollo. The region needed radiance. The heavy ghost of coal hung everywhere. Cedar Meadow must have been named in a fit of rural nostalgia, for the town was a close-built brick huddle centred on a black river and a few gaunt factories slapped up to supply Grant's murderous armies. The unexpected reality of this place, so elaborate and layered in its way, so El Grecoesque and sad between its timbered hills, beneath its grimy clouds, so remote in its raw totality from the flattering bookishness that had been up to now its sole purchase on Bech's mind, nearly led him to drive through it, up its mean steep streets and down, and on to tomorrow's Holiday Inn, near a Mennonite normal school.

But he passed a street whose name, Belleview, had been rendered resonant by over fifteen years of return book envelopes: Marvin Federbusch, 117 Belleview. The haggard street climbed towards its nominal view past retaining walls topped with stone spikes; on the slanted street corners there were grocery stores of a type Bech remembered from the Thirties, in the upper Bronx, the entrances cut on the diagonal, the windows full of faded cardboard inducements. He found number 117: corroded aluminium numerals marked a flight of cement steps divided down the middle by an iron railing. Bech parked, and climbed. He came to a narrow house of bricks painted red, a half-house actually, the building being divided down the middle like the steps, and the tones of red paint not quite matching. The view from the gingerbread porch was of similar houses, as close-packed as dominoes arrayed to topple, and of industrial smokestacks rising from the river valley, and of bluish hills gouged by abandoned quarrying. The doorbell distantly stridulated. A small shapeless woman in her sixties answered Bech's ring. 'My brother's having his rest,' she said.

Her black dress had buttons all down the front; her features seemed to be slightly rolling around in her face, like the little brass beads one maddeningly tries as a child to settle in their cardboard holes, in those dexterity-teasing toys that used to come with Cracker Jack.

'Could you tell him Henry Bech is here?'

Without another word, and without admitting him to the house, she turned away. Federbusch was so slow to arrive, Bech supposed that his name had not been conveyed correctly, or that the collector could not believe that the object of fifteen years of devotion had miraculously appeared in person.

But Federbusch, when he came at last, knew quite well who Bech was. 'You look older than on your chackets,' he said, offering a wan smile and a cold, hard handshake.

This was the voice, but the man looked nothing like it – sallow and sour, yet younger than he should have been, with not an ounce of friendly fat on him, in dark trousers, white shirt, and suspenders. He was red-eyed from his nap, and his hair, barely flecked by grey, stood straight up. The lower half of his face had been tugged into deep creases by the drawstrings of some old concluded sorrow. 'It's nice of you to come around,' he said, as if Bech had just stepped around the corner – as if Cedar Meadow were not the bleak far rim of the world but approximately its centre. 'Come on in, why don'tcha now?'

Within, the house held an airless slice of the past. The furniture looked nailed-down and smelled pickled. Nothing had been thrown away; invisible hands, presumably those of the sister, kept everything in order – the glossy knick-knacks and the doilies and the wedding photos of their dead parents and the landscapes a dead aunt had painted by number and the little crystal dishes of presumably petrified mints. Oppressive ranks of magazines – *Christian Age*, *Publishers Weekly*, the journal of the Snyder County Historical Society – lay immaculate on a lace-covered table, beneath an overdressed window whose sill was thick with plastic daffodils. In the corners of the room, exposed plumbing pipes had been papered in the same paper as the walls. The ceilings, though high, had been papered, too. Kafka was right, Bech saw: life is a matter of burrows. Federbusch beside him was giving off a strange withered scent – the delicate stink of affront. Bech guessed he had been too frankly looking around, and said, to cover himself, 'I don't see my books.'

Even this missed the right note. His host intoned, in the sonorous voice Bech was coming to hear as funereal, 'They're kept in a closet, so the sun won't fade the chackets.'

A room beyond this stagnant front parlour had a wall of closet doors. Federbusch opened one, hastily closed it, and opened another. Here indeed was a trove of Bechiana – old Bech in *démodé* Fifties jackets, reprinted Bech in jazzy Seventies paperbacks with the silver lettering of witchcraft novels, Bech in French and German, Danish and Portuguese, Bech anthologized, analysed, and deluxized, Bech laid to rest. The books were not erect in rows but stacked on their sides like lumber, like dubious ingots, in this lightless closet along with – oh, treachery! – similarly exhaustive, tightly packed, and beautifully unread collections of Roth, Mailer, Barth, Capote. ... The closet door was shut before Bech could catalogue every one of the bedfellows the promiscuous Federbusch had captivated.

'I don't have any children myself,' the man was saying mournfully, 'but for my brother's boys it'll make a wonderful inheritance some day.'

'I can hardly wait,' Bech said. But his thoughts were sad. His thoughts dwelt upon our insufficient tragedies, our dreadfully musty private lives. How wrong he had been to poke into this burrow, how right Federbusch was to smell hurt! The greedy author, not content with adoration in two dimensions, had offered himself in a fatal third, and maimed his recording angel. 'My dealer just sent some new Penguins,' Federbusch said, mumbling in shame, 'and it would save postage if ...' Bech signed the paperbacks and wound his way through ravaged hills to the

Mennonite normal school, where he mocked the students' naïve faith and humiliated himself with drunkenness at the reception afterwards at the Holiday Inn. But no atonement could erase his affront to Federbusch, who never troubled his telephone again.

In the days when Bech was still attempting to complete *Think Big*, there came to him a female character who might redeem the project, restore its lost momentum and focus. She was at first the meagrest wisp of a vision, a 'moon face' shining with a certain lightly perspiring brightness over the lost horizon of his plot. The pallor of this face was a Gentile pallor, bearing the kiss of Nordic fogs and frosts, which ill consorted with the urban, and perforce Jewish, hurly-burly he was trying to organize. Great novels begin with tiny hints – the sliver of madeleine melting in Proust's mouth, the shade of louse-grey that Flaubert had in mind for Mme Bovary – and Bech had begun his messy accumulation of pages with little more than a hum, a hum that kept dying away, a hum perhaps spiritual twin to the rumble of the IRT under Broadway as it was felt two blocks to the west, on the sixth floor, by a bored bachelor. The hum, the background radiation to the universe he was trying to create, was, if not the meaning of life, the tenor of meaninglessness in our late-twentieth-century, post-numinous, industrial-consumeristic civilization, North American branch, Middle Atlantic subdivision. Now this hum was pierced by an eerie piping from this vague 'moon face'.

Well, the woman would have to be attractive; women in fiction always are. From the roundness of her face, its innocent pressing frontality, would flow a certain 'bossiness', a slightly impervious crispness that would set her at odds with the more subtle, ironical, conflicted, slippery intelligentsia who had already established power positions in the corporate structure of his virtually bankrupt fantasy. Since this moony young (for the crispness, this lettucy taste of hers, bespoke either youth or intense refrigeration) woman stood outside the strong family and business ties already established, she would have to be a mistress. But whose? Bech thought of assigning her to Tad Greenbaum, the six-foot-four, copiously freckled, deceptively boyish dynamo who had parlayed a gag-writer's servitude into a daytime-television empire. But Tad already had a mistress – stormy, raven-haired, profoundly neurotic Thelma Stern. Also, by some delicate gleam of aversion, the moon face refused to adhere to Greenbaum. Bech offered her instead to Thelma's brother Dolf, the crooked lawyer, with his silken moustaches, his betraying stammer, and his great clean glass desk. Bech even put the two of them into bed together; he loved describing mussed sheets, and the sea-fern look of trees seen from the window of a sixth-floor apartment, and the way the chimney pots of the adjacent roofs resemble tin men in black pyjamas engaged in slow-motion burglary. But though the metaphors prospered, the relationship didn't take. No man was good enough for this woman, unless it were Bech himself. She must have a name. Moon face, Morna – no, he already had a Thelma, his new lady was cooler, aloof ... doom, Poe, Lenore. *And the only word there spoken was the whispered word, 'Lenore!'* Lenore would do. Her work? That kindly bossiness, that confident frontality – the best he could think of was to make her an assistant producer for his imaginary network. But that wasn't right: it didn't account for her supernatural serenity.

She became as real to him as the nightglow on his ceiling during insomnia. He wrote scenes of her dressing and undressing, in the space between the mussed bed-sheets and the window overlooking tree-tops and chimney pots; he conjured up a scene where Lenore primly lost her temper and told Tad Greenbaum he was a tyrant. Tad fired her, then sent Thelma around to persuade her not to write an exposé for *TV Tidbits*. Experimenting with that curious androgynous cool Lenore possessed, Bech put her into bed with Thelma, to see what happened. Plenty happened, perhaps more gratifyingly to the author than to either character; if he as male *voyeur* had not been present, they might have exchanged verbal parries and left each other's yielding flesh untouched. However, Thelma, Bech had previously arranged, had become pregnant by her ex-husband, Polonius Stern, and could not be allowed a Sapphic passion that would pull Lenore down into the plot. He cancelled the pregnancy but the moon face hung above the plot still detached, yet infusing its tangle with a glow, a calm, a hope that this misbegotten world of Bech's might gather momentum. She seemed, Lenore, to be drawing closer.

One night, reading at the New School, he became conscious of her in the corner of his eye. Over by the far wall, at the edge of the ocean of reading-attending faces – the terrible tide of the up-and-coming, in their thuggish denims and bristling beards, all their boyhood misdemeanours and girlhood grievances still to unpack into print, and the editors thirsty to drink their flesh blood, their contemporary slant – Bech noticed a round female face, luminous, raptly silent. He tried to focus on her, lost his place in the manuscript, and read the same sentence twice. It echoed in his ears, and the audience tittered; they were embarrassed for him, this old dead whale embalmed in the anthologies and still trying to spout. He kept his eyes on his pages, and when he lifted his gaze, at last, to relieved applause, Lenore had vanished, or else he had lost the place in the hall where she had been seated. *Quaff, oh quaff this kind nepenthe and forget this lost Lenore!*

A week later, at his reading at the YMHA, she had moved closer, into the third or fourth row. Her wide, white, lightly perspiring face pressed upward in its intensity of attention, refusing to laugh even when those all around her did. As Bech on the high stage unrolled, in his amplified voice, some old scroll of foolery, he outdid himself with comic intonations to make his milk-pale admirer smile; instead, she solemnly lowered her gaze now and then to her lap, and made a note. Afterwards, in the unscheduled moment of siege that follows a reading, she came backstage and waited her turn in the pushing crowd of autograph-seekers. When at last he dared turn to her, she had her notebook out. Was this truly Lenore? Though he had failed to imagine some details (the little gold hoop earrings, and the tidy yet full-bodied and somewhat sensually casual way in which she had bundled her hair at the back of her head), her physical presence flooded the translucent, changeable skin of his invention

169

with a numbing concreteness. He grabbed reflexively at her note-book, thinking she wanted him to sign it, but she held on firmly, and said to him, 'I thought you'd like to know. I noted three words you mispronounced. "Hectare" is accented on the first syllable and the "e" isn't sounded. In "flaccid" the first "c" is hard. And "sponge" is like "monkey" – the "o" has the quality of a short "u".'

'Who are you?' Bech asked her.

'A devotee.' She smiled, emphasizing the long double 'e'. Another devotee pulled Bech's elbow on his other side, and when he turned back, Lenore was gone. *Darkness there and nothing more.*

He revised what he had written. The scene with Thelma was sacred filth, dream matter, not to be touched; but the professional capacities of the moon face had come clearer – she was a school-teacher. A teacher of little children, children in the first-to-fourth-grade range, in some way unusual, whether unusually bright or with learning disabilities he couldn't at first decide. But as he wrote, following Lenore into her clothes and the elevator and along the steam-damp, slightly tipping streets of West Side Manhattan, the name above the entrance of the build-ing she entered became legible: she taught in a Steiner School. Her connection with the other characters of *Think Big* must be, therefore, through their children. Bech rummaged back through the manuscript to discover whether he had given Tad Greenbaum and his long-suffering wife, Ginger, boys or girls for children, and what ages. He should have made a chart. Faulkner and Sinclair Lewis used to. But Bech had always resisted those practical aids which might interfere with the essential literary process of daydreaming; Lenore belonged to a realm of subconscious cumulus. She would have wide hips: the revela-tion came to him as he slipped a week's worth of wastepaper into a plastic garbage bag. But did the woman who had come up to him, in fact, have wide hips? It had been so quick, so magical, he had been conscious only of her torso in the crowd. He needed to see her again, as research.

When she approached him once more, in the great hot white

tent annually erected for the spring ceremonial of the American Academy on those heights beyond Harlem, she was wearing a peasant skirt and bra-less purple bodice, as if to hasten in the summer. To be dressy she had added a pink straw hat; the uplifted gesture with which she kept the wide hat in place opened up a new dimension in the character of Lenore. She had been raised amid greenery, on, say, a Hardyesque farm in north-eastern Connecticut. Though her waist was small, her hips were ample. The sultriness of the tent, the spillage of liquor from flexible plastic cups, the heavy breathing of Bech's fellow immortals made a romantic broth in which her voice was scarcely audible; he had to stoop, to see under her hat and lip-read. Where was her fabled 'bossiness' now? She said, 'Mr Bech, I've been working up my nerve to ask, would you ever consider coming and talking to my students? They're so sweet and confused, I try to expose them to people with values, any values. I had a porno film director, a friend of a friend, in the other day, so it's nothing to get uptight about. Just be yourself.' Her eyes were dyed indigo by the shadow of the hat, and her lips, questing, had a curvaceous pucker he had never dreamed of.

Bech noticed, also, a dark-haired young woman standing near Lenore, wearing no makeup and a man's tweed jacket. A friend, or the friend of a friend? The young woman, seeing the conversation about to deepen, drifted away. Bech asked, 'How old are your students?'

'Well, they're in the third grade now, but it's a Steiner School –'

'I know.'

'– and I move up with them. You might be a little wasted on them now; maybe we should wait a few years, until they're in fifth.'

'And I've had time to work on my pronunciation.'

'I do apologize if that seemed rude. It's just a shock, to realize that a master of words doesn't hear them in his head the way you do.' As she said this, her own pronunciation seemed a bit slurred. An empty plastic glass sat in her hand like an egg collected at dusk.

Perhaps it was the late-afternoon gin, perhaps the exhilaration of having just received a medal (the Melville Medal, awarded every five years to that American author who has maintained the most meaningful silence), but this encounter enchanted Bech. The questing fair face perspiring in the violet shade of the pink hat, the happy clatter around him of writers not writing, the thrusting smell of May penetrating the tent walls, the little electric push of a fresh personality – all felt too good to be true. He felt, deliciously, overpowered, as reality always overpowers fiction.

He asked her, 'But will we still be in touch, when your sweet confused students are in the fifth grade?'

'Mr Bech, that's up to you.' In the shade of her hat, she lowered her eyes.

'To me?'

Her blue eyes lifted boldly. 'Who else?'

'How do you feel about dinner then, if we can find the flap to get out of this tent?'

'The two of us?'

'Who else?' Of *course*, he was thinking, with the voice of reason that dismally mutters accompaniment to every euphoria, *there is a rational explanation. God forbid there wouldn't be a rational explanation. I have conjured this creature, by eye-glance and inflection, from the blank crowds just as I conjured her, less persuasively, from blank paper.* 'What did you say your name was?'

'Ellen,' she said.

So he had got that slightly wrong. He had been slightly wrong in a hundred details, the months revealed. Their affair did not last until her students were in the fifth grade. It was his literary side, it turned out, his textbook presence, that she loved. Also, she really did – his instincts had been right in this – see the male sex as, sexually, second-rate. Still, she gave him enough of herself to eclipse, to crush, 'the rare and radiant maiden whom the angels name Lenore', and once again *Think Big* ground to a grateful halt.

*

An irresistible invitation came to Bech. A subsidiary of the Superoil Corporation called Superbooks had launched a series of signed classics; for an edition of *Brother Pig* bound in genuine pigskin Bech was invited to sign twenty-eight thousand five hundred tip-in sheets of high-rag-content paper, at the rate of one dollar fifty a sheet. He was to do this, furthermore, during a delightful two-week holiday on a Caribbean island, where Superoil owned a resort. He should take with him a person to pull the sheets as he signed them. This 'puller' could be a friend, or someone hired in the locality. All this was explained to Bech as to a fairly stupid child by a hollow-voiced man calling from corporation headquarters – a thousand-acre variant of Disneyland somewhere in Delaware.

As always in the face of good fortune, Bech tended to cringe. 'Do I have to have a puller?' he asked. 'I've never had an agent.'

'The answer to your question,' the man from Superbooks said, 'is one-hundred-per-cent affirmative. From our experience, without a puller efficiency tapers very observably. As I say, we can hire one on the spot and train her.'

Bech imagined her, a svelte little Carib who had been flown to emergency secretarial school, but doubted he could satisfy hereafter the first proud rush. So he asked Norma Latchett to be his puller.

Her reply was inevitable. 'Super,' she said.

In weary truth, Bech and Norma had passed beyond the end of their long romance into a limbo of heterosexual palship haunted by silently howling abandoned hopes. They would never marry, never be fruitful. The little island of San Poco was a fit stage for their end drama – the palm trees bedraggled and battered from careless storage in the prop room, the tin-and-tar-paper houses tacked together for a short run, the boards underfoot barely covered by a sandy thin soil resembling coffee grounds, the sea a piece of rippling silk, the sunshine as harsh, white, and constant as overhead spotlights. The island was littered with old inspirations – a shoal collecting the wrecks of hotels, night spots, cabañas, and eateries swamped by the brilliant lethargy. The beach resort where Bech and Norma and the twenty-eight thousand five hundred pieces of paper were housed had been built by pouring cement over inflated balloons that were then collapsed and dragged out the door; the resulting structures were windowless. All along the curve of one dark wall were banked brown cardboard boxes containing five hundred sheets each. Superoil's invisible minions had placed in the centre of the hemisphere a long Masonite table, bland as a torturer's rack, and cartons of felt-tip pens. Bech never used felt-tip pens, preferring the manly gouge and sudden dry death of ballpoints. Nevertheless, he sat right down in his winter suit and ripped through a box, to see how it went.

It went like a breeze. Arrows, to be trimmed away by the binder, pointed to the area he must inscribe. Norma, as if still auditioning for the role of helpmate, pulled the sheets with a sweet deftness from underneath his wrists. Then they undressed – since he had last seen her naked, her body had softened, touchingly, and his body, too, wore a tallowish slump that appeared unfamiliar – and went out to swim in the lukewarm, late-afternoon sea. From its gentle surface the lowering sun struck coins of corporate happiness; Bech blessed Superoil as he floated, hairy belly up. The title of his next novel, after *Think Big* was in the bag, came to him: *Easy Money*. Or had Daniel Fuchs used it during the Depression? When he and Norma left their vast bath, the soft coral sand took deep prints from Bech's bare feet, as from those of a giant.

Wake, eat, swim, sun, sign, eat, sun, sign, drink, eat, dance, sleep. Thus their days passed. Their skins darkened. Bech became as swarthy as his Brazilian jacket photos. The stack of boxes of signed sheets slowly grew on the other side of the cement dome. They had to maintain an average of two thousand signatures a day. As Norma's tolerance for sun increased, she begrudged the time indoors, and seemed to Bech to be accelerating her pulling, so that more than once the concluding 'h' got botched. 'You're slowing down,' she told him in self-defence, the third time this happened in one session.

'I'm just trying to give the poor bastards their buck-fifty's worth,' he said. 'Maybe you should pay attention to *me*, instead of trying to pull and read at the same time.' She had taken to reading a novel at their signing table – a novel by, as it happened, a young writer who had, in the words of one critic, 'made all previous American-Jewish writing look like so much tasteless matzo dough'.

'I don't need to pay attention,' she said. 'I can hear it now; there's a rhythm. Mm-diddle-um-*um*, boomity-boom. You lift your pen in the middle of "Henry" and then hurry the "Bech". You love your first name and hate your last – why is that?'

'The "B" is becoming harder and harder,' he admitted. 'Also, the "e" and the "c" are converging. Miss O'Dwyer at PS 87 tried to teach me the Palmer penmanship method once. She said you should write with your whole arm, not just your fingers.'

'You're too old to change now; just keep doing it your way.'

'I've decided she was right. These are ugly signatures. *Ugly*.'

'For God's sake, Henry, don't try to make them works of art; all Superbooks wants is for you to keep touching pen to paper.'

'Superbooks wants super signatures,' he said. 'At least they want signatures that show an author at peace with himself. Look at my big "H"s. They've turned into backward "N"s. And then the little "h" at the end keeps tailing down. That's a sign of discouragement. Napoleon, you know, after Waterloo, every treaty he signed, his signature dragged down right off the page. The parchment.'

'Well, you're not Napoleon, you're just an unemployed self-employed who's keeping me out of the sun.'

'You'll get skin cancer. Relax. Eleven hundred more and we'll go have a piña colada.'

'You're fussing over them, I can't stand it! You just *romped* through those early boxes.'

'I was younger then. I didn't understand my signature so well. For being so short, it has a lot of ups and downs. Suppose I was Robert Penn Warren. Suppose I was Solzhenitsyn.'

'Suppose you were H.D., I'd still be sitting here in this damn dark igloo. You know, it's getting to my shoulders. The pauses between are the worst – the tension.'

'Go out in the sun. Read your pimply genius. I'll be my own puller.'

'Now you're trying to hurt my feelings.'

'I'll be fine. I know my own rhythm.'

'The Henry Bech backward crawl. I'll see this through if it kills us both.'

He attempted a signature, hated the 'nry', and slashed a big 'X' across the sheet. 'Your vibes are destroying me,' he said.

'That was a dollar fifty,' Norma said, standing in protest.

'Yeah, and here's the sales tax,' Bech said, and X-ed out the preceding signature, whose jerky 'ch' linkage had disturbed him as he did it, though he had decided to let it pass. He crumpled the sheet into a ball and hit her with it squarely between the two pieces of her bathing suit.

After this, when they sat down on opposite sides of the long table, fear of this quarrel's being repeated clotted their rapport. Fear of impotence seized his hand. The small digital muscles, asked to perform the same task thousands upon thousands of times, were rebelling. Sabotage appeared on the assembly line. Extra squiggles produced 'Hennry,' and the 'B' of 'Bech' would come out horribly cramped, like a symptom of a mental disease. While the sun poured down, and the other resort guests could be heard tinkling and babbling at the thatched beach bar not far away, Bech would write 'Henry' and forget what word came next. The space between his first and last name widened as some uncappable pressure welled up between them. The whole signature kept drifting outside the arrows, though he shoved with his brain while Norma tugged the stacks of sheets into repeated readjustments. Their daily quota fell below two thousand, to seventeen hundred, then to three boxes, and then they stopped counting boxes.

'We *must* sign them all here,' Norma pleaded. 'They're too heavy to take away with us.' Their two weeks were drawing to a close, and the wall of unopened boxes seemed to grow, rustling, in the night. They sliced them open with a blade from Bech's razor; he cut his forefinger and had to pinch the pen through a Band-Aid. The pens themselves, so apparently identical at first, revealed large differences to his hypersensitive grasp, and as many as six had to be discarded before he found one that was not too light or heavy, whose flow and his were halfway congenial. Even so, one signature in five came out defective, while Norma groaned and tried to massage her own shoulders. 'I think it's writer's cramp,' she said.

'There's a paradox,' he said. 'You know, towards the end of his career Hogan would absolutely freeze over a one-foot putt.'

'Don't make conversation,' Norma begged. 'Just inscribe.'

The loudspeaking system strung through the palm trees interrupted its millionth rendition of 'Yellow Bird' to announce his name. Over the phone in the manager's office, the man from Superoil said, 'We figured you'd be a hundred-per-cent done by tomorrow, so we've arranged for a courier to jet in and ship the sheets to our bindery in Oregon.'

'We've run into some snags,' Bech told him. 'Also, the pullers are restive.'

The voice went a shade more hollow. 'What per cent would you say is still to be executed?'

'Hard to say. The boxes have grown big as freight cars. At first they were the size of matchboxes. Maybe there's ten left.'

A silence. 'Can you stonewall it?'

'I'm not sure that's the phrase. How about "hot-dog it"?'

'The jet's been commissioned; it can't be cancelled. Do the best you can, and bring the rest back in your luggage.'

'Luggage!' Norma scoffed, back at the igloo. 'I'd just as soon try to pack a coral reef. And I *refuse* to ruin my last full day here.'

Bech worked all afternoon by himself, while she sauntered on the beach and fell in with a pair of scuba divers. 'Jeff wanted me to go underwater with him, but I was scared our hoses would get tangled,' she reported. 'How many did you do?'

'Maybe a box. I kept getting dizzy.' It was true; his signature had become a cataclysmic terrain of crags and abysses. His fingers traced the seismograph of a constant earthquake. Deep in the strata of time, a hot magma heaved. Who was this Henry Bech? What had led him up, up from his seat in his row in Miss

O'Dwyer's class, to this impudent presumptive scrawl of fame? Her severe ghost mocked him every time an 'e' collapsed or a 'B' shrivelled at his touch.

Norma inspected his work. 'These are wild,' she said. 'There's only one thing to do: get some piña coladas and stay up all night. I'm game.'

'That makes one of us.'

'You bastard. I've ruined my life waiting for you to do *some*-thing and you're going to do *this*. Then that's it. This is the last thing I'll ever see you through.'

'As Joan of Arc often said to the Dauphin,' Bech said.

His dream-forgetting mechanism drew a merciful curtain over the events of that night. At one point, after the last trip to the bar had produced a bottle of rum and a six-pack of grape soda, his signature reached up from the page and tried to drag him down into it. Then he seemed to be pummelling Norma, but his fist sank in her slack belly as in muddy water. She plucked an arrow from an unsigned sheet and fended him off. The haggard dawn revealed one box still to be opened, and a tranquil sea dyed solid Day-Glo. They walked along the arc of beach holding inky hands. 'Bech, Bech', the little waves whispered, mis-pronouncing the 'ch'. He and Norma fell asleep diagonally on the bed, amid sliced cardboard. The commotion at their louvred door woke them to a surge of parched nausea. Two black men were loading the boxes on to a trolley. The bundles of opened and resealed wrapping paper looked altogether strange, indecent, and perishable out in the air, among the stark morning verities of sky and sand and sea. Bathers gathered curiously about the pyramid, this monstrous accumulation hatched from their cement egg. To Bech's exhaustion and hangover was added a sensation of shame, the same shame he felt in bookstores, or after vomiting. One of the black men asked him, 'This all there is, mon?'

'There's one more box,' Bech admitted. For the first time in two weeks, a cloud covered the sun.

'Big jet from de state of Delaware at de airport waiting for Sea Breeze Taxi deliber all dese boxes,' the other black man explained. Suddenly rain, in gleaming globular drops each big enough to fill a shot glass, began to fall. The onlookers in bathing suits scattered. The cardboard darkened. The ink would blur, the paper would wrinkle and return to pulp. The black men trundled away the mountain of Bech's signatures, promising to return for the last box.

In the dank igloo, Norma had placed the final sheaf of five hundred sheets, trim and pure, in the centre of the table. She seated herself on her side, ready to pull. Groggily Bech sat down, under the dome drumming with the downpour. The arrows on the top sheet pointed inward. Clever female fingers slipped under a corner, alert to ease it away. The two San Poco taximen returned, their shirts sopping, and stood along one wall, silent with awe of the cultural ritual they were about to witness. Bech lifted a pen. All was poised, and the expectant blankness of the paper seemed an utter bliss to the author, as he gazed deep into the negative perfection to which his career had been brought. He could not even write his own name.

Bech Third-Worlds It

In Ghana, the Ambassador was sixty and slender and spunky, and wore a suit white as himself. He bade the driver on the road from Accra to Cape Coast stop at a village where a remarkable native sculpture with uncanny mimetic sympathy created in painted plaster an ornate, enigmatic tower. Green and pink, decorated with scrolls and pineapples, the tower, as solid inside as a piece of marzipan, was guarded by life-size plaster soldiers dressed in uniforms that combined and compounded the devices of half a dozen imperial uniforms. Out of pasty plaster faces they stared with alien blue eyes towards the sea whence, beginning with the Portuguese, the white men had come. The strange structure was weathering rapidly in these tropics. Its purpose, Bech imagined, was magical; but it was their ambassadorial limousine, as it roared into the village at the head of a procession of raised dust, a tiny American flag flapping on one fender, that had the magical effect: the villagers vanished. While the little cultural delegation stood there, on the soft dirt, in the hot sun – the Ambassador, mopping his pink and impressive face; Bech, nervously picking at an eye-tooth with the nail of his little finger; the cultural attaché, a curly-haired, informative, worried man from Minnesota; his assistant, a lanky black female from Charlotte, North Carolina, coiffed in the only Afro, as far as Bech could see, in all of Africa; and their driver, a gleaming Ghanaian a full head shorter than the rest of them – the village's inhabitants peeped from behind palms and out of oval doorways. Bech was reminded of how, in Korea, the North Korean soldiers skulked on their side of the truce zone, some with binoculars, some with defiant gestures. 'Did we do something wrong?' Bech asked.

'Hell, no,' the Ambassador said, with his slightly staggering excess of enthusiasm, like a ringmaster shouting to the far rows, 'that's just the way the buggers act.'

In Seoul, at a party held in a temple converted to an official banquet hall, a Japanese poet was led up to Bech by a translator. 'I have long desired,' the translator said, 'to make the acquaintanceship of the honourable Henry Bech.'

'Why?' Bech thoughtlessly asked. He was very tired, and tired of being polite in Asia.

There was, this rude monosyllable translated, a smiling, steady answer. The translator put it, 'Your beautiful book *Travel Light* told us of Japan what to expect of the future.' More Japanese, translated as 'Young hooligans with faces of glass.' This surely meant Bech's most famous apparition, the begoggled motorcyclists in his first, now venerated and wearisome, novel.

The poet in the kimono was leaning at a fixed angle. Bech perceived that his serenity was not merely ethnic; he was drunk. 'And you,' Bech asked through the translator, 'what do *you* do?'

The answer came back as 'I write many poems.'

Bech felt near fainting. The jet lag built up over the Pacific was unshakeable, and everywhere he went, a dozen photographers in identical grey suits kept blinding him with flash bulbs. And Korean schoolgirls, in waxy pigtails and blue school uniforms, kept slipping him love letters in elevators. Two minutes off the airplane, he had been asked four times, 'What are your impressions of Korea?'

Where was he? A thin ochre man in a silvery kimono was swaying before him, upheld by a chunky translator whose eyes were crossed in a fury of attention. 'And what are your poems about?' Bech asked.

The answer was prompt. 'Flogs,' the translator said. The poet beamed.

'Frogs?' Bech said. 'My goodness. *Many* poems about frogs?'
'Many.'
'How many?'

No question was too inane, here in this temple, to receive

an answer. The poet himself intervened to speak the answer, in proud English. 'One hunnert twelve.'

The Cape Coast Castle breasted the green Atlantic like a ship; the great stone deck of the old slave fort was paved with plaques testifying to the deaths, after a year or two of service here, of young British officers – dead of fever at twenty, twenty-two, twenty-five. 'They thought that gin kept away malaria,' the cultural attaché told him, 'so everybody was reeling drunk most of the time. They died drunk. It must have been some show.'

'Why did they come?' Bech asked, in his role as ambassador from the kingdom of stupid questions.

'Same reason they came to the States,' the attaché said. 'To get out from under. To get rich quick.'

'Didn't they know' – Bech felt piqued, as if the plaques around him were a class of inattentive students – 'they would die?'

'Dead men tell no tales,' the Ambassador interrupted heartily, brandishing an imaginary whip. 'They kept the bad news mum back home and told the poor buggers fool tales about black gold. That's what they used to call this hellhole. The Gold Coast.'

The Ambassador's party went down to the dungeons. In one, a shrine seemed operative; bones, scraps of glass, burned-out candles, and fresh ash dirtied a slab of rock. In the deepest dungeon, a trough cut into the stone floor would have carried away body wastes and a passageway where the visitors now had to crouch once led the black captives, manacled, out to the ships and the New World. Bare feet had polished a path across the shelf of rough rock. Overhead, a narrow stone speaking-tunnel would have issued the commands of the captors. 'Any white man come down in here,' the Ambassador explained with loud satisfaction, 'he'd be torn apart quicker'n a rabbit.'

This grotto-like historical site still somehow echoed with, even seemed still to smell of, the packed, fearful life it had contained.

'Leontyne Price was here a year ago,' the cultural attaché said. 'She really flipped out. She began to sing. She said she had to.'

Bech glanced at the black girl from Charlotte, to see if she were flipping out. She was impassive, secretarial. She had been here before; it was on the Ghana tour. Yet she felt Bech's glance and suddenly, there in the dungeon dimness, gave it a dark, cool return. Can looks kill?

In Venezuela, the tallest waterfall in the world was hidden by clouds. The plane bumped down in a small green clearing and jauntily wheeled to the end of the airstrip. The pilot was devil-may-care, with a Cesar Romero moustache and that same Latin all-giving smile, under careful opaque eyes. Bech's guide was a languid young olive-skinned woman employed by the Creole Petroleum Corporation, or the government Ministry of Human Resources, or both. She struck Bech as attractive but untouchable. He followed her out of the plane into tropical air, which makes all things look close; the river that flowed from the invisible waterfall was audible on several sides of them. At the far edge of the clearing, miniature brown people were walking, half-naked, though some wore hats. There were perhaps eight of them, the children among them smaller but in no other way different; they moved single file, with the wooden dignity of old-fashioned toys, doubly dwarfed by the wall of green forest and the mountainous clouds of the moist, windy sky. 'Who are they?' Bech asked.

'Indians,' his lovely guide answered. Her English was flawless; she had spent years at the University of Michigan. But something Hispanic made her answers curter than a North American's would have been.

'Where are they going?'

'Nowhere. They are going precisely nowhere.'

Her emphasis, he imagined, invited Bech to question deeper. 'What are they thinking?' he asked.

The question was odd enough to induce a silky blink.

'They are wondering,' said the *señorita* then, 'who you are.'

'They can see me?'

They had vanished, the Indians, into the forest by the river, like chips of pottery lost in grass. 'Perfectly,' she told him. 'They can see you all too well.'

★

The audience at Cape Coast grew restive during Bech's long address on 'The Cultural Situation of the American Writer', and afterwards several members of the audience, dressed in the colourful robes of spokesmen, leaped to their feet and asked combative questions. 'Why,' asked a small bespectacled man, his voice tremulous and orotund over the microphone, 'has the gentleman speaking in representation of the United States not mentioned any black writers? Does he suppose, may I ask, that the situation of the black writers in his country partakes of the decadent and, may I say, uninteresting situation he has described?'

'Well,' Bech began, 'I think, yes, the American Negro has his share of our decadence, though maybe not a full share –'

'We have heard all this before,' the man was going on, robed like a wizard, his lilting African English boomed by the amplifying system, 'of your glorious Melville and Whitman, of their *Moby Dicks* and *Scarlet Letters* – what of Eldridge Cleaver and Richard Wright, what of Langston Hughes and Rufus Magee? Why have you not read to us pretty posies of their words? We beg you, Bech, tell us what you mean by this phrase' – a scornful pause – ' "American writer".'

The noise from the crowd was rising. They seemed to be mostly schoolgirls, in white blouses and blue skirts, as in Korea, except that their skin was black and their pigtails stood straight up from their heads, or lay in corn rows that must have taken hours to braid. 'I mean,' Bech said, 'any person who simultaneously writes and holds American citizenship.'

He had not meant this to be funny and found the wave of laughter alarming. Was it with him or against him?

In Korea, there was little laughter at his talk on 'American Humour in Twain, Tarkington, and Thurber'. Though Bech himself, reading aloud at the dais beside the bored Belgian chairman, repeatedly halted to get his own chuckles under control, an echo of them arose only from the American table of the conference – and these were contributed mostly, Bech feared, as tactical support. The only other noise in the vast pale-green room was the murmur of translation (into French, Spanish, Japanese, and Korean) leaking from earphones that bored Orientals had removed. Also, a yipping noise now and then escaped from the Vietnamese table. This table, labelled Vietnam though it represented the vanishing entity called South Vietnam, happened alphabetically to be adjacent to that of the United States, and, in double embarrassment, one of the delegates happened to be crazy. A long-faced man with copious black hair cut in a bowl shape, he crooned and doodled to himself throughout all speeches and rose always to make the same speech, a statement that in Vietnam for twenty years the humour had been bitter. Humour was the conference subject. Malaysian professors cracked Malaysian one-liners; the panel on Burmese scatology was very dignified. There was never much laughter, and none when Bech concluded with some deep thoughts on domestic confusion as the necessary underside of bourgeois order. '*Y a-t-il des questions?*' the chairman asked.

A young man, Asiatic, in floppy colourless shirt and slacks, stood up with fear splayed on his face and began to scream. Scream, no, he was intoning from sheets of paper held shaking in his hands. Fear spread to the faces of those around him who could understand. Bech picked up the headset before him on the dais and dialled for the English translation. There was none, and silence also gaped in French, in Spanish, in Japanese. To judge from the uplifted, chanting sounds, the young man was reciting poetry. Two policemen as young as he, their faces as smooth as their white helmets and as aloof from their bodies as the faces in Oriental prints, came and took the young man's arms. When he struggled and attempted to read on, to the end, Bech presumed, of a stanza, the policeman on his right arm neatly chopped him on the side of the neck, so his head snapped and the papers scattered. No one laughed. Bech was informed later that the young man was a Korean satiric poet.

In Kenya, on the stage at Nairobi, a note was passed to Bech, saying, *Crazy man on yr right in beret, dont call on him for any question*. But when Bech's talk, which he had adjusted since

Ghana to 'Personal Impressions of the American Literary Scene', was finished and he had fielded or fluffed the obligatory pokes about racism, Vietnam, and the American loss in Olympic basketball, a young goateed African in a beret stepped forward to the edge of the stage and, addressing Bech, said, 'Your books, they are weeping, but there are no tears.'

On a stage, everything is hysterically heightened. Bech, blinded by lights, was enraptured by what seemed the beautiful justice of the remark. At last, he was meeting the critic who understood him. At last, he had been given an opportunity to express and expunge the embarrassment he felt here in the Third World. 'I know,' he confessed. 'I would *like* there to be tears,' he added, feeling craven as he said it.

Insanely, the youthful black face opposite him, with its Pharaonic goatee, had produced instant tears; they gleamed on his cheeks as, with the grace of those beyond harm, of clowns and paupers and kings, he indicated the audience to Bech by a regal wave of his hand and spoke, half to them, half to him. His lilt was drier than the West African lilt, it was flavoured by Arabic and savannah; the East Africans were a leaner and more thin-lipped race than that which had supplied the Americas with slaves. 'The world,' he began, and hung that ever-so-current bauble of a word in the space of their gathered silence with apparent utter confidence that meaning would come and fill it, 'is a worsening place. There can be no great help in words. This white man, who is a Jew, has come from afar to give us words. They are good words. Is it words we need? Do we need his words? What shall we give him back? In the old days, we would give him back death. In the old days, we would give him back ivory. But in these days, such gifts would make the world a worse place. Let us give him back words. Peace.' He bowed to Bech.

Bech lifted enough from his chair to bow back, answering, 'Peace.' There was heavy, relieved applause, as the young man was led away by a white guard and a black.

In Caracas, the rich Communist and his elegant French wife had Bech to dinner to admire their Henry Moore. The Moore, a reclining figure of fiercely scored bronze – art seeking to imitate nature's patient fury – was displayed in an enclosed green garden where a floodlit fountain played and bougainvillaea flowered. The drinks – Scotch, *chicha*, Cointreau – materialized on glass tables. Bech wanted to enjoy the drinks, the Moore, the beauty of rich enclosure, the paradox of political opinion, but he was still unsettled by the flight from Canaima, where he had seen the tiny Indians disappear. The devil-may-care pilot had wanted to land at the unlighted military airfield in the middle of the city rather than at the international airport along the coast, and other small planes, also devil-may-care, kept dropping in front of him, racing with the fall of dusk, so he kept pulling back on the controls and cursing, and the plane would wheel, and the tin slums of the Caracas hillsides would flood the tipped windows – vertiginous surges of mosaic.

'*¡Caramba!*' the *escritor norteamericano* wanted to exclaim, but he was afraid of mispronouncing. He was pleased to perceive, through the surges of his terror, that his cool guide was terrified also. Her olive face looked aged, blanched. Her great silky eyelids closed in nausea or prayer. Her hand groped for his, her long fingernails scraping. Bech held her hand. He would die with her. The plane dived and smartly landed, under a romantic full moon just risen in the postcard-purple night sky above Monte Avila.

The Ambassador held a dinner for Bech and the Ghanaian élite. They were the élite under this regime, had been the élite under Nkrumah, would be the élite under the next regime. The relative positions within the élite varied, however; one slightly demoted man, with an exquisite Oxford accent, got drunk and told Bech and the women at their end of the table about walking behind Nkrumah in a procession. In those days (and no doubt in these), the élite had carried guns. 'Quite without warning or any tangible provocation,' the man told Bech, as gin-enriched sweat shone from his face as from a basalt star, 'I was visited by this overpowering urge to kill him. Over*powering* – my palm was itching, I could feel the little grid of the revolver handle in my fingers, I focused hypnotically upon the precise spot, in

the centre of his occiput, where the bullet would enter. He had
become a tyrant. Isn't that so, ladies?'

There was a soft, guarded tittering of agreement from the
Ghanaian women. They were magnificent, Ghanaian women,
from mammy wagon to Cabinet post, fertile and hopeful,
wrapped in their sumptuous gowns and turbans. Bech wanted
to repose forever, in the candlelight, amid these women, like
a sultan amid so many pillows. Women and death and airplanes:
there was a comfortable triangulation there, he drowsily perceived.

'The urge became irresistible,' his informant was continuing.
'I was wrestling with a veritable demon; sweat was rolling from
me as from one about to vomit. I had to speak. It happened
that I was walking beside one of his bodyguards. I whispered
to him, "Sammy. I want to shoot him." I had to tell someone
or I would have done it. I wanted him to prevent me, perhaps
– who knows the depths of the slave mentality? – even to shoot
me, before I committed sacrilege. You know what he said to
me? He turned to me, this bodyguard, six foot two at the
minimum, and solemnly said, "Jimmy, me, too. But not now.
Not yet. Let's wait."'

In Lagos, they were sleeping in the streets. Returning in a
limousine from a night club where he had learned to do the
high-life (his instructress's waist like a live, slow snake in his
hands), Bech saw the bodies stretched on the pavements, within
the stately old British colonnades, under the street lamps, without
blankets. Seen thus, people make a bucolic impression, of a type
of animal, a hairless, especially peaceful type, performing one
of the five acts essential to its existence. The others are: eating,
drinking, breathing, and fornicating.

In Seoul, the prostitutes wore white. They were young girls,
all of them, and in the white dresses, under their delicate parasols,
they seemed children gathered along the walls of the hotels,
waiting for a bus to take them to their first Communion. In
Caracas, the whores stood along the main streets between the
diagonally parked cars so that Bech had the gustatory impression

of a drive-in restaurant blocks long, with the car-hops allowed to choose their own uniforms, as long as they showed lots of leg, in several delicious flavours.

In Egypt, the beggars had sores and upturned, blind eyes; Bech felt they were gazing upwards to their reward and sensed through them the spiritual pyramid, the sacred hierarchy of suffering that modern man struggles with nightmare difficulty to invert and to place upon a solid material base of sense and health and plenty. On an island in the Nile, the Royal Cricket Club flourished under new management; the portly men playing bowls and sipping gin were a shade or two darker than the British, but mannerly and jubilant. The bowling greens were level and bright, the gin was Beefeater's, the laughter of sportsmanship ricocheted, it was jolly, jolly. Bech was happy here. He was not happy everywhere in the Third World.

A friend had fought in Korea and had told Bech, without rancour, that the whole country smelled of shit. Alighting from the plane, Bech discovered it to be true: a gamy, muddy smell swept towards him. That had been his first impression, which he had suppressed when the reporters asked for it.

As the audience in Cape Coast politely yielded up a scattered, puzzled applause, Bech turned to the Ambassador and said, 'Tough questions.'

The Ambassador, whose white planter's suit lacked only the wide-brimmed hat and the string tie, responded with a blast of enthusiasm. 'Those weren't tough questions, those were kid-glove questions. Standard stuff. These buggers are soft; that's why they made good slaves. Before they sent me here, I was in Somaliland; the Danakil – now, those are buggers after my own heart. Kill you for a dime, for a nickel-plated spoon. Hell, kill you for the fun of it. Hated to leave. Just as I was learning the damn language. Full of grammar, Dankali.'

Tanzania was eerie. The young cultural attaché was frighten-ingly with it, equally enthusiastic about the country's socialism and its magic. 'So this old guy wrote the name of the disease and my brother's name on the skin of the guava and it *sank right in*. You could see the words moving *into the centre*. I tried writing on a guava and I couldn't even make a mark. Sure enough, weeks later I get a letter from him saying he felt a lot better suddenly. And if you figure in the time change, it was *that very day*.'

They kept Bech's profile low; he spoke not in a hall but in a classroom, at night, and then less spoke than deferentially listened. The students found decadent and uninteresting Proust, Joyce, Shakespeare, Sartre, Hemingway – Hemingway, who had so enjoyed coming to Tanganyika and killing its *kudu* and sitting by its camp-fires getting drunk and pontifical – and Henry James. Who, then, Bech asked, *did* measure up to the exacting standards that African socialism had set for literature? The answering silence lengthened. Then the brightest boy, the most militant and vocal, offered 'Jack London', and rubbed his eyes. He was tired, Bech realized. Bech was tired. Jack London was tired. Everything in the world was tired, except fear – fear and magic.

Alone on the beach in Dar es Salaam, where he had been warned against going alone, he returned to the sand after trying to immerse himself in the milky, shoal-beshallowed Indian Ocean and found his wristwatch gone. There was nothing around him but palms and a few rocks. And no footprints but his own led to his blanket. Yet the watch was gone from where he had distinctly placed it; he remembered its tiny threadlike purr in his ear as he lay with his back to the sun. It was not the watch, a drugstore Timex bought on upper Broadway. It was the fear he minded, the terror of the palms, the rocks, the pale, unsatisfactory ocean, his sharp small shadow, the mocking emptiness all around. The Third World was a vacuum that might suck him in, too, along with his wristwatch and the words on the skin of the guava.

At the centre of a panel of the Venezuelan élite, Bech discussed 'The Role of the Writer in Society'. Spanish needs more words, evidently, than even English to say something, so the intervals of translation were immense. The writer's duty to society, Bech had said, was simply to tell the truth, however strange, small, or private his truth appeared. During the eternity while the translator, a plump, floridly gesturing woman, rendered this into the microphone, one panelist kept removing and replacing his glasses fussily and the rich Communist studied his own right hand as if it had been placed by an officious waiter on the table – square, tan, cuffed in white and ringed in gold. But what, the man with the restless spectacles was at last allowed to ask, of Dreiser and Jack London, of Steinbeck and Sinclair Lewis – what has happened in the United States to their noble tradition of social criticism?

It's become sexual display, Bech could have said; but he chose to answer in terms of Melville and Henry James, though he was weary, weary to death of dragging their large, obliging, misshapen reputations around the globe, rag dummies in which the stuffing had long ago slipped and dribbled out the seams. Words, words. As Bech talked, and his translatress feverishly scribbled notes upon his complicated gist, young Venezuelans – students – not too noisily passed out leaflets among the audience and scattered some on the table. The Communist glanced at one, put it face down on the table, and firmly rested his handsome, unappetizing hand upon the now blank paper. Bech looked at the one that slid to a stop at the base of his microphone. It showed himself, huge-nosed, as a vulture with striped and starred wings, perched on a tangle of multicoloured little bodies; beneath the caricature ran the capitalized words INTELECTUAL REACCIONARIO, IMPERIALISTA, ENEMIGO DE LOS PUEBLOS.

The English words 'Rolling Stone' leaped out at him. Some years ago in New York City he had irritably given an interviewer for *Rolling Stone* a statement, on Vietnam, to the effect that, challenged to fight, a country big enough has to fight. Also he had said that, having visited the Communist world, he could not share radical illusions about it and could not wish upon Vietnamese peasants a system he could not wish upon himself. Though it was what he honestly thought, he was sorry he had said it. But then, in a way, he was sorry he had ever said anything, on anything, ever. He had meddled with sublime silence. There was in the world a pain concerning which God has sct an example of unimpeachable no comment. These realizations took the time of one short, not even awkward pause in his peroration about ironic points of light; bravely, he droned on, wondering when the riot and his concomitant violent death would begin.

But the Venezuelan students, having distributed their flier, stood back, numbed by the continuing bombardment of North American pedantry, and even gave way, murmuring uncertainly, when the panel wound down and Bech was escorted by the U S I S men and the rich Communist from the hall. They looked, the students, touchingly slim, neat, dark-eyed, and sensitive – the fineness of their skin and hair especially struck him, as if the furrier eye of his uncle Mort had awakened within him and he were appraising pelts. By the doorway, he passed close enough to reach out and touch them. Had he known Spanish, Bech might have told these youngsters how grateful he, like one of those dragons in Spenser craving to be eliminated from the lists of evil, was for their attempt to slay him.

He lived. Outdoors, in the lustrous, shuffling tropical night, the Communist writer stayed with him until the U S I S men had flagged a taxi and, in response to Bech's protestations of gratitude (for being his bodyguard, for showing him his Moore), gave him a correct, cold handshake. A rich radical and a poor reactionary: natural allies, both resenting it.

To quiet Bech's fear, the State Department underlings took him to a Caracas tennis tournament, where, under bright lights, a defected Czech beat a ponytailed Swede. But his dread did not lift until, next morning, having signed posters and books for all the wives and cousins of the embassy personnel, he was put aboard the Pan Am jet at the Maiquetía airport. His government had booked him first class. He ordered a drink as soon as the seat-belt sign went off. The stewardess had a Texas accent and a cosmetically flat stomach. She smiled at him. She blamed him for nothing. He might die with her. The sun above the boundless cloud fields hurled through the free bourbon a golden arc that shuddered beside the plastic swizzle stick, upon the plastic tray. In Korea, the girls in school uniforms would slip him notes on blue-lined paper reading, *Derest Mr Bech Mr Kim our teacher assined your stori on being Jewsh in English clas it was my favrite ever I think you very famus over the world I love you.* In Nigeria, the woman teaching him the high-life had reached out and placed two firm black hands gently upon his hips, to settle him down: he had been doing a jumpy, aggressive frug to this different, subtler beat. In the air, the 747 hit some chop and jiggled, but stayed aloft. Not a drop of his golden drink spilled. He vowed never to Third-World it again, unless somebody asked him to.

Australia and Canada

Clean straight streets. Cities whose cores are not blighted but innocently bustling. Anglo-Saxon citizens, British once removed, striding long-legged and unterrorized out of a dim thin past into a future as likely as any. Empty territories rich in minerals. Stately imperial government buildings. Parks where one need not fear being mugged. Bech in his decline went anywhere but had come to prefer safe places.

The invitation to Canada was to Toronto, to be interviewed, as Henry Bech, the exquisitely unprolific author, on the television programme *Vanessa Views*. Vanessa was a squat woman with skin like orange cheesecloth, who nevertheless looked, on a twenty-three-inch screen, if not beautiful, alive. 'It's all in the eyes,' she explained. 'The people with deep sockets do terribly. To project to the camera, you must have eyes set forward in your head. If your eyes turn inward, the viewers turn right off.'

'Suppose your eyes,' Bech asked, 'turn towards each other?'

Vanessa refused to pick it up as a joke, though a female voice behind the lights and cameras laughed. 'You are an author,' Vanessa told him sternly. 'You don't have to project. Indeed, you shouldn't. Viewers distrust the ones who do.'

The two of them were caught in the curious minute before airtime. Bech, practised rough-smoothie that he was, chatted languidly, fighting down the irreducible nervousness, a floating and rising sensation as if he were, with every second ticked from the huge studio clock, being inflated. His hands prickled, swelling; he looked at his palms and they seemed to have no wrinkles. His face felt stiff, having been aromatically swabbed with something like that strange substance with which one was supposed, thirty years ago, to colour oleomargarine and thereby enhance the war effort. The female who had laughed behind the lights, he saw, was the producer, a leggy girl pale as untinted oleo, with nostrils reddened by a cold, and lifeless, pale hair she kept flicking back with the hand not holding her handkerchief. Named Glenda, she appeared harried by her own efficiency, which she refused to acknowledge, brushing aside her directives to the cameramen as soon as she issued them. Like himself, Bech felt, she had been cast by life into a role it amused her not quite to fill.

Whereas his toad-like interviewer, whose very warts were tele-genic, inhaled and puffed herself way up; she was determined to fill this attenuated nation from coast to coast. The seconds waned into single digits on the studio clock and a muffled electronic fuss beyond the lights clicked into gear and Bech's pounding heart bloated as if to choke him. Vanessa began to talk. Then, miracle that never failed, so did he.

He talked into the air. Even without the bright simulacrum of his head and shoulders gesticulating in the upper-left corner of his vision, where the monitor hung like an illuminated initial on a page of shadowy manuscript, Bech could feel the cameras licking his image up and flinging it, quick as light, from Ontario to British Columbia. He touched his nose to adorn a pensive pause, and the gesture splashed on to the shores of the Maritime Provinces and fell as silver snow upon the barren Yukon. As he talked, he marvelled at his words as much as at the electronic marvel that broadcast them; for, just as this broadcasting was an airy and flattering shell upon the terrestrial, odorous, confused man who physically occupied a plastic chair and a few cubic feet of space in this tatty studio, so his words were a shell, an unreal umbrella, above his kernel of real humanity, the more or less childish fears and loves that he wrote out of, when he wrote. On the monitor now, while his throaty interviewer described his career with a 'voice-over', stills of his books were being flashed, and from their jackets photographs of Bech – big-eared and com-bative, a raw youth, on the flap of *Travel Light*; a few years older on *Brother Pig*, his hair longer, his gaze more guarded and, it

seemed to Bech in the microsecond of its exposure, illicitly conspiratorial, seeking to strike up a mutually excusatory relationship
with the reader; a profile, frankly and vapidly Bachrachian, from
his collection of essays; and, wizened if not wiser, pouchy and
classy as a golf bag, his face, haloed by wild wool that deserved to
belong to a Kikuyu witch doctor, from the back of his 'big' novel,
which had been, a decade ago, jubilantly panned. Bech realized,
viewing the montage, that as his artistic powers had diminished
he had come to look more and more like an artist. Then, an even
older face, the shocking face of a geezer, of a shambler, with a
furtive wit waiting to twitch the licked and criminal lips, flashed
on to the screen, and he realized it was he, he as of this moment,
on camera, live. The talking continued, miraculously.

Afterward, the producer of the show emerged from behind the
cables and the cameras, told him he was wonderful, and, the
day being fair, offered to take him for a tour of the city. He had
three hours before a scheduled dinner with a Canadian poet who
had fenced with Cocteau and an Anglican priest who had prepared a concordance of Bech's fiction. Glenda flicked back
her hair absent-mindedly; Bech scanned her face for a blip
marking how far she expected him to go. Her eyes were an even
grey shallowly backed by a neutral Northern friendliness. He
accepted.

In Australia, the tour of Sydney was conducted by two girls,
Hannah, the dark and sombre prop girl for the TV talk show on
which he had been a seven-minute guest (along with an expert on
anthrax; a leader of the Western Australia secessionist movement;
a one-armed survivor of a shark attack; and an aborigine protest
painter), plus Moira, who lived with Hannah and was an
instructor in the economics of underdevelopment. The day was
not fair. A downpour hit just as Hannah drove her little Subaru to
the Opera House, so they did not get out but admired the world-
famous structure from the middle distance. A set of sails had been
the architect's metaphor; but it looked to Bech more like a set of
fish mouths about to nibble something. Him, perhaps. He gave
Hannah permission to drive away. 'It's too bad,' Moira said from

the back seat, 'the day is so rotten. The whole thing is covered in a white ceramic that's gorgeous in the sun.'

'I can picture it,' Bech lied politely. 'Inside, does it give a feeling of grandeur?'

'No,' said Hannah.

'It's all rather tedious bits and pieces,' Moira elaborated. 'We fired the Dane who did the outside and finished the inside ourselves.'

The two girls' life together, Bech guessed, contained a lot of Moira's elaboration, around the other's dark and sombre core. Hannah had moved towards him, after the show, as though by some sullen gravitational attraction such as the outer planets feel for the sun. He was down under, Bech told himself; his volume still felt displaced by an eternity in airplanes. But Hannah's black eyes had no visible backs to them. Down, in, down, they said.

She drove to a cliffy point from which the harbour, the rain lifting, gleamed like silver long left unpolished. Sydney, Moira explained, loved its harbour and embraced it like no other city in the world, not even San Francisco. She had been in San Francisco once, on her way to Afghanistan. Hannah had not been anywhere since leaving Europe at the age of three. She was Jewish, said her eyes, and her glossy, tapered fingers. She drove them down to Bondi Beach, and they removed their six shoes to walk on the soaked sand. The tops of Bech's fifty-year-old feet looked white as paper to him, cheap paper, as if his feet amounted to no more than the innermost lining of his shoes. The girls ran ahead and challenged him to a broad-jump contest. He won. Then, in the hop, step, and jump, his heart felt pleasantly as if it might burst, down here, where death was not real. Blond surfers, wet-suited, were tumbling in with the dusk; a chill wind began sweeping the cloud tatters away. Hannah at his side said, 'That's one reason for wearing a bra.'

'What is?' Moira asked, hearing no response from Bech.

'Look at my nipples. I'm cold.'

Bech looked down; indeed, the woman wore no bra and her erectile tissue had responded to the drop in temperature. The rare sensation of a blush caked his face, which still wore its television makeup. He lifted his eyes from Hannah's sweater and saw that, like fancy underpants, the entire beach was frilled, with pink and lacy buildings. Sydney, the girls explained, as the tour continued from Bondi to Woollahra to Paddington to Surry Hills and Redfern, abounds in ornate ironwork shipped in as ballast from England. The oldest buildings were built by convicts: barracks and forts of a pale stone cut square and set solid, as if by the very hand of rectitude.

In Toronto, the sight Glenda was proudest to show him was the City Hall, two huge curved skyscrapers designed by a Finn. But what moved Bech, with their intimations of lost time and present innocence, were the great Victorian piles, within the university and along Bloor Street, that the Canadians, building across the lake from grimy grubbing America, had lovingly erected – brick valentines posted to a distant, unamused queen. Glenda talked about the city's community of American draft evaders and the older escapees, the families who were fleeing to Canada post-Vietnam, because life in the United States had become, what with race and corruption and pressure and trash, impossible.

Flicking back her pale hair as if to twitch it into life, Glenda assumed Bech agreed with her and the exiles, and so a side of him lackadaisically did; but another side, his ugly patriotism, bristled as she chattered on about his country's sins and her own blameless land's Balkanization by the money that, even in its death throes, American capitalism was flinging north. Hearing this, Bech felt the pride of vicarious power – he who lived cowering on drug-ridden West Ninety-ninth Street, avoiding both the venture of marriage, though his suburban mistress was more than ready, and the venture of print, though his editor, dear old Ned Clavell, from his deathbed in the Harkness Pavilion had begged him to come up at least with a memoir. While Glenda talked, Bech felt like something immense and confusedly vigorous about to devour something dainty. He feigned assent and praised the new architecture booming along the rectitudinal streets, because he believed that this woman – her body a hand's-breadth away on the front seat of a Canadian Ford – liked him, liked even the whiff of hairy savagery about him; his own body wore the chill, the numb expectancy all over his skin, that foretold a sexual conquest.

He interrupted her. 'Power corrupts,' he said. 'The powerless should be grateful.'

She looked over dartingly. 'Do I sound smug to you?'

'No,' he lied. 'But then, you don't seem powerless to me, either. Quite masterful, the way you run your TV crew.'

'I enjoy it, is the frightening thing. You were lovely, did I say that? So giving. Vanessa can be awfully obvious in her questions.'

'I didn't mind. You do it and it flies over all those wires and vanishes. Not like writing, that sits there and gives you that Gorgon stare.'

'What are you writing now?'

'As I said to Vanessa. A novel with the working title *Think Big*.'

'I thought you were joking. How big is it?'

'It's bigger than I am.'

'I doubt that.'

I love you. It would have been easy to say, he was so grateful for her doubt, but his sensation of numbness, meaning love was at hand, had not yet deepened to total anaesthesia. 'I love,' he told her, turning his face to the window, 'your sensible, pretty city.'

'Loved it,' Bech said of his tour of Sydney. 'Want to drop me at the hotel?'

'No,' Hannah said.

'You must come home and let us give you a bite,' Moira elaborated. 'Aren't you a hungry lion? Peter said he'd drop around and that would make four.'

'Peter?'

'He has a degree in forestry,' Moira explained.

'Then what's he doing here?'

'He's left the forest for a while,' Hannah said.

'Which of you ... knows him?' Bech asked, jealously, hesitantly.

But his hesitation was slight compared with theirs; both girls were silent, waiting for the other to speak. At last Hannah said, 'We sort of share him.'

Moira added, 'He was mine, but Hannah stole him and I'm in the process of stealing him back.'

'Sounds fraught,' Bech said; the clipped Australian lilt was already creeping into his enunciation.

'No, it's not so bad,' Moira said into his ear. 'The thing that saves the situation is, after he's gone, we have each other. We're amazingly compatible.'

'It's true,' Hannah sombrely pronounced, and Bech felt jealous again, of their friendship, or love if it were love. He had nobody. Flaubert without a mother. Bouvard without a Pécuchet. Even Bea, whose sad suburban life had become a continuous prayer for him to marry her, had fallen silent, the curvature of the earth interceding.

They had driven in the darkness past palm-studded parks and golf courses, past shopping streets, past balconies of iron lace, into a region of dwarf row houses, spruced up and painted pastel shades: Bohemia salvaging another slum. Children were playing in the streets and called to their car, recognizing Hannah. Bech felt safe. Or would have but for Peter, the thought of him, the man from the forest, on whose turf the aged lion was daring to intrude.

The section of Toronto where Glenda drove him, proceeding raggedly uphill, contained large homes, British in their fussy neo-Gothic brickwork but New World in their untrammelled scale and large lawns – lawns dark as overinked etchings, shadowed by great trees strayed south from the infinite forests of the north. Within one of these miniature castles, a dinner party had been generated. The Anglican priest who had prepared the concordance asked him if he were aware of an unusual recurrence in his work of the adjectives *lambent*, *untrammelled*, *porous*, *jubilant*, and *recurrent*. Bech said no, he was not aware, and that if he could have thought of other adjectives, he would have used them instead – that a useful critical distinction should be made, perhaps, between recurrent imagery and authorial stupidity; that it must have taken him, the priest, an immense amount of labour to compile such a concordance, even of an *oeuvre* so slim. Ah, not really, was the answer: the texts had been readied by the seminarians in his seminar in post-Christian kerygmatics, and the collation and print-out had been achieved by a scanning computer in twelve minutes flat.

The writer who had cried '*Touché!*' to Cocteau was ancient and ebullient. His face was as red as a mountain-climber's, his hair fine as thistledown. He chastened Bech with his air of the Twenties, when authors were happy in their trade and boisterous in plying it. As the whiskey and wine and cordials accumulated, the old saint's arm (in a shimmering grape-coloured shirt) frequently encircled Glenda's waist and bestowed a paternal hug; later, when she and Bech were inspecting together (the glaze of alcohol intervening so that he felt he was bending above a glass museum case) a collector's edition of the Canadian's most famous lyric, *Pines*, Glenda, as if to 'rub off' on the American the venerable poet's blessing, caressed him somehow with her entire body, while two of their four hands held the booklet. Her thigh rustled against his, a breast gently tucked itself into the crook of his arm, his entire skin went blissfully porous, he felt as if he were toppling forward. 'Time to go?' he asked her.

'Soon,' Glenda answered.

Peter was not inside the girls' house, though the door was open and his dirty dishes were stacked in the sink. Bech asked, 'Does he *live* here?'

'He eats here,' Hannah said.

'He lives right around the corner,' Moira elaborated. 'Shall I go fetch him?'

'Not to please me,' Bech said; but she was gone, and the rain recommenced. The sound drew the little house snug into itself – the worn Oriental rugs, the rows of books about capital and underdevelopment, the New Guinean and Afghan artifacts on the wall, all the frail bric-à-brac of women living alone, in nests without eggs.

Hannah poured them two Scotches and tried to roll a joint. 'Peter usually does this,' she said, fumbling, spilling. Bech as a child had watched Westerns in which cow-pokes rolled cigarettes with one hand and a debonair lick. But his efforts at imitation were so clumsy that Hannah took the paper and the marijuana back from him and made of these elements a plump-tongued packet, a little white dribbling piece of pie, which they managed to smoke, amid many sparks. Bech's throat between sips of liquor burned. Hannah put on a record. The music went through its grooves, over and over. The rain continued steady, though his consciousness of it was intermittent. At some point in the rumpled stretches of time, she cooked an omelette. She talked about her career, her life, the man she had left to live with Moira, Moira, herself. Her parents were from Budapest; they had been refugees in Portugal during World War II, and when it was over, only Australia would let them in. An Australian Jewess, Bech thought, swallowing to ease his burned throat. The concept seemed unappraisably near and far, like that of Australia itself. He was here, but it was there, a world's fatness away from his empty, sour, friendly apartment at Riverside and Ninety-ninth. He embraced her and they seemed to bump together like two clappers in the same bell. She was fat, solid. Her body felt in his arms hingeless; she was one of those wooden peasant dolls, containing congruent dolls, for sale in Slavic Europe, where he had once been, and where she had been born. He asked her among their kisses, which came and went in his consciousness like the sound of the rain, and which travelled circularly in grooves like the music, if they should wait up for Peter and Moira.

'No,' Hannah said.

If Moira had been there, she would have elaborated, but she wasn't and therefore didn't.

'Shall I come up?' Bech asked. For Glenda lived on the top floor of a Toronto castle a few blocks' walk – a swim, through shadows and leaves – from the house they had left.

'All I can give you,' she said, 'is coffee.'

'Just what I need, fortuitously,' he said. 'Or should I say lambently? Jubilantly?'

'You poor dear,' Glenda said. 'Was it so awful for you? Do you have to go to parties like that every night?'

'Most nights,' he told her, 'I'm scared to go out. I sit home reading Dickens and watching Nixon. And nibbling pickles. And picking quibbles. Recurrently.'

'You do need the coffee, don't you?' she said, still dubious. Bech wondered why. Surely she was a sure thing. That shimmering body touch. Her apartment snuggled under the roof, bookcases and lean lamps looking easy to tip among the slanting walls. In a far room he glimpsed a bed, with a feathery Indian bedspread and velour pillows. Glenda, as firmly as she directed cameramen, led him the other way, to a small front room claustrophobically lined with books. She put on a record, explaining it was Gordon Lightfoot, Canada's own. A sad voice, gentle to no clear purpose, imitated American country blues. Glenda talked about her career, her life, the man she had been married to.

'What went wrong?' Bech asked. Marriage and death fascinated him: he was an old-fashioned novelist in this.

She wanly shrugged. 'He got too dependent. I was being suffocated. He was terribly nice, a truly nice person. But all he would do was sit and read and ask me questions about my feelings. These books, they're mostly his.'

'You seem tired,' Bech said, picturing the feathery bed.

She surprised him by abruptly volunteering, 'I have something wrong with my corpuscles, they don't know what it is, I'm having tests. But I'm out of whack. That's why I said I could offer you only coffee.'

Bech was fascinated, flattered, relieved. Sex needed participation, illness needed only a witness. A loving witness. Glenda was dear and directorial in her movement as she rose and flicked back her hair and turned the record over. The movement seemed to generate a commotion on the stairs, and then a key in the lock and a brusque masculine shove on the door. She turned a notch paler, staring at Bech; the pink part of her nose stood out like an exclamation point. Too startled to whisper, she told Bech, 'It must be *Peter*.'

Downstairs, more footsteps than two entered the little house, and from the grumble of a male voice, Bech deduced that Moira had at last returned with Peter. Hannah slept, her body filling the bed with a protective turnipy warmth he remembered from Brooklyn kitchens. The couple below them bumbled, clattered, tittered, put on a record. It was a Chilean flute record Hannah had played for him earlier – music shrill, incessant, searching, psychedelic. This little white continent, abandoned at the foot of Asia, looked to the New World's west coasts for culture, for company. Californian clothes, Andean flutes. 'My pale land,' he had heard an Australian poet recite, and from airplanes it was, indeed, a pale land, speckled and colourless, a Wyoming with a seashore. A continent as lonely as the planet. Peter and Moira played the record again and again; otherwise, they were silent downstairs, deep in drugs or fucking. Bech got up and groped lightly across the surface of Hannah's furniture for Kleenex or lens tissue or anything tearable to stuff into his ears. His fingers came to a paperback book and he thought the paper might be cheap enough to wad. Tearing off two corners of the title page, he recognized by the dawning light the book as one of his own, the Penguin *Brother Pig*, with that absurdly literal cover, of a grinning pig, as if the novel were *Animal Farm* or *Charlotte's Web*. The paper crackling and cutting in his ears, he returned to the bed. Beside him, stately Hannah, half-covered and unconscious, felt like a ship, her breathing an engine, her lubricated body steaming towards the morning, her smoke-stack nipples relaxed in passage. The flute music stopped. The world stopped turning. Bech counted to ten, twenty, thirty in silence, and his consciousness had begun to disintegrate when a man laughed and the Chilean flute, and the pressure in Bech's temples, resumed.

'This is Peter Syburg,' Glenda said. 'Henry Bech.'

'*Je sais, je sais bien,*' Peter said, shaking Bech's hand with the painful vehemence of the celebrity-conscious. 'I saw your gig on the tube. Great. You talked a blue streak and didn't tip your hand once. What a con job. Cool. I mean it. The medium is *you*, man. Hey, that's a compliment. Don't look that way.'

'I was just going to give him coffee,' Glenda interposed.

'How about brandy?' Bech asked. 'Suddenly I need my spirits fortified.'

'Hey, don't go into your act,' Peter said. 'I *like* you.'

Peter was a short man, past thirty, with thinning ginger hair and a pumpkin's gap-toothed grin. He might have even been forty;

but a determined retention of youth's rubberiness fended off the possibility. He flopped into a canvas sling chair and kept crossing and recrossing his legs, which were so short he seemed to Bech to be twiddling his thumbs. Peter was a colleague of sorts, based at the CBC office in Montreal, and used Glenda's apartment here when she was in Montreal, as she often was, and vice versa. Whether he used Glenda when she was in Toronto was not clear to Bech; less and less was. Less and less the author understood how people lived. Such cloudy episodes as these had become his only windows into other lives. He wanted to go, but his going would be a retreat – Montcalm wilting before Wolfe's stealthy ascent. He had a bit more brandy instead. He found himself embarked on one of those infrequent experiments in which, dispassionate as a scientist bending metal, he tested his own capacity. He felt himself inflating, as before television exposure, while the brandy flowed on and Peter asked him all the questions not even Vanessa had been pushy enough to pose ('What's happened to you and Capote?' 'What's the timer makes you Yanks burn out so fast?' 'Ever thought of trying television scripts?') and expatiating on the wonders of the McLuhanite world in which he, Peter, with his thumb-like legs and berry-bright eyes, moved as a successful creature, while he, Bech, was picturesquely extinct. Glenda flicked her pale hair and studied her hands and insulted her out-of-whack corpuscles with cigarettes. Bech was happy. One more brandy, he calculated, would render him utterly immobile, and Peter would be displaced. His happiness was not even punctured when the two others began to talk to each other in Canadian French, about calling a taxi to take him away.

'*Taxi, non,*' Bech exclaimed, struggling to rise. '*Marcher, oui. Je pars, maintenant. Vous le regretterez, quand je suis disparu. Au revoir, cher Pierre.*'

'You can't walk it, man. It's miles.'

'Try me, you post-print punk,' Bech said, putting up his hairy fists.

Glenda escorted him to the stairs and down them, one by one; at the foot, she embraced him, clinging to him as if to be rendered fertile by osmosis. 'I thought he was in Winnipeg,' she said. 'I want to have your baby.'

'Easy does it,' Bech wanted to say. The best he could do was, '*Facile le fait.*'

Glenda asked, 'Will you ever come back to Toronto?'

'*Jamais,*' Bech said, '*jamais, jamais,*' and the magical word, so true of every moment, of every stab at love, of every step on ground you will not walk again, rang in his mind all the way back to the hotel. The walk was generally downhill. The curved lights of the great city hall guided him. There was a forested ravine off to his left, and a muffled river. And stars. And block after block of substantial untroubled emptiness. He expected to be mugged, or at least approached. In his anaesthetized state, he would have welcomed violence. But in those miles he met only blinking stop lights and impassive architecture. *And they call this a city*, Bech thought scornfully. *In New York, I would have been killed six times over and my carcass stripped of its hubcaps.*

The cries of children playing woke him. The sound of the flute at last had ceased. Last night's pleasure had become straw in his mouth; the woman beside him seemed a larger sort of dreg. Her eyelids fluttered, as if in response to the motions of his mind. It seemed only polite to reach for her. The children beneath the window cheered.

Next morning, in Toronto, Bech shuffled, footsore, to the Royal Ontario Museum and admired the Chinese urns and the totem poles and sent a postcard of a carved walrus tusk to Bea and her three children.

Downstairs, in Sydney, Moira was up, fiddling with last night's dishes and whistling to herself. Bech recognized the tune. 'Where's Peter?' he asked.

'He's gone,' she said. 'He doesn't believe you exist. We waited up hours for you last night and you never came home.'

'We *were* home,' Hannah said.

'Oh, it dawned on us finally.' She elaborated: 'Peter was so moody I told him to leave. I think he still loves *you* and has been leading this poor lass astray.'

'What do you like for breakfast?' Hannah asked Bech, as

wearily as if she and not he had been awake all night. Himself, he felt oddly fit, for being fifty and on the underside of the world. 'Tell me about Afghanistan – should I go there?' he said to Moira, and he settled beside her on the carpeted divan while Hannah, in her lumpy blue robe, shuffled in the kitchen, making his breakfast. 'Grapefruit if you have it,' he shouted to her, interrupting the start of Moira's word tour of Kabul. 'Otherwise, orange juice.' *My God*, he thought to himself, *she has become my wife. Already I'm flirting with another woman.*

Bech boarded the plane (from Australia, from Canada) so light-headed with lack of sleep it alarmed him hardly at all when the machine rose into the air. His stomach hurt as if lined with grit, his face looked grey in the lavatory mirror. His adventures seemed perilous, viewed backwards. Mysterious diseases, strange men laughing in the night, loose women. He considered the nation he was returning to: its riots and scandals, its sins and power and gnashing metal. He thought of Bea, his plump suburban softy, her belly striated with fine silver lines, and vowed to marry her, to be safe.

The Holy Land

I never should have married a Christian, Bech thought, fighting his way up the Via Dolorosa. His bride of some few months, Beatrice Latchett (formerly Cook) Bech, and the Jesuit archaeologist that our Jewish–American author's hosts at the Mishkenot Sha'ananim had provided as guide to the Christian holy sites – a courtly Virgil to Bech's disbelieving Dante – kept getting ahead of him, their two heads, one blond and one bald, piously murmuring together as Bech fell behind in the dusty jostle of nuns and Arab boys, of obese Protestant pilgrims made bulkier still by airline tote bags. The incessant procession was watched by bored gaunt merchants with three-day beards as they stood before their souvenir shops. Their dark accusing sorrow plucked at Bech. His artist's eye, always, was drawn to the irrelevant: the overlay of commercialism upon this ancient sacred way fascinated him – Kodachrome where Christ stumbled, bottled Fanta where He thirsted. Scarves, caftans, olive-wood knickknacks begged to be bought. As a child, Bech had worried that merchants would starve; Union Avenue in Williamsburg, near where his uncles lived on South Second Street, had been lined with disregarded narrow shops, a Kafka world of hunger artists waiting unwatched in their cages. This was worse.

Père Gibergue had confirmed what Bea already knew from her guidebooks: the route Jesus took from Pilate's verdict to Golgotha was highly problematical, and in any case, all the streets of first-century Jerusalem were buried under twelve feet of rubble and subsequent paving. So they and their fellow pilgrims were in effect treading on air. The priest, wearing flared slacks and a short-sleeved shirt, stopped to let Bech catch up, and pointed out to him overhead a half-arch dating, it seemed certain, from the time of Herod. The other half of the arch was buried, lost, behind a grey façade painted with a polyglot array in which Bech could read the word GIFTS. Bea's face, beside the tanned face of the archaeologist, looked radiantly pale. She was lightly sweating. Her guidebook was clutched to her blouse like a missal. 'Isn't it all wonderful?' she asked her husband.

Bech said, 'I never realized what a big shot Herod was. I thought he was just something on the back of a Christmas card.'

Père Gibergue, in his nearly flawless English, pronounced solemnly, 'He was a crazy man, but a great builder.' There was something unhappy about the priest's nostrils, Bech thought; otherwise, his vocation fitted him like a smooth silk glove.

'There were several Herods,' Bea interposed. 'Herod the Great was the slaughter-of-the-innocents man. His son Herod Antipas was ruling when Jesus was crucified.'

'Wherever we dig now, we find Herod,' Père Gibergue said, and Bech thought, *Science has seduced this man. In his archaeological passion, he has made a hero of a godless tyrant.* Jerusalem struck Bech as the civic embodiment of conflicted loyalties. At first, de-planing with Bea and being driven at night from the airport to the Holy City through occupied territory, he had been struck by the darkness of the land, an intended wartime dark such as he had not seen since his GI days, in the tense country nightscapes of England and Normandy. Their escort, the son of American Zionists who had emigrated in the Thirties, spoke of the convoys that had been forced along this highway in the '67 war, and pointed out some hilly places where the Jordanian fire had been especially deadly. Wrecked tanks and trucks, unseeable in the dark, had been left as monuments. Bech remembered, as their car sped vulnerably between the black shoulders of land, the sensation (which for him had been centred in the face, the mouth more than the eyes – had he been more afraid of losing his teeth than his sight?) of being open to bullets, which there was no dodging. Before your brain could register anything, the damage would be done. Teeth shattered, the tongue torn loose, blood gushing through the punctured palate.

Then, as the car entered realms of light – the suburbs of Jerusalem – Bech was reminded of southern California, where he had once gone on a fruitless flirtation with some movie producers, who had been unable to wrap around his old novel *Travel Light* a package the banks would buy. Here were the same low houses and palm fronds, the same impression of staged lighting, exclusively frontal, as if the backs of these buildings dissolved into unpainted slats and rotting canvas, into weeds and warm air – that stagnant, balmy, expectant air of Hollywood when the sun goes down. The Mishkenot – the official city guesthouse, where this promising fifty-two-year-old writer and his plump Protestant wife were to stay for three weeks – seemed solidly built of the same stuff of cinematic illusion: Jerusalem limestone, artfully pitted by the mason's chisel, echoing like the plasterboard corridors of a Cecil B. De Mille temple to the ritual noises of weary guests unpacking. A curved staircase of mock-Biblical masonry led up to an alcove where a desk, a map, a wastebasket, and a sofa awaited his meditations. Bech danced up and down these stairs with an enchantment born in cavernous movie palaces; he was Bojangles, he was Astaire, he was George Sanders, wearing an absurd headdress and a sneer, exulting in the captivity and impending torture of a white-limbed maiden who, though so frightened her jewels chatter, will not forswear her Jahweh. Israel had no other sentimental significance for him; his father, a Marxist of a theoretical and unenrolled sort, had lumped the Zionists with all the *Luftmenschen* who imagined that mollifying exceptions might be stitched into the world's cruel and necessary patchwork of rapine and exploitation. To postwar Bech, busy in Manhattan, events in Palestine had passed as one more mop-up scuffle, though involving a team with whom he identified as effortlessly as with the Yankees.

Bea, an Episcopalian, was enraptured simply at being on Israel's soil. She kept calling it 'the Holy Land'. In the morning, she woke him to share what she saw: through leaded windows, the Mount of Olives, tawny and cypress-strewn, and the silver bulbs of a Russian church gleaming in the Garden of Gethsemane. 'I never thought I'd be here, *ever*,' she told him, and as she turned, her face seemed still to brim with reflected morning light. Bech kissed her and over her shoulder read a multilingual warning not to leave valuables on the windowsill.

'Why didn't you ask Rodney to bring you,' he asked, 'if it meant so much?'

'Oh, Rodney. His idea of a spiritual adventure was to go backpacking in Maine.'

Bech had married this woman in a civil ceremony in lower Manhattan on an April afternoon of unseasonable chill and spitting snow. She was the younger, gentler sister of a mistress he had known for years and with whom he had always fought. He and Bea rarely fought, and at his age this appeared possibly propitious. He had married her to escape his famous former self. He had given up his apartment at Ninety-ninth and Riverside – an address consecrated by twenty years of *Who's Who*s – to live with Bea in Ossining, with her twin girls and only son. These abrupt truths raced through his mind, marvellously strange, as he contemplated the radiant stranger whom the world called his wife. 'Why didn't you tell me,' he asked her now, 'you took this kind of thing so much to heart?'

'You knew I went to church.'

'The E*pis*copal church. I thought it was a social obligation. Rodney wanted the kids brought up in the upper middle class.'

'He thought that would happen anyway. Just by their being his children.'

'Lord, I don't know if I can hack this: be an adequate stepfather to the kids of a snob and a Christian fanatic.'

'Henry, this is your Holy Land, too. You should be thrilled to be here.'

'It makes me nervous. It reminds me of *Samson and Delilah*.'

'You *are* thrilled. I can tell.' Her blue eyes, normally as pale as the sky when the milkiest wisps of strato-cirrus declare a storm coming tomorrow, looked up at him with a new, faintly forced lustre. The Holy Land glow. Bech found it distrustworthy, yet, by some twist, in some rarely illumined depth of himself, flattering. While he was decoding the expression of her eyes, her mouth was forming words he now heard, on instant replay, as 'Do you want to make love?'

'Because we're in the Holy Land?'

'I'm so excited,' Bea confessed. She blushed, waiting. Another hunger artist.

'This is blasphemous,' Bech protested. 'Anyway, we're being picked up to sightsee in twenty minutes. What about breakfast instead?' He kissed her again, feeling estranged. He was too old to be on a honeymoon. His marriage was like this Zionist state they were in: a mistake long deferred, a miscarriage of passé fervour and antiquated tribal righteousness, an attempt to be safe on an earth where there was no safety.

Their quarters in the Mishkenot included a kitchen. Bea called from within it, 'There's two sets of silver. One says Dairy and the other says Meat.'

'Use one or the other,' Bech called back. 'Don't mingle them.'

'What'll happen if I do?'

'I don't know. Try it. Maybe it'll trip the trigger and bring the Messiah.'

'Now who's being blasphemous? Anyway, the Messiah *did* come.'

'We can't all read His calling card.'

Her only answer was the clash of silver.

I'm too old to be married, Bech thought, though he smiled to himself as he thought it. He went to the window and looked at the view that had sexually stimulated his wife. Beyond the near, New Testament hills the colour of unglazed Mexican pottery were lavender desert mountains like long folds in God's lap.

'Is there anything I should know about eggs and butter?' Bea called.

'Keep them away from bacon.'

'There isn't any bacon. There isn't any meat in the fridge at all.'

'They didn't trust you. They knew you'd try to do something crummy.' His Christian wife was thirteen years younger than he. Her belly bore silver stretch marks from carrying twins. She made gentle yipping noises when she fucked. Bech wondered whether he had ever really been a sexy man, or was it just an idea that went with bachelorhood? He had been a satisfactory sprinter, he reflected, but nobody up to now had challenged his distance capacity. At his age, he should be jogging.

The first sight they were taken to, by a Jewish archaeologist in rimless glasses, was the Wailing Wall. It was a Saturday. Sabbath congregations were gathered in the sun of the limestone plaza the Israelis had created by bulldozing away dozens of Arab homes. People were chanting, dancing; photographs were forbidden. Men in sidelocks were leaning their heads against the wall in prayer, the broad-brimmed hats of the Hasidim tipped askew. The archaeologist told Bech and Bea that for a millennium the wall could not be seen from where they stood, and pointed out where the massive, characteristically edged Herodian stones gave way to the smaller stones of Saladin and the Mamelukes. Bea urged Bech to walk up to the wall. The broad area in front of it had been designated a synagogue, with separate male and female sections, so they could not pass in through the fence together. 'I won't go where you can't go,' he said.

Bech's grandfather, a diamond-cutter and disciple of Spinoza, had come to the United States from the ghetto of Amsterdam in 1880; Bech's father had been an atheistic socialist; and in Bech socialist piety had dwindled to a stubborn wisp of artistic conscience. So there was little in his background to answer to the unearthly ardour of Bea's urging. 'I want you to, Henry. Please.'

He said, 'I don't have a hat. You have to have a hat.'

'They have paper *yarmulkes* there. In that basket,' the archaeologist offered, pointing. He was a short bored bearded man, whose attitude expressed no wish, himself, to approach the wall. He stood on the blinding limestone of the plaza as if glued there by his shadow.

'Let's skip it,' Bech said. 'I get the idea from here.'

'No, Henry,' Bea said. 'You must go up and touch it. You must. For me. Think. We may never be here again.'

In her plea he found most touching the pronoun 'we'. Ever since his honourable discharge from the armed forces, Bech had been an I. He picked a black paper hat from the basket, and the hat

213

was unwilling to adhere to his head; his hair was too woolly, too fashionably full-bodied. Greying had made it frizzier. A little breeze seemed to be blowing outward from the wall and twice threatened to lift his *yarmulke* away. Amid the stares of congregated Hasidic youth, their side curls as menacing as lions' manes, he held the cap to the back of his skull with his hand and approached, step by cautious step, all that remained of the Temple.

It was, the wall, a Presence. The great rectangular Herodian stones, each given a shallow border, like a calling card, by the ancient masons, were riddled with lice. Into the cracks of erosion, tightly folded prayers had been stuffed – the more he looked, the more there were. Bech supposed paper lasted forever in this Californian climate. The space around him, the very air, felt tense, like held breath. Numbly he reached out, and as he touched the surprisingly warm sacred surface, an American voice whined into his ears from a small circle of Hasidim seated on chairs nearby. 'Who is this God?' the voice was asking loudly. 'If He's so good, why does He permit all the pain in the world? Look at Cambodia, man ...' The speaker and his audience were undergoing the obligatory exercise of religious debate. The Jewish tongue, divinely appointed to be active. Bech closed his ears and backed away rapidly. The breeze made another grab at his paper *yarmulke*. He dropped the flimsy thing into the basket, and Bea was waiting on the other side of the fence.

She was beaming, proud; he had been attracted to that in her which so purely encouraged him. Amid many in this last, stalled decade of his who had wished to reshape, to activate him forcefully, she had implied that his perfection lay nowhere but in a deepening of the qualities he already possessed. Since he was Jewish, the more Jewish he became in her Christian care, the better.

'Wasn't it wonderful?' she asked.

'It was something,' was all he would grant her. Strange diseases, he thought, demand strange remedies: he, her. As they linked arms, after the separation imposed by a sexist orthodoxy, Bech apprehended Bea with refreshed clarity, by this bright, dry light of Israel: as a creature thickening in the middle, the female of a species mostly hairless and with awkward gait, her flesh nearing the end of its reproductive capacity and her brain possessed by a bizarre creed, yet pleasing to him and asking for his loyalty as unquestioningly, as helplessly as she gave him hers.

Their guide led them up a slanted road, past an adolescent soldier with a machine gun, to the top of the wall. On their left, the faithful continued to circle and pray; on their right, a great falling off disclosed the ugly results of archaeology, a rubble of foundations. 'The City of David,' their guide said proudly, 'just where the Bible said it would be. Everything,' he said, and his gesture seemed to include all of the Holy City, 'just as it was written. We read first, then we dig.' At the Gate of the Moors, their guide yielded to a courtly Arab professor – yellow face, brown suit, Oxford accent – who led them in stockinged feet through the two mosques built on the vast platform that before 70 AD had supported the Temple. Strict Jewish believers never came here, for fear of accidentally treading upon the site of the Holy of Holies, the Ark of the Covenant. Within the Aqsa Mosque, Bech and Bea were informed of recent violence: King Abdullah of Jordan had been assassinated near the entrance in 1951, before the eyes of his grandson the present King Hussein; and in 1969, a crazed Australian had attempted to set the end nearest Mecca afire, with considerable success. Craziness, down through history, has performed impressively, Bech thought.

They were led past a scintillating fountain, up a few marble stairs, to the Dome of the Rock. Inside an octagon of Persian tile, beneath a dizzyingly lavish and symmetrical upward abyss, a spine of rock, the tip of Mount Moriah, showed where Abraham had attempted to sacrifice Isaac and, failing that, had founded three religions. Here also, the professor murmured amid the jostle of the faithful and the touring, Cain and Abel had made their fatally contrasting offerings, and Mohammed had ascended to Heaven on his remarkable horse Burak, whose hoofprints the pious claim to recognize, along with the fingerprints of an angel who restrained the Rock from going to Heaven also. For reasons known best to themselves, the Crusaders had hacked at the Rock.

Great hackers, the Crusaders. And Suleiman the Magnificent, who had wrested the Rock back from the (from his standpoint) infidels, had his name set in gold on high, within the marvellous dome. The King of Morocco had donated the green carpets, into which Bea's stockinged feet dug impatiently, aching to move on from these empty wonders to the Christian sites. *Sexy little feet*, Bech thought; from his earliest amours, he had responded to the dark band of reinforcement that covers half of a woman's stockinged toes, giving us eight baby cleavages.

'Do you wish to view the hairs from the Beard of the Prophet?' the professor asked, adding, 'There is always a great crowd around them.'

Hairs of the Prophet were the kind of sight Bech liked, but he said, 'I think my wife wants to push on.'

They were led down from Herod's temple platform along a peaceable path beside an Arab cemetery. Their guide suddenly chuckled; his teeth were as yellow as his face. He gestured at a bricked-up portal in the Old City wall. 'That is the Golden Gate, the gate whereby the Messiah is supposed to come, so the Ommiads walled it solid and, furthermore, put a cemetery there, because the Messiah supposedly is unable to walk across the dead.'

'Hard to go anywhere if that's the rule,' Bech said, glancing sideways to see how Bea was bearing up under these malevolent overlays of superstition. She looked pink, damp, and happy, her Holy Land glow undimmed. At the end of the pleasant path, at the Lion's Gate, they were passed into the care of the debonair Jesuit and embarked upon the Via Dolorosa.

Lord, don't let me suffocate, Bech thought. The priest kept leading them underground, to show them buried Herodian pools, Roman guardrooms that the sinkage of centuries had turned into grottoes, and paving stones scratched by the soldiers as they played the game of kings – proof, somehow, of the historical Jesus. Père Gibergue knew his way around. He darted into the back room of a bakery, where a dirty pillar of intense archaeological interest stood surrounded by shattered crates. By another detour, Bech and Bea were led on to the roof of the Church of the Holy Sepulchre; here an ancient company of Abyssinian monks maintained an African village of rounded huts and sat smiling in the sun. One of them posed for Bea's camera standing against a cupola. Below the cupola, Père Gibergue explained with archaeological zeal, was the crypt where Saint Helena, mother of Constantine, discovered in the year 327 the unrotted wood of the True Cross. To their guide's sorrow, the young Russian Orthodox priest (his face waxen-white, his thin beard tapered to a double point: the very image, as Bech imagined it, of Ivan Karamazov) who answered their ring at the door of the Alexandra Hostel refused to admit them, this being a Sabbath, to the excavated cellar wherein had been found a worn threshold certainly stepped upon by the foot of God Incarnate.

So this is what's been making the goyim tick all these years. All these levels – roofs coterminous with the street, sacred footsteps buried metres beneath their own – afflicted Bech like a sea of typographical errors. Perhaps this was life: mistake heaped upon mistake, one protein molecule entangled with another until the confusion thrived. Except that it smelled so fearfully dead. The Church of the Holy Sepulchre was so needlessly ugly that Bech said to Bea, 'You should have let the Arabs design it for you.'

Père Gibergue overheard and said, 'In fact, an Arab family has been entrusted with the keys for eight hundred years, to circumvent the contention among the Christian sects.' Inside the hideous edifice, the priest, too, seemed overwhelmed; he sat on a bench near some rusting pipe scaffolding and said, 'Go. I will pray here while you look.' He hid his face in his hands.

Undaunted, Bea with her guidebook led Bech up a marble staircase to the site of the Crucifixion. This turned out to be a great smoke-besmirched heap or fungus of accreted icons and votive lamps. Six feet from the gold-rimmed hole where Christ's cross had supposedly been socketed, a fat Greek priest, seated in his black muffin hat at a table peddling candles, was taking a swig from a bottle in a paper bag. At Bech's side, Bea did a genuflective dip and gazed enthralled at this mass of aesthetic horrors. German tourists were noisily shuffling about, exploding flashbulbs.

'Let's go,' Bech muttered.

'Oh, Henry, why?'

'This frightens me.' It had that alchemic stink of medieval basements where vapours condensed as demons and pogroms and autos-da-fé. Torquemada, Hitler, the tsars – every despot major or minor who had tried to stunt and crush his race had inhaled these Christly vapours. He dragged Bea away, back down to the main floor of the church, which her guidebook itself admitted to be a *conglomeration of large and small rooms, impossible to consider as a whole*.

Père Gibergue unbowed the tan oval of his head. He asked hopefully, 'Enough?'

'More than,' Bech said.

The Jesuit nodded. 'A great pity. This should be Chartres. Instead . . .' He told Bea, 'With your camera, you should photograph that, what the Greeks are doing. Without anyone's permission, they are walling up their sector of the nave. It is barbarous. But not untypical.'

Bea peered through a gilded grate into a sector of holy space crowded with scaffolding and raw pink stone. She did not lift her camera. She had been transported, Bech realized, to a realm beyond distaste. 'We cannot go without visiting the Sepulchre of Christ,' she announced.

Père Gibergue said, 'I advise against it. The line is always long. There is nothing to see. Believe me.'

Bech echoed, 'Believe him.'

Bea said, 'I don't expect to be here ever again,' and got into line to enter a little building that reminded Bech, who joined her, of nothing so much as those mysteriously ornate structures that used to stand in discreet corners of parks in Brooklyn and the Bronx, too grand for lawn mowers but unidentified as latrines; he had always wondered what had existed inside such dignified small buildings – mansions in his imagination for dwarfs. The line moved slowly, and the faces of those returning looked stricken.

There were two chambers. The outer held a case containing a bit of the stone that the Angel is said to have rolled away from the mouth of the tomb; a German woman ahead of Bech in line kissed the cracked glass top of the case and caressed herself in an elaborate spasm of pious gratification, eyeballs rolling, a dovelike moan bubbling from her throat. He was relieved that Bea was better behaved: she glanced down, made a mental note, and passed by. He gazed upon the whitish hair pinned up above the damp nape of her neck as if seeing it for the last time. They were about to be separated by an infamous miracle.

The inner chamber was entered by an opening so small Bech had to crouch, though the author was not tall. Within, as had been foretold, there was 'nothing to see'. Smoking lamps hanging thick as bats from the low ceiling. A bleak marble slab. No trace of the original sepulchre hewn from the rock of Golgotha. In the confines of this tiny space, elbow to elbow with Bech, another stocky Greek priest, looking dazed, was waving lighted tapers held cleverly between his spread fingers. The tapers were for sale. The priest looked at Bech. Bech didn't buy. With a soft grunt of irritation, the priest waved the lighted tapers out. Bech was fascinated by this sad moment of disappointed commerce; he imagined how the wax must drip on to the man's fat fingers, how it must sting. A hunger artist. The priest eyed Bech again. The whites above his dolefully sagging lower lids were very bloodshot. Smoke gets in your eyes.

Back in their room at the Mishkenot, he asked Bea, 'How's your faith?'

'Fine. How's yours?'

'I don't know much about places of worship, but wasn't that the most God-forsaken church you ever did see?'

'It's history, Henry. You have to see through external accidents to the things of the spirit. You weren't religiously and archaeo-logically prepared. The guidebook warns people they may be disappointed.'

'Disappointed! Disgusted. Even your poor Jesuit, who's been there a thousand times, had to hide his face in his hands. Did you hear him complain about what the Greeks were doing to their slice of the pie? Did you hear his story about the Copts swooping down one night and slapping up a chapel that then couldn't be taken away for some idiotic superstitious reason?'

'They wanted to be close to the Holy Sepulchre,' Bea said, stepping out of her skirt.

'I've never seen anything like it,' Bech said. 'It was garbage, of an ultimate sort.'

'It was beautiful to be there, just beautiful,' Bea said, skinning out of her blouse and bra in one motion.

How, Bech asked himself, out of a great materialist nation containing one hundred million fallen-away Christians had he managed to pick this one radiant aberrant as a bride? *Instinct*, he answered himself; his infallible instinct for the distracting. At the height of the love-making that the newly-weds squeezed into a shadowy hour before they were due to go out to dinner, the bloodshot eyeball of the unsuccessful taper-selling priest returned to him, sliding towards Bech as towards a demon brother unexpectedly encountered while robbing the same tomb.

The dinner was with Israeli writers, in a restaurant staffed by Arabs. Arabs, Bech perceived, are the blacks of Israel. Slim young men, they came and went silently, accepting orders and serving while the lively, genial, grizzled, muscular intellectuals talked. The men were an Israeli poet, a novelist, and a professor of English; their wives were also a poet, a novelist, and a professor, though not in matching order. All six had immigrated years ago and therefore were veterans of several wars; Bech knew them by type, fell in with their warmth and chaffing as if back into a party of uncles and cousins. Yet he scented something outdoorsy, an unfamiliar toughness, a readiness to fight that he associated with Gentiles, as part of the psychic kit that included their indiscriminate diet and their bloody, lurid religion. And these Jews had the uneasiness, the slight edge, of those with something to hold on to. The strength of the Wandering Jew had been that, at home nowhere specific, he had been at home in the world. The poet, a man whose face appeared incessantly to smile, broadened as it was by prominent ears and a concentration of wiry hair above the ears, said of the Wailing Wall, 'The stones seem smaller now. They looked bigger when you could see them only up close.'

The professor's wife, a novelist, took fire: 'What a reactionary thing to say! I think it is beautiful, what they have done at the Kotel Ha. They have made a sacred space of a slum.'

Bech asked, 'There were many Arab homes?'

The poet grimaced, while the shape of his face still smiled. 'The people were relocated, and compensated.'

The female novelist told Bech, 'Before '67, when the Old City was theirs, the Jordanians built a hotel upon the Mount of Olives, using the old tombstones for the soldiers' barracks. It was a vast desecration which they committed in full view. We felt very frustrated.'

The male novelist, whose slender, shy wife was a poetess, offered as a kind of truce, 'And yet I feel at peace in the Arab landscape. I do not feel at peace in Tel Aviv, among those Miami Beach hotels. That was not the idea of Israel, to make another Miami Beach.'

'What was the idea, then?' asked the female novelist, teasing – an overweight but still-dynamic flirt among hirsute reactionaries. There is a lag, Bech thought, between the fading of an attractive woman's conception of herself and the fading of the reality.

The male novelist, his tanned skin minutely veined and ponderously loose upon his bones, turned to Bech with a gravity that hushed the table; an Arab waiter, ready to serve, stood there frozen. 'The idea,' it was stated to Bech in the halting murmur of an extreme confidence, 'is not easy to express. Not Freud and Einstein, but not Auschwitz, either. Something ... in between.'

Bech's eye flicked uneasily to the waiter and noticed the name on his identification badge: SULEIMAN.

The poetess, as if to lighten her husband's words, asked the American guests, 'What have been your impressions so far? I know the question is foolish, you have been here a day.'

'A day or a week,' the female novelist boisterously volunteered, 'Henry Bech will go back and write a best-selling book about us. Everybody does.'

The waiter began to serve the food – ample, deracinated, Hilton food – and while Bech was framing a politic answer, Bea spoke up for him. He was as startled as if one of his ribs had suddenly chirped. 'Henry's in raptures,' she said, 'and so am I. I can't believe I'm here, it's like a dream.'

'A costly dream,' said the professor, the youngest of the men and the only one wearing a beard. 'A dream costly to many men.' His beard was as red as a Viking's; he stroked it a bit preeningly.

'The Holy Land,' Bea went on, undeterred, her voice flowing like milk poured from above. 'I feel I was born here. Even the air is so *right*.'

Her strangeness, to her husband at this moment, did verge on the miraculous. At this table of Jews who, wearied of waiting for the Messiah, had altered the world on their own, Bea's voice with its lilt of hasty good news came as an amazing interruption. Bech answered the poetess as if he had not been interrupted. 'It reminds me of southern California. The one time I was there, I felt surrounded by enemies. Not people like you,' he diplomatically amended, 'but up in the hills. Sharpshooters. Agents.'

'You were there before Six-Day War,' joked the female professor; until then, she had spoken not a word, merely smiled towards her husband, the smiling poet. It occurred to Bech that perhaps her English was insecure, that these people were under no obligation to know English, that on their ground it was his obligation to speak Hebrew. English, that bastard child of Norman knights and Saxon peasant girls – how had he become wedded to it? There was something diffuse and eclectic about the language that gave him trouble. It ran against his grain; he tended to open books and magazines at the back and read the last pages first.

'What shall we do?' the flamboyant female novelist was urgently asking him, evidently apropos of the state of Israel. 'We can scarcely speak of it any more, we are so weary. We are weary of war, and now we are weary of talk of peace.'

'The tricky thing about peace,' Bech suggested, 'is that it doesn't always come from being peaceable.'

She laughed, sharply, a woman's challenging laugh. 'So you, too, are a reactionary. Myself, I would give them anything – the Sinai, the West Bank. I would even give them back East Jerusalem, to have peace.'

'*Not* East Jerusalem!' the Christian in their midst exclaimed. 'Jerusalem,' Bea said, 'belongs to everybody.'

And her face, aglow with confidence in things unseen, became a cause for wonder among the seven others. The slim, shy poetess, whose half-grey hair was parted in the exact centre of her slender skull, asked lightly, 'You would like to live here?'

'We'd love to,' Bea said.

Bech felt he had to step on this creeping 'we' of hers. 'My wife speaks for herself,' he said. 'Her enthusiasm overwhelmed even the priest who took us up the Via Dolorosa this afternoon. My own impression was that the Christian holy sites are hideously botched. I liked the mosques.'

Bea explained with the patience of a saint, 'I said to myself, I've waited for this for thirty-nine years, and I'm not going to let anybody, even my husband, ruin it for me.'

Sunday-school pamphlets, Bech imagined. Bible illustrations protected by a page of tissue paper. Bea had carried those stylized ochre-and-moss-green images up from infancy and, when the moment had at last arrived, had placed them carefully upon the tragic, eroded hills of Jerusalem and pronounced the fit perfect. He loved her for that, for remaining true to the little girl she was. In the lull of silence her pious joy had induced, Suleiman came and offered them dessert, which the sated Israelis refused. Bech had apple pie, Bea had fig sherbet, to the admiration of their hosts. Young in marriage, young in appetite.

'You know,' he told her in the taxi back to the Mishkenot, 'the Holy Land isn't holy to those people tonight the way it is to you.'

'I know that, of course.'

'To them,' he felt obliged to press on, 'it's holy because it *is* land at all; after nineteen hundred years of being pushed around, the Jews have a place where they can say, OK, this is it, this is our country. I don't think it's something a Christian can understand.'

'I certainly can. Henry, it saddens me that you feel you must explain all this to me. Rodney and I once went to a discussion group on Zionism. Ask me about Herzl. Ask me about the British Mandate.'

'I explain it only because you've surprised me with your own beliefs.'

'I'll keep them to myself if they embarrass you.'

'No, just don't offer to immigrate. They don't want you. Me, they wouldn't mind, but I have enough problems right now.'

'I'm a problem.'

'I didn't say that. My work is a problem.'

'I think you'd work very well here.'

'Jesus, no. It's depressing. To me, it's just a ghetto with farms. I *know* these people. I've spent my whole life trying to get away from them, trying to think bigger.'

'Maybe that's your problem. Why try to get away from being Jewish? All those motorcycles, and Cincinnati, and Saint Bernard – you have to make it all up. Here, it'd be real for you. You could write and I could join a dig, under Father Gibergue.'

'What about your children?'

'Aren't there kibbutz schools?'

'For Episcopalians?'

She began to cry, out of a kind of sweet excess, as when angels weep. 'I thought you'd like it that I love it here,' she got out, adding, 'with you.'

'I *do* like it. Don't you like it that I like it in Ossining, with you?' As their words approached nonsense, some dim sense of what the words 'holy land' might mean dawned on him. The holy land was where you accepted being. Middle age was a holy land. Marriage.

Back in their room in the Mishkenot, a calling card had been left on a brass tray. Bech looked at the Hebrew lettering and said, 'I can't read this.'

'I can,' Bea said, and turned the card over, to the Roman type on the other side.

'What does it say?'

Bea palmed the card and looked saucy. 'My secret,' she said.

I never should have married a Christian, Bech told himself, without believing it. He was smiling at the apparition of his plump Wasp wife, holding a calling card shaped like a stone in Herod's wall.

Wifely, she took pity. 'Actually, it's somebody from the *Jerusalem Post*. Probably wanting an interview.'

'Oh God,' Bech said.

'I suppose he'll come again,' Bea offered.

'Let's hope not,' Bech said, blasphemously.

Macbech

Bea on her mother's side was a Sinclair, and a long-held dream of hers had been to visit the land of her ancestors – the counties of Sutherland and Caithness in the eastern Scots Highlands. Bech, now legally established in the business of making her dreams come true, and slightly enriched by the sale of a forgotten *Collier's* chestnut to a public-television series promoting Minor Masters of the American Short Story, volunteered to take her there, as a fortieth-birthday present. They parked their crumbling mock-Tudor manse in Ossining and its three juvenile inhabitants with a house-sitting young faculty couple from Mercy College and flew that May to London, entraining north to Edinburgh and thence to Inverness. Bech liked Great Britain, since its decline was as notorious as his, and he liked trains, for the same reason. The farther north they went, the strangely happier he became.

His happiness first hit him in Edinburgh, as he lugged their suitcases up a mountainous flight of stairs from the sunken glass-and-iron sheds of Waverley Station. As he turned on to North Bridge, at the far end of which their hotel waited, his eyes confronted not metropolitan rectangles but a sweeping green shoulder of high and empty land named, Bea read at his straining side from out of her blue guidebook, Arthur's Seat. Burdened by baggage as he was, Bech felt lifted up, into the airy and the epic. Scotland seemed at a glance ancient, raw, grimy, lush, mysterious and mannerly. Like Bech it was built solid of disappointments. Lost causes abounded. Defenders of the Castle were promptly hanged outside the Portcullis Gate, witches were burned in bundles, Covenanters were slaughtered. In Holyrood Palace, the red-haired Queen of the Scots, taller than one had expected, slipped in her brocaded slippers down a spiral stone staircase to visit the handsome boy Darnley, who, devoid of all common sense, one evening burst into her little supper room and, with others, dragged off her pet secretary David Rizzio and left him in the audience chamber dead of fifty-six stab wounds. *The alleged indelible stain of blood, if it exists, is concealed by the floor covering. Jealousy of Rizzio's political influence, and perhaps a darker suspicion in Darnley's mind, were the probable motives for the crime.* Dried blood and dark suspicions dominated the Caledonian past; nothing sinks quicker in history, Bech thought, than people's actual motives, unless it be their sexual charm. In this serene, schizophrenic capital – divided by the verdant cleavage of a loch drained in 1816 – he admired the biggest monument ever erected to an author, a spiky huge spire sheltering a statue of Sir Walter Scott and his dog, and he glanced, along the slanting Royal Mile, down minuscule alleys in the like of which Boswell had caught and clipped his dear prostitutes. 'Heaven,' Bech kept telling Bea, who began to resent it.

But Bech's abrasive happiness grew as, a few days later, the windows of their next train gave on the gorse-blotched slopes of the Grampians, authentic mountains green and grey with heather and turf. In Inverness, they rented a little cherry-red car in which everything normally on the right was on the left; groping for the gear-shift, Bech grabbed air, and peering into the rear-view mirror, saw nothing. Bea, frightened, kept reminding him that she was there, on his left, and that he was driving terribly close to that stone wall. 'Do you want to drive?' he asked her. At her expected answer of 'Oh, no,' he experimentally steered the short distance to Loch Ness; there they stood among the bright-yellow bushes on the bank, hoping to see a monster. The water, dark even in the scudding moments of sunlight, was chopped into little wavelets each shadow of which might be a fin, or a gliding nostril. 'It could be,' Bech said. 'Remember the coelacanth.'

His fair wife touched his arm and shivered. 'Such dark water.'

'They say the peat, draining into it. Tiny black particles suspended everywhere, so all these expensive cameras they lower down can't see a thing. There could be whales down there.'

Bea nodded, still staring. 'It's much bigger than anybody says.'

Married peace, that elusive fauna swimming in the dark also, stole back upon them at the hotel, a many gabled brick Guests beside the pretty river Ness. After dinner, in the prolonged northern light, they wandered across a bridge and came by chance upon a stadium where a show for tourists was in progress: Scots children in kilts performed traditional dances to the bagpipes' keening. The couple loved, when they travelled, all children, having none of their own. Their marriage would always be sterile; Bea had been willing, though nearing the end of her fourth decade, but Bech shied from paternity, with its overwhelming implication of commitment. He aspired to be no more than one of mankind's uncles, and his becoming at a blow stepfather to Bea's twin adolescent girls, Ann and Judy, and to little Donald (who had at first called him 'Mr Bech' and then 'Uncle Henry'), was bliss and burden enough, in the guardian-ship line. His books and in his fallow years his travels were his children, and by bringing Bea along he gave her what he could of fresh ties to the earth. Some of the Scots performers were so small they could barely hop across the swords laid flat on the grass, and some were tugged back and forth in the ritual patterns by their older sisters. Watching the trite, earnest routines, Bea beside Bech acquired a tranced smile; tears had appeared in her blue eyes without cancelling the smile, an unsurprising combination in this climate where sun and shower and rainbow so swiftly alternated. In the sheltered bleachers where they sat they seemed the only tourists; the rest were mothers and fathers and uncles, with children's raincoats in their laps. As Bech and Bea returned to their hotel, the still-twilit sky, full of hastening clouds, added some drops of silver to the rippling river that looked utterly pure, though it was fed by the black loch.

Next day they dared drive left-handedly along the crowded coast road north, through Dingwall and Tain, Dornoch and Golspie. At Dunrobin Castle, a downpour forbade that they descend into the famous formal gardens; instead they wandered unattended through room after panelled room, past portraits and stag horns and framed photographs of turn-of-the-century weekends, the Duke of Sutherland and his stiff guests in white flannels, holding tennis rackets like snowshoes. '*Its name,*' Bech read to Bea from the guidebook, '*may mean "Robin's Castle", after Robert, the sixth Earl of Sutherland, whose wife was a daughter of the barbarous Alexander, Earl of Buchan, a young son of King Robert II and known as the "The Wolf of Badenoch"*'. Now there's *history,*' he said. ' "The barbarous Alexander." The third Duke of Sutherland,' he went on, paraphrasing, 'was the largest land-owner in Western Europe. Almost the whole county of Suther-land, over a million acres. His father and grandfather were responsible for the Clearances. They pushed all these poor potato farmers out so they could graze sheep – the closest thing to genocide in Europe up to Hitler, unless you count the Armenians in Turkey.'

'Well, don't blame me,' Bea said. 'I was just a Sinclair.'

'It was a man called John Sinclair who brought the Cheviot sheep north into Caithness.'

'My mother's branch left around 1750.'

'The Highlanders were looked at the same way the Victorians saw the Africans – savage, lazy, in need of improvement. That's what they called it, kicking the people out and replacing them with sheep. Improvement.'

'Oh look, Henry! Queen Victoria slept in this bed. And she left her little lace gloves.'

The bed had gilded posts but looked hard and small. *Uneasy lies the head.* Bech told Bea, 'You really don't want to face it, do you? The atrocities a castle like this is built on.' He heard his father in him speaking, and closed his mouth abruptly.

Bea's broad maternal face was flustered, pink, and damp in the humidity as rain slashed at the leaded windows overlooking the North Sea. 'Well I hadn't thought to face it *now*, just because I'm a little bit Scotch.'

'Scots,' he corrected.

'The Sinclairs didn't order the Clearances, they were victims like everybody else.'

'They had a castle,' Bech said darkly.

'Not since the seventeenth century,' Bea said back.

'I want to see the Strath Naver,' he insisted. 'That's where the worst of the Clearances were.'

Back in the car, they looked at the map. 'We can do it,' Bea said, her wifely composure restored. 'Go up through Wick and then around John o'Groats and over through Thurso and then down along the Strath Naver to Lairg. Though there won't be much to see, just empty land.'

'That's the point,' Bech said. 'They moved the poor crofters out and then burned their cottages. It was the women, mostly, who resisted. The sheriff's men got drunk and whacked them on the head with truncheons and kicked them in their breasts.'

'It was a terrible, terrible thing,' Bea said, gently outflanking him. Her face looked luminous as harsh rain drummed on the roof of their little red English Ford, where everything was reversed. Her country, his patriotism. Her birthday, his treat. How strange, Bech bothered to notice, that his happiness in Scotland should take the form of being mean to her.

The Sinclairs had farmed, and perhaps a few did still farm, these great treeless fields of Caithness whose emerald sweep came right to the edge of the perilous cliffs. The cliffs, and the freestanding towers the sea had created from a millennial merging of those eroded ravines called gills, were composed of striations of grey sandstone as regular as the pages of a book. Down on the shore, vast, slightly tilted flagstones seemed to commemorate a giant's footsteps into the sea, or to attest to the ruin of a prodigious library. No fence prevented a tourist or a cow from toppling off and hurtling down the sheer height composed of so many accreted, eroding layers; paths had been beaten raggedly parallel to the cliff edge, leading to cairns whose explanatory legend was obscured by lichen and to, in one spot, an unofficial dump, where newspapers and condensed-milk cans had been deposited upon the edge of the precipice but had not all fallen in. Gulls nested just underneath the lip of the turf and in crannies straight down the cliff face; their white bodies, wings extended in flight, speckled the windy steep spaces between the surface of the twinkling sea and the edge where Bech and Bea stood. The plunging perspectives made her giddy, and she shrieked when, teasing, he took a few steps forwards and reached down as if to steal a gull egg. The mother gull tipped her head and peered up at him with an unimpressed pink eye. Bech backed away, breathless. For all his boyish bravado, his knees were trembling. Heights called to him. *Fall. Fly.*

The wind so fierce no trees spontaneously grew in this northernmost county of Britain was a bright May breeze today, setting a blush on Bea's cheeks and flaring Bech's nostrils with the scent of salt spray. The Vikings had come to this coast, leaving ruin behind, and flaxen-haired infants. The houses of the region were low, with roofs of thatch or slate, and squared slabs of ubiquitous flagstone had been set upright and aligned into fences along field boundaries. But the primary feel of this land was of unbounded emptiness, half-tamed and sweet, with scarce a car moving along the A9 and not another walking man or woman to be seen this side of the green horizon, beyond which meadows gave way to brown moors where peat was dug in big black bricks out of long straight trenches, and the emptiness began in earnest. Every cemetery they stopped at had its Sinclairs; Bea was excited to be on ancestral territory, though less ecstatic than she had been in Israel. Bech had felt crowded there, and here, in the many-pocketed tweed jacket he had bought along Princes Street and the droop-brimmed plaid bog hat purchased just yesterday in Wick, he felt at home. 'This is my kind of place,' he told Bea from the cliff edge, his breath regained and his knees again steady.

'You're just paying me back,' she said, 'for liking the Holy Land so much.'

'That was overdeveloped. This is just right. Thousand-acre zoning.'

'You look ridiculous in that hat,' she told him unkindly, uncharacteristically. The wind, perhaps, had whipped a shine into her eyes. 'I'm not sure the jacket suits you, either.'

'They feel great. "Blow, winds, and crack your cheeks!" '

'They give you that troll look.'

'What troll look?'

'That troll look that –'

He finished for her. 'That Jews get in tweeds. Shit. I've really done it. I've married an anti-Semite.'

'I wasn't going to say that at all.' But she never did supply what she had been going to say, and it was not until they were snuggled in their bed on the musty third floor of the Thurso Arms that the monsters in the deep space between them stopped shifting. The little brick city fell away beneath the gauze curtains of their windows like a town in one of the drabber fairy tales. They made love dutifully, since they had been given a double bed. There was no doubt, Bea did resent his taking Scotland so readily – so greedily – into himself. The stones and grass of this place, its pinnacles and cobbles and weatherswept greys, its history of constant, though turbulently contested, loss in relation to the cushioned green land to the south ... weren't the Scots one of the ten lost tribes of Israel? Like the Jews, the Celts had been pushed aside from the European mainstream yet not thrown quite free of it: permitted, rather, to witness closely its ruthless forward roar and to harbour in wry hearts and pinched lives a criticism that became – beyond Spinoza and Hume, Maxwell and Einstein – America. Or so it seemed while Bea slept and Bech lay awake relishing the sensation of being, on the northern edge of this so thoroughly annotated island, in a kind of magical margin, the sky still white though the time approached midnight. From beneath his window arose the unexpected sound of raucous teen-age horseplay, a hungry scuffling and hooting that further enriched his mystical, global sensations. For surely, if Bech's own narrow and narcissistic life was miracle enough to write about, an interlocked miracle was the existence, wherever you went on a map, of other people living other lives.

Except, it seemed, in the Highlands. Often where a place name sprouted on the dotted red line of the road, there seemed to be nothing, not even the ruined walls of a single house. Nothing was left of men but this name on the map, and the patches of brighter green where, over a century ago, potato patches had been fertilized. Otherwise, mile after mile of tummocky brown turf unrolled with no more than an occasional river or lake for punctuation, or one of those purple-green protuberances, neither mountain nor hill, for which the only name could be 'ben'. Bech and Bea had driven west from Thurso above the sea and turned south along the Strath Naver, scene of the most infamous of the Clearances. Atrocity leaves no trace on earth, Bech saw. Nature shrugs, and regroups. Perhaps in Poland there were stretches made vacant like this. There seemed no trace of man but the road itself, which was single-track, with widened spots at intervals where a car could pull over to let another pass. The game did not take long to learn: when two vehicles approached, the drivers accelerated to reach the farthest possible turnout short of collision. Bea maintained that that wasn't the way the game was played at all; rather, drivers courteously vied for the privilege of pulling over and letting the other driver pass with a wave of cheerful gratitude. 'Do you want to drive?' he asked her.

'Yes,' she answered, unexpectedly.

He stopped the car and stepped out. He inhaled the immaculate Highland air. Small white and pink flowers starred the violet reaches of moor. The clouds leaned in their hurry to get somewhere, losing whole clumps of themselves. There were no sheep. These, too, had been cleared away. As Bea drove along, her chin tipped up with the mental effort of not swerving right, he read to her about the Clearances. '*We have no country to fight for. You robbed us of our country and gave it to the sheep. Therefore, since you have preferred sheep to men, let sheep defend you!*' he read, a lump in his throat at the thought of an army of sheep. Jewish humour. 'That's what they said to the recruiters when they tried to raise an army in the Highlands to help fight the Crimean War. The lairds were basically war chieftains, and after the Scots were beaten at Culloden and there was no more war, the crofters, who paid their rent mostly with military service, had nothing to offer. The lairds had moved to London and that nice part of Edinburgh we saw and needed money now, and the way to get money was to rent their lands to sheep farmers from the south.'

'That's sad,' Bea said absently, pulling into a patch of dirt on the left and accepting a grateful wave from the flaxen-haired driver of a rattling old lorry.

'Well, there's a kind of beauty to it,' Bech told her. 'The Duke of Sutherland himself came up from London to see what was the matter, and one old guy stood up in the meeting and told him, *It is the opinion of this county that should the Tsar of Russia take possession of Dunrobin Castle and of Stafford House next term we couldn't expect worse treatment at his hands than we have experienced in the hands of your family for the last fifty years.*' Bech chuckled; he thought of ancestors of his own, evading enlistment on the opposite side of the same war. His mother's people had come from Minsk. History, like geography, excited and frightened him with the enormousness of life beyond his dwindling own.

Bea blinked and asked, 'Why are you so enthusiastic about all this?'

'You mean you aren't?'

'It's sad, Henry. You're not looking at the scenery.'

'I am. It's magnificent. But misery must be seen as part of the picture.'

'Part of *our* picture, you mean. That's what you're rubbing my nose in. You bring me here as a birthday present but then keep reminding me of all these battles and evictions and starvation and greed, as if it applies to *us*. All right. We're mortal. We're fallible. But that doesn't mean we're necessarily cruel, too.' One of the leaning, hurrying clouds was darker than the others and suddenly it began to rain, to hail, with such ferocity that Bea whimpered and pulled the car to a halt in a wide spot. The white pellets danced upwards from the red hood as if sprung from there and not the sky; the frown within the air was like what the blind must confront before the light winks out entirely. Then the air brightened; the hail ceased; and through the luminous mist of its ceasing a rainbow appeared above the shadows of a valley where a cultivated field formed a shelf of smooth verdure. They had come down from the remotest Highlands into an area where cultivation began, and telephone wires underlined the majesty of the subarctic sky. They both climbed out of the little car, to be nearer the rainbow, which, longer in one leg than the other, receded from them, becoming a kind of smile upon the purple-green brow of a ben. Bech luxuriated in the wild beauty all around and said, 'Let's buy a castle and murder King Duncan and settle down. This is where we belong.'

'We do *not*,' Bea cried. 'It's where *I* belong!' He was startled; fear must have shown on his face, for an anxious wifely guilt blurred hers as, close to tears, she still pressed her point: 'That's so *typical* of you writers – you appropriate. My own poor little Scottishness has been taken from me; you're more of a Scot now than I am. I'll have nothing left eventually, and you'll move on to appropriate somebody else's something. Henry, this marriage was a horrible mistake.'

But the sheer horror of what she was saying drove her, her blurred round face pink and white like that of a rabbit, into his arms. He held her, patting her back while her sobs moistened his tweed shoulder and the rainbow quite faded in the gorse-golden sun. She was still trying to explain herself, her outburst. 'Ever since we got married –'

'Yes?' he encouraged, noting above her sunny head that the lower slopes of the mountain, for aeons stark moor, had been planted in regiments of fir trees to feed the paper mills of the south.

'– I've felt myself in your mind, being di*gest*ed, becoming a *char*acter.'

'You're a very real person,' he reassured her, patting mechanically. 'You're my Christian maiden.' In deference to the prickly spine of feminist feeling that she had grown beneath his hands, he quickly amended this to: 'God's Christian maiden.'

Bech Wed

The house in Ossining was a tall mock-Tudor with an incongruous mansard roof, set on a domed lawn against a fringe of woods on an acre and a half tucked somewhere between the Taconic State and the Briarcliff–Peekskill parkways. Its exterior timbers were painted the shiny harsh green of park benches and its stucco had been aged to a friable tan; the interior abounded in draughty wasteful spaces – echoing entrance halls and imperious wide staircases and narrow windowless corridors for vanished servants to scuttle along. Bea and Rodney while their marriage thrived had fixed it up, scraping the white and then, next layer down, the dusty-rose paint off the newel posts and banisters until natural oak was reached; they had replaced all the broken glass and fragmented putty in the little greenhouse that leaned against the library, re-tiled the upstairs bathrooms, re-plastered the backstair walls, and laid down a lilac hedge and a composition tennis court. As their marriage ran into difficulties, the scraping stopped halfway up the left-hand banister and the tennis court was taken over by the neighbourhood children and their honey-limbed baby-sitters. Now Bech was installed in the mansion like a hermit crab tossed into a birdhouse. The place was much too big; he couldn't get used to the staircases and the volumes of air they arrogantly commandeered, or the way the heat didn't pour knocking out of steam radiators from an infernal source concealed many storeys below but instead seeped from thin pipes sneaking low around the baseboards, pipes kept warm by personalized monthly bills and portentous, wheezing visits from the local oil truck. In the cellar, you could see the oil tanks – two huge rust-brown things greasy to the touch. And here was the furnace, an old converted coal-burner in a crumbling overcoat of plastered asbestos, rumbling and muttering all through the night like a madman's brain. Bech had hardly ever visited a basement before; he had lived in the air, like mistletoe, like the hairy sloth, Manhattan subgenus. Though he had visited his sister in Cincinnati, and written his freshest fantasy, *Travel Light*, upon impressions gathered during avuncular visits there, he had never in his bones known before what America was made of: lonely outposts, log cabins chinked with mud and moss.

Insulation was a constant topic of conversation with the neighbours, and that first winter Bech dragged his uprooted crab tail back and forth to the building-supply centre along Route 9 and hauled home in Bea's sticky-geared Volare station wagon great rolls of pink insulation backed by silver paper; with a hardening right hand he stapled this cumbersome, airy material between the studs of an unused and never plastered third-floor room, intended for servants or storage, and made himself, all lined in silver imprinted with the manufacturer's slogans, a kind of dream-image, a surreal distillation, of his cloistered forsaken apartment high above the windswept corner of Ninety-ninth and Riverside. Here, his shins baking in the intersecting rays of two electric heaters, he was supposed to write.

'Write?' he said to Bea, who had proposed this space allocation. 'How do you do that?'

'You know,' she said, not to be joshed. 'It'll all come back to you, now that you're settled and loved.'

His heart, which had winced at 'settled', fled from the word 'loved' so swiftly that he went momentarily deaf. These happy conditions had nothing to do with writing. Happiness was not the ally but the enemy of truth. Dear Bea, standing there in her slightly shapeless housedress, her fair hair straggled out in the dishevelment of utter sincerity, seemed a solid obstacle to the translucent on-running of the unease that was Bech's spiritual element, his punctilious modernist diet. Too complacent in her seventh-hand certainty, descended from Freud, that she held between her soft thighs the answer to all his questions, Bea assumed that the long sterile stretch of his unwed life before her had been, simply, a mistake, a wandering in a stony wilderness cluttered with women and trips. He doubted it was that simple. Being an artist was a matter of delicate and prolonged manoeuvre; who could tell where a false move lay? Think of Proust's, think of Rilke's, decades of procrastination. The derangement of the senses, Rimbaud had prescribed. Didn't all of Hart Crane's debauchery find its reason in a few incandescent lines that burned on long after the sullen waves had closed upon his suicide?

'What you must do,' Bea told him, even as her blue Scots eyes slid sideways towards some other detail of housekeeping, 'is go up there first thing every day and write a certain number of pages – not too many, or you'll scare yourself away. But do that number, Henry, good or bad, summer or winter, and see what happens.'

'Good or bad?' he asked, incredulous.

'Sure, why not? Who can tell anyway, in the end? Look at Kafka, whom you admire so much. Who cares now, if *Amerika* isn't as good as *Das Schloss*? It's all Kafka, and that's all we care about. Whatever you produce, it'll be Bech, and that's all anybody wants out of you. *Mehr Licht; mehr Bech!*'

He hadn't known she knew all this German. 'I don't admire Kafka,' he grumbled, feeling a child's pleasurable restiveness. 'I feel him as an oppressive older brother. He affects me the way his father affected him.'

'What you're doing,' Bea told him, 'is punishing us. Ever since *The Chosen* got panned, you've been holding your breath like an angry baby. Enough now. Finish *Think Big*.'

'I was thinking of calling it *Easy Money*.'

'Good. A much better title. I think the old one intimidated you.'

'But it's about New York. How can I write about New York when you've taken me away from it?'

'All the better,' Bea briskly said, patting her hair in closer to the luminous orb of her face. 'New York was a terrible place for you, you were always letting yourself get sidetracked.'

'Who's to say,' he asked, giving his old aesthetic one more try, 'what a sidetrack is?'

'Simple. It's the one that doesn't lead anywhere. Do what you want with your talent. Hide it under a bushel. I can't stand here arguing forever. From the sounds out back, Donald and his friends are doing something terrible to the dog.'

It was true, Donald and two pals from a house across the lane were trying to play rodeo with Max, a sluggish old golden retriever that Rodney and Bea had bought as a puppy. He had yelped when lassoed and then, as the boys were being scolded, hung his tail, ashamed of having tattled. Bech had never lived in close conjunction with a dog before. He marvelled at the range of emotion the animal could convey with its tail, its ear, and the flexible loose skin of its muzzle. When he and Bea returned from the supermarket or an expedition to the city, old Max in his simple-minded joy would flog the Volare fenders with his tail and, when his new master bent down to pat his head, would slip Bech's hand into his mouth and try to pull him towards the house – retrieving him, as it were. The grip of the dog's teeth, though kindly meant, was firm enough to give pain and to leave livid marks. Bech had to laugh, trying to pull his hand free without injury. Max's muzzle rumpled with fond determination as he kept tugging the stooping, wincing man towards the back door; his ears were rapturously flattened, and cats slid off the porch to rub at Bech's ankles jealously. Cats came with this house, and rodent pets of Donald's that died of escaping from their cages. The three children all had noisy friends, and Bea herself would spend many a morning and afternoon entertaining housewives from the neighbourhood or from Briarcliff Manor or Pleasantville – old friends from the Rodney days, curious perhaps to glimpse the notorious author (in the suburbs, at least since *Peyton Place*, all authors are *sui generis* notorious) whom Bea – *Bea*, of all people – had somehow landed. If these visitors were there for morning coffee, they gave Bech little more than bright-eyed, wide-awake smiles above the crisp dickies stuck in their cashmere sweaters; but if he came upon them amid the lengthening shadows of the cocktail hour, slouched around second drinks in a murky corner of the timbered living room, these Gentile housewives would dart towards him blurred, expectant glances and, merriment waxing reckless, challenge him to 'put' them 'in' a book. Alas, what struck him about these women, in contrast to the women of his travels and of Manhattan, was just their undetachability from these, to him, illegible Westchester surroundings.

Without so many inducements to flee upstairs, Bech might never have settled into his silver room. But it was the one spot in the vast house where he did not seem to be in the middle of a tussle, or a party, or a concert. The twin girls especially could not bear to be out of range of amplified music. They were fifteen when Bech became their stepfather – rather bony, sallow girls with Rodney's broad forehead and solemn, slightly bulging grey eyes. They lolled on the sofa or upstairs in their room reading fat novels of witchcraft and horror in Maine while bathed in the clicking thud and apocalyptic lyrics of reggae. Donald, who had inherited more of Bea's curves and shades of humid pink, was ten, and for a time carried everywhere with him a battery-powered CB unit on which he attempted to chat with truckers rolling north beyond the woods. The sound of traffic, though kept at a distance, neverthless permeated Westchester County, its pitch more sinister, because concealed by greenery, than the frank uproar of Manhattan. Marrying Bea, who had drifted into his life in the wake of her stormy sister, Bech had ignorantly climbed aboard an ark of suburban living whose engines now throbbed around him like those of a sinking merchant ship in Conrad. There was no ignoring noise in these environs. In New York, there were walls, precincts, zones and codes of avoidance; here in Ossining every disturbance had a personal application: the ringing phone was never in someone else's apartment, and the child crying downstairs was always one's own. A kind of siege crackled around the gawky half-green house, so conspicuous on its hillock of lawn – a siege of potentially disastrous groans in the plumbing and creaks in the woodwork, while the encircling animal world gnawed, fluttered, and scrabbled at the weakened structure. Invisible beetles and ants powdered the basement floor with their leavings, and Bech was astonished at how much infiltrating wildlife lurked in even a thoroughly tamed and mortgaged stretch of woods. Squirrels or was it bats danced over his head in the silver room, above the ceiling with its fantasy map of stains, within those dusty constructional gaps that merged with the teeming treetops via holes he could never spot from the ground or a ladder. Even in the summer he kept his room's one window closed against the distracting variety of birdcalls. That second spring a colourless small bird had built a nest in a chink of the eaves of the mansard roof and bewitched Bech with the incessancy of its trips to the nest. A fluffy beating of wings, an arousal of tiny cheeping, a momentary silencing of the cheeping with wriggling food, and then a beating of the wings away again. So much fanatic labour, to add a few mousy birds to the world's jungle. One morning, suddenly, there was silence from the nest; the fledglings had flown. A loneliness enveloped the writer's aerie, with its old army-green desk from Ninety-ninth Street, its tinny electric heaters, its bookshelves of raw pine attached to the studs with screwed-in L-brackets, its cardboard boxes of confused but accumulating manuscript. For Bech had, even before their Scots trip, taken root in his birdhouse; he had accepted Bea's advice and was pecking his way steadily through the ghostly tangle of *Think Big*.

Bech's fourth and, as critical diction has it, 'long-awaited' novel existed in several spurts, or shoals, of inspiration. The first had come upon him in London, during a brief fling with a petite heiress and gossip columnist named Merissa, and took the envisioned form of an ambitious and elegiac novel directed, like *Anna Karenina* and *Madame Bovary*, towards the heroine's suicide. The heroine was to have Merissa's exquisite small bones and feline adaptability but to be squarely, winsomely, self-ruinously American. Her name came to him with an oddness bespeaking a profoundly subconscious imperative, as Olive. Bech managed about sixty handwritten pages, dealing mostly with Olive's education at a Southern girls' college where the stench of horse manure incongruously swept through the curried green campus and the idyllic vista of young women of good family striding to class in smart skirts and high heels. But when it came time in the novel to bring her to that capital of ruined innocence, New York City, he was at a loss for what professional field he should mire her in. The only one he knew first-hand, that of publishing, inspired great distaste in our author when encountered in fiction; he did not much like involution, indeed, whether met in Escher prints, iris petals, or the romantic theme of incest. Yet all those glass boxes weighing on the heart of the city – what was done inside them, what empires rose and fell? He could not imagine. Stalled, Bech let a year slide by as he responded to invitations and filled out questionnaires from doctoral candidates. Then, one iron-cold winter afternoon, with steam pouring lavishly from the radiator valves, Bech to counter his claustrophobia turned on television, and met there a young actress's face uplifted beseechingly towards that of an aseptic-capped doctor, whose soothing baritone yet had a menacing rumble to it. Turning the channel, Bech eavesdropped upon the staccato conversation of two vexed women as they swiftly circulated among the furniture of a Texas-scale living room. Clicking past a channel of electronic ticker tape and another of Spanish sitcom, he found on the third major network a teen-aged girl screaming and snuffling about an abortion while California cliffs soared past the windows of her convertible. Here, Bech realized, was an empire, a kingdom as extensive and mystically ramified as a Chinese dynasty; the giant freckled figure of boyish, ruthless Tad Greenbaum swam into his cerebrum, trailing those of pliant, pill-popping Thelma Stern, Tad's mistress; her diabolical ex-husband, the enigmatic Polonius Stern; and her unscrupulous though insouciant lawyer-brother, Dolf Lessup. A world of searingly lighted soundstages and intimately dark cutting rooms, of men frantically reaching out from within a closed expensive world of glass desks and deep carpets and dim French restaurants towards the unseen millions sitting lonely in shabby rooms, offered itself to Bech as a wilderness sufficiently harsh to memorialize, and one wherein all his ignorances could be filled in with bits from those old Hollywood movies about making Hollywood movies. For some pages, his path lit alternately by klieg lights and *crêpes flambées*, the author moved through this luminous maze, until all lights failed and he went dry again. For the fact was that power, and the battle for it, utterly bored Bech. Then he met Ellen, a Steiner School teacher, and by the glow of her intelligent, unsmiling moon face he revised some of the yellowing old shoals. Olive, his heroine, became Lenore, and not so vulnerable and innocent as when she had been conceived, towards the end of the still-sexist Sixties. Today's young woman would sooner commit murder than suicide. And television soap opera had become, disconcertingly, the rage, a cliché. More trips mercifully intervened. Bech had passed fifty, and his hair had become a startling blob of white in the publicity photographs, and his work in progress, *Think Big*, had been so often mentioned in print that collectors wrote him in some exasperation over their inability to procure a copy. It was this mess of hopeful beginnings, it was this blasted dream, that Bea now ordered him to make come true.

What did she know of art? She had been an honours student at Vassar, majoring in economics. Her father, old Judge Latchett, recently dead, had run the quickest docket in the East. Her sister, the difficult Norma, ill-disguised prototype of Thelma Stern, had had a testy and judgemental tongue. Bea's softness, which had lured him, sheathed an instinctive efficiency; at heart she was still that good child who would check off Toothbrushing, Breakfast, and Toidy on the chart provided before going off each day to school. 'Writing isn't like that,' he protested.

'Like what?'

'Like toothbrushing and breakfast and doing toidy. The world doesn't need it that way.'

She thought, her face in repose round and unsmiling, like that of his character Lenore. '*You* do, though,' she said. 'Need it. Because you're a writer. At least that's what you told me you were.'

Bech ignored the suggestion that he had deceived her, for the many years of their courtship. He pursued his argument: 'To justify its existence writing has to be extraordinary. If it's ordinary it's less than worthless; it's clutter. Go into any bookstore and try to breathe. You can't. Too many words produced by people working every morning.'

'You know,' Bea told him, 'Rodney wasn't that crazy about being a bonds analyst, either. He would have loved to play tennis all day, every day. But up he got, to catch that 7:31, rain or shine; it used to break my heart. I'd hide in bed until he was gone, it made me feel so guilty.'

'See,' Bech said. 'By marrying me, you've freed yourself from guilt.' But every time she brandished Rodney's example at him, he knew that he had given the world of power a hook into his flesh.

'Donald keeps asking me what you *do*,' Bea went on ruthlessly. 'The girls were asked at school if it was true you were insane. I mean, thirteen years without a word.'

'Now you're hurting me.'

'You're hurting *us*,' she said, her face going pink in patches. 'Rodney feels sorry for me, I can tell over the phone.'

'Oh *fuck* Rodney. What do I care about the Rodneys of the world? Why'd you ever leave him if he was so great?'

'He was a pill; but don't make me say it. It's you I love, obviously. Forget everything I said, I *love* it the way you keep yourself pure by never putting pen to paper. There's just one little thing.'

'What's that?'

'Never mind.'

'No, tell me.' He loved secrets, had loved them ever since his father whispered to him that his mother was bad-tempered that day for a reason that had nothing to do with them, and that some day when Henry grew up he would understand. It was not until Bech was about thirty-eight, and lying in bed beside a lovely sleeping girl called Claire, that Bech realized his father had been referring to menstruation.

'We need the dough,' Bea said.

'Oho. Now you're really talking.'

'This is a big house to heat, and they say fuel oil's going to go to a dollar a gallon. And some slates fell off the north side after that big wind last week.'

'Let's sell this barn and move back to the Apple, where the living is easy.'

'You know I would, if it weren't for the children.'

He knew nothing of the kind, but enjoyed making her lie. He enjoyed, indeed, these contentious conversations, bringing out the Norma in Bea, and would have continued had not the front-door bell rung. It was Marcie Flint, another driven veteran of the suburban quotidian, come to compare second marriages over coffee. Bech fled upstairs, past all the tumbled toys and blankets of the children's bedrooms, to his third-floor retreat. He scratched out *Think Big* on page one of his mauled manuscript and penned the words *Easy Money*. He changed his heroine's name back to Olive. Ripe with reckless scorn, he began anew.

As Bech typed, countering with his four-finger syncopation the nervous rustling of the Rodentia overhead, and as spring's chartreuse buds and melting breezes yielded to the oppressive overgrowth of summer, in turn to be dried and tinted according to the latest fall fashions and returned to the frost-bound earth, memories of Manhattan weather washed through him unpredictably, like pangs of bursitis. There, the seasons spoke less in the flora of the hard-working parks than in the costumes of the human fauna, the furs and wool and leather boots and belts and the summer cotton and clogs and in these recent condition-conscious years the shimmering tanktops and super-shorts of the young women who rose up from the surfaces of stone as tirelessly as flowers out of mud. New York was so *sexy*, in memory: the indoorness of it all, amid circumambient peril, and the odd good health imposed upon everyone by the necessity of hiking great distances in the search for taxis, of struggling through revolving doors and lugging bags heavy with cheesecake and grapefruit up and down stairs, the elevator being broken. On this island of primitive living copulation occurred as casually as among Polynesians, while Scarlatti pealed from the stereo and the garbage truck whined its early-morning song two blocks away. Bech remembered, from that cosy long decade of his life before the onset of Claire, how he had gone home from a publishing party with a *Mademoiselle* editor and how in her narrow kitchen her great silvery breasts had spilled from her loosened shantung dress into his hands as simultaneously their

mouths fused in the heat of first kiss and his eyes, furtively
sneaking a look at his surroundings, filled with the orbs of the
glossy red onions hung on a jutting nail above this overflowing
lady's sink. He remembered how Claire, slender as a fish, would
flit naked through the aquarium light of his own rooms as a short
winter day ended outside in a flurry of wet snow collecting flake
by flake on the ridges of the fire escape. She had been studying
dance in those remote days, and in the dimness as Ravel latticed
the air with rhythm could have been practising in a flesh-coloured
leotard but for the vertical smudge of her pubic hair; unlike the
dark triangle that was standard her pussy formed a gauzy little
column as of smoke. Of the mistress succeeding Claire, Bech
entertained fewer nostalgic memories, for she had been Norma
Latchett, now his sister-in-law. Norma occasionally visited them,
dirtying every ashtray in the house with a single lipsticky
cigarette each and exuding a rapacious melancholy that
penetrated to Bech even through the dungeon walls of the kin-
ship taboo that now prevailed between them. Judge Latchett,
having sent so many to their reward, had gone to his, and the
sisters' mother was legally incompetent; so Norma now faintly
stank to Bech of family depressingness, as Wasps know it. It was
the romantic period before Norma that with a sweetness
bordering on pain welled up to flood the blank spaces in his
ragged manuscript; it now seemed a marvel worth confiding that
through those publicly convulsed years under two lugubrious
presidents the nation had contained catacombs of private life.
Bech at his green steel desk retrieved that vast subterrain detail
by detail and interwove the overheard music of a tranced time
with the greedy confusion his characters bred. They were, but
for Olive and some lesser *shikse* mistress, Jewish, and here, in
this house built and repeatedly bought by Protestants, and
presently occupied save for himself by blonds, and haunted by
the tight-lipped ghost of Rodney Cook, Jewishness too became
a kind of marvel – a threadbare fable still being spun, an energy
and irony vengefully animating the ruins of Christendom, a
flavour and guile and humour and inspired heedlessness truly
superhuman, a spectacle elevated the promised Biblical notch

above the rest of the human drama. His own childhood, his Brooklyn uncles and West Side upbringing, he now saw, through the precious wrong end of the telescope, to be as sharp and toy-like as once the redneck motorcycles of the Midwest had seemed, when the telescope was pointed in the other direction. Day by day his imagination caught slow fire and smouldered a few pages to the grey of typescript. He had determined not to rewrite, in his usual patient-spider style, or even to reread, except to check the colour of a character's hair or sports car. Where the events seemed implausible, he reasoned that a novel about Green-baum Productions might legitimately have the texture of a soap opera; where a character seemed thin and unformed, he re-assured himself that later episodes would flesh him out; where a gap loomed, Bech enshrined yet another erotic memory from that past enchanted by the removes of time and his Ossining exile. He cast off as spiritual patrons finicky Flaubert and Kafka and adopted the pragmatic fatalism of those great native slapdashers Melville and Faulkner. Whatever faults he was bundling pell-mell into his opus he saw as deepening his revenge upon Bea. For his uncharacteristic gallop of activity was among other things spiteful – fulfilment of a vow to 'show' her. 'I'll show you!' children would sometimes shout, near tears, beneath his window.

Downstairs, when the day's dizzying flight with the smirched angels of his imagining was over, a brave new domestic world awaited Bech. For lunch he might eat several drying peanut-butter-and-jelly sandwich halves that Donald and a playmate had spurned an hour before. As summer ripened, vegetables from Bea's garden – beans, broccoli, zucchini – might be lying on the butcher-block kitchen counter and could be nibbled raw. That there was great nutritional and moral benefit in raw, home-grown vegetables was one of the Christian notions he found piquant. If Bea was around, she might warm him soup from a can and sit at the round kitchen table and sip some with him. Luncheon meat might be in the refrigerator or not, depending upon the vagaries of her shopping and the predations of Ann's and Judy's boyfriends. It was a contrast of chaos to the provender of

Bech's bachelor days, when the stack of delicatessen salami occupying in lonely splendour the second shelf of his refrigerator went down at the inexorable rate of three slices a day, like a book being slowly read through. Dinner in those days he usually ate out; or else, in the emergency of a blizzard or an irresistible TV special, he heated up a frozen Chinese meal, the heart of the egg roll still deliciously icy. Here, wed, he confronted great formal meals planned by Bea as if to fatten him up for the kill, or else fought for scraps with barbaric adolescents.

Ann's and Judy's boyfriends struck him as a clamorous and odorous swarm of dermatological disasters, a pack of howling wolves clad in the latest style of ragbag prep, their clothes stretching and ripping under the pressure of their growing bodies, their modes of courtship uniformly impossible to ignore, from the demonstrations of football prowess arranged on the September lawn to the post-midnight spin-outs of their parents' Mercedeses on the gravel drive after some vernal dance. The twin girls themselves – Ann a touch more pensive and severe than Judy, Judy the merest shade more womanly than Ann, as if the fifteen minutes by which she had preceded her into the world insured an everlasting edge of maturity – were much at school. Bech was irritably conscious of their presence most during those evenings when, bored by homework, they would collapse together into whispering and giggles, making in the house an everywhere audible, bottomless vortex of female hilarity that fed endlessly upon itself and found fresh cause wherever it glanced. Bech could only imagine that he was somehow the joke, and feared that the entire house and his life with it would be sucked down into their insatiable mirth, so sinisterly amplified by twinnishness. Whereas little Donald, his companion in the error of being male, stirred in him only tender feelings. In the child's clumsy warrior energy he saw himself at heart; standing above the sleeping boy's bed at night, he took the measure of his own grotesque age and, by the light of this dream-flushed, perfect cheek, his own majestic corruption. Donald returned on the pumpkin-coloured school bus around four, and sometimes he and Bech would play catch with a baseball or football, the forgotten motions returning strangely to Bech's shoulders, the rub and whack of leather to his hands. Or, before the fall chill caused the backyard pools to be drained and the tarpaulins tugged into place, the two of them and Bea might go swimming at a neighbour's place to which Bea's old friendship gave them access, and where the hostess would emerge to keep them company and offer them a drink. These old friends of Bea's, named Wryson or Weed or Hake or Crutchman – sharp English names that might have come off the roster of a sailing ship – had their charms and no doubt their passions and disappointments and histories, but seemed so exotic to Bech, so brittle and pale and complacently situated amid their pools and dogwoods and the old Dutch masonry of their retaining walls, that he felt like a spy among them and, when not a silent spy, a too-vigorous, curly-haired show-off. Exquisite and languid as a literary practitioner, he was made to feel among Bea's people vulgar and muscular, a Marx brother about to pull up a skirt or grind out a cigar in a finger bowl. An evening amid such expectations wearied him. 'I don't know,' he sighed to Bea. 'They're just not my crowd.'

'You don't give them a chance,' she said, driving him home along the winding lanes. 'You think just because they don't live in apartment houses and have metal bookcases crammed to the ceilings and grandparents that came from a *shtetl* they're not people. But Louise Bentley, that you met tonight, had something really terrible happen to her years ago, and Johnny Hake, though I know he can get carried away, really *did* pull himself back from the abyss.'

'I don't doubt,' Bech said. 'But it's not my abyss.' Money, for example, as these Wasps possessed it, seemed something rigid and invisible, like glass. Though it could be broken and distributed, acquired and passed on, it quite lacked organic festiveness. Whereas money under Jewish hands was yeasty; it grew and spread and frolicked on the counting table. And their bizarre, Christmassy religion: many of Bea's crowd went to church, much as they faithfully played tennis and golf and attended rallies to keep out developers. Yet their God, for all of his colourful history and spangled attributes, lay above Earth

249

like a whisper of icy cirrus, a tenuous and diffident Other Whose tendrils failed to entwine with fibrous blood and muscle; whereas the irrepressible Jewish God, the riddle of joking rabbis, playing His practical jokes upon Job and Abraham and leading His chosen into millennia of mire without so much as the promise of an afterlife, this God beside whom even the many-armed deities of the Hindus appeared sleek and plausible, nevertheless entered into the daily grind and kibitzed at all transactions. Being among the goyim frightened Bech, in truth; their collective chill was the chill of devils.

He felt easier in downtown Ossining, with its basking blacks and its rotting commercial streets tipped down sharply towards the Hudson and its chunky Gothic brick-and-cornice architecture whispering to Bech's fancy of robber barons and fairy tales and Washington Irving. Washington Heights, he supposed, once looked much as Ossining did now. He had not expected such a strong dark-skinned presence on the streets so far up the Hudson, or the slightly sleepy Southern quality of it all – the vacant storefronts, the idle wharfs, the clapboarded shacks and rusting railroad spurs and Civil War memorials. Throughout the northeastern United States, he realized, there were towns like this, perfected long ago and filled with ice cream and marching music, only to slide into a sunstruck somnolence, like flecks of pyrite weeping rusty stain from the face of a granite escarpment. Ossining, he learned, was a euphemism; in 1901, the village fathers had changed the name from Sing Sing, which had been pre-empted by the notorious prison and long ago had been stolen from the Indians, in whose Mohican language 'Sin Sinck' meant 'stone upon stone'. Stone upon stone the vast correctional facility had arisen; electrocutions here used to dim the lights for miles around, according to the tabloids Bech read as a boy. The coarsely screened newspaper photos of the famed 'hot seat' at Sing Sing, and the movie scene wherein Cagney is dragged, moaning and rubbery-legged, down a long corridor to his annihilation, had told the young Bech all he ever wanted to know about death. He wondered if denizens of the underworld still snarled at one another, 'You'll fry for this', and supposed not. The lights of

Ossining no longer dimmed in sympathy with snuffed-out murderers. The folks downtown looked merry to Bech, and the whole burg on a play scale; he had the true New Yorker's secret belief that people living anywhere else had to be, in some sense, kidding. On that sloping stage between Peekskill and Tarrytown he enjoyed being enrolled in the minor-city minstrelsy; he often volunteered to run Bea's errands for household oddments, killing time in the long dark unair-conditioned drugstore, coveting the shine on the paperbacks by Uris and Styron and marvelling at the copious cosmetic innocence of commercial America. His light-headedness on these away-from-home afternoons strengthened him to burrow on, through that anfractuous fantasy he was weaving among the lost towers of Gotham.

He remembered the great city in the rain, those suddenly thrashing downpours flash-flooding the asphalt arroyos and overflowing the grated sewer mains, causing citizens to huddle – millionaires and their mistresses companionable with bag ladies and messenger boys – under restaurant canopies and in the recessed marble portals of international banks, those smooth fortresses of hidden empery. In such a rain, Tad Greenbaum and Thelma Stern are caught without their limousine. For some time, remember, Thelma has been resolved to leave Tad but dreads and postpones the moment of announcement. The taxis splash past, their little cap lights doused, their back seats holding the shadowy heads of those mysterious personages who find cabs in the worst of weathers: when the nuclear weapons begin to fall, these same shadows will be fleeing the city in perfect repose, meters ticking. Thelma's dainty Delman's, high gold heels each held to her feet by a single ankle strap, become so soaked as she wades through the gutter's black rivulet that she takes them off, and then scampers across the shining tar in her bare feet. No, cross that out, her feet are not bare, she would be wearing pantyhose; with a madcap impulse she halts, beneath the swimming DONT WALK sign, and reaches up into her shantung skirt and peels herself free, disentangling first the left leg, then the right. Now her feet are truly bare. Tomboyishly she, who as the lithe Lessup girl had run wild in the hills of Kentucky, wads the drenched nylon and chucks it overhand into one of those UFO-like trash barrels the filth-beleaguered metropolis provides. Tad, catching up to her, his size thirteen iguana-skin penny loafers still soggily in place, laughs aloud at her reckless gesture. Her gold shoes follow into the bin; his immense freckled baritone rings out into the tumult of water and taxi tyres and squealing hookers caught loitering in their scarlet stretch pants a few doors up Third Avenue with no more for shelter than a MASSAGE PARLOUR sign. 'I – want – *out*,' she suddenly shouts up at him. Her raven hair is pasted about her fine skeletal face like the snake-ringlets of Medusa.

'Out – of – *what*?' Tad thunders back.

Still the pedestrian sign says DONT WALK, though the traffic light on the avenue has turned red. The ghostly pallor of her face, upturned towards his in the streaming rain, takes on an abrupt greenish tinge. 'Out – of – *you*,' she manages to shout at last, the leap of her life, her heart falling sickeningly within her at the utterance; Tad's face looms above her like a blimp, bloated and unawares, his chestnut mop flattened on his wide freckled brow and releasing down one temple a thin tan trickle of the colour-freshener his hair stylist favours. He is just a boy growing old, she thinks to herself, with a boy's warrior brutality, and a boy's essential ignorance. Without such ignorance, how could men act? How could they create empires, or for that matter cross the street?

Their sign has changed from red to white, a blur spelling perilously WALK. Tad and Thelma run across Third Avenue to take refuge in the shallow arcade of a furrier. The street surface is a rippling film; wrappers are bunched at the clogged corner grate like bridesmaids' handkerchiefs. Feeling tar on the soles of her feet and being pelted by rain all the length of her naked calves has released in Thelma an elemental self which scorns Tad and his charge cards and his tax breaks. He, on the other hand, his Savile Row suit collapsed against his flesh and an absurd succession of droplets falling from the tip of his nose, looks dismal and crazed. 'You bitch,' he says to her in the altered acoustics of this dry spot. 'You're not going to pull this put-up-or-shut-up crap again; you know it's just a matter of time.'

Meaning, she supposes, until he leaves Ginger – Ginger Greenbaum, that stubborn little pug of a wife, always wearing caftans and muu-muus to hide her thirty pounds of overweight. Thelma marvels at herself, that she could ever sleep with a man who sleeps with that spoiled and pouting parody of a woman, whose money (made by her father in meat packing) had fed Tad's infant octopus. It seems comic. She laughs, and prods with a disrespectful forefinger the man's drenched shirtfront of ribbed Egyptian cotton. His stomach is spongy; there comes by contrast into her mind that taut body of her slender Olive, their gentle mutual explorations in that exiguous, triangular West Side apartment where the light from New Jersey enters as horizontally as bars of music and overlays with such long shadows the breathing silence of the two intertwined women.

Tad slugs her. Or, rather, cuffs her shoulder, since she saw it coming and flinched; the blow bumps her into a wire burglar-guard behind which a clay-faced mannequin preens in an ankle-length burnoose lined with chinchilla. The rain has lessened, the golden taxis going by are all empty. 'You were thinking of that other bitch,' Tad has shrewdly surmised.

'I was not,' Thelma fervently lies, determined now to protect at all costs that slender other, that stranger to their city; she has remembered how the subtle crests of Olive's ilia cast horizontal shadows across her flat, faintly undulant abdomen. 'Let's go back to your place and get dry,' she suggests.

And Henry Bech in his mind's eye saw the drying streets, raggedly dark as if after a storm of torn carbon paper, and each grate exuding a vapour indistinguishable from leaks of municipal steam. And the birds, with that unnoticed bliss of New York birds, have begun to sing, to sing from every pocket park and potted kerbside shrub, while sunlight wanly resumes and Thelma – all but her sloe eyes and painted fingernails hidden within the rustling, iridescent cumulus of a bubble bath in Tad's great sunken dove-coloured tub – begins to cry. It is a good feeling, like champagne in the sinuses. His own sinuses prickling, Bech lifted his eyes and read the words *Apply this side towards living space* on the aluminium-foil backing of his room's insulation. He turned his attention out the window towards the lawn, where little Donald and a grubby friend were gouging holes in the mowed grass to make a miniature golf course. Bech thought of yelling at them from his height but decided it wasn't his lawn, his world; his world was here, with Tad and Thelma. She emerges from the bathroom drying herself with a russet towel the size of a ping-pong-table top. 'You big pig,' she tells Tad with that self-contempt of women which is their dearest and darkest trait, 'I love your shit.' He in his silk bathrobe is setting out on his low glass Mies table – no, it is a round coffee table with a leather centre and a stout rim of oak, and carved oaken legs with griffin feet – champagne glasses and, in a little silver eighteenth-century salt dish bought at auction at Sotheby's, the white, white cocaine. Taxi horns twinkle far below. Thelma sits – whether in bald mockery of the impending fuck or to revisit that sensation of bare-foot mountain-girl uncontrollability she had experienced on the rainswept street, it would take a psychologist and not a mere novelist to discern – naked on an ottoman luxuriously covered in zebra hide. Each hair is a tiny needle. Bech shifted from buttock to buttock in his squeaking chair, empathizing.

By such reckless daily fits, as seven seasons slowly wheeled by in the woods and gardens of Ossining, the manuscript accumulated: four emptied boxes of bond paper were needed to contain it, and still the world set forth seemed imperfectly explored, a cave illumined by feeble flashlight, with ever more incidents and vistas waiting behind this or that stalagmite, or just on the shadowy far shore of the unstirring alkaline pool. At night sometimes he would read Bea a few pages of it, and she would nod beside him in bed, exhaling the last drag of her cigarette (she had taken up smoking, after years on the nicotine wagon, in what mood of renewed desperation or fresh anger he could not fathom), and utter crisply, 'It's good, Henry.'

'That's all you can say?'

'It's loose. You're really rolling. You've gotten those people just where you want them.'

'Something about the way you say that –'

'Well what am I supposed to do, whoop for joy?' She doused her butt with a vehement hiss in the paper bathroom cup half-full of water she kept by her bedside in lieu of an ashtray, a trick learned at Vassar. 'All those old sugarplums you fucked in New York, do you really think I enjoy hearing about how great they were?'

'Honey, it's *fant*asy. I never knew anybody like these people. These people have money. The people I knew all subscribed to *Commentary*, before it went fascist.'

'Do you realize there isn't a Gentile character in here who isn't slavishly in love with some Jew?'

'Well, that's –'

'Well, that's life, you're going to say.'

'Well, that's the kind of book it is. *Travel Light* was *all* about Gentiles.'

'Seen as hooligans. As barbaric people. How can you think that, living two years now with Ann and Judy and Donald? He just adores you, you know that, don't you?'

'He can beat me at Battleship, that's what he likes. Hey, are you crying?'

She had turned her head away. She rattled at her night table, lighting another cigarette with her back still turned. The very space of the room had changed, as if their marriage had passed through a black hole and come out as anti-matter. Bea prolonged the operation, knowing she had roused guilt in him, and when she at last turned back gave him a profile as cool as the head on a coin. She had a toughness, Bea, that the toughness of her sister, Norma, had long eclipsed but that connubial solitude revealed. 'I've another idea for your title,' she said, biting off the words softly and precisely. 'Call it *Jews and Those Awful Others*. Or how about *Jews and Jerks*?'

Bech declined to make the expected protest. What he minded most about her in these moods was his sense of being programmed, of being fitted tightly into a pattern of reaction; she wanted, his loving suburban softy, to *nail him down*.

Frustrated by his silence, she conceded him her full face, her eyes rubbed pink in the effort of suppressing tears and her mouth a blurred cloud of flesh-colour sexier than any lipstick. She put an arm about him. He reciprocated, careful of the cigarette close to his ear. 'I just thought,' she confessed, her voice coming in little heated spurts of breath, 'your living here so long now with me, with *us*, something nice would get into your book. But those people are so vicious, Henry. There's no love making them tick, just ego and greed. Is that how you see us? I mean us, people?'

'No, no,' he said, patting, thinking that indeed he did, indeed he did.

'I recognize these gestures and bits of furniture you've taken from your life here, but it doesn't seem at all like me. This idiotic Ginger character, I hate her, yet sometimes whole sentences I know I've said come out of her mouth.'

He stroked the roundness of the shoulder that her askew nightie strap bared, while her solvent tears, running freely, released to his nostrils the scent of discomposed skin moisturizer. 'The only thing you and Ginger Greenbaum have in common,' he assured her, 'is you're both married to beasts.'

'You're not a beast, you're a dear kind man –'

'Away from my desk,' he interjected.

'– but I get the feeling when you read your book to me it's a way of paying me *back*. For loving you. For marrying you.'

'Who was it,' he asked her, 'who told me to do a few pages a day and not worry about *le mot juste* and the capacity for taking infinite pains and all that crap? Who?'

'Please don't be so angry,' Bea begged. The hand of the arm not around her shoulders and holding a cigarette, the hand of the arm squeezed between and under their facing tangent bodies, found his dormant prick and fumblingly enclosed it. 'I love your book,' she said. 'Those people are so silly and wild. Not like us at all. Poor little Olive.'

His voice softened as his prick hardened. 'You talk as though this was the first time I've ever written about Jews. That's not so. *Brother Pig* had that union organizer in it, and there were even rabbis in *The Chosen*. I just didn't want to do what all the

others were doing, and what Singer had done in Yiddish anyway.'

She snuffled, quite his Christian maiden now, and burrowed
her pink nose deeper into the grizzly froth of his chest while her
touch lower down took on a quicksilver purity and slidingness.
'I have a terrible confession to make,' she said. 'I never got
through *The Chosen*. It was assigned years ago in a reading group
I belonged to up here, and I tried to read it, and kept getting
interrupted, and then the group discussed it and it was as if I
had read it.'

Any guilt Bech might have been feeling towards her eased.
Claire had read *The Chosen*; it had been dedicated to her. Norma
had read it twice, taking notes. He rolled across Bea's body and
switched off the light. 'Nobody who did read it liked it,' he said
in the dark, and kneeled above her, near her face.

'Wait,' she said, and dunked her cigarette with a sizzle.
Something like a wet smoke ring encircled him; tightened,
loosened. What beasts we all are. What pigs, Thelma would say.
I love your shit.

Bea found him a typist – Mae, a thirty-year-old black woman
with an I BM Selectric in a little ranch house the colour of faded
raspberries on Shady Lane; there was a green parakeet in a cage
and a small brown child hiding behind every piece of furniture.
Bech was afraid Mae wouldn't be able to spell, but as it turned
out she was all precision and copy-editing punctilio; she was in
rebellion against her racial stereotype, like a Chinese rowdy or
an Arab who hates to haggle. It was frightening, seeing his
sloppily battered-out, confusingly revised manuscript go off and
come back the next weekend as stacks of crisp prim typescript, with a carbon on onionskin and a separate pink sheet
of queried corrigenda. He was being edged closer to the dread
plunge of publication, as when, younger, he would mount in a
line of shivering wet children to the top of the great water slide
at Coney Island – a shaky little platform a mile above turquoise
depths that still churned after swallowing their last victim – and
the child behind him would nudge the backs of his legs, when
all Bech wanted was to stand there a while and think about it.

'Maybe,' he said to Bea, 'since Mae is such a whiz, and must need the money – you never see a husband around the place, just that parakeet – I should go over it once more and have her retype.'

'Don't you dare,' Bea said.

'But you've said yourself, you loathe the book. Maybe I can soften it. Take out that place where the video crew masturbates all over Olive's drugged body, put in a scene where they all come up to Ossining and admire the fall foliage.' Autumn had invaded their little woods with its usual glorious depredations. Bech had begun to work in his insulated room two springs ago. Spring, summer, fall, winter, spring, summer, fall: those were the seven seasons he had laboured, while little Donald turned twelve and Ann, so Judy had tattled, lost her virginity.

'I loathe it, but it's you,' Bea said. 'Show it to your publisher.'

This was most frightening. Fifteen years had passed since he had submitted a manuscript to The Vellum Press. In this interval the company had been sold to a supermarket chain who had peddled it to an oil company who had in turn, not liking the patrician red of Vellum's bottom line, managed to foist the firm off on a West Coast lumber-and-shale-based conglomerate underwritten, it was rumoured, by a sinister liaison of Japanese and Saudi money. It was like being a fallen woman in the old days: once you sold yourself, you were never your own again. But at each change of ownership, Bech's books, *outré* enough to reassure the public that artistic concerns had not been wholly abandoned, were reissued in a new paperback format. His long-time editor at Vellum, dapper, sensitive Ned Clavell, had succumbed to well-earned cirrhosis of the liver and gone to that three-martini luncheon in the sky. Big Billy Vanderhaven, who had founded the firm as a rich man's plaything in the days of the trifling tax bite and who had concocted its name loosely out of his own, had long since retired to Hawaii, where he lived with his fifth wife on a diet of seaweed and macadamia nuts. A great fadster, who had raced at Le Mans and mountain-climbed in Nepal and scuba-dived off Acapulco, 'Big' Billy – so called sixty years ago to distinguish him from his effete and once socially prominent cousin, 'Little' Billy Vanderhaven – had apparently cracked the secret of eternal life, which is Do Whatever You Please. Yet, had the octogenarian returned under the sponsorship of that Japanese and Saudi money to take the helm of Vellum again, the effect could have been scarcely less sensational than Henry Bech turning up with a new manuscript. Bech no longer knew the name of anyone at the firm except the woman who handled permissions and sent him his little cheques and courtesy copies of relevant anthologies, with their waxen covers and atrocious typos. When at last, gulping and sitting down and shutting his eyes and preparing to slide, he dialled Vellum's number, it was the editor-in-chief he asked for. He was connected to the snotty voice of a boy.

'You're the editor-in-chief?' he asked incredulously.

'No I am not,' the voice said, through its nose. 'This is her secretary.'

'Oh. Well could I talk to her?'

'May I ask who is calling, please?'

Bech told him.

'Could you spell that, please?'

'Like the beer but with an "h" on the end like in "Heineken".'

'Truly? Well aren't we boozy this morning!'

There was a cascade of electronic peeping, a cup-shaped silence, and then a deep female voice saying, 'Mr Schlitzeh?'

'No, no. Bech. B-E-C-H. Henry. I'm one of your authors.'

'You sure are. Absolutely. It's an honour and a pleasure to hear your voice. I first read you in Irvington High School; they assigned *Travel Light* to the accelerated track. It knocked me for a loop. And it's stayed with me. Not to mention those others. What can I do for you, sir? I'm Doreen Pease, by the way. Sorry we've never met.'

From all this Bech gathered that he was something of a musty legend in the halls of Vellum, and that nevertheless here was a busy woman with her own gravity and attested velocity and displacement value. He should come to the point. 'I'm sorry, too.' he began.

'I *wish* we could get you in here for lunch some time. I'd love to get your slant on the new format we've given your reprints. We're just crazy about what this new designer has done, she's *just* out of the Rhode Island School of Design, but those stick figures against those electric colours, with the sateen finish, and the counterstamped embossing –'

'Stunning,' Bech agreed.

'You know, it gives a *un*ity; for me it gives the shopper a handle on what *you* are all about, you as opposed to each individual title. The salesmen report that the chains have been really enthusiastic: some of them have given us a week in the window. And that ain't just hay, for quality softcover.'

'Well, actually, Mrs – Miss? – Miz? –'

'Doreen will do fine.'

'It's about a book I'm calling.'

'Yess?' That was it, a single spurt of steam, impatient. The pleasantries were over, the time clock was running.

'I've written a new one and wondered whom I should send it to.'

The silence this time was not cup-shaped, but more like that of a liqueur glass, narrow and transparent, with a brittle stem.

She said, 'When you say you've written it, what do you mean exactly? This isn't an outline, or a list of chapters, you want us to bid on?'

'No, it's finished. I mean, there may be some revisions on the galleys –'

'The first-pass proofs, yess.'

'Whatever. And as to the bid, in the old days, when Big – when Mr Vanderhaven was around, you'd just take it, and print it, and pay me a royalty we thought was fair.'

'Those *were* the old days,' Doreen Pease said, permitting herself a guffaw, and what sounded like a puff on her cigar. 'Let's get our dominoes all in line, Mr Bech. You've finished a manuscript. Is this the *Think Big* you mention in interviews from time to time?'

'Well, the title's been changed, tentatively. My wife, I'm married now –'

'I read that in *People*. About six months ago, wasn't it?'

'Two and a half years, actually. My wife had this theory about how to write a book. You just sit down –'

'And do it. Well of course. Smart girl. And you're calling me to ask who to send it to? Where's your agent in all this?'

He blushed – a wasted signal over the phone. 'I've never had one. I hate people reading over my shoulder.'

'Henry, I'm cutting my own throat saying this, but if I were you I'd get me one, starting now. A book by Henry Bech is a major development. But if you want to play it your way, send it straight here to me. Doreen Pease. Like the vegetable with an "e" on the end.'

'Or I could bring it down on the train. I seem to live up here in Westchester.'

'Tell me where and we'll send a messenger in a limo to pick it up.'

He told her where and asked, 'Isn't a limo expensive?'

'We find it cuts way down on postage and saves us a fortune in the time sector. Anyway, let's face it, Henry: you're top of the line. What'd you say the title was?'

'*Easy Money*.'

'Oh yesss.'

The hiss sounded prolonged. He wondered if he was tiring her. 'Uh, one more thing, Miss Pease, Doreen. If it turns out you like it and want to print it –'

'Oh, Christ, I'm sure we'll want to, it can't be that terrible. You're very sweetly modest, Henry, but you have a name, and names don't grow on trees these days; television keeps coming up with so many new celebrities the public has lost track. The public is a conservative animal: that's the conclusion I've come to after twenty years in this business. They like the tried and true. You'd know that better than I would.' She guffawed; she had decided that he was somehow joshing her, and that all her worldly wisdom was his also.

'What I wanted to ask,' Bech said, 'was would I be assigned an editor? My old one, Ned Clavell, died a few years ago.'

'He was a bit before my era here, but I've heard a ton about him. He must have been a wonderful man.'

'He had his points. He cared a lot about not splitting infinitives or putting too much vermouth into a martini.'

'Yess. I think I know what you're saying. I'm reading you, Henry.'

She was? He seemed to hear her humming; but perhaps it was another conversation fraying into this line.

'I think in that case,' Doreen decided, 'we better give you over to our Mr Flaggerty. He's young, but very brilliant. *Very*. And sensitive. He knows when to *stop*, is I think the quality you'll most appreciate. Jim's a delicious person, I *know* you'll be *very* happy with him.'

'I don't have to be *that* happy,' Bech said, but in a burble of electronic exclamations their connection was broken off. Neither party felt it necessary to re-place the call.

The limo arrived at five. A young man with acne and a neo-Elvis wet look crawled out of the back and gave both Ann and Judy, who crowded into the front hall, a lecherous goggle eye. Bech began to fear that he was guarding treasure, with these blooming twins. Rodney, their biological father, after a period of angry mourning for his marriage, had descended into the mid-Manhattan dating game and exerted an ever feebler paternal presence. He showed up Sundays and took Donald to the Bronx Zoo or a disaster movie, and that was about it. The only masculine voices the children heard in the house belonged to Bech and the old man who came in a plastic helmet to read the water meter. But now that his book was submitted and, as of November, 'in the works', the homely mock-Tudor house tucked against the woods no longer felt like a hermitage. Calls from Vellum's publicity and production departments shrilled at the telephone, and a dangerous change in the atmosphere, like some flavourless pernicious gas, trickled through the foundation chinks into the heated wastes spaces of their home: Bech, again a working author, was no longer quite the man Bea had married, or the one his stepchildren had become accustomed to.

Vellum Press (the 'The' had been dropped during a streamlining operation under one of its former corporate owners) had its offices on the top six floors of a new Lexington Avenue skyscraper and lacteal white of ersatz-ivory piano keys; the architect, a Romanian defector famous in the gossip press for squiring the *grandes dames* of the less titled jet set, had used every square inch of the building lot but given the skyline a fillip at the top, with a round pillbox whose sweeping windows made the publisher's offices feel like an airport control tower. When Bech had first published with Vellum in 1955, a single brownstone on East Sixty-seventh Street had housed the operation. In those days Big Billy himself, ruddy from outdoor sport, sat enthroned in a leather wing chair in what had been two fourth-floor maid's rooms, the partition broken through. He would toy with a Himalayan paper-knife and talk about his travels, his mountain-climbing and marlin-fishing, and about his losing battle with the greed and grossly decayed professional standards of printers. Bech enjoyed these lectures from on high, and felt exhilarated when they were over and he was released to the un-dogmatic, ever fresh street reality of the ginkgos, of the polished nameplates on the other brownstones, of the lean-legged women in mink jackets walking their ornamentally trimmed poodles. Ned Clavell's office had been a made-over scullery in the basement; from its one narrow window Bech could see these same dogs lift a fluffy hind leg, exposing a mauve patch of raw poodle, and daintily urinate on the iron fencing a few yards away. Ned had been a great fusser, to whom every page of prose gave a certain pain, which he politely tried to conceal, or to explain with maximum politeness, his hands showing a tremor as they shuffled sheets of manuscript, his handsome face pale with the strain of a hangover or of language's inexhaustible imperfection. His voice had had that hurried briskness of Thirties actors, of Ronald Colman and George Brent, and meticulously he had rotated his grey, brown, and blue suits, saving a double-breasted charcoal pinstripe for evening wear. A tiny gold rod had pressed the knot of his necktie out and the points of his shirt collar down; he wore rings on both hands, and had never married. Bech wondered now if he had been a homosexual; somehow not marrying in those years could seem a simple inadvertence, the omission of a dedicated man. 'Piss off, you bitch!' he used to blurt out, from beneath his pencil-line moustache, when one of the poodles did its duty; and it took years for Bech to realize that Ned did not mean the dog but the woman with taut nylon ankles who was overseeing the little sparkling event. Yet Ned had been especially pained by Bech's fondness for the earthier American idioms, and they spent more than one morning awkwardly bartering tits, as it were, for tats, the editor's sharpened pencil silently pointing after a while at words he took no relish in pronouncing. Dear dead Ned: Bech sensed at the time he had his secret sorrows, his unpublished effusions and his unvented appetites, but the young author was set upon his own ambitions and used the other man as coolly as he used the mailman. Now the man was gone, taking his decent, double-breasted era with him.

Through the great bowed pane of Mr Flaggerty's office the vista of the East River and of Queens' waterfront industrial sheds was being slowly squeezed away by rising new construction. Flaggerty also was tall, six three at least, and the hand he extended was all red-knuckled bones. He wore blue jeans and an open-necked shirt of the chequered sort that Bech associated with steelworkers out on their bowling night. He wondered, *How does this man take his authors to restaurants?* 'It's super Doreen is letting me handle you,' Flaggerty said.

'I've been told I'm hard to handle.'

'Not the way I hear it. The old-timers I talk to say you're a pussycat.'

This young man had an uncanny dreamy smile and seemed content to sit forever at his glass desk smiling, tipped back into his chair so that his knees were thrust up to the height of his stacked In and Out baskets. His lengthy pale face was assembled all of knobs, melted together; his high brow especially had a bumpy shine. His desk top looked empty and there was no telling what he was thinking as he gazed so cherishingly at Bech.

Bech asked him, 'Have you read the book?'

'Every fucking word,' Flaggerty said, as if this was unusual practice.

'And –?'

'It knocked me out. A real page-turner. Funny *and* gory.'

'You have any suggestions?'

Flaggerty's wispy eyebrows pushed high into his forehead, multiplying the bumps. 'No. Why would I?'

'The language didn't strike you as – a bit rough in spots?' One of Ned Clavell's favourite phrases.

This idea seemed doubly startling. 'No, of course not. For me, it all worked. It went with the action.'

'The scene with Olive and the video crew –'

'Gorgeous. Raunchy as hell, of course, but with, you know, a lot of crazy tenderness underneath. That's the kind of thing you do so well, Mr Bech. Mind if I call you Henry?'

'Not at all. Sock it to me, Jim.' Bech still had not got what he wanted – an unambiguous indication that this fellow had pondered the manuscript. He had the strange sensation, talking to Flaggerty, that his editor had not so much read the book as inhaled it: that Bech's book had been melted down and evaporated in these slice-of-pie-shaped offices and sent into the ozone to join the former contents of aerosol cans. Here, in Vellum's curved and pastel halls, languidly drifting young women in Vampira make-up outnumbered any signs of literary industry; the bulletin boards were monopolized by tampon and lingerie ads torn out of magazines, with all their chauvinistic implications under-lined and annotated in indignant slashing felt-tip. Flaggerty's walls were white and mostly blank, but for a grainy blowup of Thomas Wolfe about to board a trolley car. Otherwise they might be sitting in a computer lab. Bech asked him, 'How do you like the title?'

'*Easy Money?*' So he had got that far. 'Not bad. Might confuse people a little, with all these how-to-get-rich-in-the-coming-crash books on the market.'

'The original title was *Think Big*, but I found it hard to work under. I couldn't get going really until my wife told me to scrap the title.'

'*Think Big*, huh?' Flaggerty's eyes, deep in their sockets of bone, widened. 'I like it.' They were beryl: an acute pale cat colour. 'Don't you?'

'I do,' Bech admitted.

'It comes at you a little harder somehow. More *zap*. More subliminal leverage.'

Bech nodded. This tall fellow for all his languor and rural costume talked Bech's language. They were in business.

BECH IS BACK! was to be the key of the advertising campaign. Newspaper ads, thirty-second radio spots, cardboard cutouts in the bookstores, posters showing Bech as of over a decade ago and Bech now. *Fifteen Years in the Making* was a subsidiary slogan. But first, nine months of gestation had to be endured, while proofs languished in the detention cells of book production and jacket designs wormed towards a minimum of bad taste. Back in Ossining, Bea was frantic over the loss of Ann's virginity. If only it had been Judy, she explained, she wouldn't be so shocked; but Ann had always been the good one, the A student, the heir to Rodney's seriousness.

'Maybe that's why,' Bech offered. 'It takes some seriousness to lose your virginity. Always flirting and hanging out with the cheerleaders like Judy, you get too savvy and the guys never lay a glove on you.'

'Oh, what do you know? You've never had daughters.'

'I had a sister,' he said, hurt. 'I had a twenty-one-year-old mistress once.'

'I bet you did,' Bea said. 'Typical. You're just the kind of thing Rodney and I hoped would never happen to our girls.'

The twins were seventeen. They would be eighteen on Valentine's Day. The deflowerer, if Judy could be believed, was one of the speckled crowd crunching around in the driveway with their fathers' cars. 'I don't see that it's any big deal,' Bech said. 'I mean, it's a peer, it's puppy love, it's not rape or Charles Manson or anybody. Didn't I just read in a survey somewhere that the average American girl has had intercourse by around sixteen and a half?'

'That's with everybody figured in,' Bea snapped. 'The ghettos and Appalachia and all that. If I'd wanted my girls to be ghetto statistics I would have moved to a ghetto.'

'Listen,' Bech said, hurt again. 'Some of my best ancestors grew up in a ghetto.'

'Don't you *understand*?' Bea asked, her face white, her lips thinned. 'It's a de*file*ment. A woman can never get it *back*.'

'What would she do with it if she could get it back? Come on, sweetie. You're making too fucking much of this.'

'Easy for you to say. Easy for you to say anything, evidently. Do you think this would have happened if that book of yours hadn't been in the house, all that crazy penthouse sex you cooked up out of your own sordid little flings?'

'I didn't know Ann had read it.'

'She didn't have to. She heard us talking about it. It was in the air.'

'Oh, please. It doesn't take a book of mine to put sex in the air.'

'No, of course not. Don't blame books for anything. They just sit there behind their authors' grins. You act as though the world is one thing and art is another and God forbid they should ever meet. Well, my daughter's virginity has been sacrificed, as I see it, to that damn dirty book of yours.'

Bech had never seen Bea like this before, raging. What frightened him most were her eyes, unseeing, and the mouth that went on, a machine of medium-soft flesh that could not be shut off. This face that had nested in every fork of his body floated like some careening gull in the wind of her fury, staring red-rimmed at him as if to swoop at the exposed meat of his own face. 'Jesus,' he offered with mild exasperation. 'The kid is seventeen. Let her fuck if that's what she wants.'

'It's *not* what she wants, how could she want one of those awful boys? She *does*n't want it, that's the point; what she wants is to show *me*. Her mother. For leaving her father and screwing you.'

'I thought it was Rodney who left.'

'Oh, don't be so literal, you know how these things are. It takes two. But then my taking up with you, so quickly really, in that house on the Vineyard that time, and the way we've been here, so h-happy with each other' – her face was going from white to pink, and drifting closer to his – 'I never thought of how it must

267

look to them. The children. Especially the girls. Don't you see, I've made them face what they shouldn't have had to face so early, their own mother's' – now her face was on his shoulder, her breath hot on his neck – 's-sexuality! And of *course* they hate it, of *course* they want to do self-destructive things out of spite!' He was in her grip, no less tight for her being grief-stricken. As her storm of remorse worked its way through Bea's fragile, Christian nervous system, tough, Semitic Bech, dreamer and doer both, author of the upcoming long-awaited *Think Big*, pondered open-eyed the knobbed and varnished and lightly charred mantel of their fieldstone fireplace. Above it there was an oil painting, with a china-blue, single-clouded sky, of a clipper ship that Bea's maternal great-grandfather had once captained, depicted under full sail and cleaving a bottle-green sea as neatly crimped by waves as an old lady's perm; upon it, two phallic clay candlesticks, one by Ann and one by Judy, executed by the twins in some vanished summer's art camp at Briarcliff and now by consecrated usage set on either end of the mantelpiece; beside it, a fishing rod with broken reel that Donald had chosen to lean forever in the corner where the fieldstones met the floral-wall-papered wall. Bourgeois life: its hooks came in all sizes.

He patted Bea's back and said, 'And for all this you blame me?'

'Not you, *us*.'

Like Adam and Eve. The first great romantic image, the Expulsion. The aboriginal trinity of producer, advertiser, and consumer. This woman's fair head was full of warping myths. Her sobbing had become its own delicious end, a debauchery of sorts, committed not with him but with Rodney's ghost, to the accompaniment of spiritual stride piano played by that honorary member of many a Jew-excluding organization, Judge R. Austin Latchett.

Tad slugs her. Bech looked around for cold water, and threw some. 'What about birth control?' he asked.

Bea looked up out of her tear-mottled face. 'What about it?'

'If the kid's humping, she better have it or you'll really have something to cry about.'

Bea blinked. 'Maybe it was only one time.'

Bech flattened a tear at the side of her nose, tenderness returning. 'I'm afraid it's not something you do only once. You get hooked. Have you ever talked to the girls about all this?'

'I suppose so,' Bea said vaguely. 'I know at school they took hygiene ... It's *hard*, Henry. For a long time they're so young it wouldn't make any sense and then suddenly they're so old you assume they must know it all and you'd feel foolish.'

'Well, there're worse things than feeling foolish.' It was hard for him, on his side, to believe that this woman needed his advice, his wisdom. The music of female mockery, and of its Southern cousin female adulation, had played in his ears for five decades; so it was hard for him to hear this shy wifely tune, this gentle halting request for guidance in a world little more transparent in its fundamental puzzles to female intuition than to male. 'You must talk to her,' Bech advised firmly.

'But how can I let her know I know anything without betraying Judy?'

The prototypical maze, Bech remembered reading somewhere, was the female insides. He tried to be patient. 'You don't have to let her know. Just tell her as an item of general interest.'

'Then I should be talking to them both at the same time.'

She had a point there, he admitted to himself. Aloud he said, 'No. In this area being a twin doesn't count anymore. You can imply to Ann you've had or will have the same conference with Judy, but for now you want to talk privately with *her*. Listen. The girl must know she's gotten in deep, she *wants* to hear from her mother. She's not going to grill you about what you know or how you know.'

The more persuasively he talked, the more slack and dismayed her expression grew. 'But what do I say ex*act*ly, to start it off?'

'Say, "Ann, you're reaching an age now when many girls in our society enter into sexual relations. I can't tell you I approve, because I don't; but there are certain medical options you should be aware of." '

'It doesn't sound like me. She'll laugh.'

'Let her. She's a little girl inside a woman's body. She's

269

suddenly been given the power to make a new human life out of her own flesh. It's more frightening than getting a driver's licence. She's more frightened than you are.'

'How do you know so much?'

'I'm a man of the world. People are my profession.'

A new thought struck Bea. 'Don't boys like that use things?'

'Well, they used to, but in this day and age I expect they're too spoiled and lazy. They don't like that snappy feeling.'

'But if I begin to talk contraception with her so calmly, it amounts to permission. I'm saying it's *fine*.' Panic squeezed this last word out thin as a wire.

'Well, maybe it is fine,' he said. 'Think of Samoa. Of Zanzibar. Western bourgeois civilization, don't forget, is a momentary aberration in the history of *Homo sapiens*.'

She heard the impatience of his tone, his boredom with wedded worry and wisdom. 'Henry, I'm sorry. I'm being stupid. It's just I'm so scared of doing the wrong thing. For some reason I can't think.'

'Well,' he began in a deep voice, for the third time. 'It's easy to give advice where it's not your own life and death. On the matter of my book, you were very hard-headed.'

'And you resent it,' she pointed out, dry-eyed at last.

After this fraught discussion of sexuality, it seemed to Bech, Bea pulled back, she who had once been so giving and playful, so honestly charmed to find this new, hairier, older, more gnarled and experienced man in her bed. Now when at night, finished reading, he turned off his light and experimentally caressed her, she stiffened at his touch, for it interrupted her inner churning. Even under him and enclosing him, she felt absent. 'What are you thinking about?' he would ask.

It would be as if he had startled her awake, though the whites of her eyes gleamed sleeplessly in the Ossining moonlight. Sometimes she would confess, blaming herself for both the girl's sin and this its frigid penance, 'Ann.'

'Can't you give it a rest?'

'God in Heaven, I wish I could.'

At Vellum, lanky laconic Flaggerty had a young female

assistant, a quick black-haired girl fresh from Sarah Lawrence, and Bech wondered if it was her hands that showed in the Xeroxes the firm sent him of his galley sheets. Whoever it was had held each sheet flat on the face of the photocopier, and in the shadowy margins clear ghosts of female fingers showed, some so vivid a police department could have analysed the fingerprints. Bech inspected these parts of disembodied hands with interest; they seemed smaller, slightly, than real hands, but then womanly smallness, capable of Belgian embroidery and Romanian gymnastics, is one of the ways by which the grosser sex is captivated. He looked through the photocopied fingers for the hard little ghost of a wedding or engagement ring and found none; but then she might have been employing only her right hand.

At last Bea did take Ann aside, on an evening when Judy was working late on the senior yearbook, and they had their conversation. 'It was just as you predicted,' Bea told Bech in their bed. 'She wasn't angry that I seemed to know, she seemed relieved. She cried in my arms, but she wouldn't promise to stop doing it. She isn't sure she loves the boy, but he's awfully sweet. We agreed I'd make an appointment with Doctor Landis to get her fitted for a diaphragm.'

'Well then,' he said. 'After all that fuss.'

'I'm sorry,' Bea apologized. 'I know I've been distracted lately. You want to make love now?'

'In principle,' Bech said. 'But in practice, I'm beat. Donald made me bowl six strings with him over at Pin Paradise and my whole shoulder aches. Also I thought I'd take the train into town tomorrow.'

'Oh?'

'There're some things I want to go over on the galleys with Flaggerty. It's better if we can hash it out right there, and I want to be sharp. He's deceptive – all lazy and purring and next thing he's at your throat.'

'I thought you said he never had any suggestions. Unlike that other editor you had years ago.'

'Well, he didn't, but now he's developing some. I think he was babying me before, since I'm a living legend.'

'O K, dear. If you say so. Love you.'

'Love you,' Bech echoed, preparing to fold his mind into a dark shape, a paper airplane to be launched with a flick from the crumbling cliff of consciousness.

But Bea broke into his dissolution with the thought, spoken aloud towards the ceiling, 'I worry now about what Judy will say. Somehow I don't think she'll approve. She'll think I've been too soft.'

His sweet suburban softy, Bech thought sibilantly, and slept.

At his suggestion next day Flaggerty introduced him to his assistant. 'Arlene Schoenberg,' Flaggerty said, stooping in his shirt of mattress ticking like some giant referee overseeing a jump-off between two opposing players at a midget basketball game. The girl was small, slender, and sleek, with hair in a Lady Dracula fall, a chin one centimetre longer than strictly necessary, and sable eyes fairly dancing, in their web of sticky lashes, with delight at meeting Henry Bech.

'Mr Bech, I've admired you for *so* long –'

'I feel like old hat,' Bech finished for her.

'Oh, *no*,' the girl said, aghast.

'So you tote bales for Mr Jim here,' Bech said.

'Arlene has all the moves,' Flaggerty said, shuffling, about to blow the whistle.

Bech had held on a half-second longer than necessary to her hand. Her dear small busy clever hand. It was much whiter than in the Xeroxes, and decidedly pulsing in his.

He glided back to Ossining as the early-winter dusk enwrapped the signal lights, the grudged wattage of the station platform, the vulnerable gold of the windows of homes burning in the distance, all softened by the tentative wet beginnings of a snowfall. His head and loins were light with possibility merely, for Flaggerty had taken him to lunch at a health-food restaurant where no liquor was served and, when they had returned, Arlene Schoenberg was absent on a crosstown errand. Bech drove his old Ford – only thirty-three thousand miles in eighteen years of ownership – home through the cosmic flutter. He was met by a wild wife. Bea pulled him into the downstairs bathroom so she could impart her terrible new news. 'Now Judy wants one too!'

'One what?' Bea's eyes, after his brooding upon Arlene's dark, heavily lashed ones all through the lulling train ride, looked so bald and blue, Bech had to force himself to feel there was a soul behind this doll's stare.

'One *dia*phragm!' Bea answered, putting the lid hard on her desire to scream. 'I asked her if she was making love to anybody and she said No and I told her they couldn't fit one in with her hymen intact and she said she broke hers horseback-riding years ago, and I just have no idea if she's lying or *not*. She was *aw*fully cocky, Henry; I know now I did the wrong thing with Ann, I *know* it.' Bea uttered all this in a choked tearful rush; he had to hug her, there in the downstairs bathroom, the smallest room in the big house.

'You did the right thing,' he had to say, for she had followed his advice.

'But why did Ann have to run right away and *tell* her?' Bea asked, betrayed.

'Bragging,' Bech offered, already bored. He felt this woman's mind narrowing in like the vortex in a draining bathtub towards an obsession with her daughters' vaginas. There must be more to life than this. He asked Bea, 'What would Rodney have done in this situation?'

It was the wrong name to invoke. 'This situation wouldn't have *hap*pened if Rodney were still here,' Bea said, making little fists and resting them on Bech's chest in lieu of thumping him.

'Really?' he asked, wondering whether this could be so. Rodney had gone from being a pill and a heel to become *in absentia* the very principle of order – the clockwork God of the Deists, hastily banished by the Romantic rebellion. 'Could he really have stopped the girls from growing up?'

Bea's face was contorted and clouded by a rich pink veil of mourning for Rodney. Beyond a certain age, women are not enhanced by tears. Bech shrugged off her absent-minded grip upon him and snapped, 'Here's a simple solution. Tell Judy she has to go out and get fucked first before you'll buy her a diaphragm.'

Get a diaphragm the old-fashioned way, ran through his mind. *Earn it.* He left her weeping in the tiny room with its honourable solid turn-of-the-century plumbing and surveyed the weather from the bay windows. It was snowing hard now, thick as a ticker-tape parade. The mass of woods behind the house was toned down almost out of sight, and in the near foreground the spherical aluminium bird-feeder suspended from the old grape arbour swung softly back and forth like a bell buoy in a whispering white sea. Donald was outside trying to toboggan already on the fresh-fallen inch, and the twin girls were huddled giggling on the long orange sofa in the TV den, which had been intended a hundred years ago as a library. On its shelves Bech's books still waited to be integrated with the books already there. Rodney had been a history buff, and collected books on sailing. The girls' faces looked feverish with secrets. Their giggling stopped when Bech loomed in the doorway. 'Why don't you two little angels,' he asked them, 'stop giving your mother a hard time with your nasty little cunts?'

'Fuck you, Uncle Henry,' Judy managed to get out, though their four grey eyes stared in fright.

Rather than wax more ogreish, he climbed the stairs to his silver room and read proof for the hour before dinner. Mortimer Zenith, a minor character who took on an unexpected menace and dynamism in the third chapter, is outlining to poor fat, battered, snuffly, alcoholic Ginger Greenbaum the potential financial wonders of a divorce. Mortimer, too, has his designs on the lovely Olive, once he gets his own game show, which he is hoping Ginger will back, once she gets her share of Tad's money. Ginger, muddled and despairing though she is, cannot quite imagine life without Tad, whose scorn and long absences are somewhat mitigated by the afternoon consolations of Emilio, the young Filipino horsetrainer on their newly acquired Connec-ticut estate. What caught Bech's eye as he wrote, and now as he rewrote on proof, was the light at the great windows of the Greenbaum penthouse, while Mort and Ginger murmur and car horns – he crossed out 'twinkle' – bleat ever more urgently ten storeys below. The sky has sifted out of its harsh noon cobalt a kind of rosy brown banded behind the blackening profiles of the skyscrapers, here and there a cornice or gargoyle flaming in the dying light from the west. Rush hour, once again. Bech suddenly sees a pigeon alight on the sill outside, causing both scheming, curried heads to turn around simultaneously. At his own window, the outdoors was an opaque grey blanket. Individual pellets of snow ticked at the icy panes, like a tiny cry for help. Downstairs, a trio of female voices was lifted in pained chorus, chanting the scandal of Bech's brief exchange with the twins. The front door slammed as Donald came in frozen, his voice loud with complaint at the toboggan's performance Happiness was up here, as the tendrils of emendation thickened along the margins and the electric heaters glazed Bech's shins with warmth. He glanced again at his window and was surprised not to see a pigeon there, with its cocked head and Chaplin-tramp style of walking, beady eye alert for a handout. *Tick. Tick.* Blizzards are ideal for doing proof, he thought. Socked in. Byrd at the South Pole. Raleigh in the Tower.

The storm felt sexy, but beneath the goosedown puff Bea whimpered to him, 'I'm sorry, sweetie. This thing with the girls has exhausted me. Judy and Ann and I had a big cry about everything but it still all feels so up in the air.' Wind softly whirred in the chimney of their bedroom fireplace, with its broken damper. Gently his hand sought to tug up the flannel of her nightie. 'Oh, Henry, I just *can't*,' Bea pleaded. 'After all this upset I just feel *dirty* down there.' When her breathing slowed to a sleeper's regularity, and the house sighed in all its walls as the storm cuffed its frame with rhythmic airy blows, Bech in his meteorological rapture masturbated, picturing instead of his own thick hand that small, dark, dirty xeroxed one.

The snow descended for forty-eight hours, and they were snowbound for another two days. The pack of pimply wolves attracted to this house by Ann and Judy's pheromones assembled now not in their fathers' cars but on cross-country skis and in one especially well equipped case on a Kawasaki snowmobile; the boys, puffed up by parkas to the size of that cheerful monster made out of Michelin tyres, clumped in and out of the front hall, tracking snow and exhaling steam. Bea's immediate neighbours, too, tracked in and out, swapping canned goods and tales of frozen pipes and defrosted food lockers. The oral tradition in America was not quite dead, it seemed, as sagas of marooned cars, collapsed gazebos, and instant Alps beside the ploughed parking lots downtown tumbled in. The worst privation in Ossining appeared to be the few days' non-delivery of *The New York Times*; withdrawal symptoms raged at breakfast tables and beset stolid bankers as they heaved at the snow in their driveways, recklessly aware of bubbles of ignorance in their bloodstreams that might reach their hearts. All day long, while feathers whipped from the spines of drifts and children dug tunnels and golden retrievers bounded up and down in the fluff like dolphins, people in hushed tones discussed the scandal of it, of being without the *Times*. Television stations flashed pictures of the front page, to reassure outlying districts that it was still being published, and the *Citizen Register* (serving Ossining, Briarcliff, Croton, Buchanan, Cortlandt) expanded its World/Nation section, but these measures only underlined the sense of dire emergency, of being cut off from all that was real. Bech retreated from the *Times*less hubbub to his silver-lined room, adding tendrils to his proofs like a toothpicked avocado pit sending down roots into a water glass. For the first time, he began to think he might really have something here. Maybe he really was back.

The gestation period of nine months dictated that *Think Big* be a summer book, and that helped it; it didn't have to slug it out with that muscle-bound autumnal crowd of definitive biographies or multi-generational novels with stark titles like *Lust* or *Delaware* and acknowledgement pages full of research assistants, nor with their hefty spring sisters, the female romancers and the feminist decriers of the private life. *Think Big* in its shiny aqua jacket joined the Popsicles and roller coasters, baseball games and beach picnics as one of that summer's larky things; 'it melts in your mouth and leaves sand between your toes,' wrote the reviewer for the *East Hampton*

Star. 'The squalid book we all deserve,' said Alfred Kazin in *The New York Times Book Review*. 'A beguilingly festive disaster,' decreed John Leonard in the daily *Times*. 'Not quite as *vieux chapeau* as I had every reason to fear,' allowed Gore Vidal in the *New York Review of Books*. 'Yet another occasion for rejoicing that one was born a woman,' proclaimed Ellen Willis in the *Village Voice*. 'An occasion for guarded wonder,' boomed Benjamin De Mott in *Partisan Review*, 'that puts us in grateful mind of Emerson's admonition, "Books are the best of things, well used; abused, among the worst."' 'An occasion,' proposed George Steiner in the *New Yorker*, 'to marvel once again that not since the Periclean Greeks has there been a configuration of intellectual aptitude, spiritual breadth, and radical intuitional venturesomeness to rival that effulgence of middle-class, *Mittel*-European Jewry between say, Sigmund Freud's first tentative experiments with hypnosis and Isaac Babel's tragic vanishing within Stalin's Siberian charnel houses.'

People simply opined, 'A blast, if you skip the scenery,' and featured Bech and Bea repairing their grape arbour in his-and-hers carpenter coveralls. Even before the sparkling notices came rolling in, the fair-weather flags had been up. Bech was photographed by Jill Krementz, caricatured by David Levine, and interviewed by Michiko Kakutani. The Book-of-the-Month Club made *Think Big* its Alternate Alternate choice for July, with a Special Warning to Squeamish Subscribers. Bantam and Pocket Books engaged in a furious bidding of which the outcome was a well-publicized figure with more zeros than a hand has fingers. 'Bech Is *In*!' *Vogue* splashed in a diagonal banner across a picture of him modelling a corduroy coat and a ribbed wool turtleneck. 'Bech Surprises' was *Time*'s laconic admission in a belated follow-up piece, they having ignored *Think Big* during publication week in favour of a round-up of diet cook books. What surprised Bech, that remarkably fair summer, was seeing his book being read, at beaches and swimming pools, by lightly toasted teenagers and deep-fried matrons and even by a few of his male fellow commuters during his increasingly frequent trips to New York. To think that those shuttling eyes were consuming the delicate, febrile interplay of Tad and Thelma, or of Olive and Mort, or of Ginger and her Filipino, while lilacs droopy with bloom leaned in at the open upper half of the stable door and the smell of oats mingled with human musk – the thought of it embarrassed Bech; he wanted to pluck the book from its readers' hands and explain that these were only his idle dreams, hatched while captive in Sing Sing, unworthy of their time let alone their money.

Having taken Donald swimming one day at the pool of Bea and Rodney's old club, Bech saw a bronze and zaftig young woman on a plastic-strap chaise holding the book up against the sun, reading it through her rhinestone-studded sunglasses. 'How's it going?' he asked aloud, feeling guilty at the pain he must be giving her – the squint, the ache in her upholding arm. She lowered the book and stared at him, dazed and annoyed; it was as if he had awakened her. He saw from the tightening of her zinc-white lips that she made no connection between the world she had been immersed in and this stocky, woolly male intruder in outmoded plaid trunks, and that if he did not instantly move away she would call for the lifeguard. Yet she had an appealing figure, and must have an emptiness within, which his book was in some sense filling. He was his own rival. He came to flinch at the sight of his aqua jackets; they were as vivid to his sensitized sight as swimming pools seen from an airplane. He had filled the world with little distorting mirrors. *Think Big* was in its sixth printing by September, and Big Billy telegraphed in congratulation from Hawaii, GROW OLD ALONG WITH ME THE BEST IS YET TO COME.

He couldn't even take Arlene Schoenberg to lunch in an unprestigious Italian restaurant without some nitwit asking him to sign a scrap of paper – usually one of those invitations to a 'health club' staffing topless masseuses that are handed out all over sordid midtown. Every time an autograph-seeker approached, it put more stardust in Arlene's eyes and set seduction at another remove. The world, by one of those economic balancings whereby it steers, had at the same time given him success and taken from him the writer's chief asset, his privacy.

Her little fascinating hands enticingly fiddled with her knife and fork, caressed her Campari-and-soda, and dropped to her lap. After a moment, like an actress taking a curtain call, one of them returned into sight to scratch with a fingernail at an invisible itch on the side of her slightly long chin. She asked him where he got his ideas, from real life or out of his imagination. She asked him if he thought a writer owed anything to society or just to himself. She asked him if he had always been such a neat typist and good speller; now, her little brothers and sisters, none of them could spell, it was really shocking, you wonder if there will be any books at all in twenty years, the terrible way it's going. Bech told her that credit for his typing and spelling should go to Mae, a dark genius his wife had found for him in Ossining. In an attempt to steer Miss Schoenberg's fascination away from his professional self, he talked a good deal about his wife. He gave Bea credit for finally settling him down in front of a typewriter and getting him to finish his book. He further confessed, putting the intimacy level up a notch, that when he had married her he had not realized what a worrier she was: she had seemed, in contrast to her difficult sister, Norma, so calm and understanding, so, well, motherly. And indeed she had proved motherly: she thought about her kids all the time, and nearly went wild when one of her daughters began to – Bech hesitated, for this starstruck minx was also somebody's daughter, and the word 'fuck' or 'screw', running ahead as a kind of scout, might startle her into a defensive posture – 'misbehave', he said. As he spoke, the house in Ossining, with its dome-shaped lawn and coarse green exoskeleton and cool silver-lined retreat, became uncomfortably real. The storm windows were only half up. Some insulation needed to be taped and restapled in his study. Bech wondered if the magic appeal of those Xeroxed hands, haunting the edges of his duplicated galleys, might not have been a mirage peculiar to that cloistered environment. Certainly Miss Schoenberg, as she sat perkily across from him in her sparrow-coloured sweater, gave signs of being common.

'It must be terribly exciting to be a writer's wife,' she said. 'I mean, she must never know what you're thinking.'

'Oh, I expect she knows as much as she wants to.'

'I mean, when you look at her, she must feel she's being X-rayed. You write about women so well, she must feel naked.'

Campari-and-soda always gave Bech the same sensation as swallowing aspirin: that burny feeling at the top of the oesophagus. Thinking of naked, he stared glumly at Arlene's thready sweater and found it utterly opaque. Did she have breasts in there, or typewriter spools? She was wearing a thin gold chain which nobody had ripped off her neck yet. And she was going on, 'Writers have such rich fantasy lives, I think that's what makes them so fascinating to women.'

'Richer, you think, than, say, Mr Flaggerty's fantasy life?'

It was an inspired stab. She said petulantly, 'Oh *him*, all he fantasizes about is the Mets and then the Jets. Really. And where to get good Mexican brown like they used to groove on at college when he was picketing the ROTC and marching with Dylan and all that.'

'You seem,' Bech ventured, 'to know him pretty well.'

For the first time, her eyes lost their starry celebrity shine and submitted to an amused and sexual narrowing. 'Well enough. He's a good boss. I've had worse.'

Bech nostalgically wished he were back home raking the lawn. But Arlene Schoenberg was just getting relaxed, her shapely hands deftly twirling green fettucini on to a fork. The restaurant skills of New York women: like praying mantises roving the twigs of a creosote bush. He should have had more Gothamesque eating-out in his book. And the way the tables are moving out into the streets, into the soot. His silence brought a slow smile to Arlene's face, showing a provocative rim of gum. 'See,' she said. 'I have no idea what you're thinking.'

'I was wondering,' he told her, 'if there was a way we could get Vellum to pay for this lunch. Can you forge Flaggerty's signature, or aren't you that friendly yet?'

Her eyes became solemn bright circles again. 'Oh, no.'

'OK, then. On me. What else can I do for you?'

'Well' – she absent-mindedly, tuggingly fiddled up a loop into her gold chain and squeezed her finger in it so that the tip turned bright red – 'that brother I was telling you about, you know, *did* want me to ask you if you could possibly talk to his seventh-grade class, it's a special school for dyslexics out towards Glen Cove, they'd be *so*, you know –'

Bech saw his opportunity and took it. He patted her bare hand as it lay distracted on the checked tablecloth. 'I'd like to,' he told her, 'but I can't. The last time I spoke in a school I got involved in a disastrous affair with a woman who only cared about the literary me. She spurned the man. Wasn't that rotten of her?'

'I'd have to know the circumstances,' Arlene Schoenberg prudently said, as if there had never been a sexual revolution, and pulled back her hand to cope further with the fettucini.

On the walk from the restaurant back to the Vellum offices, they passed the Doubleday window, which held a pyramid of *Think Big*s. Bech always pitied his books, seen in a bookstore; they looked so outnumbered. He had sent them forth to fight in inadequate armour, with guns that jammed. These unbought copies were beginning to fade and warp in the daily slant of sun. On the train home, he saw how many of the yellowing trees were already bare. Soon it would be a year since he had finished the book Bea had got him to sit down and write. Their household had changed: the girls were off at college, Ann at MIT and Judy at Duke, and little Donald no longer wanted his stepdad to take him places. Each fall they used to go to one Ossining High School football game together, played by mostly black players on a field where you could smell the torn earth and hear each cheerleader's piping voice fragile against the sky. This year the boy, newly thirteen, had looked disdainful and begged off. His father's snobbery was welling up through his genes. Rodney had taken Donald instead to the Harvard – Princeton game, at Palmer Stadium.

The house crackled in its timbers and joints, now that the furnace was on again and a heat differential applied torque. Workmen were busy inside the house and out; since Bech's book had made a million dollars, the north face of the mansard roof was being given new slates and the grand front staircase was being fully refinished, after ten years of a half-scraped left-hand banister. The television crew of *Sixty Minutes* had come and rearranged all the furniture, exposing how shabby it was. Within the many rooms Bech had been somewhat avoiding Bea; she wanted mostly to talk about their household expenditures, or to complain that Donald kept climbing on the roofers' scaffolding after they had gone for the day. 'He has these horrible new delinquent friends, Henry. With Ann and Judy off I thought we'd be so relaxed now.'

'How did that ever work out, by the way, with the diaphragms?'

She looked blank. If there was one thing Bech resented about women, it was the way they so rapidly forgave themselves for the hysteria they inflicted on others. He prompted, 'You remember, Judy wanted one too, but she was still a virgin ...'

'Oh. Yes. Didn't I tell you? It was very simple, I don't know why we didn't think of it. Doctor Landis fitted Ann for one, and then gave me a prescription for two the same size. After all, they *are* twins.'

'Brilliant,' Bech sighed.

'Sweetie, could you spare a minute and look at these Sloane's catalogues with me? What I'd like to do around the fireplace is get sort of a conversation-pit feeling without having it look like a ski lodge. Do you think boxy modern looks silly on a big Oriental?'

The hinges of his jaw ached with a suppressed yawn. 'I think,' he said, 'the room looks nice enough now.'

'You're not focusing. The staircase being all new and shiny shows everything else up. If it's the cost you're worried about, Sheila Warburton says with things so unsettled in the Middle East *any* Oriental you buy is a better investment than stocks, than gold –'

'I love those old wing chairs,' Bech said. In the evenings he would sit in one, his feet up on an inverted bushel basket that was meant to hold wood, and read; he was reading Thomas Mann on Goethe, Wagner, Nietzsche, Schopenhauer, and Freud these nights. What chums they all turned out to have been!

'Those chairs were Rodney's mother's, and he really should have them back now that he has a bigger apartment.'

'Bea, you know we don't *have* the million dollars yet, it's just a bunch of bits in Vellum's computer. I won't get my first royalties till next August.'

'That was another thing Sheila Warburton said: you were crazy not to ask for a whopping advance, with inflation the way it is.'

'*Damn* Sheila Warburton, and that pompous Paul as well. Nobody knew the book would take off like this. In the old days a respectable author *never* asked for an advance; that was strictly for the no-talents starving down in the Village.'

Standing contemplative in her room of imagined furniture, Bea was hard to rattle. She slowly woke to his tone of indignation and came and embraced him. She had been raking leaves in an unravelling ski sweater that smelled muskily of leafmould and lank autumn grass. 'But these aren't the old days, Henry,' she said, tickling his ear with her breath. 'It costs a fortune to live down in the Village now. And you aren't the old Henry, either.' She shuddered in happiness, and in her spasm gave him a squeeze. 'We're all so *proud* of you!'

If there was another thing Bech resented about women it was the way they enveloped – the way they yearned, at moments of their convenience, to dissolve the sanitary partition between I and Thou. Assimilation, the most insidious form of conquest. He was becoming a shred of leafmould. 'I don't know about that book.' he began.

'The book is wonderful,' she interrupted, with breathy impatience. 'When do we do another?'

'Another?' The thought sickened him. A whole new set of names to invent, a theme to nurture within like a tumour, a texture to maintain page after page ... His suburban softy, his plot of earth, was insatiable.

'Sure,' Bea said briskly, backing off. 'The storm windows are up, you've done all the publicity the media can stand, you've said the same things to twenty different interviewers, what are you going to do with your days?'

'Well, there've been some invitations to read at colleges. Some little agricultural college in West Virginia sounded interesting, and an Indian school in South Dakota –'

'Oh you've *done* all that,' Bea said. 'You don't need to go expose yourself for peanuts any more, or fuck those little coeds in the Ramada Inn. Don't think I don't know really why you did all that speaking.' Her sideways glance was both hostile and flirtatious, a common marital combination.

And he resented female knowingness, its coy invasion, its installation of an *Oberführer* in every province of his person. His mind, body, mouth, genitals – Bea had possessed them all and set up checkpoints along every escape route. His 'triumph' (to quote *Vogue* again) was more deeply hers than his; that night in bed, when she insisted on copulating, it was, he felt, with the body of her own triumphant wifeliness that she came to climax, cooing above him and then breaking into that ascending series of little yips that had the effect, on this occasion at least, of swallowing up his own climax as something relatively trivial. More and more Bea favoured the female-superior position. As the air in the bedroom seasonally cooled, she kept on her nightie, becoming in the dark a tent of chiffon and lace and loose blonde hair, an operatic apparition whose damp grip upon him was swaddled and unseen as she pulled him up forcefully into manhood, into achievement, into riches and renewed fame, into viscid fireworks and neural release. She collapsed on to his chest panting.

'I feel so satisfied with you,' she confided.

'And I with you,' he responded, trusting the formal grammar to shade his inevitable and as it were pre-shaped rejoinder.

She heard the shadow. 'Aren't you pleased?' she asked. 'Not only about the book but about *us*? Tell me.'

'Yes, I'm pleased. Of course.'

'You were such a sad person then, Henry.' Then. Before their marriage had infiltrated every cell and extracted daily wordage and nightly semen.

'I was?'

'*I* thought so,' Bea said. 'You used to frighten me. Not just sad. Other things, too. A lovely man, but, I don't know, sterile. You're so sweet with Donald.'

Her arm across his chest was wonderfully heavy. He felt pegged down, and the image of Donald was another luminous nail. 'We get along,' he admitted. 'But the kid's growing up.'

Bea would not allow even so faint a discord to be the final note. 'He loves you,' she uttered, and as she slept he could see by moonlight that a smile remained on her face, rounding the cheek not buried in the pillow.

In his dream he is free. The landscape seems European – low grey sky, intense green fields, mud underfoot, churned and marked by tyre treads and military boots. He has escaped from somewhere; fear is mixed sourly with his guilt, guilt at having left all those others behind, still captive. Yet in the meantime there are the urgencies of escape to cope with: dogs pursuing him are barking, and a hedge offers a place to hide. He squeezes in, his heart enormous and thumping. Candy wrappers litter the ground underfoot. The hedge is too wintry and thin; he will be discovered. In that thick grey European wool overhead, a single unseen bomber drones. It is, he instinctively knows, his only hope, though it will bring destruction. He awakes, and recognizes the drone as the furnace, floors below. The neighbourhood dogs have been harrying something, a raccoon perhaps, and downstairs Max had sleepily joined in with a gruff bark or two. Yet terror and guilt were slow to drain from Bech's system.

That afternoon, Bea had to pick up Donald after school and take him to the orthodontist and then to buy some school clothes; he had outgrown last year's. The child's smile had sprouted touching silver bands, and the first few pimples, harbingers of messy manhood, marred the skin that had once seemed perfect. They would not be home until six at the earliest. Bech roamed the great house with a vague sense of having lost something, a Minotaur restless in his maze. Around four, the doorbell rang. He expected to open it upon a UPS deliveryman or one of Bea's Ossining sipping companions; but the woman on the porch was Bea's sister, Norma Latchett.

Where middle age had brought out Bea's plumpness, it had whittled Norma down, making her appear even more stringy, edgy, and exasperated than formerly. Her dark hair was turning grey and she was not dyeing it but pulling it back from her brow severely. Yet her black wool suit was smart, her lipstick and eye shadow were this fall's correct shade and amount, and across her face, when it proved to be he who opened the door, flickered all the emotions of a woman first alarmed by and then measuring up to judgement by a former lover. 'Where's Bea?' she asked.

Bech explained, and invited her in to wait until six or so.

Norma hesitated, clutching her pocketbook and looking slightly too trim, like the Avon lady. 'I'm heading north to give a talk in Poughkeepsie and thought I'd say hello. Also I have some papers for Bea to sign. You two never come to the city any more.'

'Bea hates it,' Bech said. 'What are you giving your talk about? Come in, for heavens sake. Just me and Max are here, and we aren't biting today.'

'Oh, the usual thing,' Norma said, looking vexed but entering the great varnished foyer. Since the workmen had done the refinishing it gleamed like the cabin of a yacht. 'Those awful icons.' For years, Norma had held jobs off and on in museums, and in these last ten years, as hope of marriage faded, had put herself seriously to school, and become an expert on Byzantine and Russian Orthodox art. Icons becoming ever more 'collectible', she included bankers as well as students in the audience for her expertise. She lit a cigarette whose paper was tinted pale green, and looked switchily about for an ashtray.

'Let's go into the living room,' Bech said. 'I'll build a fire.'

'You don't have to entertain me, I could push on to Vassar and make the art department chairman give me dinner. Except I hate to eat before I talk, the blood all rushes to your stomach and makes you very stupid.'

'I don't think anything could make you *very* stupid,' he said gallantly, remembering as he followed her in past the pompous staircase how her body concealed surprising amplitudes – her hips, for instance, were wide, as if the pelvic bones had been spread by a childbirth that had never occurred, and so that her thighs scarcely touched, giving her a touching knock-kneed look, naked or in a bathing suit. He took three of the logs he had split last winter in hopes that the exercise would prolong his life, and laid a fire while she settled into one of the wing chairs, his favourite, the one covered in maroon brocade, that he usually read in. The match flared. The crumpled *Times* caught. The pine kindling began to crackle. He stood up, asking, 'Tea?' His heart was thumping, as in last night's dream. The house in all its rooms held silent around them like the eye of a storm. Max padded in, claws clicking, and dropped himself with a ponderous sigh on the rug before the quickening flames. One golden eye with a red lower lid questioned Bech before closing. 'Or a real drink?' Bech pursued. 'I'm not sure we have white crème de menthe. Bea and I don't drink that much.' Norma had, he remembered, a fondness for vodka stingers, for Black Russians, for anything whose ingredients one was likely not to have.

'I never drink before I talk,' she said sharply. 'I'm wondering, if I'm going to stay, if I should bring my slides in from the car. You leave them in a cold car too long, they sometimes crack in the heat of the projector.'

As Bech retrieved the grey metal box from the trunk of her car, Max trotted along with him, letting one of Norma's tyres have his autograph and running a quick check on the woodchuck trying to hibernate underneath the porch. In returning, Bech closed the front door on the dog's rumpled, affronted face. Three's a crowd.

The slides tucked safely beneath her chair, beside her outsize alligator purse, Norma asked, 'Well. How does it feel?'

'How does what feel?' This time her cigarette was violet in tint. They must come mixed in the box, like gumdrops.

'Having pulled it off.'

'What off ?' The nylon sheen of her ankles picked up an orange glimmer from the fireplace flames; her eyes held wet and angry sparks.

'Don't play dumb,' she said. 'That book. She got you to make a million. Busy Bea, buzz, buzz.'

'She didn't get me to do anything, it just happened. Is happening. They say there's going to be a movie. Sure you don't want any tea?'

'Stop being grotesque. Sit down. I have your chair.'

'How can you tell?'

'The look on your face when I sat here. It didn't just happen, she's bragging all the time about how she got you your little *room*, and told you to write a few pages every *day*, and keep going no matter how *rot*ten it was, and how now the money's rolling in. How does it feel, being a sow's ear somebody's turned into a silk purse?'

He had thought they might trade a few jabs with the big gloves on; but this was a real knife fight. Norma was furious. The very bones in her ankles seemed to gnash as she crossed and recrossed her legs. 'Did you read the book?' Bech mildly asked her.

'As much as I could. It's lousy, Henry. The old you would never have let it be published. It's slapdash, it's sentimental, it's *cosy*. That's what I couldn't forgive, the cosiness. Look how everybody loves it. You know that's a terrible sign.'

'Mm,' he said, a syllable pressed from him like a whistle from the chimney, like a creak from the house.

'I don't blame you; I blame Bea. It was she who forced it out of you, she and her cosy idea of marriage, to make a monument to herself. What if the monument *was* made of the bodies of all your old girl friends, *she's* the presiding spirit, she's the one who reaps the profit. Top dog. Bea always had to be top dog. You should have seen her play tennis, before she got so fat.' Norma's eyes blazed. The demons of vengeance and truth had entered this woman, a dazzling sight.

'Bodies of old girl friends –?' Bech hesitantly prompted.

'Christ, Henry, it was a pyre. Smoke rising to heaven, to the glory of big fat Bea. Thanks by the way for calling me Thelma, so all my friends can be sure it's me.'

'Thelma wasn't exactly ...' he began. And, thinking of Bea herself, her soft body in bed, the way her eyelids and nose looked rubbed and pink when she was sad or cold, he knew that the rebirth and growth of *Think Big* weren't quite as Norma had described them, making something sudden and crass out of all those patient months spent tapping away amid the tree-tops and the flying squirrels. Still, she put the book in a fresh harsh light, and a fresh light is always liberating. 'Bea *is* pleased about the money,' he admitted. 'She wants to refurnish the entire house.'

'You bet she does,' Norma said. 'You should have seen the way she took over the dollhouse my parents had meant for both of us. She's greedy, Henry, and materialistic, and small-minded. Why does she keep you out here with these ridiculous commuters? The real question is, Why do you permit it? You've always been weak, but weak in your own way before, not in somebody else's. I guess I better have tea after all. To shut me up.' She pinched her long lips tight to dramatize and turned her head so her profile looked Pre-Raphaelite against the firelight. Some strands of her hair had strayed from severity, as if a light wind were blowing.

He perched forward on the lemon-coloured wing chair and asked, 'Didn't you at least like the part where Mort Zenith finally gets Olive alone in the beach cabaña?'

'It was cranked oút, Henry. Even where it was good, it felt cranked out. But don't mind me. I'm just an old discarded mistress. You've got Prescott and Cavett with you and they're the ones that count.'

In the barny old kitchen, its butcher-block counter-tops warping and its hanging copper pans needing Brillo, the tea water took forever to boil: Bech was burning to get back to his treasure of truth, arrived like an arrow in Ossining. He was trembling. Dusk was settling in outside. Max woofed monotonously at the back door, where he was usually at this hour let in and fed. When Bech returned with the two steaming cups and a saucer of Ritz crackers to the living room, Norma stood up. Her wool suit wore a fuzzy corona; her face in shadow loomed featureless. He set the tray down carefully on the inverted bushel basket and, giving the response that seemed expected, held and kissed her. Her mouth was wider and wetter than Bea's and, by virtue of longer acquaintance, more familiar. 'I have a question for you,' he said. 'Do you ever fuck before you talk?'

They were so careful. They let Max in and closed the kitchen door. Upstairs, they chose Donald's bed because never made, it would not show mussing. The boy's shelves still held the stuffed toys and mechanical games of childhood. A tacked-up map of the world, in the projection that looks like a flattened orange peel, filled Bech's vision with its muted pinks and blues when his eyelids furtively opened. *So this is adultery*, he thought: this homely, friendly socketing. An experience he would have missed, but for marriage. A sacred experience, like not honouring your father and mother. Good old Norma, she still had a faintly sandy texture to her buttocks and still liked to have her nipples endlessly, endlessly flicked by the attendant's tongue. She came silently, even sullenly, without any of Bea's angelic coos and yips. They kept careful track of the time by the clown-faced plastic clock on Donald's maple dresser, and by five-thirty Bech was downstairs pouring Kibbles into Max's bowl. The dog ate greedily, but would never forgive him. Bech cleared away the telltale untasted tea, washed and dried the cups, and put them back on their hooks. What else? Norma herself, whom he had last seen wandering in insouciant nudity towards the twins' bathroom for a shower, was maddeningly slow to get dressed and come back downstairs; he wanted her desperately to go, to disappear, even forever. But she had brought in her big reptilian pocketbook some documents connected with old Judge Latchett's estate – the release of some unprofitable mutual-fund shares – that needed Bea's signature. So they waited together in the two wing chairs. Bech took the maroon this time. Max went and curled up by the front door, pointedly. Norma cleared her throat and said, 'I *did*, actually, like that bit with Zenith and your heroine. Really, it has a lot of lovely things in it. It's just I hate to see you turn into one more scribbler. Your paralysis was so beautiful. It was ... statuesque.'

Her conceding this, in softened tones, had the effect of making her seem pathetic. A mere woman, skinny and ageing, hunched in a chair, his seed and sweat showered from her. In praising his book even weakly she had shed her dark magic. Bad news had been Norma's beauty. She was getting nervous about the talk she had to give. 'If they aren't back by six-fifteen, I really *will* have to leave.'

But Donald and Bea returned at six-ten, bustling in the door with crackling packages while the dog leaped to lick their faces.

Donald's face had that stretched look of being brave; he had been told he must keep wearing retainers for two more years. Bea was of course surprised to find her sister and her husband sitting so primly on either side of a dying fire. 'Didn't Henry at least offer you a drink?'

'I didn't want any. It might make me need to pee in the middle of my lecture.'

'You poor thing,' Bea said. 'I'd be impossibly nervous.' She knew. Somehow, whether by the stagy purity of their waiting or the expression of Max's ears or simple Latchett telepathy, she knew. Bea's blue eyes flicked past Bech's face like a piece of fair sky glimpsed between tunnels high in the mountains. And little Donald, he knew too, looking from one to the other of them with a wary brightness, feeling this entire solid house suspended above him on threads no more substantial than the invisible currents between these tall adults.

White on White

No sooner had the great success of *Think Big* sunk into the general social consciousness along the upper East Side than engraved invitations had begun to arrive at the Bechs' Ossining house. After Bech moved out, Bea in her scrupulous blue handwriting would forward these creamy stiff envelopes, including those addressed to 'Mr and Mrs', to Bech's two drab sub-let rooms on West Seventy-second Street. (Bech had taken these rooms in haste, renting from a disreputable friend of Flaggerty's, and though he deplored the tattered old acid-trip decor – straw mats, fringed hassocks – he was surprised by how much better he slept here than in bucolic splendour, surrounded by cubic yards of creaking, solid-black space for whose repair and upkeep he had become at least half responsible.) Many of his invitations he dropped into the plastic waste-basket, after lovingly thumbing them as examples of the engraver's art and the stationer's trade; but he tended to accept those that carried with them the merest hint or stray thread of old personal connection. His marriage having dissolved around him like the airy walls of a completed novel, anyone who knew Bech 'when' interested him, as a clue to his past and hence to his future.

Mr and Mrs Henderson Hyde, III
and
Colortron Photographics, Inc.
request the pleasure of your company
at a party, honouring the publication of
White on White
by Angus Desmouches, esquire

White on White

on Friday, the thirteenth of April
at six o'clock

R.s.v.p.   *Suggested dress*
124-7777   *All white*

Bech remembered being photographed by the young and eager Angus Desmouches for *Flair*, long defunct, in the mid-Fifties, when *Travel Light* was coming out, to a trifling stir. The youthful photographer had himself looked at first sight as if seen through a wide-angle lens, his broad, tan, somehow Aztec face and wide head of wiry black hair dwindling to a pinched waist and tiny, tireless feet; clicking and clucking, he had pursued Bech up and down the vales and bike paths of Prospect Park, and then for contrast had taken him by subway to lower Manhattan and posed him stony-faced among granite skyscrapers. Bech had scarcely been back to the financial district in the decades since, though now he had a lawyer there, who, with much well-reimbursed head-wagging, was trying to disentangle him and his recent financial gains from Bea and her own tough crew of head-waggers. In a little bookshop huddled low in the gloom of Wall Street Bech had flipped through a smudged display copy of *White on White* ($128.50 before Christmas, $150 thereafter): finely focused platinum prints of a cigarette butt on a plain white saucer, a white kitten on a polar-bear rug, an egg amid feathers, a naked female foot on a tumbled bedsheet, a lump of sugar held in bared teeth, a gob of what might be semen on the margin of a book, a white-hot iron plunged into snow.

Bech went to the party. The butler at the door of the apartment looked like a dancer in one of the old M-G-M musical extravaganzas, in his white tie, creamy tails, and wing collar. The walls beyond him had been draped in bleached muslin; the apartment's regular furniture had been replaced with white wicker and with great sailcloth pillows; boughs and dried flowers spray-painted white had been substituted for green plants; most remarkably, in the area of the duplex where the ceiling formed a dome twenty feet high, a chalky piano and harp shared a platform with a tall vertical tank full of fluttering, ogling albino tropical fish. Angus Desmouches bustled forward, seemingly little changed – the same brown pug face and gladsome homosexual energy – except that his crown of black hair, sticking out stiff as if impregnated with drying paste, had gone stark white. So stark Bech guessed it had been dyed rather than aged that colour; his eyebrows matched, it was too perfect. The years had piled celebrity and wealth upon the little photographer but not added an inch to his waist. He looked resplendent in a satin plantation suit. Bech felt dowdy in an off-white linen jacket, white Levi's and tennis shoes he had made a separate trip out to Ossining to retrieve.

'Gad, it's good to press your flesh,' Desmouches exclaimed, seeming in every cubic centimetre of his own flesh to mean it. 'How long ago was that, anyway?'

'Nineteen fifty-five,' Bech said. 'Not even twenty-five years ago. Just yesterday.'

'You were such a sweet subject, I remember that. So patient and funny and wise. I got some delicious angles on especially the downtown take, but the foolish *fool*ish magazine didn't use any of it, they just ran a boring head-and-shoulders under some weeping *wil*low. I've always been afraid you blamed *me*.'

'No blame,' Bech said. 'Absolutely no blame in this business. Speaking of which, that's some book of yours.'

The other man's miniature but muscular hands fluttered skyward in simultaneous supplication and disavowal. 'The idea came to me when I dropped an aspirin in the bathtub and couldn't find it for the longest time. The idea, you know, of exploring how little contrast you could have and still have a photograph.' His hands pressed as if at a pane of glass beside him. 'Of taking something to the *li*mit.'

'You did it,' Bech told the air, for Desmouches like a scarf up a magician's sleeve had been whisked away, to greet other guests in this white-on-white shuffle. Bech was sorry he had come. The house in Ossining had been empty, Donald off at school and Bea off at her new job, being a part-time church secretary under some steeple up towards Brewster. Max had been there, curled up on the cold front porch, and had wrapped his mouth around Bech's hand and tried to drag him in the front door. The door was locked, and Bech no longer had a key. He knew how to get in through the cellar bulkhead, past the smelly oil tanks. The house, empty, seemed an immense, vulnerable shell, a *Titanic* throttled down to delay its rendezvous with the iceberg. Its emptiness did not, oddly, much welcome him. In the brainlessly short memories of these chairs and askew rugs he was already forgotten; minute changes on all sides testified to his absence. Bea's clothes hung in her closet like cool cloth knives seen on edge, and in the way his remaining shoes and his tennis racket had been left tumbled on the floor of his own closet he read a touch of disdain. He turned up the thermostat a degree, lest the pipes freeze, before sneaking back out through the cellar and walking the two miles to the train station, through the slanting downtown, where he had always felt like a strolling minstrel.

The drinks served at this party were not white, nor was the bartender. An ebony hand passed him the golden bourbon. The host and hostess came and briefly cooed their pleasure at Bech's company. Henderson Hyde may have been a third but he came from some gritty town in the Midwest and had the ebullient urbanity of those who have wrapped themselves in Manhattan as in a sumptuous cloak. His wife, too, was the third – a former model whose prized slenderness was with age becoming gaunt. Her great lipglossed smile stretched too many tendons in her neck; designer dresses hung on her a trifle awkwardly, now that they were truly hers; her tenure as wife had reached the expensive stage. Tonight's gown, composed of innumerable crescent slices as of quartz, suggested the robe of an ice-maiden helper that Santa had taken on while rosy-cheeked Mrs Claus looked the other way. Until he had married Bea, Bech had imagined that Whitsuntide had something to do with Christmas. Not at all, it turned out. And there was an entire week called Holy Week, corresponding to the seven days of Pesach. They were in it, actually.

'Smash of a book,' said Hyde, giving the flesh above Bech's elbow a comradely squeeze as expertly as a doctor taps the nerves below your kneecap.

'You got through it?' Bech asked, startled. His funny bone tingled.

Mrs Hyde intervened. 'I told him all about it,' she said. 'He couldn't get to sleep for all my chuckling beside him as I read it. That scene with the cameramen!'

'It's top of the list I'm going to get to on the Island this summer. Christ, the books keep piling up,' Hyde snarled. He was wearing, Bech only now noticed in the sea of white, a brilliant bulky turban and a caftan embroidered with the logo of his network.

'It's hard to read anything,' Bech admitted, 'if you're gainfully employed.'

Somebody had begun to tinkle the piano: 'The White Cliffs of Dover'. *There'll be bluebirds over* . . .

'So sorry your wife couldn't be with us,' Hyde's wife said in parting.

'Yeah, well,' Bech said, not wanting to explain, and expecting they knew enough anyway. 'Easy come, easy go.' He had meant this to be soothing, but an alarmed look flitted across Mrs Hyde III's gracious but over-elastic features.

The harp joined in, and the melody became 'White Christmas'. *Just like the ones we used to know* . . . A man of his acquaintance, a fellow writer, the liberal thinker Maurie Leonard, came up to him. Maurie, though tall, and thick through the shoulders and chest, had such terrible, deskbound posture that all effect of force was limited to his voice, which emerged as an urgent rasp. Metal on metal. Mind on matter. 'Some digs, huh?' he said. 'You know how Hyde made his money, don'tcha?' More than a liberal, a radical whose twice-weekly columns were deplored by elected officials and whose bound essays were removed from the shelves of public-school libraries, Maurie yet took an innocent prideful glee in the awful workings of capitalism.

'No. How?' Bech asked.

'Game shows!' Maurie ground the words out through a mirth that pressed his cheeks up tight against his eyes, whose sockets were as wrinkled as walnuts. *Hyde-Jinks, Hyde-'n'-seek*. Haven't you heard of 'em? Christ, you just wrote a whole book about the TV industry!'

'That was fiction,' Bech said.

Maurie, too, exerted pressure on the flesh above Bech's elbow, muttering confidentially, 'You wouldn't know it to look at the uptight little prick, but Hyde's a genius. He's like Hitler – the worst thing you can think of, he's there ahead of you already. Know what his latest gimmick is?'

'No,' Bech said, beginning to wish that this passage were not in dialogue but in simple expository form.

'Mud wrestling!' Maurie rasped, and a dozen wrinkles fanned upwards from each outer corner of his Tartarish, street-wise eyes. 'In bikinis, right there on the boob tube. Not your usual hookers, either, but the girl next door; they come on the show with their husbands and mothers and goddamn gym teachers and talk about how they want to win for the hometown and Jesus and the American Legion and the next thing you see there they are, slugging another bimbo with a fistful of mud and taking a bite out of her ass. Christ, it's wonderful. One or two falls and they could be fucking stark naked. Wednesdays at five-thirty, just before the news, and then reruns Saturday midnight, for couples in bed. Bech, I defy you to watch without getting a hard-on.'

This man loves America, Bech thought to himself, *and he writes as if he hates it*. 'Easy money,' he said aloud.

'You can't imagine how much. If you think this place is OK, you should see Hyde's Amagansett cottage. And the horse farm in Connecticut.'

'So what I wrote was true,' Bech said to himself.

'If anything, you understated,' Leonard assured him, his very ears now involved in the spreading folds of happiness, so that his large furry lobes dimpled.

'How sad,' said Bech. 'What's the point of fiction?'

'It hastens the Revolution,' Leonard proclaimed, and in fare-well, with hoisted palm: 'Next year in Jerusalem!'

Bech needed another drink. The piano and harp were doing 'Frosty the Snowman', and then the harp alone took on 'Smoke Gets in Your Eyes'. The room was filled up with whiteness like a steam bath. At the edge of the mob around the bar, a six-foot girl in a frilly Dior nightie gave Bech her empty glass and asked him to bring her back a Chablis spritzer. He did as he was told and when he returned to stand beside her saw that she had on a chocolate-brown leotard beneath the nightie. Her hair was an unreal red, and heavy, falling to her shoulders in a waxen Ginger Rogers roll; her bangs were cut even with her straight black eyebrows. She was heavy all over, Bech noticed, but comely, with a marmoreal humourless gaze. 'Whose wife are you?' Bech asked her.

'That's a chauvinistic approach.'

'Just trying to be polite.'

'Nobody's. Whose husband are you?'

'Nobody's. In a way.'

'Yeah? Tell me the way.'

'I'm still married, but we're split up.'

'What split you up?'

'I don't know. I think I was bad for her ego. Women now I guess need to do something on their own. As you implied before.'

'Yeah.' Her pronunciation was dead level, hovering between agreement and a grunt.

'What do *you* do, then?'

'Aah. I been in a couple a Hendy's shows.'

Ah. She was a mud wrestler. Maurie Leonard in his enthusiasm for the Revolution sometimes got a few specifics wrong. The mud wrestlers *were* hookers. The give-away-nothing eyes, the calm heft held erect as a soldier's body beneath the frills. 'You win or lose?' Bech asked her. He had the idea that wrestlers always proceeded by script.

'We don't look at it that way, win or lose. It's more like a dance. We have a big laugh at the end, and usually dunk the referee.'

'I've always wondered, what happens if you get mud in your eyes?'

'You blink. You the writer?'

'One of the many.'

'I saw you on Cavett. Nice. Smooth, but, you know, not too. You gonna stick around here long?'

'I was wondering,' he said.

The girl turned her face slightly towards him – a thrilling sight, like the soft sweep of a lighthouse beam or the gentle nudging motion of a backhoe, so much smooth youth and health bunched at the base of her throat, where her nightie's lace hem clouded the issue. He felt her heavy gaze rest on the top of his head. 'Maybe we could go out get a snack together afterwards,' she suggested. 'After we circulate. I'm here to circulate.'

'I am too, I guess,' Bech said, his body locked numbingly around its new secret, a kind of cancer, a rampant multiplication. Men and women: what a grapple. New terms, same old pact. 'Name's Lorna,' his mud wrestler told him, and moved off, her leotard suspended like a muscular vase within the chiffon of her costume. He remembered Bea's soft nighties and the bottom dropped out of his excitement, leaving an acid taste. Better make the next drink weak, it looked like a long night.

'Shine On, Harvest Moon' had become the tune, and then one he hadn't heard since the days of Frankie Carle, 'The Glow Worm'. *Glimmer, glimmer*. The music enwrapped as with furling coils of tinsel ribbon the increasingly crowded room, or rooms; the party was expanding in the vast duplex to a boundary whereat one could glimpse those rooms stacked with the polychrome furniture that had been temporarily removed, rooms hung with paintings of rainbows and flayed nudes, bursts of colour like those furious quasars hung at the outer limits of our telescopes. In the mass of churning whiteness the mud wrestlers stood firm, big sturdy girls wearing silver wigs and rabbit-fur vests and shimmery running shorts over those white tights nurses wear, or else white gowns like so many sleepwalking Lady Macbeths, or the sterilized pyjamas and boxy caps of laboratory workers dealing with bacteria or miniaturized transistors; in the pallid seethe they stood out like caryatids.

Bech had to fight to get his bourbon. The piano and the harp were jostled in the middle of 'Stardust' and went indignantly silent. Like a fuzzy sock being ejected by the tumble-dryer there was flung toward Bech the shapeless face of Vernon Klegg, the American Kafka, whose austere minimalist renderings of kitchen spats and dishevelled mobile homes were the rage of writers' conferences and federal and state arts councils. There was at the heart of Klegg's work a haunting enigma. Why were these heroines shrieking? Why were these heroes going bankrupt, their businesses sliding from neglect so resistlessly into ruin? Why were these children so rude, so angry and estranged? The enigma gave Klegg's portrayal of the human situation a hollowness hailed as quintessentially American; he was published with great faithfulness in the Soviet Union, as yet another illustrator of the West's sure doom, and was a pet of the Left intelligentsia everywhere. Yet one did not have to be a very close friend of Klegg's to know that the riddling texture of his work sprang from a humble personal cause: except for that dawn hour of each day when, pained by hangover and recommencing thirst, Klegg composed with sharpened pencil and yellow-paper pad his few hundred beautifully minimal words – nouns, verbs, nouns – he was drunk. He was a helpless alcoholic from whom wives, households, faculty positions, and entire neighbourhoods of baffled order slid with mysterious ease. Typically in a Klegg *conte* the hero would blandly discover himself to have in his hands a butcher knife, or the broken top fronds of a rubber plant, or the buttocks of a pubescent baby-sitter. Alcohol was rarely described in Klegg's world, and he may himself not have recognized it as the element that kept that world in perpetual centrifugal motion. He had a bloated face enlarged by a white bristle that in a circle on his chin was still dark, like a panda marking. In this environment he seemed not unsober. 'Hear you turned down Dakota Sioux Tech,' he told Bech.

'My wife advised me to.'

'Didn't know you still had a wife.'

'My God, Vern, I don't. I plumb forgot.'

'It happens. My fourth decamped the other day, God knows why. She just went kind of crazy.'

'Same with me,' Bech said. 'This modern age, it puts a lot of stress on women. Too many decisions.'

'Lord love 'em,' Klegg said. 'Who are all these cunts standing around like cops?'

'Mud wrestlers. The newest thing. Wonderful women. They keep discipline.'

'About time somebody did,' Klegg said. 'I've lost the bar.'

'Follow the crowds,' Bech told him, and himself rotated away from the other writer, to a realm where the bodies thinned, and he could breathe the intergalactic dust. A stately creature swaddled in terrycloth attracted him; her face was not merely white, it was painted white, so that her eyes with their lashes stared from within a kind of mask. She smiled in welcome, and her red inner lips and gums seemed to declare an inner face of blood.

'Hey man.'

'Hey,' he answered.

'What juice *you* groovin' on?'

'Noble dispassion,' he answered.

Her hands, Bech saw, were black, with lilac nails and palms. She was black, he realized. She was truth. The charm of liquor is not that it distorts perceptions. It does not. It merely lifts them free from their customary matrix of anxiety. America at heart is black, he saw. Snuggling into the jazz that sings to our bones, we feel that the Negro lives deprived and naked among us as the embodiment of truth, and that when the castle of credit cards collapses a black god will redeem us. The writer would have spoken more to this smiling apparition with the throat of black silk beneath her mask of rice, but Lorna, his first mud wrestler, sidled up to him and said, 'You're not circulating.' Her hair was as evenly, incandescently red as the glowing coil of the hot plate he cooked his lonely breakfasts on.

'Is it time to go?' he asked, like a child.

'Give it another half-hour. This is just fun for you, but Hendy makes us girls tow the line. If I skip off early it could affect my ratings.'

'We don't want that.'

'No we don't, ol' buddy.' Before she went off again her body purposely and with only peripheral menace brushed Bech's; in the lightness of the contact her breast felt as hard as her hip. A word from Bech's deep past rose and occurred to him. *Kurveh.* The stranger who comes close.

The piano and harp were interrupted again, this time in the middle of 'Stars Fell on Alabama'. Henderson Hyde was up on the piano bench, making a speech about Angus Desmouches's extraordinary book. '. . . horizons . . . not since Atget and Steichen . . . rolling back the limits of the photographic universe . . .' The albino fish in the vertical tank flurried and goggled, alarmed by the new vibrations. They were always in profile. On edge they looked like knives, like Bea's clothes in the closet. *Why is a fish like a writer?* Bech asked himself. *Because both exist in only two dimensions.* Since seeing through the black woman's white paint and obtaining for himself a fourth bourbon (neat: the party was running out of water), Bech felt the gift of clairvoyance growing within him. Surfaces parted; he had achieved X-ray vision. The white of this party was a hospital johnny beneath which lungs harboured dark patches and mud-packed arteries sluggishly pulsed. Now Angus Desmouches was up on the piano bench, saying he owed everything to his mother's sacrifices and to the nimbleness and sensitivity of his studio assistants too numerous to name. Not to mention the truly wonderful crew at Colortron Photographics. A limited number of signed copies of *White on White* could be purchased in the foyer, at the pre-Christmas price. Thank you. You're great people. Really great. The albino crowd flared and fluttered, looking for its next crumb. In the mass of white, heads and shoulders floated like photos on the back flaps of dust jackets. Bech recognized two authors, both younger than he, more prolix and polished, and saw right through them. Elegantly slim, diamond-laden Lucy Ebright, she of dazzling intellectual constructs and uncanny six-hundred-page forays into the remoter realms of history: in her work a momentous fluency passed veils of illusion before the reader's eyes everywhere but when, more and more rarely, her own threadbare Altoona girlhood was evoked. Then as it were a real cinder appeared at the heart of a great unburning fire of invention. For the one thing this beautiful conjurer of the world's riches truly understood was poverty; the humiliation of having to wear second-hand clothes, the inglorious pain of neglected teeth, the shame of watching one's grotesque parents grovel before the possessors of jobs and money – wherever such images arose, even in a psychoallegorical thriller set in the court of Kublai Khan, a jarring authenticity gave fluency pause, and the reader uncomfortably gazed upon raw truth: *I was poor.* Lucy was chatting, the sway of her long neck ever more aristocratic as her dreams succeeded in print, with the brilliant and engaging Seth Zimmerman, whose urbane comedies of sexual entanglement and moral confusion revealed to Bech's paternal clairvoyance a bitter, narrow, insistent message. *I hate you all,* Seth's comedies said, *for forsaking Jesus.* A Puritan nostalgia, an unreasonable longing for the barbaric promise of eternal light beyond the slate-marked grave, a fury at all unfaith including his own gave Zimmerman's well-carpentered plots their uncentred intensity and his playful candour its hostile cool. Both rising writers came up to Bech and in all sincerity said how much they had adored *Think Big.*

'I just wished it was even longer,' Lucy said in her lazy, nasal voice.

'I wished it was even dirtier,' Seth said, snorting in self-appreciation.

'Aw, shucks,' said Bech. Loving his colleagues for their alabaster attire and for having like him climbed by sheer desperate wits and acquired typing skill up out of the dreary quotidian into this apartment on high, he nevertheless kept dodging glances between their shoulders to see if his new friend in her nightie and wig were approaching to carry him off. The piano and harp, running out of white, had turned to 'Red Sails in the Sunset' and then 'Blue Skies'. Radiant America; where else but here? Still, Bech, sifting the gathering with his inspired gaze, was not quite satisfied. Another word occured to him. *Treyf,* he thought. Unclean.